WHAT I KNOW

About Ben Eccles.

BY

ABRAHAM PAGE.

PHILADELPHIA:
J. B. LIPPINCOTT & CO.
1869.

CONTENTS.

CHAPTER X.

CHAPTER XI.

CHAPTER XII.

CHAPTER XIII.

CHAPTER XIV.

CHAPTER XV.

CHAPTER XVI.

CHAPTER XVII.

CHAPTER XVIII.

CHAPTER XIX.

PREFACE BY MR. PAGE'S EXECUTOR.

The following paragraph occurs in Mr. Page's will:

"I have written these stories in the solitude of my own home. Although there are among my acquaintance many gentlemen and ladies of extensive reading and refined literary taste, there is not one amongst them who can be called a 'literary person,' whom I might consult. It is the natural result of our institutions and mode of life, that we should occupy ourselves with our own personal and domestic affairs rather than with developing literature, science, or art for the public; and although in some respects this is to be regretted, it is undoubtedly but a small loss, which has a noble compensation in the preservation of our individuality. The doctrine that: 'The Individual should be sacrificed to the Public,' is one of those bastard truths which are produced from an illegitimate union of society—universal equality. Really, natural society is that which tends to preserve and strengthen individuality in all its members, and allows no subserviency or sacrifice either to itself or of the individual. Individual modesty is of far more general importance than public amusement, and of far greater public benefit than is the transient instruction of the public. To consult my friends about my writing would bring about publicity and fifty other embarrassments I dread, while giving me no actual assistance; for, although each could give me his or her own opinion, and very severely chaste opinion, upon the morality and reasoning, the grammar and rhetoric, and other intrinsic merits, not one could form an idea from experience as to the popular merits of the works. I, in some respects a mere country bumpkin, have therefore had to be guided by my own unaided judgment; feeling that so long as I adhered to truth and natural sentiment, I must please, even the public. I trust and defer to the judgment of my executor, and feel sure that his regard for my memory will make him a severe critic."

My venerated friend imposed upon me a task which I should perform with great caution, even if I did not distrust my own powers so much as to be unwilling to undertake it at all. I could easily designate the passages in this book, for instance, which please me most; but I will not do so, and would be very loth to disturb those which do not so well accord with my own opinions or taste; for a discerning public might decide that I was unfortunate, both in my selection of pleasing passages, and in my discovery and criticism of the faulty. I will therefore waive the task. I have added to this volume only two or three explanatory notes, and a syllabus to each of the chapters—both of which additions I thought might please the reader.

I will venture upon but one criticism concerning the matter of the book. It may be thought that my dear old friend has touched too often upon points of religion; and some may find the additional fault that those points are just those which are most controverted. I beg leave to differ with both objections.

The story of a life is incomplete unless the moral and religious nature of that life be given; for not only is that the most important portion of the life itself, but, disguise it as we may, every living rational man is engaged in a moral and religious struggle from the time he first begins to reflect until the close of his life. Because we see our friends light-hearted and apparently careless of all serious affairs is no reason that they are not engaged actively and continuously in that struggle. The elements of conflict are within and around every one; none can avoid them while he lives, and many seek relief for them in the *long* sleep of death. Depend upon it, your most giddy neighbor is at times as gravely and perhaps far more violently occupied in this conflict than is the wisest of his friends.

The other objection, that the points he has touched upon are those most controverted is, in fact, equally untenable. Faith and prayer are the two grand necessities of man. They are moral food and light, and moral exercise and air, and his moral nature can exist without them quite as ill as his life and health can exist without light and air, physical exercise, and substantial food. If there be controversy upon these two points it is a controversy between Christianity and heathenism; no, I will not say that, for the heathen seek for faith, and pray as well as Christians; it is a controversy between the good and the evil, the instinctive and the stupid, in the man's own nature;

and, however he may seek to controvert faith and prayer as spoken of by Mr. Page, his own faith in his own doctrine wavers, and he finds himself praying in spite of himself. Mr. Page has set forth no new faith, but has simply explained the nature and method of faith, as every Christian from St. Paul to our day has understood it, and he only tries to render the natural action and emotion of prayer more satisfactory and pleasing.

And he has touched upon these matters of religion, simply so far as they were necessary to the proper diagnosis and prognosis of the character and conduct of his hero. It is more a psychological than a religious story, and because the good old writer has not been mystical or transcendental, but has used words of the most common sort and of the plainest meaning, to speak of what every one must feel, and, at least partly, understand, it must not be supposed that his work is any the less valuable.

This much I have felt that I might venture to say. The story itself, as a story, and its manner of being told, I leave with the reader. I, the executor, am not aware of any other Ben Eccles, Susan, Alice, Dr. Sam, or Charley Bowman, in literature—to say nothing of Aunt Polly, and the others. They are, for the most part, of Southern growth. Although the bases of their characters exist wherever there are men and women, the organization and state of the society in which they lived peculiarly modified those bases, and created with them characteristics. Whoever knows human nature will find it normally though peculiarly developed in them.

In my preface to Mr. Page's life of himself, I stated that I did not feel myself qualified to meddle with the old gentleman's grammar or style; and in this book also I have carefully let those matters alone, having found nothing in them revolting to my own knowledge or taste—though it is possible that they may be obnoxious to severe criticism.

The reception of his "Life and Opinions" by the public has been such as would have greatly gratified their author; although the many flattering words the book has received from his friends would have made him suspect that friendship rather than its intrinsic merits dictated them. I happen to know, that though Mr. Page was fond of approbation, he generally suspected it, and always felt rather more humbled than elated by it. "Some natures," I have heard him say, "grow in strength by approbation, as others gain energy from opposition; but I have yet to see the earnest man who is thoroughly contented with his work, however much it may be praised. When he compares it with what he desired it to be, contrasts its dull execution with his vivid conceptions, he is disappointed with himself. The glowing passion he tried to describe appears vapid, and he cannot himself again be affected by it; the plot he thought so ingenious and delicate is awkward and stale; he can find innumerable faults with the diction which expressed his ideas exactly and so neatly; his wit is paltry, and his pathos mere sentimentality. Under these circumstances, praise sounds to him toned with compassion for what he feels to have been his failure; and, though he would be overwhelmed by blame, the encouragement he finds in praise rather excites a tender humility than a bold pride."

Such, I think, would be my feelings if I were an author, though I might not be able to express them so well.

It is my present intention to publish next Mr. Page's story of "The Quines"—a family he seems to have observed very closely. It will depend, however, very much upon the state of the public affairs, and consequently the private prosperity of the country, and upon whether the stories told by the old gentleman meet with as much favor as his "Life and Opinions" has received.

JOHN CAPELSAY,

OF NATCHEZ,

Executor.

WHAT I KNOW ABOUT BEN ECCLES.

CHAPTER I.

WHICH IS THE LONGEST IN THE BOOK.

I MUST be allowed great latitude in telling what I know about Ben Eccles, and may as well acknowledge at the outset that many things I will say about his opinions and feelings are but conjectures founded upon the facts he has told me, and upon what I know to be his disposition and character. Although he is at this moment in the house with me, and I could consult him about everything I write here, it would make him uncomfortable to know I was writing about him, and I therefore will not arouse his suspicions by continued questions.

If I were writing a work of fiction, I would perhaps commence in this way:

One dark afternoon in early winter a brisk northeast wind blew the sand and withered leaves about the sparsely built streets of a small town in the interior of North Carolina. It was a cheerless time and a cheerless place. Not a soul was to be seen abroad; even the hogs had gathered into their beds under some of the unoccupied houses, the little wooden church, and the school-house; a few shivering cows could be seen with roughened coats and drooping heads browsing among the stunted oaks and huckleberry bushes around the inclosures. Pine trees and scrubby black-jack oaks came up to the very backs of the small yards and gardens on the main street, and sand and yellow clay composed the soil for such a growth.

It will always be a puzzle to the traveler why a town should have been commenced on such a spot, unless it were that healthiness was the first consideration of the founders, and they thought that general desiccation was favorable to health. But though it was a county town its growth seemed to have been checked, years before the time of which I am writing, and the scattered one-storied wooden houses stood paintless and racked, each surrounded by a dilapidated paling or board fence, with here and there a gate hanging open on one wooden hinge, or a gateway stopped up with rails; a rail or two on forks, or a couple of wooden blocks answering for a stile.

From one of the two chimneys of one of these wooden houses at the farther end of the main street the smoke poured lazily forth; but presently its volume became larger and more brisk as though a few pine knots had been added to the fire; and there was a sound of female voices, and a lively bustle within, and a male voice was to be heard on the back gallery calling: "Sally! you Sally!" to the negro cook and woman of all work whose abode was the kitchen in the back yard.

"She ain't here, master; she gone to the spring!" shouted her little son, Tom, running to the kitchen door.

"You Sally!" called the male voice at its strongest

pitch: "run after her, Tom, and tell her to come to her mistress, quick!"

And with that the man re-entered the house, and presently emerged from the front door, kicking a shivering hound off the shuck door-mat on the gallery, and, as he went, buttoning up the overcoat which hung upon his tall slender form, took his way hurriedly over the stile and down the street where he soon arrived at the door of old Mrs. Wobbles, good old Mrs. Wobbles, the granny of the neighborhood, who in a few minutes afterwards, well muffled up, and bearing a bundle tied in a large striped cotton handkerchief, accompanied him as fast as she could along the sandy road to his house again. After they had entered all became as quiet as before on the street; but the other chimney soon began to send forth smoke, and Sally hastened in and out to and from the kitchen; and then as the gray of the evening came on, the man came out on the front gallery puffing nervously at a cob pipe, and after walking up and down until its contents were consumed, knocked the ashes out on the bannisters and went in again. As the night darkened the dogs of the town seemed, now and then, to wake up, and bark and howl in concert, and the cold wind rushed through the pines and rattled the dead leaves on the black-jacks and the wooden shutters and doors of the house, and the man sat in the front room alone, on a stool, leaning with his head in his hands in front of the fire, half asleep, half awake, until just before midnight the faint cry of an infant's voice roused him up, and old Mrs. Wobbles presently came into the room smiling, and reaching for her pipe in the chimney corner, as she said:

"Well, Mr. Eccles, you're a lucky man. It's all over; right as a trivet."

"Which is it, Mrs. Wobbles?" inquired Mr. Eccles, with a nervous smile.

"As fine a boy as you ever see, Mr. Eccles, but a mighty small chance of a feller. His grandma's a dressin' of him now, an' I thought I would come in and kind o' take a little smoke. It's awful tiresome, Mr. Eccles. You don't think so; but you jest try it once. Jane, your wife, is a narvous critter, an' if it hadn't a been for her ma I don't know what I should a done; but——"

"May I go in and see Jane now, Mrs. Wobbles?" asked Mr. Eccles, with an undecided movement toward the door.

"Wait a bit, sir. Miss Robbins, your ma-in-law, will let you know when you can come in."

And Mrs. Wobbles having lit her pipe and established herself comfortably before the fire in a large split-bottomed rocking-chair, soothed herself into silent meditation like one who has accomplished a great and arduous work, and Mr. Eccles was fain to take his seat again, and await the bidding of his ma-in-law; for he was not a man to take liberties, or to assert his way, particularly at a time like this, and in the presence of two such authorities as Mrs. Wobbles and Mrs. Robbins.

But at last Mrs. Robbins came to the door on tiptoe, and beckoned to him, and he went into the room where his wife was calmly asleep, and saw at her side a little bundle of blanket which the grandmother took in her arms; and turning down one corner, she showed him the little red and mealy face of the "mighty small chance of a feller," his heir, and my hero.

Mr. Eccles, though a very nervous and imaginative man, was not given to know exactly what he thought or felt at any particular moment, but I fancy that he felt a slight disappointment and sinking of the heart when he beheld that all his hopes amounted to only this tiny specimen. It seemed a very small matter to have made so much fuss about, and he could hardly realize to himself that *this* could ever be a boy to romp and hurrah, to wear pants and go to school, to learn books, and to fight, ride, and work, and finally to be proud of.

If I were writing fiction, I say, I would perhaps commence it with this scene, but as I am writing fact I must candidly confess that I know nothing at all about the birth of Ben Eccles, except that it was at some village in North Carolina, and that it was about the winter of the year 1800. I know, moreover, that his mother, after giving birth to two other children who did not live long, died when he was five or six years old, leaving him the only child and stay of a father broken in health. Captain Benjamin Eccles, the father, was a lawyer, and from his appearance, and all I could ever learn about him, was, in many respects, such a man as his son afterwards proved to be. After the death of his wife, he dawdled and lingered about home for two or three years, and then came out to Yatton, where he commenced the practice of his profession, but in two years more died of consumption, leaving his son almost destitute and friendless.

The Captain had brought with him to Yatton, Sally,

the cook, a kindly negro woman, who had grown portly and sleek over her kitchen fires; and Tom, her son, now about twelve years old—both black negroes. For three hundred dollars he had bought from Squire Harkness a small frame-house which stood near the edge of the town, that is to say, about six hundred yards from the court-house—for the population of Yatton at that time did not exceed six hundred white and black, and the accommodations for them were scattered over but a small surface of ground.

The house was between my father's residence and the main portion of the town, and fronted on the big road, as the street was to be considered there, having only two or three houses on one side of it; the other side being already an old field washed into gullies with here and there a pine bush growing on some island in the gullies where the cattle could not conveniently tread it down. It was a plain weather-boarded house with the usual front and back galleries, and around the front yard was the universal picket fence which was extended on each side to about a hundred yards to the rear inclosing the log kitchen, a chicken-pen, and a small vegetable garden. The kitchen building was of two rooms, one of which was occupied by Sally and Tom. The house had in it three rooms: one, a bed-room, was occupied by Ben and his father; another, adjoining it, served as a dining and sitting-room and library; and the third, a small room formed by inclosing one end of the back gallery, was used as a pantry and general store-room for provisions and other household goods.

Back of the garden extended another old field, washed

into still deeper gullies, in fact, into deep ravines, along one of which, near the fence, ran a spring branch which took its rise from a bold spring about two hundred and fifty yards above, nearer town, which supplied several other households, besides that of Mr Eccles, with water for all purposes. The neighboring washing was done there, as was shown by the two or three large iron kettles swung upon poles supported by forks; and after breakfast every Monday morning that the weather was fair, Sally, accompanied by Tom, to keep up the fire, lugged her tub and the soiled clothes of the family to the little shed at the spring where she met with plenty of company in the other negro women who came for the same purpose, with whom a boisterous laughing and gossip were kept up until it was time to go home and prepare dinner, by which time the washing was generally concluded and could be packed in the tubs and carried home to be hung out to dry.

So much for Ben's residence and surroundings, and I have been thus minute in my description because I have no doubt but that the scenes in which he was placed at this time had much to do with giving tone to his disposition. For a long time after he came to Yatton his father, Sally, and Tom were almost his only friends, and he seemed a lonely little fellow. But I doubt if he felt the loneliness. He was even then a silent little body, looking questions to strangers out of his great gray eyes rather than asking them with his lips, and always intent upon some work in the garden or yard or on the spring branch—delving at a bed for radishes or cabbage, contriving a kennel for his dog, a sleeping place for his cat, or miniature mill-ponds; not one of which designs was destined ever to be wholly completed, though zealously worked at day after day.

I suppose that I was attracted to observe the boy more than I should otherwise have done by the attachment taken to him by my own little son, whom I was destined to lose but a short time afterwards. My little boy, who lived generally at his grandfather's, always loved best to play with boys older than himself, and Ben was so gentle with him, and at the same time seemed to him so bold and adventurous in jumping, climbing, walking on stilts, and other such boyish pranks, that he greatly admired and loved him. He used often to say to me: "Pa, Ben's such a good boy; aint he? But when I'm a big boy I'll beat him climbing and riding; wont I?"

It was after my son died that Ben's lone condition impressed itself most strongly upon me. I suppose it was by association and sympathy; but it always made me sad to see him in winter, cleanly but thinly clad, with his jacket ragged at the elbows, and his hands far down in his pockets to keep them warm, walking briskly, with his shoulders raised, along beside his father to his office in town; or to see him in summer, sitting alone on the front step, or in the office getting his lessons, which he said to his father, who could ill afford, and could not bear, to send him to school.

I pitied the father, and would have helped him if I could; but what can one do for a stranger, not absolutely destitute, and who is broken in heart and health? You may indeed sympathize with him, but he has no sympathy with you, because he does not know the bitterness of your heart, and is too wholly absorbed with his own sorrows to intermeddle with your joys—if, indeed, you have them. Our offices were but a few doors apart, and little Ben, who seemed to consider me his friend, and sometimes came to my office door for a timid chat, was a bond of acquaintance between us, which made his father rather more unreserved with me than with any other person in the town—excepting always my father, to whom he, with his grief and poverty, and need of friendship, was a real blessing.

That blessed father of mine—whom I have never tried to emulate, because I never possessed his vigor of brain or simplicity of heart, and could not bear to merely mimic; and to copy another's conduct without possessing his qualities is only mimicry—the dear old gentleman, I say, was never so happy as when some one else was utterly miserable, and he could relieve him. And Captain Ben Eccles was about as miserable and helpless as a man—even though raised in the piney-woods of North Carolina—well can be. I do not mean that the pine forests, whether of North Carolina or Georgia, do not sometimes produce remarkably intelligent, brave, and shrewd men; but my observation leads me to believe that they do not generally produce tough men, in soul or body. I am neither a learned psychologist nor a scientific physiologist, and am not prepared to discuss the different effects of differing soils, climates, productions, habits, and customs upon the souls and bodies of men. I merely record it as the result of my observation, that men raised, as was Captain Eccles, in those piney-woods districts generally lack fortitude and endurance. They are easily discouraged and easily killed, particularly when they are away from home.

However this may be, my father took a lively interest in Captain Eccles. The state of the man's health was peculiarly within the province of his knowledge and skill, while the poor fellow's circumstances and condition of mind appealed strongly to his feelings. He had no need to use art to attract the confidence of others; the manifest qualities of his soul were officious for him. His perfect integrity, great intelligence, and kindly nature, shown in every action, seemed to draw the weak to him as one who would always sympathize with them, and upon whom they could lean with perfect trust. He was ready to meet them half way, and it would have been a hard soul which could have avoided going the other half. The consequence was that very soon after the Captain came to the town, he had been noticed by my father; and by the mutual attractions of strength and weakness, sorrow and sympathy, an acquaintance had been formed as gratifying to the one as it was helpful to the other.

It must not be supposed that Captain Eccles was deficient in sense or knowledge of the world—that is, as far as one raised in a North Carolina country village could know the world. There are some qualities of human nature which are best learned in Southern country villages (I suppose the rule holds good elsewhere), and a lawyer has the best opportunity of learning them thoroughly. But those qualities are of the smaller and baser sort. Indeed, I do not know but that to see human nature in its naked meanness such a village is the very best place. But a lifelong contact with this little world is apt to contract one's ideas to its caliber; to make the lawyer shrewd and suspicious rather than liberal and philosophic; in other words, to make him cunning rather than intellectual and learned in his profession. Captain Eccles had a thorough knowledge of all the turns and twists of special pleading, and of all the art of getting out of witnesses what they least wished to divulge, or getting it in the form least favorable to his adversary. He was also possessed of a fair share of rough common-sense impressiveness which did good service with a jury. But he was wholly unaccustomed to polished society; and though he had those good manners which a fair intelligence and a good heart always supply, he was out of place among ladies of refinement and men of the great world. Add to this the facts of his being a stranger, poor, in bad health, and with a deep grief oppressing him, and it may be readily imagined that he did not add much animation or interest to my father's family circle, into which he was speedily introduced. He was welcomed, of course, by my mother and sisters, but welcomed with pity, as one of our father's weaknesses (so the girls irreverently termed his special pets, who were always ailing), as one on whom benefits were to be conferred.

Let what the poets will be said about pity, it always argues inferiority in its object, and unless it be infused with much more active feelings it is nigher akin to contempt than to love. For my own part, I should vastly dread being thought a bore if I should find myself an object of pity to a lot of women folk, though they would be ready to move heaven and earth for my relief.

"Ma," I have heard Bel say of an afternoon when Captain Eccles had paid a visit to the house, "Captain Eccles is in the parlor."

"Well, my dear," my mother would answer, looking up from her sewing, "go down and entertain him a little while; for you see I am very busy just now. Poor man!"

"No, ma; it's Julia's turn to do that. I went the last time, and oh!" with a sigh, "how tired I got! It was a whole hour before you came. And, besides, ma," suddenly becoming enlivened, "I am very busy too. You know I am just fitting the body of my Swiss. Really, I do wish the man would stay at home!"

"You should be more charitable, my dear. Recollect that he has no friends here. You should be glad of an opportunity to cheer him up a little. Poor man!"

"Why don't you go then, ma?" said Miss Bel, impertinently; "to cheer him up would be all very well if it did not bore me so. You and pa are better than I am, and it doesn't bore you; does it? I know pa delights in it. How I do wish he was here. I'll go and send Jim to find him. Brother, please do go down and stay with the poor man a little while, till pa comes. Julia has to help me, and it would never do to make the poor man wait; it might hurt his feelings. You can send little Ben up stairs to ma, and to play with David. David! David!" calling my son from Julia's room where he would be busy with his playthings. "Ben's here!" And off she would march, as though the difficulty were all settled to our mutual satisfaction, leaving me no alternative but to follow her plan. My little boy would come scampering, and calling eagerly,

"Ben! Ben! Papa, where is Ben? I want to see Ben, papa. Where is he?"

But in a few months Captain Eccles' visits became more and more rare until little Ben had to come alone; for the walk was too much for his father. The hollow cheeks and the panting breath, shown in the last few visits, awakened all the warm and active benevolence of the ladies, and Captain Eccles was no longer a bore. He was a greatly suffering man, and though, in fact, more animated than he was before, they knew that at last death was really near him. Little Ben was required by them to come every day for some nice or wholesome thing they had prepared with their own hands to suit his palate, and their own servants were continually on the go to and from his house. My father spent several hours of every day with him, and put knowledge and ingenuity to active work for methods of making more smooth his path to the grave. One of our negro men was required to stay at his house every night, in case he should be wanted, and brother Eldred and I and several brother Masons (for I must not omit to state that the Captain was a Mason, and that almost every gentleman of our town and county was a zealous member of that order) visited him, at first in a friendly, unceremonious way, and then day and night as his nurses. He was grateful, but thought all these attentions very strange and useless. He said he felt better, and more at himself, than he had for years past. True, he was a little weak; but that would pass off when the weather became cooler and more bracing; and his cough, too, was better than it had been: though it was perhaps a little more frequent, it did not give him so much pain. Oh, he was decidedly better, and next spring would take a trip to North Carolina, and put Ben to school near his grandfather's, and settle up some business he had left unsettled when he came away.

Then it was that my father's greatness showed itself. I only admired it then—now that I am old, I call it greatness. We could nurse the man's sick body as gently and as efficiently, perhaps, as he; but he was away above us and beyond us in his knowledge of the sick man's heart, and his sympathy with the sick man's soul; and he set himself naturally to the task we but faintly appreciated and could not perform. Captain Eccles had to learn that he was dying, and had to be cheered along the darkening road until he reached the point from which he must pass on alone; and my father knew, far better than any man I ever saw, the cheer, the only cheer which could be given. His heart knew it even better, if it could be, than his head, and he gave it clearly and firmly as it could be understood and borne, lovingly and gently, as though he were persuading his own soul to take the last unavoidable step without fear.

I shall have been but a sorry bungler if you, having read my own life, do not understand and appreciate my father's character. True greatness consists not so much in doing grand and wonderful things as in doing right things. That man is greatest who does his duties best and confers most benefits upon his fellows. With this criterion, in speaking of warriors, artists, and scientific men who have excelled, it is necessary to qualify their greatness by adding its particular nature. A man may be a great conqueror who is a sordid, mean, malignant villain. One may be great as an artist or savant, who is beneath the social notice of a mere peasant. But where will you find a greater man than one who, by the grasp of his intellect and the gentle sympathies of his heart, fully appreciates the dignity and the needs of his fellow-men, and devotes his life to supporting and perfecting the one and supplying the other! My father was such a man. He was no sectarian in religion, politics, or in social life. Learned in the prejudices of sects, and in the actual teachings of Holy Scripture, of profane writings, of observation, and experience far beyond most men, he was a man whose organization was so perfect and so delicate that he sympathized with everything that could suffer, and, consequently, with everything that lived. Above all, he appreciated the wonderful dignity and the majestic sufferings of the twofold organization of man, God's chiefest work, for whose salvation the Son of God had himself to suffer and to die. As a physician, he for many years applied himself to the relief of man's body, and as a companion, he always had a care for his soul. As though he and his fellows were wandering in the twilight, along a way he knew the best, he warned them of the obstacles, assisted them when they stumbled, and encouraged them when they grew disheartened or bewildered. Though he lived in only a little country village, thousands had to bless him for good deeds done during his long lifetime, and I have no doubt but that hundreds shall bless him throughout eternity.

I do not know exactly how he introduced the subject of death to Captain Eccles, but believe that it was in a conversation about the importance of making a will; of which act some persons have a superstitious dread. At any rate, he did introduce it, and as the Captain gradually became convinced of the certainty of his speedy death, he became also imbued with hope of the life hereafter.

I am not fond of describing death-bed scenes, for although we all have once to pass that dreadful hour, unless our souls be suddenly shot into eternity as from a catapult, I am not at all convinced that such descriptions benefit the living, either while they are in health or when they come to die. The fact is, that the greatest sinners often die like saints, and the best saints like hopeless sinners. We can predicate nothing of the manner of a man's death upon the manner of his life. His nervous system has more to do with it than his soul; and though it may flatter the vanity or feed the prejudices of the members of some sect of religion or philosophy, or the partisans of some national conflict or political clique, to know that some one of their co-workers has died a brave or triumphant death, they are apt neither to live the better for it, nor can they control the manner of their own natural death. It is possible that a Frenchman might rehearse his death-bed speeches beforehand, and, if he kept his senses, act according to the rehearsal, but I imagine that with most men when the supreme hour comes vanity and affectation are forgotten in awe of the mighty King of Terrors.

After all his preparation, Captain Eccles died suddenly to us all, and even, I presume, to himself. His little son was in the house at the time, and did not shriek and weep, as most children would have done, but looked stunned and frightened. Awe, rather than grief, oppressed him at first, and he went about on tip-toe, looking up at first the one and then the other of us as we talked low and passed him, as though to realize from us what all this great woe meant. My father had his little trunk of clothes carried to our house, and sent him there to remain until the funeral should be ready. My little son, young as he was, seemed to know that his friend had a great sorrow and could not play with him, and approached him only with open-eyed, silent sympathy.

The lad moped about the house, or sat dull and tearless upon the steps, away from every one. My mother and sisters patched and mended and brushed up his slender wardrobe, so that he made a decent appearance at the funeral, which took place at our family burying ground. He stood by his father's open grave, calm and sad, until Mr. Snow pronounced the words, "earth to earth," and the first clods rattled from the sexton's spade upon the coffin; and then the poor child shuddered and fell fainting upon the ground. It was not until in the deep silence of that night, when nature had somewhat recovered from its depression, that he began to weep. He waked up weeping, and after hours had passed sobbed himself to sleep again. He seemed to dread being heard; and then, and always after, when he wept it racked my heart to see him weep so silently, —as though his grief were his own and he had to bear it alone, without sympathy.

Although it may be accounted inartistic in a story-teller, let me here, in the first chapter, confess that though Ben Eccles is my principal character I never loved him. Although I liked and like him very much, I have always pitied, and therefore could not love him in the strong sense in which only that term should be used. To confer benefits on another is a sure way to make one like, but however pure and honest and admirable that other may be, it is just as sure a way of preventing love, particularly if the sexes be the same and the natures of the two be different. It is not true that we love our opposites—unless we be ourselves of the lower nature. Man loves that which he thinks admirable, and weakness is not admirable even in a boy-baby. Though that boy-baby be your own, if you love it you do so in spite of its weakness; you had much rather it were bold and wilful and noisy. A man of strong nature loves the woman whose qualities of soul command his respect on account of their strength and purity. If he love a weak woman at all, it is in spite of her weakness and on account of other attractions which are powerful to him.

Of course I am not speaking of loving our opposites in bodily construction. I grant you that fat men generally marry lean women; tall men, short women; blue-eyed men, dark-eyed women; and *vice versa*—but that is a wise provision in the economy of nature for another purpose than spiritual. But for it the human race would have long since been divided into four distinct races: red-headed giants and black-haired giants, red-headed pigmies and black-haired pigmies; or, rather, into as many races as there are hereditary peculiarities in the human form; for instance, red-headed, slender giants, and red-headed, fat giants; black-haired, slender, cross-eyed giants, and black-haired, fat, cross-eyed giants, etc.

Nor am I speaking of opposites in mere mental power or quality—though, even in that, average men generally marry average women, and no man knowingly and voluntarily marries a fool. The principle I wish to establish is, that we love only what we would wish to resemble; in other words, what we admire and respect; and unless one be of the inferior nature he is not apt to love his opposite. The weak, vacillating man loves a strong, firm man; but the converse rarely follows, unless there be other causes than sympathy for the affection. The strong attracts the weak, but the weak does not attract the strong by its mere weakness.

Now, I know very well that I lay myself liable to be called presumptuous and vain, in giving such a reason for not loving Ben Eccles—and there comes up another conventional humbug of a saying to be combated. Men gravely commend the maxim, know thyself; and quote with approbation Pope's line, "the noblest study of mankind is man;" and yet when one has really studied himself and his fellow-man, and has learned that he has merits or qualities not possessed by another, or that he can excel his fellows in one or more matters, if he by chance let his having that knowledge come to the world, he is called vain and presumptuous, and is ridiculed as one who blows his own trumpet.

Is it not laughable to analyze the feelings which give rise to many of the maxins and habits of this world which pass current, and meet you pat and bold as truth at every turn? Because men do not like to have their inferiorities exposed, they make a sin of one's showing himself, even by innuendo, their superior. But a man does not necessarily boast when he shows a knowledge of his own excellencies, nor does that knowledge, if he be reasonable, make him vain; for he must understand that though he excel one he does not excel all.

Let me, however, state in my defence—for I am an old man, and a vain old man is the most pitiable of human contradictions—that the reason I do not *love* Ben Eccles, is not that I am braver, purer, or perhaps more intellectual than he, but simply that my nature is harder than his, more reasonable, and less sensitive: although, if it can give my critics any satisfaction, I confess that I am by no means so hard or so reasonable as some men I have seen, whom I did not pity, but respected and admired, and therefore loved.

CHAPTER II.

TELLS HOW THE ORPHAN WAS DISPOSED OF, AND GIVES A FEW INCIDENTS OF HIS CHILDHOOD.

CAPTAIN ECCLES left a will which was a very simple affair in itself, but it constituted my father his executor, and the guardian of little Ben; neither of which duties was so simple. If the property had been large the administration of it would have been easier though the accountability were increased; but it was so small that only the nicest kind of care could make it produce anything for the boy. Nor is it a simple or slight matter to have the care of another person's child thrust upon one. It is true that the responsibility is not felt to be so great as when the child is one's own; but the annoyance is not so mitigated by affection. A man takes care of his own child as he does of himself; the motive is selfish; but to take care of another's child demands the highest exercise of benevolence; and benevolence, I have often thought, is more generally passive than active in this world. If the way to hell be paved with good intentions, certainly the paths and the abode of misery are fenced by good wishes. I have known very many wicked men, but never yet have seen one who was devoid of benevolence. Such a man may exist, and so may there be men born without selfishness; but I have never met one in whom I detected such a monstrosity of disposition. What a happy world this would be if all the good wishes of even the worst of its inhabitants were put in execution!

Ben's house was rented out, and my father employed at his own house Sally and her son, for whom he charged himself with fair wages. They were much attached to their young master, and he to them. Sally he had always called mammy, and she had from his infancy exercised a "mammy's" care and authority over him.

The peculiar relation of the black "mammy" to her master's children has never, that I know of, been particularly described, and yet in nothing do I find the singular nature of the negro so exactly and strongly marked. In almost every Southern country family there is one of the negro women, generally the cook or the nurse, who stands by common consent as the "mammy." She is so called by all the white children of the family, and her authority over them is nearly as great as that over her own children, and they obey her almost as implicitly as their own mother, and often more willingly. But her authority over the white children is manifested in a very different way from that over her own; and I have often observed that she loved them even better. This will not appear strange to one who knows the negro well, and is one of the characteristics in which the nature of that race differs from what we commonly call human nature. Whether the story of Ham be true or a fable, and whether the negro have descended from Ham or another, one thing is certain, that from the days of Ham, so far as there has been any observation of the facts, the race has been wanting in natural affection. A negro woman will become furious if another beat her child, but almost invariably she will herself beat and ill treat it most abominably. One of the greatest troubles the Southern planter has is to make the negro mothers take proper care of their children; and that such a proportion of them should live is only due to the care and authority of their masters. In the marital relation the same lack of affection exists; and neither its laxity nor the neglect of the children is due to the state of slavery. It is due to their nature, as is always seen whenever they are found not in a state of slavery. Negroes do not lack strong feelings, and their affections are warm enough; but they lack moral stamina; and their affections are generally volatile. Their appetites and passions are furious, and their principles are weak—when they exist at all. They neither respect themselves nor each other.

These facts being predicated, it is not difficult to understand that the negro "mammy" often (I will even say generally) has a warmer affection for the white children than for her own. She respects them as her superiors not only in station, but in nature also, and therefore is more careful and loving towards them: and in this matter of respecting and loving her superiors she is just like most other women and men, whatever their race.

Sally was therefore very much attached to Ben, and would whale Tom on his account upon the slightest provocation. In fact Tom knew by sad experience that his Mas' Ben was to be respected in all his humors, which, fortunately for him, were neither very variable nor exacting. Mas' Ben was allowed to eat in peace his potato roasted for him by his mammy in advance of the dinner, and his especial hot biscuits were duly respected. Nor did the difference in the ages of the two boys perceptibly vary the respect which would have been required for the one and paid by the other if their ages had been the same, though I must do Tom the justice to say that he too loved his little master, and obeyed him almost as much for his own sake as for fear of Sally. On the other hand, when Sally told Ben to go out of the kitchen, or to come in out of the wet, or to go to bed, he went; and that not alone, because he was by nature bidable; Sally would most assuredly have spanked him if he had not obeyed her reasonable orders. The good soul would spank him, and if he wept over-much, would become compunctious and console him for his pain, whereas the louder Tom yelled the harder she would thrash him, and then would send him ignominiously howling after chips, or to bed.

My father's old cook was my mammy, and the mammy of my brothers and sisters. My son—who claimed Martha, my cook, as his mammy—called her grandmammy, and as he had found out that she used to thrash me he respected her authority hugely. The first day that Sally went to the house she was installed as cook, for my father's cook happened to be sick. Ben soon made his way to her, and was taken in her arms, wept over, and condoled with.

"Come to Sally, honey! She's been a honin' to see her boy for two days. You ain't got nobody but Sally now; Sally an' Tom to take care of you—don't cry, my chile; you mus' try an' be a man."

"Oh, mammy!" said the weeping boy, "I don't want to be a man! I want to be with my pa!"

"Yes, my chile, an' so you shill, in de happy lan' whar dey's pleasu's evermo'. But you mus' be good now. You' po' pa was a good man, an' he's done gone to heav'n, an' lef' us here a little while longer. But you mus'nt cry; you mus' bear up. I'll be with you, my po' chile; me an' Tom's here."

And so the interview went on at length until Sally's volatile spirit sought some distraction from the sorrowful theme, and she exclaimed:

"Why, hi! Bless de chile, if he ain't got on a new jacket! an' new shoes too, bless de Lord! Why, you's a comin' out! Who guv' em to you?"

"Ma-a-a-my!" drawled Tom, running into the kitchen.

"Ma-a-a-my! yes, it's mammy! ma-a-a-my!" exclaimed Sally to her offspring, her admiration changing to wrath. "What you doin' here? Don't you see yer Mas' Ben, you ill-mannered whelp, you?"

"How d'ye do, Mas' Ben?" said Tom, going up sheepishly, and giving Ben his hand.

"Yes. How d'ye do, Mas' Ben!" said Sally, sneeringly, to Tom; and then changing her tone, "Whar dem chips, I say? Whar dem chips I sont you fur? Ef you don't git along out o' dis kitchen and fotch me dem chips in a hurry, I skin you alive! you dratted——" and she made a rush at Tom, who cleared the door at a double-quick, and soon reappeared with an armful of sticks and chips, and beckoned to Ben to go off with him to hunt hens' nests.

Ben for a few months led an even existence at my father's, a loving and loved companion for my little son. His grief gradually disappeared from the surface, and sank deep into his heart. Of such childish griefs, cast by fate, with childish hopes and joys, all afterwards forgotten in their particulars, are the foundations of our characters made; they give shape to the whole superstructure. And poor little Ben had sorrow upon grief; first, his own loss, and then a woe which smote me as its chief victim. Hardly had his smiles reappeared in transient gleams when that dreadful scourge, scarlet fever, came, and took away my youngest brother, my sister Julia, and my dear little boy.

Let me pass that time by; I have not the courage to recall its details. I could do so. When at any time I would go back to my early days I have to fix my eyes straight upon the object I would revisit, nor once turn them into the gloomy chambers which open on either side, whence come to me the faint moans and whispering bustle around the dying, lest I should enter there with one of the shadowy forms I meet, and be again placed under the power of agony, to see and hear, and wring my hands, and weep, without the power to withdraw, until the bier, and hearse, and open grave have received their dead, and the pitiless pattings of the heavy spades upon the very breasts of my loved ones dismiss me from the spell. Therefore I will resist the allurements of fondly sorrow, and speak only of Ben, who, when my little son and my brother Joseph died in quick succession, thought that time had reached its allotted point, and all the living were surely now given over to death and eternity. The child was silent and unsteady like one dazed, and when the fever seized him, too, an unresisting victim, he bore its tortures as though it were his allotted part, in which he had no share but to suffer and submit without a murmur. It was a sharp and long tossing and torment the fever gave him, and while it was going on, one of his gentle nurses, Julia, left his side. It was not until weeks afterwards, when the storm was over, and he sat with us, silent and trying to rearrange our scattered hopes and objects in life, that he learned he would never see her here on earth again.

I will not curse the scarlet fever; for who am I that I should arraign the immutable and irresistible course of Nature, and curse it for any of its effects! but of all the mortal epidemic diseases to which poor man may be subjected without his own immediate fault, it is the only one for which I have never yet been able to find any compensation—except the comfort that having had it one no longer has to dread it. The small-pox can be prevented. The yellow fever generally renews the constitution of the man who has had it, so that however *blasé* and worn out he may have been by ill health or dissipation, he is made again capable of enjoying his life; and if it should become endemic, or a regular disease of the country, it would lose its terrors, and could in many respects be deemed a blessing to the native inhabitants at least. Cholera, in most instances, also seems to make the life fresh and vigorous. But the scarlet fever, besides being more virulent and fatal than either of these, often leaves behind it deafness, sometimes blindness, occasionally dumbness, and a long list of *sequelæ* which destroy beauty, and may torment the victim all through a long life.

Ben escaped with an attack of the dropsy, during which he was plentifully dosed with jalap and cream of tartar. In a few weeks, however, from the time the fever left him he was well; but his little companion was gone; the voices about the house were more hushed, and he commenced in a very lonely way his new life; for he was as though he had commenced to live in a new element. The past was past, and he was now an orphan doubly desolate among strangers—kind persons it was true, quite as kind and far more able to assist the requirements of his boyish nature than any he had ever known; but they were strangers.

All except Sally and Tom: and he showed a great disposition to spend his whole time with them. But that did not meet his guardian's views. Sally was very devoted, but her place was the kitchen or the wash-tub. Tom also was devoted, but was a mischievous black scamp, who would have been very willing to pass a whole existence hunting eggs, chinquepins, and rabbits, and setting bird-traps with his young master. Ben had to be educated in books, according to my father's idea, and fitted to become a useful man, or, at any rate, to make his own living.

I may be pardoned for saying: first, that I do not believe in book-education at all for the generality of mankind; second, that I do not think that ordinary book-education adds to the usefulness, as it certainly detracts from the happiness, of a large majority even of the more intellectual part of mankind; and, thirdly, that I do believe that the man who earns his own living by honest manual labor adds more to the stock of human comfort, which is the soul of most human happiness, than all the scholars, except those who by their learning find out new or readier means to add to those comforts.

I do not believe in book-education (beyond reading, writing, and the first rules of arithmetic) for the mass of the human race, because to acquire it takes up too much time from what is more useful; but principally because the mass of the human race are not intellectually capable of profiting by it. Even reading, writing, and the first rules of arithmetic are more than the large majority can profit by, and are, at best, a dangerous experiment. It has been my fate to dwell with books all my life; they have been my dear companions, my solace in grief, the chiefest sources of my pleasures. I have read and studied all systems of philosophy, from Aristotle down to Kant, and, here recently, to Comte; and it may be because my mind is naturally narrow, or it may be because it has become weakened by age, but, at any rate, now I often ask myself: What is the use? Comte, the latest light, is no wiser than Aristotle. Neither of them, nor all of them, with all their knowledge and ability, with all their subtlety and rhetoric, has ever gone beyond the rules of common sense. They have been for the most part wiseacres, who hardly understood themselves, and were totally incomprehensible to the mass of mankind, even to most of the better sort. They have, none of them, invented anything useful and new, but have only given names to things in common use from the creation of reason and man. Their inventions of the Inductive system and the Deductive system remind me of Molière's *Bourgeois Gentilhomme*, who was overjoyed to find that he always spoke in prose. But, granting that they have made prodigious discoveries, what do their teachings, except those which are plain common sense, profit, when it is found that each in succession tries to destroy the ideas of his predecessors?

The fact is their Philosophies are a muddle, and will muddle the brain of every one who tries to indoctrinate himself in them thoroughly. Man is, after all their learning, forced to rely on FAITH, and HARD WORK at the *practical* arts, sciences, and labors of life. Even if the Philosophies were true, which, except in two or three points, they cannot be, they are not of the slightest practical use; whereas steam, and electricity, and minerals, and metals, and plants, and all the visible and invisible objects and powers of nature, are of real and vital importance, and the workers in them, and the discoverers of the laws which govern them and their relations to each other, are the truly useful portion of mankind. Better and cheaper clothing, food, and medicine are the three great wants of man. Labor and death are the curses upon the race, and whatever lightens labor, makes life more enjoyable, or delays death, is what the race must aspire to. All the rest is very well in its place—as an amusement. I may, if I be rich and perform all my duties, pass my leisure time in discussing the Ego and the Non Ego, the Atomic Theory, the Spasmodic Theory (which is one of my own and is very true), the Inductive and the Deductive, if I please, and no one can blame me. But what possible good can it do me, except to amuse?

This may be regarded by the prejudices of the world as a heresy. But the fact is that I have studied all these things until they made head and heart ache and found myself presently afterwards still perplexed and ignorant; and that Ben Eccles, poor fellow, did the same thing with no better result; and that every other honest man of common sense who studies the same things will confess the same failure.

Mathematics and the kindred topics are useful because they are either immediately practical, or they lead to what is practical and useful, and books upon such subjects are necessary for the preservation of the observations which have been made, for the use of those who can profit by them. But what a small proportion of the human race can understand those observations and put them to any practical use, even if they had time to acquire the learning! And so I can go on and enumerate every other branch of human learning even of the most practical kinds, and about each the same interrogative observation may be made.

The French understand this matter better than we do and have already taken a step or two in the right direction. Their schools of design, attached to several of their great manufactories, where their workmen are taught to develop all the talent nature has given them to an immediately practical use; their *conservatoire*, where music is taught practically and on a large scale; are the beginning of the right work. The way to educate the masses is by showing them what they can see and understand. The object of education is to give mere useful ideas ; and one grain of practical instruction is worth a thousand pounds of book puzzlement.

If we further take into consideration the awful harm which superficial knowledge in religion, politics, medicine, and law always produce, and the very small class who have the time, disposition, and intellect to become profound in those most universal and necessary branches of knowledge, we find the class of even intellectual men who ought to be taught in books to be very limited in number. To hear brutal heresy in religion and politics, go among the farm laborers, the carpenters, and other partly educated artisans throughout Christendom. To hear follies in medicine and law, go to the thousands of jack-leg lawyers and doctors who swarm in America to get a living as nearly as possible without work. In Europe the apprenticeship and examinations exclude ignoramuses (though they do not keep out fools) from those professions.

I am thoroughly convinced—more now than ever—that the two articles of my non-belief, and the one of my belief with which I commenced this topic, are true. But my father did not think so, and the consequence was that he looked around for the best school to which Ben could be sent. My opinion was that if he were put at a trade it should be better for him. It is my opinion still; but the reader will be better able to judge after he has read all of this book

To encourage his patience I here promise that I will not again, if I can avoid it, enter into a display of my own opinions about dry subjects, but will confine myself to the life, opinions, and adventures of Ben, and of his friends, enemies, and acquaintance.

CHAPTER III.

DESCRIBES SOME FRIENDS BEN WAS ABOUT TO MAKE: AND TELLS OF OTHER MATTERS IMPORTANT TO BE KNOWN BY THE WORLD.

TWENTY-FIVE miles from Yatton, just over in the adjoining county, lived the Reverend Dr. Alexander McCleod. He was originally from the north of Ireland, and belonged to one of those families in which Presbyterianism has almost become hereditary—just as Puritanism has actually become with some of our Northern brethren. A materialist would say that the peculiar religious belief had expanded or desiccated some fibres of the brain or heart, and that the expansion or desiccation has after three or four generations become so constitutionally impressed as to be transmitted. However that may be, Dr. McCleod was a strong Calvinistic Presbyterian, and though some of his tenets might appear to most men hard and repulsive, I who knew him well can say that a more kindly or better man in every respect I never knew.

But there was great prejudice against him. He had married a widow of large property, who had already five children, and by her he had a son and a daughter. Mrs. McCleod was one of the best of women; pious, gentle, affectionate, intelligent, and energetic; and she loved her husband and all of her children devotedly. But where there is a large property and two sets of children in the house, what can you expect? The elder set, and their relations, hated the doctor, of course. He was rigid, and that was bad enough, but he had also by his marriage and virility materially subdivided the property, and the consequence was that there was war; not outspoken hostility,—love and respect for the mother prevented that,—but that kind of domestic armed neutrality which engenders more hatred, malice, and slander, than open strife could create.

For a small but active representation of Hell upon earth commend me to a family in which there are disputes about property. And the more intellectual and refined the family, the more aggravated the hell; for the grosser stock would fight it out and end it in some way, whereas the others exercise their imaginations, inflamed by passions, exaggerate the slightest faults, and conjure up enormities of the penitentiary and gallows grades, while the fear of the world keeps their hands and legs tied.

It appears that when the old gentleman first got the property into his hands he was very gentle, and much inclined to be liberal, but the relatives of the elder children had stepped in on their behalf and demanded the most unreasonable concessions, and he had become fretted, and at last had fixed himself immovably upon his legal rights, and would neither bestow nor concede anything not strictly demanded by law or Christian charity. His wife took his part, and soon, from fighting for him, she had to defend herself.

All this, however, by-the-by. I only speak of it in order that the characters of the doctor and his family may be the better understood; for, in the first place, it has in itself nothing to do with the course of my story; and, in the next, the dissension was very quiet and decent, because the children loved their mother, and she loved her husband, and the relatives did not live in the immediate neighborhood.

In sober truth there was very little of the attractive to a young person about the doctor. He was a tall and heavily built man, with a narrow forehead, keen dark-blue eyes, and dark hair, a firm mouth and square, heavy jaws generally bristling with a thick, stiff beard, which he made it a rule to shave off about once in two weeks, and was fond of rasping with the thumb and fingers of his left hand. His voice was deep and sonorous, and he rarely raised or hastened it even when annoyed or angry. In fine, his expression, voice, and manner were austere, and were well calculated to repel the young who did not know him well. Infants were pleased with him, because nature has supplied their feebleness with an instinct more keen and infallible than the reason of the older, who are able to protect themselves; but boys generally dreaded "old Mac," as they called him to each other. They dreaded his manner even after they had found out the great benevolence of his heart.

But he was just the man for Mrs. King; who found herself a widow with four strapping boys and a girl, a large and troublesome plantation, and a natural veneration for preachers. She was a bright-eyed little woman, affectionate, neat, and thorough in everything she did. The doctor's office attracted her, the solidity of his character suited her, and his goodness of heart completely won her; and, as she suited him quite as well, they married. Although he was only a poor Presbyterian preacher, and she was a rich widow, such was the manliness of his character that I doubt if any person ever really believed in his heart that he married her (at any rate, principally) for her money; but the bickerings came, and the children, after awhile, and the prejudice, as I have before related, and the good doctor had taken up a position, head out, at bay, in a moral fence corner, so that, as one of the cooler relatives irreligiously remarked, "neither the law, nor the devil himself could get at him."

All but the youngest of the elder set of children were off at school, and I pass over any description of them, and come to Miss Mary Hart, better known as Aunt Polly, who was of much more interest to Ben Eccles. She was a second cousin to Mrs. McCleod, and had come to live with her soon after her marriage to her first husband, and had continued with her ever since, the most industrious, sympathetic, and faithful of friends. She was a tall, raw-boned, dark-faced woman, with heavy eyebrows, and a large mouth well filled with long and strong teeth. Surely she was no beauty to look at, but children and chickens, ducks, pigs, cows, and everything about the place that could feel gratitude or kindness disputed her love, and never knew that she was ugly. The children of the family hardly seemed to know whether she or their mother had the stronger claim upon them; and although she never usurped authority she was as implicitly obeyed by white and black as though she were sole mistress. The house negroes and those about the yard always came to her when they were sick, and the negro children always shunned her when they had been in mischief.

I do not know that Aunt Polly ever imitated Jeptha's daughter, nor do I judge from her disposition that she ever did, but the most of our race are discontented with their lot in life, and it is usually supposed that old maids regret it most. It has been my good fortune to be acquainted with a large number of that class in my life, and I must bear testimony to the fact that, as a general thing, they are the most beneficent and contented of mortals.

There is a notable difference between them and old bachelors. They are generally old maids because they have sacrificed their selfish desires to others they have loved better than themselves; whereas old bachelors are generally those who have loved themselves better than anybody else. In ninety cases out of a hundred, the family which possesses an old maid possesses a great blessing. She is the good providence of the children; the best of companions for the girls just growing up, the most wisely indulgent of friends for the boys from childhood to manhood; and the source of most of the order and comfort about the establishment. The mother is mother of the children, but she is the mother of the family.

Aunt Polly was a housewife in this sense. What if she were fussy sometimes! Did she not have the whole little world she lived in to keep in order? And can a world be governed by mortal without confusion? And what if old maids do have whims, as they are called! Their imaginations are generally more pure, their ideas more refined, and their general knowledge of the fitness of things more accurate than can be expected in those in more intimate and narrow relations. A mother may be led by prejudice to mistake what is most fitting for *her* daughter or son to do, but the old maid knows what is best fitted for all daughters and sons to do; her views are not limited by the narrow bounds of relationship. I speak, of course, of general abstract fitness and propriety, and of that she is the very best of all arbiters for herself and for other persons. And yet (and it is conclusive proof of the super-excellence of old maids) I never knew one who was not led by the nose by the nephew or niece, cousin, or other pet or pets she had taken into special fondness.

However, we shall hereafter learn more of Aunt Polly. There was another personage in the doctor's family whom I must describe. I am painting Ben Eccles, and must paint at the same time the scene in which he moves. Otherwise, the picture will be as meaningless as would be the one of the youth in the spelling-book without the rocks in the foreground and the temple of fame in the distance.

This person, Mr. Theophilus McCleod, was a personage only in his relation to Ben. He was the doctor's youngest brother, but resembled him in very little. He had been brought out from the Old Country to be started in life in this, and as he had turned his thoughts to medicine rather than to divinity, the doctor had given him a home, and had set him up as a schoolmaster while he was making his preliminary studies. I shall sufficiently describe him by saying that he was of low stature, had blue eyes, a ruddy complexion, an Irish mouth, that he talked with a broad brogue; and that to punish a child excited and frightened him more than it did the child.

The school-room in which Mr. Theophilus presided was built of logs, in one corner of the yard, about a hundred yards from the family residence. It fronted on the plantation road which swept around the fence, leading, to the right, through the woods to the quarters, and across Big Sandy Creek to the fields, and to the left, after passing the fence turned to the north, towards the main road, some two miles off, which passed from Yatton to Rosstown. Just across the road a grove of broad-spreading beeches, and Spanish oaks, and hickories, from among which the undergrowth had long ago been cut, formed a grand play-ground, which stretched along the level and down a gentle slope for a quarter of a mile before it changed to be the denser forest of the Big Sandy bottom, where the thick bushes and tangled vines were the homes and covert of wild turkeys, deer, 'coons, 'possums, and squirrels innumerable. The boys and negroes told stories to each other of panthers and bears there too; but they had been long before driven farther down the creek to the swamp along the river. That they ever had been there, though, was sufficient cause for wariness and sudden alarm to those who found themselves in the dark forest far from the clearings.

The large yard around the house was well shaded by oaks beneath which Aunt Polly's chickens, turkeys, guinea-chickens, ducks, and pigeons flew and scratched, cackled, quacked, and pot-racked, giving animation, and denoting abundance and comfort. The back yard too, in which were the kitchen and out-houses for the servants, was filled with the feathered pets, whose coops and ranges of nests in barrels and boxes were here and there against the fence, and all about. I do not wish to give an exaggerated idea of the number of Miss Polly's favorites, but Ben has told me that the first time he saw her in the yard holding a large tin-pan, and scattering the wetted bran to them as she clucked, and called at the top of her voice: Chick! chick! chickee!! he thought the sky had rained pigeons, and the earth had developed itself into chickens, turkeys, ducks, and guinea-chickens. The pigeons came sailing down upon her from their cote, lighting upon her person, and covering the very pan, while the chickens and other fowl came fluttering and shrieking from all quarters, gathering about her a tumultuous mass of heads and feathers.

I have in a preceding paragraph spoken of the House negroes and the Yard negroes. I might also, if it had been a proper place, have added the Quarter negroes—for all three sets are commonly found upon a plantation in the far South. To those who live in the South this is all very simple, but as my book may possibly be read by others, it will be well that I shall give a few words about our plantation economy.

The economy of our plantations is Waste; greater waste of labor, time, and materials, than can be found elsewhere in Christendom. It may be that the castles in feudal times equalled, but they did not exceed it. To make this apparent, I will describe, as an example, the doctor's residence on his plantation.

The "big house"—as the residence of the white family is always called, whatever its size—was a wooden building of one story, with broad front and back galleries, and a steep roof in which were set dormer windows, which gave light and air to two large garret bed-rooms. A broad passage, in which were the stairs of the upper rooms, ran from the front to the rear, in the centre, and into it opened the dining-room, parlor, and main bed-rooms. A wing at each end of the front gallery contained another bed-room, which opened upon it, and also upon the yard. One of these rooms was occupied by Miss Polly, and the other was allotted to strangers, or to two of the boys when all were at home. A small building in the front yard, called "the office," also contained a bed-room, appropriated to the two eldest boys.

This was a small and modest enough establishment, but to keep it in order and supply its demands there were two negro women, Melissa and Ann, who acted as chambermaids; Big Jane and Little Sue, seamstresses; Mary Thompson, the head nurse; Jenny, about fifteen years old, who nursed little Flora McCleod; and Tom, about the same age, who accompanied and played with Jimmy McCleod, six years old, and occasionally blacked his master's boots. Then there were Old Mathilda (mammy, *par excellence*), a fat old negress who had retired from active service as cook, and only acted as a sort of *chef*, while her daughter, Aunt Sally Ann, assisted by her sister, Little Sis, who was herself a mother, and by her son Jim and Little Sis's son Simon, and another grandson of Mammy's, attended to the kitchen.

These were all the house servants proper, if we except Big Molly, the dairy-woman, Little Jane, her assistant, and the two boys who drove up the cows, and kept off the calves while milking was going on; they were, perhaps, more properly yard servants. Big Molly's husband, Old Tom, whose house was just back of the yard, was the general minder of what was called "the house stock." Black Tom and Sam Fox were the hostlers. Uncle Jacob was the head gardener, and had as his regular assistant his son, young Jacob, and occasionally, in the spring and fall, two other men from the quarter.

Here were twenty-two servants, without including their children and grandchildren too young to be put at regular work, who were employed in the house, yard, and house-garden, to do what four or five white servants could have done far better and more speedily than they. And they thought they worked hard! The most condign punishment, physical and moral, to which they could be subjected was to be sent half a mile off to the quarter, and to take their place in the field with the seventy or eighty other hands, who contentedly spent their lives there doing, except in picking cotton, what in a more favorable climate twenty white men would have done more effectually.

I have made this digression because I wish to place upon record something detailed about the manners and customs of my own people in my own time. The time will come when all this shall be changed; because we are living in an active, working world, adverse to all such fools' paradises. Even if the outer world does not touch it, it will change itself, for it will starve itself out by its own increase.

These digressions are also necessary to my history. To judge properly a man's character, disposition, acquirements, and acts, it is essential that one should know the state of society in which he lives, and his exact position in that society. It is said that some men impress their characters upon an age, but if we are to understand that they are as original as new creatures, and of their own vast power impress that originality upon a nation or a world, it is pure humbug. A man is in all respects the result of what has preceded him; and though his genius may soar ever so high, it rises from the spot which his predecessors had reached; though he be ever so wicked, he but culminates the wickedness of his ancestors, and concentrates the vices of his age and country. Warriors, politicians, lawgivers, scientific men, all start from that goal and only carry a little farther the tendencies and knowledge of their respective ages.

From the time of Adam to this there has been but one original man—the Man, Christ Jesus—and his originality was only in so far as he was divine, and taught and acted divinely. We are not taught that his merely human knowledge and manners differed from those of the age and country in which he lived. Even *his* divine mission was begun at the very time best suited for it; the time for which it was prophesied; the time when the political power of the Jews was about to be extinguished, and, consequently, could not interfere; the time when Peter and John and Luke, the Physician and one of the most perfect of all writers, existed, and when Paul could appear, though he came "as one born out of due time." Nor did he impress the age in which he lived; but as a divine being he, at the best time, brought a redemption apart from which there neither was nor can be any possible redemption, and he taught truths which, necessary for all, were accepted by some of his own age, and for the reception of which all the progress of subsequent ages has only tended to fit the whole race.

Ben Eccles should not have been the Ben Eccles I knew if he had lived under any other circumstances; and what he actually did become I must be allowed to show as artistically as I can. If I had set out merely to tell an entertaining or exciting story, I would not have chosen him as my hero. Indeed, if I proposed to accomplish only those objects I would certainly throw aside my pen, and leave the task of amusing the world to the many, whose youthful imaginations are more attractively creative than my wearied memory is retentive of facts.

CHAPTER IV.

TELLS ABOUT BEN'S JOURNEY TO SCHOOL, AND HOW HE FARED ON HIS ARRIVAL.

BEN'S little hair trunk had been packed the night before by my mother and sister Bel. His wardrobe was for the most part new, and had been made up by them in the fashion and of the material best suited for his new career. It seems to me that I can yet see the little fellow's six white-bosomed shirts, and three check shirts, and his little pants with the flaps in front, packed neatly together with the heavy woolen clothes, and his small store of books, of which he was both proud and fearful; and in thinking of them I remember how I used to hate new clothes when I was of his age. There was something so stiff and unfamiliar about them that I was never pleased until they were well rumpled and a little dirty.

But to return to Ben; his trunk was packed, and after breakfast one bright morning in October it was tied behind my father's barouche, driven by old Silas, and he took a tearful leave of those who had been so good to him, and started to begin a new life in a new scene among total strangers.

The dusty road passed up and down long hills, and over level stretches, sometimes through lanes of dark-gray ugly worm fence, and then through pleasant woods just taking on the hues of autumn; and though the journey was an event, beyond the sudden whirr of a covey of partridges flushed from their wallowing in the warm dust by the horses as they went around some sudden bend in the road, or the playful leapings of the gray squirrels as they searched among the dead leaves for the beech nuts and acorns now beginning to fall, or the stealthy running of some veteran fox-squirrel making for the lofty tree in which he had his abode, or the grating of the wheels over the gravel, and the stopping of the horses to drink as they plashed through the beds of the two or three creeks along the route, it was not eventful. Silas, dressed in his best, was taciturn. He was rather silent on most occasions when driving, but now, and he with his "Sundays" on, it was rather beneath his dignity to be on very talkative terms with a little boy, and that boy a stranger and poor. He was a kind-hearted old fellow in the main, but he knew his own position, which was neither more nor less than an exaggerated reflex of his master's position. That master was the guardian of the orphan, and Silas was therefore the boy's patron. If the boy had been the favored son of some favored friend of the master, Silas would have been obsequious for his patronage. So Ben generally sat in silence, putting his head out of the carriage on this side or that as birds, or squirrels, or passing negroes attracted his notice. But the old man occasionally broke out into soliloquy when a suitable topic was presented:

"Mighty small chance o' cotton dat! Wonder what dey plants dem red hills fur; dey got plenty bottom lan'. Don' know nother. It's dry dis yea', but las' yea' de bottoms drownded out, an' de hills make all de cotton. Reckon ole Mr. Smith think he fooled bof ways. Wonder what he do nex' yea'."

And Silas grinned a grim smile to think of the perplexity of Mr. Smith at such changing cropping seasons.

"There's pretty cotton, Uncle Silas!" exclaimed Ben, as they came to a field in the Baker Creek bottom.

"Le'me see!" said Silas, presently, to himself. "Le'me see! I don' know dat fiel'. Mus' be Squire Hopper's; but when dey clar it? Dat mus' be de fiel' Squire Hopper's Joe done tell me 'bout yea' befo' las'. He say it was gwine to make bale to de acre yea' in an' yea' out. Look like, Joe's right. Done been fo' yea' nex' Chris'mus sence I pass' along dis road." And then he turned back and addressed Ben: "Do dey have sech cotton in No'f Ca'lina whar you come from?"

And as Ben could not answer that question in the affirmative with any assurance of certainty, Silas became a little enlivened, and put several other posers to him, as: whether he knew his folks in North Carolina? If his grandfather was rich? What made his father come out to Georgia? and wound up by letting him know that in his (Silas') opinion, he (Ben) was one of the most fortunate of mortals to have fallen into the hands of the man who was his guardian.

"You take kea," said Silas. "Dey likes you dar at de house; dat is, dey will like you ef you does right. But you take kea! Ole master sen' you to school, an' he 'spec' you to larn. You can't fool *him!* You can't fool Mas' Abe nother. You can't poke you' finger in none of 'ems eye."

"I'm going to be good, and learn, Uncle Silas," said Ben, a little alarmed.

"You better mun; you better," replied Silas, gravely shaking his head. "You ever hea' how ole master sarve dat boy John Higgins? He was so deb'lish dey couldn't keep him at de house, an' he run away from school, an' he play hob all de time; an' master talk to Mas' Abe about him, an' he jes take him to de court an' he been bine him out to ole Mr. Small, de shoemaker; an' ole Small make him work! I tell you he do! Eh, eh! de ole man keep de strap gwine *every* day. 'I make you work, you dog-gone little raskil! I make you work! you cut up bobbery here, dam' you, I skin you alive!' strap, strap! strap, strap! an' John Higgins done foun' his match I tell you. Hello! yonder de road to Doctor McCleod's, I tought we git dar arter awhile!"

It was about noon when Ben was driven up to the doctor's front gate. Miss Polly's guinea-fowls were going about the yard in pairs and bevies jerking their heads forward and back, ejaculating pot-rack! pot-rack! here and there, a cock flapped his wings and crowed, and a hen was cackling and shrieking in the back yard, and pigeons strutted and cooed on the house roof. The haze of Indian summer was just beginning to settle in the air, and in the bright sunshine, shorn of its more fervid ray's, the bees hummed leisurely, as though their season of labor was well-nigh at an end. The hum of a spinning-wheel was heard from one of the outhouses, but no human being was visible, and little Ben felt more and more like a stranger when he got off the carriage, and stood at the gate, as old Silas untied his trunk.

The noise of the iron latch as the gate was opened

roused the fat old house-dog, which came waddling leisurely down the walk from the front steps wagging his tail, and barking huskily and doubtfully. Aunt Polly hearing him, presently looked out of her door, and seeing Ben come to the steps, went on the gallery to meet and welcome him. She kindly took him by the hand, and asked if he were not little Ben Eccles, then ushered him into the broad passage which served as parlor and sewing-room in warm weather, but which now happened to be vacant, asked him to sit down, and went off to announce his arrival to the doctor and family. A negro girl presently came with a waiter, and presented him with a glass of cool water, and then in a few minutes the doctor, and Mrs. McCleod, and Miss Jane King, about his own age, and Flora, and Jimmy, all came in to make his acquaintance. Silas was ordered to take the trunk up stairs, and to then take the carriage around to the carriage-house, and the horses to the stable. And Ben went up stairs to see his trunk properly placed, and then when he had returned felt that one step in his career was accomplished, and that although the doctor was a little awful in appearance, his words and glance were kindly, and that Mrs. McCleod and Aunt Polly were both good women, and that the children were good natured, and altogether that he ought to feel well pleased.

These details are not too unimportant to be narrated. What boy of eleven years of age ever yet went away from familiar faces to live among strangers but was either very painfully or very pleasantly impressed by every, even the minutest, incident of his reception? And not only boys but men and women have that same almost morbid sensitiveness when they first enter a strange circle in which they have for some time to dwell in intimate relations. The bride when she first enters her husband's family; the husband when he first visits his bride's relatives, if they should be strangers; the clerk when he first takes his place with his fellow-clerks; even the prisoner when he is first ushered into his penitentiary or military prison; every one has a soul, like some flowers, laid open to receive the faintest impressions, and upon the first touch it closes upon rankling festers or precious drops of refreshing dew.

Silas, to Ben's mortification, after dinner showed his negro nature—for I contend that in some respects (though not, perhaps, in this particular instance) the race are not possessed of what we term human nature, as applied to the whites. Miss Polly had asked him, soon after he arrived, whether his master had instructed him to come home that evening, and he had answered: "Master didn't tell me adsactly, ma'am. He 'lowed I mus' misgovern by sarcumstances; an' de hosses is mighty tired an' blowed, ma'am."

Now the fact was that my father had expressly told him that unless the roads were in very bad order, or unless some accident should happen, he must return that same afternoon; and the roads were good, though dusty, and not the slightest accident had happened to carriage, horses, or harness. But Silas wished to pay a visit while he was about it. There were a hundred negroes on the place, the most of whom he knew slightly, while his master's reputation secured him a hearty welcome from them all. He wished to hear the news, and he wished to communicate all he knew. The temptation was too great for him not to "misgovern" very liberally, and he did his best to persuade himself that it would be too hard on the horses to return at once.

So, when Ben inquired after dinner if the carriage was ready to start, the doctor asked him what instructions Dr. Page had given about Silas' return, and Ben, who had heard them, told him. The old gentleman at once sent for Silas.

"What did you tell Miss Polly, sir, about your going home this evening?" asked he in his stern manner.

"I 'lowed to her, sir, dat de hosses was mighty hot an' blowed, an' master tole me I mus' misgovern by sarcumstances, sir."

"You're a pretty fellow to misgovern by circumstances, sir! When do you expect to start home?"

"I 'lowed to start early in de mornin', sir."

"Early in the morning? Why, to-morrow is the Sabbath, and do you expect to leave my house and travel on Sunday? Go and fetch the horses here, sir!"

And Silas went and brought the horses, and the doctor examined them.

"Why, sir, they look as though they had not traveled a step to-day. Go and hitch them in the carriage, sir; and be off from here in a half hour! Do you hear?"

So Silas ignominiously missed his visit, and Ben was deeply impressed by the stern, unanswerable manner of the doctor, which seemed to admit neither argument nor entreaty.

It being Saturday, and consequently the holiday, Mr. Theophilus had gone to Rosstown to see the world, and to fulfill some little commissions for his sister-in-law and Aunt Polly, so that it was reserved for another day for Ben to make his acquaintance.

The afternoon passed off pleasantly enough watching, with wonder, Miss Polly among her pets, and investigating the garden, school-house, and play-ground with the children. After the supper (not tea) table was removed the prayer-bell rang. All the white family assembled in the passage, and the house and yard servants, each with a stool or chair, also came and took their seats, and the doctor read and commented upon a long chapter in the Bible, keeping an eye all the while upon his congregation. As one or the other would nod, he would pause and say: You, such a one, stand up! Ben has told me that he often afterward saw as many as half a dozen, with himself, white and black (for the doctor was impartial), standing up at once. The singing would arouse all effectually, but when they got upon their knees for the prayer the drowsiness would again visit the brains of some, who would be sound asleep when the prayer was over, and would be allowed to sleep after all the rest had risen and gone out, when the silence would rouse them, and they would try to sneak out of the room, conscious that the doctor's eye was upon them, and glad if they were not "kept in" and made to stand motionless for ten minutes or more, and then dismissed with a box on the ear, or a sarcastic word, which hurt the worse of the two.

Then came bedtime, and Aunt Polly went with Ben to see if all was in order for him, and to point out which he was to occupy of the three little single beds in the room. As soon as she had bidden him good night and had left, he hurriedly undressed, blew out the light, and got into bed. It was no new thing, alas, for the poor little fellow to spend the night by himself, and wearied by the excitements of the day, he soon fell into a dreamless sleep, to be waked in the morning by the jangling of the bell which rang at sunrise for all to get up; and by the time he was dressed and had overhauled his trunk the bell rang again for morning prayers, to which he descended; and then followed breakfast, and after breakfast a catechism lesson which the doctor set him to get by heart; then came dinner, and after dinner the recitation of the catechism lesson, and reading aloud a chapter in the Bible by all the family—each a verse at a time—and then a saunter in the garden and about the yard. Then came night, and supper, and prayers, as before; and oh! how tired the little fellow was when he got to his bed! and what a dull and weary day Sunday was!

It was the first of many Sundays just like it the boy had to spend at that place; and I verily believe that to this day he dreads when Sunday comes—although he would think it a great sin to admit to himself its distastefulness.

That Sunday question has been very much vexed, and although I do not intend to bore the reader by discussing it at this time, I will remark that, in my opinion, its strict ceremonial observance does as much harm to Christianity as its total non-observance does to religion and health. Virtue, it seems to me, lies in all cases in the just mean between nothing and vice. "The Sabbath was made for man," and he should spend it so as to profit by it in the manner in which it was intended he should profit; not so as either to be bored, or to neglect its uses.

CHAPTER V.

IN WHICH MR. PAGE SHOWS THAT THERE ARE MORE WAYS THAN ONE OF TELLING A STORY; AND DESCRIBES BEN'S SCHOOLMATES.

BESIDES Ben and Jane King, Mr. Theophilus had four other scholars, all of whom came promptly to the school-house by nine o'clock Monday morning. As their influence upon Ben's character, and, as will be hereafter seen, the influence of some of them upon his life, was great, it is necessary that I shall describe them, though I confess that I am weary of this pen and ink sketching of portraits. I fear that doing so much of it at the outset will make me appear like the Dutch leaper Washington Irving has told us of, who took a start of six miles to jump over the mountain, and when he arrived at the foot had to sit down and rest.

Nevertheless, it will be admitted by all that I must tell my story just as it naturally presents itself to my mind. There are very few men the principal incidents in whose lives cannot be told in four or five sentences; while for the most of them one sentence is enough. But what would become of story-telling if no greater scope were allowed? And what would become of a story-teller if he were to be rigidly governed by the rules laid down by others for their kind of stories? Scott has told his stories, and Bulwer, Dickens, and Thackeray tell theirs, and though each has differed widely from the others, each has done admirably well. That proves that there are at least four good ways of telling a story: why may there not be more?

The old Greek and Latin poets and dramatists were most excellent—What an admirable chance I have here to display my learning! But it is one of my strongest desires to avoid the exposure of such flimsy ware. Every school-boy or literary young woman who keeps a commonplace book could pile learning upon my learning, so that my cheap commodities should be crushed. I therefore lump the matter and say, without discriminating, that the old Greek and Latin authors were most excellent: but who has ever yet done great things by imitating them? French dramatists tried it; and where will you find anything more painfully wearisome, in spite of the grandeur of many of its ideas, than the classic French school of tragedy and comedy? It frets me, and makes me stretch myself and yawn to remember it.

No. It is well to have all classic learning, ancient and modern; but to imitate none of it in style: and as for matter, it is best to forget its particulars as soon as possible, and have its excellencies so assimilated with your own mind as that you shall not be able to tell whether an idea is your own, or that of Aristophanes or Schiller. When a thoughtful man has reached this point, his writings can be called neither pedantic nor dull, for they will possess what is called originality, and be at the same time free of affectation.

A story-teller must, above all others, be left free to go his road in his own way. His first requisite is to have a good story, and his next is to tell it naturally and well. He is like a man who invites you to take a ride with him in strange localities, and visit persons who are strangers to you. Though he be but a gump himself, he may keep you amused all the while (some of the best story-tellers I have ever known had no sense otherwise), and if he be a wise and sensible man he will point out each object necessary to understand the locality, will pause with you to admire what is admirable in the view, will bring out by judicious management the peculiarities, whether laughable or sad, of your new acquaintance, and will moralize just enough to keep your heart as well as your senses and intellect observant; so that when you leave him you shall exclaim: What a delightful ride I have had! and what a pleasant friend I have found! I will go with him again if he invite me!

I know that these wise and sensible guides are not those most sought after nowadays. The Jehus are most popular who shout and whip at full speed, at the risk of all necks. But no matter for that; in the end the more quiet drivers shall have had the most passengers—as they always have the best.

Alas! while I know that I am no Jehu, I fear that I lack some of the entertaining qualities of their rivals, and greatly fear that before our journey is half over I shall have to nudge my fellow-traveler to keep him awake, even if he should have the patience to continue with me so far on the journey, or to its end.

However, I will do my best, and my executor shall judge both of my story and of its telling, and will give it to the world, or withhold it, as may seem to him best. Let me then go on and describe Charles and Henry Bowman, George Barnes, and Samuel Stockdale, the four schoolmates whose acquaintance Ben Eccles made that Monday morning.

It is a very extraordinary coincidence that all of the first-class liars I have ever known have had either red or sandy hair. The observation of others may have been different, but I speak only of my own acquaintance. Understand me well. I do not mean mere ordinary liars; for the bulk of the lying done in the world is by the dark haired, as they constitute the bulk of the people. I mean extraordinary liars; geniuses in lying; men who have vivid imaginations, who talk a great deal, and who do not care, and for the most part do not actually know, whether they be telling truth or falsehood.

I do not think that the number of facts I have observed would warrant my founding an *ergo* upon the subject; and theories are very dangerous, for men are apt to fix them in their minds as definite conclusions. Besides, I neither wish to be unjust, nor to subject myself rashly to the ill will of the red and sandy-headed, by theorizing upon the connection between hair of those shades and temperament, the connection between temperament and imagination, between imagination and memory, memory and morals. No, no: it would be inexcusable to propound moral theories upon the color of hair, the squinting of eyes, or any other physical peculiarity. Why should I have my memory cursed by the unfortunate as the inventor of a *Theory* against them, whether it should prove true or false—a point which the present accumulation of statistics does not allow me to decide! Who knows, too, but that my grandniece, the only one of my family, but myself, now living, may marry, and that her husband, or the husband or wife of some child or grandchild of hers, may "breed back," as the stock-men say, and leave the only representative of my branch of the Page family a red-headed, cross-eyed, knock-kneed little body who may, or may not, be either a liar, malicious, or weak-minded?

The utmost the facts in my possession warrant me in saying is that, when a man with a sandy or red head starts to lying he is apt to excel at it. Charles G. V. Bowman had sandy hair, and he had a remarkable gift of lying. His hair also curled, and therefore (Plutarch and several others of the ancients, as well as most of the moderns, who have discussed that important point about the hair, warrant me in using that therefore), I say, because his hair curled, *therefore* he was a lively liar. His light-blue eyes were rather small, but he was a very handsome boy of fifteen, almost as handsome as the Stanley Ruggles of my own boyhood.

His brother Henry was two years the younger; had dark hair and gray eyes, and was already of the larger stature; but he was slow in body and mind, good-natured, but passionate and stupidly headstrong. They were the sons of Col. Bowman, whose home plantation was about three miles from Dr. McCleod's. He had two other large plantations, one adjoining his home place, and one down on the river, and was a rich man. He was rather ignorant, willful, and pompous; had a great estimation of rich men, and, consequently, a low esteem for the poor. He was charitable enough when it came to giving, but had no sympathy with poverty or suffering. His sons had been raised in his doctrines, and had imbibed his feelings. Their mother was a weakly sort of woman, and had little control over them.

So much for the two Bowmans. The father of George Barnes lived six miles from the doctor's, upon a plantation much smaller than either of Col. Bowman's three places, and as George was a fat, slow-minded, good-natured boy of about Henry's age, he was, of course, the butt of the Bowmans, who patronized him. Sam Stockdale was of altogether different clay. He was the son of old Dr. Stockdale, of Rosstown, who neither was nor wished to be rich, and who had a hearty contempt for such men as Col. Bowman. Sam, who was a slim, silent, dark-eyed boy, of good parts, solid character, and generous heart, had inherited his father's independence and contempt for little-mindedness. George and Sam boarded at Dr. McCleod's, and were Ben's roommates. They went home every Friday evening, and remained until Monday morning.

Ben was the youngest of the boys, and his reception was just in accordance with their characters. The Bowmans were supercilious, George was stupidly friendly, and Sam was polite and manly.

Having described Ben's schoolmates as well as his school, it would be useless to narrate in detail their little adventures, and how they got along together. I am not writing a Sunday-school book, or a history for good little boys, but a grave philosophic work for grown folk. It has been necessary to describe the childhood of Ben Eccles; but after the few additional details I will give in this chapter, I will no longer concern myself about him until he shall have reached a more mature age.

Indeed, it is hardly necessary that I should even mention the few additional details of his school-boy days, beyond saying that he remained five years at Dr. McCleod's house; that in the second year Mr. Theophilus left the school for a medical college, and his place was taken by Jamie McDougal, a Scotchman, who was almost as well indoctrinated and as firm in church matters as the doctor himself, but whose conduct when he sometimes got off to town was in total contrast to his knowledge. The practiced reader of stories will have jumped at once to the other facts. Of course Aunt Polly was the dearest old lady in the world, and Ben worshiped her while she petted Ben; of course Charley Bowman tried to tyrannize over him, and Sam Stockdale became his protector; of course Jane grew to be a nice young lady, and was sent away to a girl's school; and of course all of the other little incidents which naturally grew out of the characters and circumstances of the parties.

There is one incident, however, which the practiced reader will not have guessed, and that I will relate in a very few words. After Ben had been at school three years, that is when he was about fourteen, upon the occasion of a revival at the Spring Hill Church, four miles from the doctor's, which he, with the family, constantly attended, he became very much impressed with religion, and joined the church.

This act is the key-note to his subsequent history, and although it is here related at the close of a chapter, the reader will have ample opportunity to reflect upon its consequences.

CHAPTER VI.

INTRODUCES TO THE READER A SURE-ENOUGH LADY, AND TELLS OF SEVERAL MATTERS HE WOULD BE SORRY NOT TO HAVE KNOWN.

ABOUT four miles from Yatton, near the Rosstown road, lived the widow Garthwaite. She was a good woman, but hardly one of those the apostle called "widows indeed," for she was rich, and had a widow's eye to the main chance. I knew her well from her girlhood; we went to school together, and as she was several years the elder and was very pretty, I was for awhile a little in love with her. She married Tom Garthwaite five years before I was grown, and he died seven years after the marriage, leaving her a rich widow with three children, the two eldest of whom died soon after their father. She was still young enough, and had plenty of offers. Why she never married again I had not the means of knowing. Tom had been a rough, spreeing man, and it was whispered among the ill-natured that the kindest act he ever did his wife was his involuntarily leaving her a widow.

How that was I do not know; but I do know that it was a rough, spreeing age and country, and that the widow might well fear the sobriety of almost any man there whose rank in life fitted him for her husband; unless it might have been some preacher, and she was one of the few women I have ever known who did not think them always the best men in the world. The fact is, that at that time almost every preacher who came to the South was a Yankee in search of a fat salary, with the subadmitted (to himself) ultimate chance of a rich wife; and Mrs. Garthwaite being gifted by nature with a good deal of strong common sense, and also with a fair share of the desire to take care of her own, and not being oppressed either by nature or education with much superstition, could not admire a man for the sake of his office. Indeed, she was one of those who are curious to know how such a one became an *officer;* whether merely by appointment of an earthly power, or by a commission from the only Head of the Church. She was in advance of her age, and was therefore not in the highest favor with either preachers or with most of her own sex, who, though they respected and liked her, used to talk about her as a sort of free thinker.

And yet a more correct woman in all her deportment, or one who was more firmly convinced of the fundamental truth of Christianity, it would be hard to find. Her charity, too, to proper objects, was notable. The only question with her was whether the object were a proper one. Her poor neighbors she esteemed most proper objects, so did she the Rev. Mr. Snow; but I am firmly convinced that the Tract Society, for instance, never "saw the color of her money."

I must not be misunderstood with regard to Mrs. Garthwaite. She was by no means what would be called nowadays "a strong-minded woman." She was as womanly as a woman well could be, but not weakly so. My dear father used to say that she laughed more cheerily than any other woman in the county, and that no woman with a hard heart or a bad conscience could laugh so pleasantly. As she was not fond of preachers because they were preachers, and there was not one of them who commanded her respect for his other qualities, she used to come to him for advice in all her spiritual troubles (and often in those of a temporal nature), and he knew and greatly esteemed her good sense, and the true piety and nobility of her character and disposition.

Her house was a great staring frame building of two stories, which had been planned by Tom Garthwaite when half drunk, and had been built without her being consulted in the matter. It stood near the big road, upon a hill in an old, worn-out field, and except a few china-trees near the front gate, and a few young oaks set here and there, and trying to live and grow in the yellow clay, and some shrubbery planted around the house, there was neither tree nor bush within a quarter of a mile. Tom used to say that "he'd be d—d if he didn't have the breeze if any came about, and he'd be doubly d—d if he would have the gnats and musquitoes."

I must be pardoned for repeating this gross remark,

but it tells a whole history; not only about Tom's manners and character, but about the climate, insect life, etc., of the country. It is much insisted that a writer shall condense.

Mrs. Garthwaite did not like the situation or the construction of the house, and she was abundantly rich to afford to live in town or anywhere she pleased; but the place was quite as healthy as any she could find for herself or her daughter, Susan, and was near enough to town to give her plenty of society if she wished any beyond that in the immediate neighborhood, which was excellent. Taking the *pros* and *cons* altogether, as she was a prudent woman, and averse to troubling "well enough," she remained at the house and made the best of it.

And very excellent was the best of it she made—at least to her friends and visitors. Some way or another her mutton, raised on the short grass of the yellow hills, was declared by every one to be the finest in the county, and she had the reputation of having it barbecued as no one else could cook it. Then her butter was always plentiful, come rainy season or drouth, and come grass or "weed" was always golden and sweet; and her honey was the whitest of any, and had the crispest comb, in which it was almost crystallized; and her coffee was the most fragrant and clearest, and her waffles and biscuits were the lightest. I declare it almost gives me an appetite to think of the delicious meals I used to get there, and the exquisitely neat manner in which they were served; and when I think of her smiling, hearty welcome, and remember the airy bed-rooms with their elegant furniture and downy pillows, and snowy sheets fragrant with rosemary, old as I am, I think I should greatly enjoy a few days again at Mrs. Garthwaite's.

But these were everyday affairs which Mrs. Garthwaite, with the means at her command, could no more avoid than a bee could help making its cell a hexagonal, and keeping its hive clean and neat. I verily believe that had she been lost in a desert she would have trained the branches of the shrub beneath which she crouched into symmetry, and so as to give the greatest surface of shade, and the sand around it she would have lightened and smoothed before she died.

It was at the children's parties, to which she often treated her daughter, that her best was at its most glorious best. If the weather were fine and pleasant, what need for growing shade-trees for out-door shelter, when the thousands of trees in the neighboring groves offered their branches for arbors! And if it were foul or cold there were no roomier parlors, and not a broader passage, or more capacious galleries in the county than were in "The Barn," as she had named her house. The weather or season could be no drawback at Mrs. Garthwaite's, and most of the children of the town and its vicinity knew it, and felt sure of pleasure when they were invited there. She had two negro men who were good fiddlers; another, Abe, who was a chronometric enthusiast upon the tamborine; Tom, who thought himself an artist upon the triangle; and still another, "James Gladden, sir, I thank'e," who was perfectly up to every phase of a cotillion and a reel. Whether under an arbor or in the house they were almost unwearied in their music; and well they might be, for when children are the dancers, and have entered into the spirit of it, the sets succeed each other very quickly.

I myself never was a dancer; not that I lacked activity or the choregraphic faculty; I never was, as I once heard it remarked at a ball about a young man who had boasted of his strength and activity, "too strong to jump and too active to dance." But the fates decreed that beyond the simplest reel or cotillion I never should acquire a skill; and, consequently, I never much enjoyed children's parties when I was a child. I enjoy them now. There is just as much puppyism and coquetry displayed there as at the balls of grown folk, and the ill-nature, vanity, and selfishness are more remarked, because children are less hypocritical. The same young lady who now replies when asked to dance by one of the ineligible: "Excuse me, sir, I am engaged for every set," would have said when a child: "No, I won't dance with you, my ma don't want me to." But, on the other hand, one will often see at a children's party more chivalrous gallantry and more gentle modesty than he is apt to find among older persons, for the reason that these qualities are more called forth by the frank rudeness of others; and it is a very excellent opportunity of judging the raising and conjecturing the future characters and dispositions of the young guests.

From Mrs. Garthwaite's parties the most quarrelsome boors always went away soothed and happy. She had a way about her, a gentleness and an authority, a sympathy and a knack, which would have kept in order an assembly of young monkeys with burnt tails so that not a squeal would have been heard but that it should have immediately been followed by grimaces of pleasurable content.

I have met with few persons who resembled her in this respect to any great degree; but I have met a few, and they were always ladies, and very intelligent and refined ladies. A coarser nature, or one less accustomed to the ways and amenities of life, could not have the sympathy and authority; a nature less profoundly and exquisitely hypocritical could not have the gentleness and knack. A great blundering, combative man, however elegant in manners and insincere in heart, could never accomplish it.

The reason for this difference can easily be understood by any one who has reflected upon the character of "the sex." A woman who, with her sensitive knowledge of right and wrong and perfect purity of imagination, always acted and spoke as she thought and felt, would be as much out of place in society as death in the ball-room. Mankind and womankind would flee from her as a pest. She is forced to be a hypocrite, and is willingly and naturally a hypocrite all her life, not to deceive, but to avoid giving useless pain. She is a hypocrite to her husband if she be a good wife, and to her children if she be a good mother. Above all is she a hypocrite to her acquaintance if she esteem them, and if she herself be really amiable and good. Why, bless my soul, one or two of the very dearest and most sympathetic female friends I have ever had and loved I knew all the time in my inmost heart cared nothing for me in their inmost hearts. But were they any the less my friends for that? They were married women, or else I was married and they were not, and was I to ask their warm affection? Was I to seek to supplant their husbands, or to induce them to supplant my wife? They were my good friends, always ready to enter into my likes and dislikes, to keep my secrets, to advise me wisely when I needed advice, and should I not have been a pretty fool if I had not been contented with their hypocrisy when it was of such a character? My experience and observation lead me to believe that a woman (and the more intelligent she is the more strictly is it true) either loves with all her heart and soul—and in that case loves her husband, or her lover—or she does not love at all. Her friendship is hypocrisy; but an hypocrisy so natural, so beneficent, and so deceptious to herself, that it is very beautiful and sweet, and the man towards whom it is exercised should think himself blessed and be contented. Let him not seek for more than the sweet hypocrisy unless he intend marriage. If he do, he will not only be a fool, but will be laughed at by the fair one as a fool.

Moralizing is apt to be the vice of the old.

From what I have said of Mrs. Garthwaite it will be seen that her daughter, Susan, had an excellent mother, in every sense of the word excellent, as applied to a country lady who did not set herself up as a saint, a genius, or a heroine. The daughter was pretty much what her name, Susan, denoted. It is a great mistake to suppose that persons, particularly girls, are named, either by their parents, or by truthful writers, according to their characters, dispositions, and appearance. They really seem in the greater number of instances to take their qualities from their names. I could instance the name Mary, and all its sweet associations;

but that was the name of my darling wife, and it could be plausibly suspected that my affection supplied me with my theory. But leaving that aside I could go on and moralize very prettily upon the subject of names, and I have promised myself to guard against that vice of composition. I avoid it now, only remarking that though I hardly believe that the name really affects the character, I do really believe that had I been named Clarence I should not have lived sober and to my present age.

But however that may be—and it is very difficult to leave the theme and go on with the story, particularly as it is just now about a little girl—Susan was a real Susan; had dark-blue eyes, long brown curls, rosy, plump cheeks, a pretty mouth, a nose very slightly *retroussé*, was very amiable, and had plenty of spirit. In appearance she, as girls are apt to do, rather resembled her father than her mother, and her mind and disposition were also much like his, only greatly softened. In spite of his headstrong willfulness he was a good-hearted, generous fellow, with good hard sense, and his intemperance had not yet become so constitutional as to affect the minds and bodies of his children disastrously. I would gladly make Susan out as superior as her mother in every respect, but I am forced to stick to facts as they were. She was nevertheless a very sweet and lady-like child, who was as perfectly at her ease and as solicitous for the pleasure of every one around her as an intelligent, good-hearted girl entirely accustomed to her position could be.

The practiced reader is now ready to jump to conclusions, and exclaim, she's just the girl to suit Ben Eccles when they both grow up!

I grant it at once; it is useless to try to deceive a reader who is thoroughly conversant with books and human nature. She did just exactly suit Ben Eccles, and he fell desperately in love with her at one of the parties he attended when on a holiday visit to my father's. It was a boy's love, but none the less strong and true for that, and none the less sensitive, and shrinking, and hopeful, and absorbing. And after he had seen more of her, and had become more accustomed to his love—the love of a boy of fourteen for a girl of eleven—he gloried in it and reveled in it, and built all sorts of gorgeous castles in the air as abodes for the loved one. Not only so, but on one Christmas occasion when the two Bowmans and Sam Stockdale happened to be in Yatton on a visit to friends (I will hereafter tell about the relatives of the Bowmans), and were invited to the party at Mrs. Garthwaite's, he was proud to introduce them, and to show himself before them as a hero for the nonce, with the avowed and hopeful prospect of being in the future a permanent hero in the most brilliant and important of all the achievements of the battle of life.

If any one think that I speak too gravely and earnestly of this young passion, I must ask him to remember, reflect, and wait.

It would never do for me to so anticipate my story and gratify the overweening vanity of the practiced reader as to state at once that she returned or did not return the ardor of her young lover. But I will say so much as that she of course knew of his preference almost as soon as it was conceived, that she knew all his sad history, and that she felt very kindly for the gentle, enthusiastic, imaginative, poor little beau.

Pshaw! This was not the only or the most momentous love affair which was commenced or concluded at Mrs. Garthwaite's children's parties. After night came on there was always a dance for the young folk of larger growth, who kept it up in mirth and decent jollity until the latest hour to which custom allowed them the privilege. Was it not there that Dr. Stanhope and Kate Stirling agreed to make a match? and Peter Talliafero and Mary Singleton, who had fallen out, made it up again, to be married at the end of a month? And was it not there that——

But why recall these scenes and events! The actors in them have almost every one departed, and I doubt if one of them, in preparing himself or herself to take the dark cold journey, ever for a moment cast a thought back to the cheerful lights and merry sounds in Mrs. Garthwaite's house. Of all the actors of my acquaintance Ben alone remains, and I alone of all the spectators remember the light, and life, and pleasure of those happy times.

CHAPTER VII.

BRINGS BEN'S BUSINESS AFFAIRS UP TO DATE: AND DISPOSES OF ONE OF HIS PEDAGOGUES.

THE Lodge in Yatton of course communicated the death of Captain Eccles to his Lodge in North Carolina, and at my father's request I also wrote to Ben's grandfather, Mr. Matthew Robbins, telling him exactly the state of affairs and the condition and prospects of the boy. It was a long time before the answer came to my letter. I have it yet, and it was as follows, in a round, formal hand:

——— N. Carla. March 10, 18—

Dr Sir

Your estd favr of the 3d Aug. ult. has been received, and contents noted.

Captain Benjamin Eccles married my daughter against my will, but now that they are both dead I have no more to say. Having recently made a purchase of negroes my means are at present limited, and it will be impossible for me to make any advances.

Capt. Eccles' executor must do the best he can for the child.

This is written for me by Mr. Ashe, merch't, of this place.

Respy yr obt servt to command

MATTHEW ROBBINS

per J. A. ASHE.

To ABRAHAM PAGE ESQ

YATTON GA.

It seemed to me that this letter manifested a grasping, unfeeling disposition, but it was all we heard from Ben's grandfather or family for four years. Then, just before my father's death, I received another letter, written by a different person, for Mr. Robbins, in which the old man manifested some anxiety to know how his grandson was doing, and suggested the idea that he should soon be required to come on there. After the death of my father I became his administrator, and the administrator *de bonis non* of Captain Eccles' estate, and Ben's guardian; and not many months afterwards received another letter from North Carolina informing me of the death, intestate, of old Mr. Robbins, and of the fact that his estate, consisting of a small plantation and some negroes, was to be equally shared by Ben and a younger cousin, who were the sole heirs. As the estate would be more profitable to the heirs by being kept together than by either being divided in kind or sold and the proceeds divided, and as I learned that the administrator in North Carolina was an honest and capable man of business, it was arranged that it should be carried on as before until the younger of the two should come of age. Within a year intelligence came of the death of the young cousin, leaving Ben sole heir of a property which, though not large, might be easily increased, and was, at any rate, large enough to support him comfortably. Other arrangements had then to be made with regard to the administration.

I will not inflict upon the reader a detail of all these business matters. The facts I have stated have been given merely as a necessary part of Ben's history, and I have given them as briefly as possible. I have been the more inclined to make the matter short, because I have feared that the pat manner in which it all fell out for his benefit might be taken for the stale ingenuity of a story-maker, instead of the narrative of facts by a plain story-teller. How easy it would be for me, if I wished to excite sympathy, to make Ben out a poor young nobleman of nature, and a brilliant genius, who is loved for his fine qualities, or despised for his poverty. In the one case I could minister to the morbid love of excitement and admiration of a superior nature to which the world is given; and in the other I could gratify the sympathy of the world by describing suffering merit; or its envy, by portraying the blind, haughty folly and wickedness of a "bloated aristocracy" of wealth; and both sympathy and envy are very common in the world. There are, however, too many records existing, and too many witnesses now living to testify to the exact truth, for me to indulge my fancy in the matter and my desire to please.

At the end of Ben's fifth year it was concluded by Dr. McCleod to break up the school at his house. After his brother, Mr. Theophilus, left, he had kept it up for the sake of Ben, in whom he took a great interest, and for his own little son, James, who was then nine years old, and had been crammed with Ruddiman's Rudiments and *Historia Sacræ*, until he had become able to bolt portions of Cæsar—most indigestible meals for a young stomach. Mr. McDougal was a good Latin scholar; in fact, he knew more about Latin than he did about English. He was one of those book-educated men who pride themselves upon their learning, and despise the unlearned in books as an inferior portion of humanity.

"Hoot, mon!" he would exclaim to Ben—but I must be excused imitating his Scotch brogue—"a man who is not learned in all the Elements is no man at all. He is little better than the beasts that perish, the Scriptures tell us about. He eats, and drinks, and works, and his horses and oxen do the same. It's when he becomes acquainted with the sacred oracles of polite learning that he commences to live as a man."

It is generally some idle, good-for-nothing drone we hear using that kind of argument—a kind of argument which has antiquity to support it. The practical spirit of the age, and every earnest man who has caught that spirit, has learned to estimate "polite learning" at its true value. As an end it is of all things the most valueless; it should be sought for only as a means. Such scholars as was Jamie McDougal will go scanning and parsing through the fields, and declaiming from Seneca or Homer in the workshops of life, despising those who do not understand them, and yet whose labor is burdened for their support: for every non-producer is supported by the producers.

One Sunday morning McDougal asked Ben, "What is the chief end of man?"

"To glorify God," answered Ben promptly, "and to enjoy him forever." And then he added quickly, "What is 'to glorify God,' Mr. McDougal?"

"Hm!" ejaculated Mr. McDougal, straightening himself, and looking a little dictatorial and a little puzzled. "Hm! What is the next question, sir, in your Catechism?"

"The next question is," answered Ben, "What rule hath God given to direct us how we may glorify and enjoy him?"

"And what is the answer, sir?" asked Mr. McDougal.

"The Word of God," answered Ben, glibly, "which is contained in the Scriptures of the Old and New Testaments, is the only rule——"

"That will do, sir," said Mr. McDougal. "Now, doesn't the Scripture say: 'Whether therefore ye eat, or drink, or whatsoever ye do, do all to the glory of God.' And what more do ye want?"

Ben wanted and wished a great deal more, but he feared to make himself ridiculous by asking questions for the further explanation of what to his teacher seemed so perfectly satisfactory. So he determined to study out the matter for himself, and learn what it was to glorify God, and what was the rule upon the subject contained in the Scriptures of the Old and New Testaments. It puzzled him many a long day when he grew older, until it grew to be the great puzzle and maze of his mind.

I only introduced this conversation in this place as an example of Mr. McDougal's shallowness, and to draw from it a positive refutation of the idea some good persons have of the utility of classical learning as a part of general education. If it be true, as I think it is, that man was created for the glory of God, and that his chief object should be to glorify God, it seems to me that of all men the unpractical bookworm comes farthest from the object. A few, a very few men have "a gift that way." To delve among Greek and Latin roots or arbitrary signs, is their one talent, and by its cultivation to the utmost they certainly—though generally unintentionally—glorify God who gave it to them. Other men, and still very few, have in addition to that gift the talent to make plain to all by translations and commentaries the learning they acquire, and they glorify God when they do that. But to present classical learning to the minds of mankind as being a thing which is valuable in itself and to God's glory, apart from the practical lessons it may teach, is a great error. There is no part of learning which may not at some time be practical and thus valuable; and it is to be regretted that every man has not all learning. But the question of education is one of utility, and must be treated of as it affects the mass of men who are created for the glory of God. Ninety-nine men out of a hundred have neither the taste, nor the capacity, nor the time to acquire classical learning, and even if they had the taste, capacity, and opportunity, it would, except in the rarest cases, be a total waste of time, which might be employed to the glory of God in benefiting themselves and their fellows.

Jamie McDougal was impressed with the idea that learning in Latin and Greek was intrinsically valuable, "and made a man of him," and he studied hard under the Dominie of the little village in which his parents lived; and when the time came they pinched and starved to send him to Edinburgh, and to keep him there till he finished his studies, and thought themselves repaid by his ability to read Tacitus and Homer without a dictionary, to dispute with the Dominie about Greek particles, and to puzzle him with problems in Conic Sections. And here was Jamie McDougal, strayed off to the antipodes, a drunken schoolmaster who had never benefited himself or another human being. He could neither plough, sow, nor reap; could not drive a nail without mashing his fingers, or drive a horse without upsetting the vehicle.

It is easy enough to say that this was the fault of Jamie McDougal; but that is a mistake. It was the fault of the system, a system which is only now in these late practical days going out of vogue. Men are beginning to see that to glorify God more than barren learning and passively doing no wrong, are required. Energetically putting to practical use the talents He has given them to discover and make profitable use of the laws and objects of nature He has created, is one of the manners in which they glorify His wisdom, power, and goodness; actively doing right to each other and benefiting themselves and each other by labor in what they find to do for living and for pleasure, is to glorify His holiness, justice, and truth.

Jamie McDougal did none of these things. He did wonders with a slate and pencil, and was perfectly familiar with the Ancients, but that was all. During the first year of his stay at the doctor's he made periodical visits to Rosstown, where he would get quietly drunk Friday evening, and remain so till Sunday morning, when he would begin to sober off, so as to return all right to his school Monday morning. And so he went on for several months undetected by the doctor, who was not suspicious, and rarely went to the town, or heard from there. But at last the frolics were prolonged over Monday; and then got still more flagrant.

He even came to his duties two or three times before he was quite sober, and suspicion being aroused, the whole truth came out, and he was discharged, and the school was broken up.

Ben, who was now my ward, told me about the man's dissipation with many expressions of horror.

Now, I knew the boy's heart, and that he was perfectly sincere in his views of the enormity of McDougal's offences: but somehow or another it has always given me a pang when I have seen and heard a boy express too much horror at the vices of the appetites of others. Apart from its too great resemblance to the acts and protestations of a hypocrite, it is, when most sincere, a sign of weakness in the boy. The same qualities which in their strength make him rigidly righteous allow him to run to the greatest excesses when they become weakened.

CHAPTER VIII.

BEN ECCLES QUITS SCHOOL, AND GOES TO COLLEGE: AND COMES HOME AND STARTS IN HIS PROFESSION.

SO Ben had to leave his school and the place which had been his pleasant home for five years—a long time at his age. The Bowmans and Sam Stockdale had long ago been sent off to college, and their places had been taken by other boys, sons of neighboring gentlemen. Ben and George Barnes alone remained of the old set. The breaking up was unlooked for, and word had to be sent to me before Ben could be disposed of. He had parted sadly with the boys after many hand-shakings and promises to write to each other. The day before old Silas was to come for him he went around and made presents of what he could to his favorites among the negro boys, reviewed and bade farewell to the dogs, and play-ground, and garden, and each familiar spot, gave Jimmy his ball and fishing-rods, and helped Aunt Polly to pack his little trunk.

Ah, Aunt Polly! she was the hardest of all to leave. She had taken him to her heart and had been mother, aunt, and elder sister to the poor orphan. She had stood between him and many a whipping from his masters and the doctor; had protected him from slights and neglect; had soothed his wounded feelings; had sympathized with his hopes and fears, his enthusiasms and depressions. Her long bony fingers had kept his clothes always whole and in the nicest order. He had found her many a Saturday night sitting up darning his socks for the next day and peering at her work through her iron-rimmed spectacles, which she only wore when working by candle-light, and in which he thought she looked so funny. It never occurred to his mind that she was an ugly old woman. To him she was beautiful, or, what is still better, kind, loving, and pleasant; without flaw or defect. That is the kind of beauty which never fades, but becomes more and more perfect the longer it is contemplated.

Silas came over night with the barouche—which I had borrowed from my mother for the occasion—and brought a note from me to the doctor. Ben was to start the next morning after an early breakfast. The prayers that night seemed to him more impressive than they ever did before—impressive of the flitfulness and vanity of all earthly things. The doctor referred to the parting, and prayed God to bless the boy in all his future career, and Ben sobbed silently while on his knees, and when bedtime came and he gave the dear kind friends his last good-night kiss, he could contain his grief no longer, but wept outright before them all.

The next morning he waked with a load upon his heart. But breakfast was soon over; the last leave was taken, and he started to Yatton. For two or three miles his grief made him disinclined to take any interest in the journey, but when the thought struck him: how changed were his circumstances since his first trip with Silas along that road; he found much cause for cheerfulness and hope. Then, he was poor, and had a heart almost empty; now, his future was assured, and he had a heart filled with loved objects, and knew that he was loved by them. Besides, he was going to the object of his fondest devotion; or, at least, he was going to the vicinity of her mother's, for she was away at school; and might he not chance to see her? Who knew? She might be at home on a holiday, or something might have occurred, or might soon occur to fetch her there. When he had first traveled that road, five years ago, only a moment to look back upon, he was only eleven years old and was friendless; now he was sixteen and knew and loved Susan. In five years more he should be of age and Susan should be a young lady, and if she only loved him then he should be the very happiest of mortals.

Of his own constancy, until then, he had no fear. He would certainly be true to her; it were treason to even doubt himself; and he would be a great man for her sake.

He was heedless of the miles as they followed each other. Up hill and down hill, forest and field, were all the same to him, as he was absorbed in his happy thoughts. Silas hardly knew what to make of his mood, and tried several times to enter into conversation, but in vain. He no longer addressed him as "you!" and "little boy!" and "I say!" when he wished to attract his attention, but called him "Mas' Ben," now that he had property of his own, and was of the imposing age of sixteen. (That is another point in which negro nature resembles human nature: Money is to them "respectability.") At last, however, he hit upon a theme which made Ben's blood tingle, and fully aroused him.

"Mas' Ben!" said Silas, as they were passing near Mrs. Garthwaite's; "Dey say ole Miss Gart'waite's mighty lonesome. Miss Susan been gone to Augusty mos' six mon's. Dey say she comin' home Chris'mus."

Ah, how many weary months till Christmas! And where should he be when Christmas came? Far away at some school, perhaps. He would not go away to school! But how could he become a great man, and worthy of Susan if he should not go! It was a dreadful predicament; but he would see his guardian about it. Blessed guardian, if he would only bring his hopes to pass!

If any one suppose that in supplying these thoughts and emotions to Ben Eccles (and I confessed in the outset that it would be frequently necessary for me to say and think a good deal for him), if any one suppose, I say, that in these thoughts and emotions I have exceeded probability, he must certainly have forgotten his own youth, or have had a youth not worth remembering. There is no estimating the brilliancy and complexity of the day-dreams in these early days of youth when passion is first felt, and the imagination is still pure and unlimited by stern realities, or, rather, is uncontrolled even by possibilities. In truth, the intelligent and imaginative boy of sixteen is wiser in his day and generation, has more knowledge and more energy in proportion to his age, than the man of forty. If it were not so, if men grew in knowledge, wisdom, and energy as rapidly from sixteen to forty as they do from ten to sixteen, there would be no bounds to their acquirements. The greatest men of the past would sink into utter insignificance beside such Godlike force.

Pooh! why do I, so old-man-like, try to justify my attributing strong feelings and thoughts to Ben Eccles at sixteen! When he presented himself to me that afternoon on the street near my office he had a chew of tobacco in his mouth, and his pants were braced up and strapped down far tighter than my own; his boots had higher heels and longer toes than mine; and his voice, with but an occasional, faint, gosling inflection, was manly, though not full—it never was. Modest and quiet as he was, constitutionally, he already thought his feelings and thoughts those of a man. He possibly gave me credit for knowing a little more about law and business than he did, but in point of scholarship he no doubt suspected my superiority, and in the matters of love and sentiment he possibly denied it. I should not have been at all astonished if he had at once asked my consent to his marriage, or proposed to manage his own affairs. He was modest and quiet, as I have said, but a fair average boy of sixteen must be treated as a man, or he does not understand you, his dignity is wounded; and the parent or guardian who does not pay the most delicate attention to his boy's feelings, and avoid in every way wounding his self-respect, does a great and permanent injury.

A day or two after his arrival we had a grand consultation. I asked him what he wished to do now, and what occupation or profession he wished to pursue in life. He deferred to my judgment, but said that his desire was to study and practice law. I advised him to give the subject a further consideration, and in the mean time to go to college until it should be time to commence his legal studies, if he insisted upon being a lawyer; and I pointed out to him the great necessity in that profession for all the learning he could acquire, be it ever so much or so varied. In short, we talked the whole matter over, and he agreed to go at once to Columbia College in South Carolina, which was then the great Southern university for our part of the South. As soon as his wardrobe could be prepared he went, and from time to time I heard good reports of his conduct and progress. The remainder of the session carried him through the Freshman Class, and he then went through the Sophomore and Junior Classes. Finding himself over nineteen years old when he was about half through his "Senior" year, he became restless about his law studies. He was very anxious, he said, to obtain his license as a lawyer by the time he was twenty-one, and graduation was nothing. In fact, the last year at college amounted to nothing, he argued, and he wished I would allow him to come to Yatton and begin his legal studies at once. I consented, and he came to my house, and in a day or two took his place in my office as my student.

Upon his first arrival he was, of course, afflicted with college ways. He had a collection of pipes, chibouks, hookahs, clay pipes of various shapes, wooden pipes, and cob pipes, to one and the other of which he was, I thought, rather too devoted. And he had a choice assortment of boots and shoes, and fancy coats, vests and pants—all of which I thought too fancy. But he had become so sensitive that it was painful, even in jest, to disapprove of any of his ways; and, besides, I knew that they would all gradually wear into the fashion of those around him. All I did was to caution him against the abuse of tobacco. To use it was all very well, and so long as it did him no injury he was right to use it, or any other thing his soul or appetite desired. He had no right, however, to use it to excess.

And so Ben Eccles was at last launched in his career. So he may be said to have commenced life, and hereafter my story is to be of a more manly cast, and I must change my manner of telling it accordingly.

Of his early companions, Sam Stockdale was off at Philadelphia attending the medical lectures, and the two Bowmans were set up by their father as planters. George Barnes was still a nobody, and no one could conjecture if he should ever become a somebody, or, if he did, what sort of a somebody he should be.

CHAPTER IX.

BEGINS WITH A PSYCHOLOGICAL STUDY, AND ENDS WITH A DESCRIPTION OF THE ROSSTOWN FEMALE COLLEGE.

I HAVE several times said that Ben was very sensitive, and I have also said that he joined the church at Spring Hill, near Dr. McCleod's. The shrewd student of human nature could write a whole history from these two facts, and, according as he was satirical or charitable, could place his hero in the most ludicrous or most affecting situations. His sensitiveness was morbid, not healthy, and his religion was, so far, a religion of the conscience and affections, and was not yet adjusted by the intellect, that is to say, he felt rather than fully understood. Now while it is certainly true that a man had better be sensitive than callous, and had better have a mere religion of the conscience and affections than have no religion at all, it is also true that Ben was in a condition of exquisite difficulty, through which he could pass only in suffering tortures. For the sensitiveness he could gain some relief by solitude, but that very solitude would add poignancy to the terrible conflict in which his religious feelings were bound to plunge him.

I am speaking plain English, and am talking about a state of mind which has been felt by millions now living, and shall yet be felt by millions in every generation. With a man of intellect, though he may be no genius, or may have no particularly bright talents, when religion gets into the heart or conscience (by religion, I mean a sense of dependence upon and accountability to God), it has to be understood and placed in its proper symmetry by the head. It is a warfare from which there is no discharge. All the whys and the wherefores have to become plain, and that cannot be, most generally, without a dreadful struggle, which often endures a lifetime, but which, at any rate, lasts a longer or a shorter time according to the temperament and capacity of the individual, and rather his temperament than his capacity.

If I were writing a religious story I would use all the technical names for this conflict, and describe it learnedly and with scholarly precision from its inception to its end. But I am not writing a religious story. So far from it I will avoid religious topics as much as I can, and although the course of my story should necessarily lead me to refer to them, I will do so as to mere matters of fact.

Cato, the censor, had a saying which I could not for a long time after I read it fully understand: that "he liked a young man who blushed more than he did one who turned pale." I think I understand him now, and that Ben was a good example of the truth of the observation. The man who blushes is gay and careless, and has quick but evanescent feelings—only his head is affected—but the man who turns pale is terribly in earnest and feels deeply—the blood rushes to his heart, gathers around the seat of life. Ben turned pale, and never blushed. His feelings were mortal.

One day on entering my office I found him pale and

nervous, though he pretended to be perfectly unconcerned. As I had just spoken to Susan and her mother who were in town doing some shopping in preparation for Susan's speedy departure for her new school at Rosstown, from which she had returned only the day before on some feminine exigency in the clothing line, and I reckoned that Ben had seen them too, and hence his paleness, I remarked:

"Well, Ben, I just now saw some old friends of yours; Mrs. Garthwaite and her daughter."

"I thought I saw the carriage pass just now, sir."

"Why, I should have thought, young sir, that you would have been all anxiety to render your thought a certainty. At your age, I spied, and inquired, and found out, and then I acted," said I, rather boastingly, for the truth was that I had been almost as nervous as he now was about the girl I loved.

"I'll go directly, sir," said he. He had been sitting there at least a half hour trying to make up his mind to face Miss Susan and her mother, and had I not thus urged him on they would perhaps have left town without his having dared to budge from the office. As it was, he went at once, and in about an hour returned all smiling and happy, and said that he had seen the ladies to their carriage, and that they had invited him out to spend the evening.

There was a great big, staring, bran-new schoolhouse at Rosstown, where young ladies were taught all the 'onomies and 'ologies, with music, painting, and the use of the globes, by a Yankee couple, or, rather, by a German music-teacher named Von Corlein, and his Yankee wife. They were a queer couple; she, an energetic, smart, full-blooded Yankee woman, with no end of a "system" and the newest and most minute and inflexible rules and regulations; he, a slender, soft, spectacled German, who had no system at all, except such as his wife might establish, but who founded himself upon that as the newest and most wonderfully perfect of all systems. It is to be supposed that as they were husband and wife they understood each other's speech, although he spoke German, of which she did not know a dozen words, and neither of them spoke English—at least, her English was so very Northern that the good people around Rosstown for some time had difficulty in understanding it, which was, of course, their fault, not hers, as she was fresh from the very central abode of civilization.

I said they were a queer couple. I should have rather said it was a queer match. Their marriage was evidently, beyond usual marriages, a speculation. He married a school-mistress, and she married a music-teacher, with the mutual idêa of personal advantage in the establishment of the Rosstown Female College. Their assistants, every one a she professor, were selected with care, they said; but they were all the sisters and cousins of Mrs. Von Corlein. That only proved that the Hitchins family from which she sprang was both extensive and erudite—not that they were poor, in want of situations, and, posssibly, humbugs.

However, the college got a great name for the thoroughness in teaching art, science, and the belles-lettres to be accomplished there, and for the elegance of deportment there to be inculcated. The science of CALISTHENICS, which was announced far and near in large caps in the "Rosstown Gazette," and in the circulars sent to patrons and desired patrons, and discussed in italics, with many exclamation and interrogation points, by the citizens talking on the streets, was, I imagine, the great card of the enterprise. It was a new name to the people, and therefore involved vastly more than simple exercise. The *science* was the thing, and the most religious of patrons could not object to the necessary motions of dancing, as it was not dancing, but Calisthenics, a purely scientific accomplishment, invented for the express purpose of extracting the sin from dancing. But that was only one of its moral advantages. The healthy mind in the healthy body was insisted upon by the Academicians, until it almost got to be believed that no man's daughter could be a real woman unless she had the agility of a rope-dancer, with the pluck and science of a prize-fighter, and the graceful looseness of an acrobat (only very high-sounding names were given to the exercises necessary to produce that state of things), and it was fully impressed upon all that at the Rosstown Female College alone she could be made perfect.

When ladies called to see Mrs. Von Corlein about placing their daughters at her school, she would pass briefly over geography and grammar, reading and writing, to fall back upon Calisthenics, which Mr. Von Corlein could bear witness were revived in Germany from the ancient Greeks, and were now all the rage at the North. No young lady could be said to be fully accomplished without one or more courses in the science, which was not only an accomplishment in itself, but was the necessary prelude and accompaniment of all other accomplishments. And she would go out of the room and presently return with her younger sister, Miss Anchisia Hitchins, a rosy-cheeked, great-mouthed young woman, with prodigious arms and breadth of loin, whom she would introduce as the Calisthenician professor, and with whom she would discuss the most complicated manœuvres, which afterwards, when stripped of their technicalities, turned out to be the most common of girls' amusements; for instance, skipping the rope was, in their parlance, *soter ly cord;* battledore and shuttle-cock, was *judy volant,* etc. etc. A Frenchman would have been as much mystified as were the Rosstownians.

There was a furor in town and county about the college. The young men fresh from college talked to each other learnedly, and to the despair of the unlearned, about *το καλον*, and laughed with vague meaning at each other as though they had been only partly raised up to it. Girls begged their mothers and coaxed their fathers to send them to the college. What if the bill were a little higher than ever school bill was before! was there not superior mental and moral training perfected by Calisthenics? Little boys looked on and listened in wonder, and thought the feminine seience would ever be occult to them. I will warrant that there are now in Rosstown and the county a half dozen, at least, of old men who remember the impressions made upon them when they were children by the wonderful word "Calisthenics," as taught at the Rosstown Female College.

There was another word strangely and therefore attractively applied. It was not a school, or even a seminary; still less was it an academy. It was a college, with its corps of professors, all shes, it's true, but still professors; and at the next meeting of the legislature it should have a charter. It would have its regular commencements, and graduating classes, and speaking, and singing, and instrumental music, and diplomas!

For once Rosstown was ahead of the world. The Rosstownians, when at Yatton, spoke pityingly of our limited facilities for female education, and commended to us the "system" of the college in which mental and moral training was assisted and perfected by Calisthenics. When at home they talked complacently about the superior advantages of their town, as though it would some day rival Boston. The "Gazette" lauded to the skies the enterprising spirit of the Rosstownians, and declared that "the thanks and the unyielding support of the nation, and of Rosstown in particular, are due to the energetic, learned, accomplished, scientific, and artistic Principals of the Rosstown Female College, who are as elegant in manners as sound and commanding in intellect, and have a breadth of understanding, a height of genius, a length of foresight, and a depth of wisdom unsurpassed by any of the whole corps of educational evangelists." In the Methodist church—the Von Corleins were, to a man, or, rather, to a professor, strong Methodists, and as that was about the most enthusiastic congregation in Rosstown, had rather placed the college under Methodist auspices; though Mr. Von was slightly inclined (Mrs. Von confessed, aside, to the Presbyterians) to the Calvinistic school; and Miss Anchisia frequently attended the Episcopal services; and Miss Joanna, a cousin, the professor of ancient languages, had been led by her investigations of the verb *βαπτιξω* to look with charity, to say the least, upon the immersing school; and if there had been Catholic families about, I expect that the Miss Hitchins, who taught French, would have had her missal: but, as I was saying, in the Methodist church on the Sunday before the Monday on which the first session of the college was to commence, Old Father Bright (whom I best remember by his exclaiming, one day, in a sermon upon the Parables, that "People mustn't make a figure go on all fours") hinted, in no obscure terms in his prayer, that the enterprise was worthy of the blessing of Heaven, and ought to, and must receive it.

The college building had been speedily erected, by subscription, upon a vacant lot just on the edge of the town. It was a large two-storied wooden building, painted white, with the school-rooms and parlor, refectory, Mrs. Von's apartment, and other domestic arrangements, on the lower floor, and the dormitories up stairs. A broad gallery was in front, up stairs and down. It was, by far, the largest dwelling-house in Rosstown, not excepting the tavern, and was for that reason an additional source of town pride. And it was soon filled with scholars. Yatton was represented there, and so were Barville, and Graystown, and Shoccoville also, although it had a rival academy of its own. Scholars had come from far and near, attracted by the new system, and among them, at last, was Susan Garthwaite. She was now over sixteen, and in the natural course of things had but a year or two more to go to school. The school in Augusta was excellent, and her progress there had been marked, but she had been there *so* long, and it was *so* dull, and *so* far away, and, besides, Calisthenics were *so* new, and the chance for superior polish at Rosstown was *so* much greater, that her mother concluded that she should spend the last year or eighteen months of her school-life with Mr. and Mrs. Von. She had started there in the winter, and now that summer was coming on she had made a visit to her mother's for the important purpose of purchasing and preparing the additional necessaries and krinkum-kranks for summer: hence her presence in town; hence Ben's nervousness, and hence his going to Mrs. Garthwaite's to spend the evening.

CHAPTER X.

A FEW WORDS ARE SAID ABOUT BOARDING-SCHOOLS; SUSAN'S COLLEGE CAREER IS BRIEFLY DESCRIBED, AND SHE HERSELF IS DESCRIBED MORE PERFECTLY; CONCLUDING WITH A GOOD WORD FOR LOVE.

IT would be absurd for one as old as I am to attempt to enter into the spirit of a girls' boarding-school, and describe the manner of life, the little cliques and cabals, the quarrels and jealousies, the harmless scandals, and the devoted, undying friendships which characterize such institutions. I can with a good conscience thank Heaven that if I had a daughter I would not have her sent to a boarding-school. True, it is something like the Pharisee's thanking God that he was not as other men are; nevertheless, I think that the man who has sense enough to keep his daughter away from such institutions has good cause for thanks to Heaven.

I know that this sounds very harsh and sweeping, and that it will be said that some of the very best of persons preside over such schools, and that their schools have turned out this and that excellent scholar —all of which may be true enough. And yet I firmly believe, and I think the experience of this and of all past ages will agree with me, that any large assemblage of young persons of either sex, to live together at a school or college, is productive of harm, sometimes great injury, as it is certainly irremediable injury.

But enough of that. I cannot reform the world. Colleges and boarding-schools will still exist, and be patronized by a people who think that instruction means education, and that instruction in books is the great object in life.

I presume that no girl ever passed more unscathed through the ordeal of boarding-schools than did Susan Garthwaite. She was to the day of her death a pure woman—a thing which I attribute, however, to her common sense and lack of imagination rather than to the influences which surrounded her at her schools. When I speak of her as a pure woman and speak of the evils of boarding-schools and such like, every one of sense understands that I do not mean that any of her companions were impure girls or women, in the sense of actually lacking in virtue. I mean that she knew so little evil that she could not even understand a *double entendre*, and used most innocently many proper expressions which almost invariably had cant and vulgar meanings attached to them when used among men. Her knowledge was pure; her imagination was pure; and all things were pure to her.

She had her dearest friends among the scholars, of course; she must be a very bad-hearted girl who has not; but I doubt if she had any confidant among them. Her mother had instilled into her that most necessary lesson for a young person who goes to mix with others in the great or a small world; a lesson first taught ages ago, but which requires reteaching to every successive generation: to treat her best friend as though she would some day be her worst enemy, and her worst enemy as though she should some day be her best friend.

This rule, proper for either sex, is most essential for woman in all stages of her growth. Naturally incapable as she is, except to a husband, a lover, or her child, or parents, of that sublime friendship which was felt by Damon and Pythias, she is yet fond of playing at friendship, and fond of talking, and therefore of saying what she really does not mean, and in point of keeping to herself what she hears is not to be completely relied on. It is self-evident, therefore, that she should be very guarded in her speech and conduct—a rigid state of things incompatible with the gushingness of the relations between confidants.

I afterwards knew and highly esteemed some of Susan's dearest friends, but as they are not especially concerned in my story I shall pass them by.

The nearest approach to an adventure Miss Susan had during her stay at the college was when she was a "Senior," on the occasion of the large dancing-party given at Col. Christmas', to which she and five of the other older girls were invited.

The first mention of the proposition to decapitate the French king hardly caused so much horror and contention in the Assembly as did this ball in the college. The question almost became national in its importance and the excitement it engendered in the community. To say that Mrs. Von was horror-struck is not sufficiently to describe her feelings. Her horror was a stage horror, and she glanced to this side and that to see its effects, and judge of the proper succession of the intensities and modifications. For awhile Mr. Von, the excitable little German, encouraged her; so did the Misses Hitchins, or the Professor Hitchinses; so did old Mr. Bright, and Mrs. Bright, and the Misses Bright—though *they* were rather lukewarm, as they considered dancing to be only one of the *mala prohibita*, which needed but the name of Calisthenics to become a virtue; so did several other dear good people of the real salt of the earth, who had received a savor of Puritanism they had never lost. What! the Rosstown Female College to have representatives in a ball-room! a private ball-room, truly, but still a ball-room; the Devil's front parlor! and those representatives the very pick and choice of the college! It was an outrage, a pestilent scandal, an unheard-of attempt at sullying the purity of the system, which combined high moral æsthetics with all the practical branches!

But those who encouraged Mrs. Von were not themselves encouraged. Mrs. Garthwaite, when she learned her daughter's desire to go to the party which was given at the house of one of her best friends, who was also one of the first gentlemen in the country, and whose family were most refined and excellent persons, gave her consent at once; and not only so, came herself to Rosstown expressly to go with her daughter. Four of the other ladies, whose daughters were invited, also consented. The better portion of the town-folk were decidedly opposed to any strait-laced nonsense about girls not going to Col. Christmas' house, party or no party. So Mr. Von cooled down, and Mr. and Mrs. Bright and the others thought that, well, perhaps they were too hasty, and the Miss Hitchinses returned to their normal state, and, of course, Mrs. Von had to compose her features and mind.

It was a great triumph to the rebellious Susan to go with her mother as the leader of the band of insurgents to the Colonel's ball; and vastly did she and they enjoy themselves. They put in public exercise their lessons in Calisthenics, to their own delight and the admiration of others. Mr. Charles Bowman begged to renew his acquaintance made years ago, when both were children, and he danced with Susan. Dr. Sam Stockdale, who was settled in Rosstown practicing his profession, did the same thing. The tip of the Rosstown *ton* sought to make her acquaintance, and the young gentlemen among them entreated her hand for the dance.

To say that Susan was a pretty girl is rather cold praise. She was beautiful. Her dark-brown hair shaded a brow around which intelligence and virtue and goodness wreathed their clustering graces; a crown far more glorious than that which decked the victor in the Isthmian games. To speak more to the point, she had a correctness and delicacy of feature and a soft radiance of bloom, with which her intelligence and gentle dignity and goodness were in perfect harmony. Her rounded and active form was exquisitely graceful, whether in movement or repose. A man could not help loving her; not that she would encourage him, for her simple and sincere nature was utterly ignorant of any of the arts of coquetry; but the thousand graces circling her about beckoned him on, and she was unconsenting, while he was made captive.

Pshaw! one would think that I had got a leaf from Ben Eccles' diary.

And yet, can anything be more bewitching even to an old man, than a pure, beautiful, and gentle girl? The sweetest dream I have of heaven is that I shall there meet just such a one, a pure, beautiful, and gentle girl, my Mary; the superior here of Susan Garthwaite in beauty and in the bright intelligence which almost rivaled light in its quickness and clearness; but, above all, her superior, in my estimation, because she loved me. She loved me! Blessed be the God of Love for making man in his own image, and all nature in accord! It is love which adds brightness to the sunbeam, beauty and fragrance to the flower, symmetry to form, and harmony to sound; which deprives the thunder-cloud of its terrors, turns despair to hope, and takes the sting away from death. It gives pleasure to the toils of life, and always stands as the crown of their reward. Man aspires to be wise, admires justice and holiness, seeks after knowledge, and strives for power over nature, but he feels Love; it alone can completely fill his nature, it alone of all his attributes is always present, and it alone can be made nearly perfect here on earth. His wisdom may prove folly; his justice, cruelty; his holiness, sinful weakness; his knowledge, a vain boast; and of his power he may despair; but his Love knows neither despair, cruelty, sinfulness, folly, nor vain boasting. It is always the very perfection of perfection; makes crooked things, straight; rough places, smooth; ugliness, beautiful; stupidity, intelligent; and even vice it often transforms to virtue. Man could neither bear to live, nor living bear to die without it. And when in addition to his own exquisite feeling of that perfect sense he knows that all of it with which another is endowed, and she one of the most lovely and loving of God's loving creatures, is bestowed upon him as its object, he feels a pride of his own dignity and an appreciation of his own blessedness as a man, which no other contemplation of his nature can impart. My Mary loved me, and I felt proud and blessed in her love. Old as I am I still feel the pride, and throughout eternity I hope to feel the blessedness.

CHAPTER XI.

IS ALTOGETHER ABOUT MR. ECCLES.

BEN studied hard and got his license at the time he had appointed for himself. His gilt sign, "BENJAMIN ECCLES, ATTORNEY & COUNSELOR AT LAW," was tacked on the shutter of one of my office windows which always stayed open—because one of its hinges was broken. We were very careless about our offices. I doubt if there were three of the nine in town which had serviceable locks on the doors. Our libraries were almost in common, and all of our most valuable papers were kept either at our own houses, or at the clerk's office, or the bank.

It is not to be expected that I should cudgel my brains to remember his first cases. There was really nothing remarkable about his professional career, though the "American Lawyer's Mirror," or some such periodical, applied to him many years later for his biography, which it proposed to publish together with his portrait, he having only to supply five hundred dollars towards insuring the perfection of the work; a small bonus which brought out the lives and portraits of a large number of "the most remarkable men of the country." Old Colonel Jenks had his portrait and biography done up, and his wife and son were vastly proud of him always afterwards, as one of the great public men of the nation. I do not know but that it impressed me with a higher esteem for the old gentleman, although I had known him all my life, and knew that the whole story was only "founded on fact." I knew most of the petty cases, and sharp practice, and close bargains, which had constituted "the heroic struggle which raised him from poverty to opulence, etc. etc." But the narrative of the struggle was very affecting, and was calculated to fire the youthful hearts of his son and grandsons with emulation.

It is my candid opinion that no matter how worthless may have been a man who dies and leaves a family, it is the bounden duty of his Lodge, or Bar, or Board, or Council, or Committee—and if he belong to none of these, then it is the duty of the people of his town or county—to call a meeting and pass resolutions of the most laudatory character about him; and that it is also the duty, the solemn and beneficent duty, of the epitaphs upon the tombstones of such men to lie, lie with pious fervor about them. It is almost equivalent to an "ancestry" for giving self-respect to descendants. This is the only sense in which the old Latin maxim "de mortuis, etc.," is true.

Poor Ben was in fact not a very great man in his own estimation. Sometimes his ambition and self-esteem would get the better of his judgment, and persuade him that he could attain renown in any pursuit requiring brains. Sometimes, too, he thought himself handsome. The spasms of conceit I would detect by his conversation, and the accesses of vanity by his conduct and dress. I myself have no doubt but that his conceit was well founded. He only lacked the one little quality, hardness. His vanity was not without good cause either. He was very good looking; had dark-gray eyes, brown hair, a very intelligent and amiable face, and a tall, graceful form. Though not remarkably handsome, he certainly had a very pleasing appearance; and, except his chewing tobacco and smoking, he was remarkably neat in all his habits and ways. He prided himself a good deal upon his moustache—a sandy growth which contrasted strangely, but he thought not unpleasantly, with his dark hair—and in those youthful days he preserved a reasonable degree of solicitude about the fashion and fit of his boots and gloves, for he considered his feet and hands his best features.

His conversation, when unrestrained, was always very pleasing. Whatever the subject, he was earnest about it. Every fact seemed to undergo in his mind a kind of transmutation, and came forth bran-new, with a sparkle of the comic, or a tinge of the sad, and an entirely original association with other facts. He had his full share of humor, sometimes pungent, often grotesque, but always amiable. Yet his most joyful bursts could often be changed to shame and confusion by a want of sympathy in his audience, or the detection of a sneer of disapproval in some blockhead of the company who aped a character for wisdom, or was envious of the speaker.

Do not be startled, dear reader, and think that I am about to inflict a dose of cant upon you when I inform you that he had a class in the Sunday-school; that he was a sort of pet with the Rev. Mr. Snow, and deputy lieutenant for Mrs. Snow; and that he attended all the prayer meetings, and monthly concerts, and night services as well as day services of the church. Nor need you be alarmed when I tell you that, sometimes, at the various meetings, he was called upon to pray, and that he did pray earnestly and intelligently. You wish to know Ben Eccles, and I must, therefore, tell you all about him; but I have no intention to go any further into this branch of the subject than to state bare facts. I have already told you that he had religion of the heart and conscience, and you are to see, and should wish to see, how he acted in such a condition.

I often noticed in the office that he would every now and then lean his head for some moments upon his open book, or on the table, and seem wrapped in reverie. One day I observed to him that he did not appear to chew so much tobacco as usual, and asked him if he had lost his taste for it. He told me that he liked it still, only too much.

"Why, does it injure your health, Ben?" I asked.

"No, Mr. Page," he answered, "it doesn't injure my health that I know of; but I think I shall have to give it up."

"That's strange," said I. "If it doesn't injure you, I'm sure it injures no one else; and if you like it so much, why not continue to use it?"

"The truth is, Mr. Page," answered he, looking doubtful, and a little confused, "I have been questioning myself whether I had the right to chew."

"The right to chew!" exclaimed I, in surprise. "Why, what new doctrine is this you wish to start, Ben?"

"It is no new doctrine at all, sir," he answered;

"but the Apostle tells us that: 'Whether therefore ye eat, or drink, or whatsoever ye do, do all to the glory of God.'"

"Well, Ben," said I, "what has that to do with the matter?"

"Why, sir," he answered, looking earnestly at me, "I can't see how my chewing tobacco redounds to the glory of God, and am, therefore, in great doubt about it."

Here was a revelation to me, and Heaven knows how deeply I sympathized with the poor fellow. But I could do nothing. All the reasoning and teaching of all the preachers in the world could avail him nothing in his then morbid state of mind and conscience. He had to work the problem out by degrees, and for himself. His reason could not work it out, for though his reason were a thousand times convinced, a thousand times new doubts would arise, and the conviction would have each time to be made anew, and still always be mingled with lurking doubt.

One communion Sunday I noticed that Ben at the close of the sermon slipped out of the church, and before the ceremony commenced returned with his moustache shaved cleanly off. I never mentioned to him that I noticed it, for I knew the cause and pitied him for it.

It cannot injure the course of my story, and may perhaps add to its clearness and interest, if I shall here at once in a few words precise the difficulty in which the young man was. I know it partly because he told me of it afterwards himself, and I understand it because, perhaps, I once felt something of it myself, but, at any rate, because I have observed it in many other persons besides Ben Eccles.

Ben was a Christian. He said he had faith, and felt that he had faith, and he also said and felt that he had no other hope of salvation than the atonement of Christ, which he appropriated to himself by faith. He was a hard Bible student and was as well instructed in the Scriptures as any young man I have ever known, and very far better than most old men who were his superiors in the length of time since they had first professed their faith, and in the comfort they derived from it. He not only studied the Scriptures themselves, but every commentary upon them, and every other religious work he could lay his hands upon. And yet, Ben did not understand. He had faith, trusted only in the atonement of Christ, and yet—and yet, he was trying to work out his own salvation. His faith had not set him free from the covenant of works. He did not *realize*, had not made it a living, active portion of his faith, that, while his own works were necessary, they were only necessary as being the only legitimate proofs of his faith. They still, practically, appeared to him to be necessary in the sense of eking out his faith; of making it effectual for salvation as a sort of *addendum;* and, therefore, his conscience was raw.

I do not know how to make my meaning more clear. There is a vast number of good persons in the world who calmly believe, or say they believe, just what Ben unconsciously believed with such an agonizing effect. As I am not writing a religious story I do not intend to enter into long argument with them. I merely wish to state facts, and they can do the doctrinal controversy. As a student of the human heart, anxious to arrive at truth with regard to all human motives, I wish to describe the state of belief which brought about a certain course of conduct and certain other effects. What may appear very rational and simple to others was not so to Ben. He could not have faith and feel that he had still to make up a deficiency for his salvation by works, and have peace of mind; whatever others may do. For my own part, if I thought that my salvation depended upon anything I could or should think, say, or do, as making up the measure for my salvation beyond and in addition to the atonement made by Christ, I should certainly think my chances for heaven very small, and live in continual fear that I might die suddenly, or in a delirium, or in a state of idiocy or coma, with some little thing left undone or some little sin not fully accounted for, and thus be lost forever.

Feeling, then, as I have described, Ben Eccles was miserable. Doubts and fears continually tormented him, and as his spirits lost their tone the doubts, and fears, and misery increased. Tobacco was his greatest want, and the occasion of his acutest pangs of conscience. He had innocently enough taken up the habit, just as boys in our country are apt to do. To use tobacco is certainly rather a dirty habit, but it, or some equivalent, seems to be necessary to the human race, as almost every people on earth indulge it. I have no doubt but that it is productive of great good by soothing the nervous system, or in some other way. It is certainly a great comfort and an active pleasure, and when it is not productive of immediate or marked ill effects—which any man of sense can perceive for himself in his own case—I think that its use should be indulged. I will go further than that, and say that as the pleasures of this life are all the good we have of the body in this life, I think it the duty of every man to get just as much pleasure as he can, so that he neither injure himself nor any one else by his pleasure; and that, therefore, if tobacco be likely to give him pleasure he should prove whether it will injure him or not, and if it do not, should enjoy it—and give God the glory.

Ben had taken up the habit, I say, innocently enough, and, as it did him no injury, he had continued it for years, so that it had actually become a necessity, and, in fact, did him great good. But here came those doubts and fears. I have seen him, after heroically denying nature's cravings for a day or two, sit for hours impassive arguing to himself while he held his ready chew between his fingers. Nature cried out for it, and was in revolt for it, and conscience kept whispering that he could not glorify God by chewing tobacco, "and whatsoever ye do, do all to the glory of God;" and he would close his eyes and silently pray, and would argue and convince himself to the point that the precious morsel would be almost at his lips, and he would let his hand fall again. And so it would go on until at last desperate, rebellious, but groaning in the agony of his mind, the chew would be taken, and he would jump up and enter hurriedly into random conversation, or busy himself about some occupation, to stifle and forget the tormenting doubts.

And so it went on for hours day after day, with, at

first, occasional intermissions for a week or two, and sometimes a month or two, during which he would be apparently assured and at peace. But where is the human mind which can pass uninjured by a conflict like this if long continued? One of three things must happen if the man live: either "full assurance of faith," or despair and recklessness, or insanity. There is no compromising the contest; though it often endures for years before it is decided at last.

The reader thinks, no doubt, by this time, that if my story be true it is a queer sort of story to be chosen for narration; and that if it be a fiction I have created a before unheard-of hero for a novel and have got him into a strange predicament. But never fear, gentle reader; whatever shall happen to Ben there is a great deal of bright sunshine and many a pleasant scene before you. It was necessary you should hear all this I have been telling you, and now that it is told thank me that you are well through with it. There are few story-tellers who would not have engaged you for at least three long chapters upon this very explanation, and here you are clear for but part of a short chapter.

An old man may be permitted to praise himself when he has for once avoided garrulity; and if you still think that I have said too much upon this subject reflect, O reflect, upon the tremendous force I have had to exert upon myself not to say more!

CHAPTER XII.

INTRODUCES MISS ALICE CHARLTON TO THE READER AS A RIVAL TO SUSAN GARTHWAITE IN HIS AFFECTIONS.

IT is now time that I shall introduce into my story another character whom I have not before mentioned, because it was only now that she commenced to be mingled with its incidents.

Aunt Polly Hart, like several other homely old maids whom I have known, had a charming niece, the daughter of her youngest sister. This niece's name was Alice Charlton; she was about a year older than Susan Garthwaite, and had been recently left an orphan by the death of her mother, who had lived at Shoccoville. Her father had died when she was eight years old, and her mother had been a widow about ten years. After her mother's death she came to live with Aunt Polly at Dr. McCleod's; a welcome guest to the whole family, for besides that she was Aunt Polly's dear and only niece, and was amiable, and pleasant both to sight and hearing, she was admirably educated both in books and in all the details of domestic life. To be useful seemed to run in Aunt Polly's family, and Alice, besides being almost as good a housekeeper as her aunt, possessed a number of feminine accomplishments which had been invented or introduced since the old lady's youth. Notably, she had a very considerable talent for drawing, a talent which is no rarer in our country than in Italy or than it was in Greece in its happiest days, but which is seldom cultivated.

The piano is almost enough to make one regret modern civilization. It was right that man in his progress of investigating the laws of mechanics and sound should invent it, but the invention should have been kept secret except to those who were engaged in the higher walks of art and science. It might have been allowed for one to be kept as a curiosity in every chief museum and among the mechanical apparatus of every university and national school of science, just as each has a huge electrical machine, but that is quite as far as the abominable complication should ever have been extended. The cheap manufacture of them is almost as glaring a wrong in the Yankee nation as is Puritanism in religion and politics, cheating and braggadocio.

If one could arrive at the exact amount of money spent each year, for, say, the last twenty-five years—since 1835—in pianos and music upon the piano, he would find a sum total which would be almost as great as that for the Tract and Foreign Missionary Societies combined—and with just about the same benefit.

Let me not, however, stray away from a pleasant subject to inveigh against the sinful waste of capital (time and money) for afflicting children who have no ear for music and grown folk who have a correct ear and taste. Alice Charlton had a pleasant voice, whether she talked or sang, but she wasted no time in attempting the impossible (correctly producing fine music) upon a piano. She had a talent for drawing and she cultivated that. It is an art which requires only a pencil and paper, or a piece of chalk, or even a stick, for its machinery, which may be exercised at all times and in all places, and which is lasting in its products; and her efforts were deemed little short of the miraculous in her narrow circle of friends. A girl who draws well is always a wonder in our country, even to those who could do just as well, or better, if they would only attempt and persevere at it.

It was not long till she had Flora McCleod as an ardent pupil in the beautiful art, and even if she had been otherwise objectionable she should have received the benedictions of the old doctor for keeping the girl quiet and amused.

Two or three weeks after Alice came to live with her aunt, she attended with her the church at Spring Hill. A visit to a country church is always novel, however well one may be accustomed to it. The large frame building perched on blocks, and situated on a hill near the big road away from habitations, and surrounded by the great trees of the primeval forest; the neighing horses hitched here and there in the wood; the little groups of persons near the doors and about under the trees; the horsemen as they arrive, turning aside to some favorite hitching tree, dismounting, and advancing to the group in which they see some friend, and switching as they go the dust from their disordered dress; the variety of vehicles, from the huge family carriage to the gig hung high on wooden springs, and the one-horse cart with chairs in it for seats; the buxom country damsels with their short riding-skirts of yellow nankin riding up to the horse-block, and shaking all over as they nimbly dismount; the boys in their Sunday-go-to-meetings, and new brogans with the store shine still upon them, strutting about from group to group, and insatiably visiting the spring in the bottom; the graces of the young men as they think themselves remarked by some fair arrival as she passes into the church, or go to assist some other to dismount, or alight from her vehicle; the business air of the preacher when he arrives and enters the church without turning to the right or left to salute the crowd which then streams in after him,—all is still novel, however often one may see it, and once seen is never forgotten.

It was in such a scene as this, one bright Sunday morning, that Alice Charlton, paying her first visit to the Spring Hill church, was remarked by Mr. Charles Bowman, Ben's former schoolmate, a young and thriving planter of the neighborhood, who wondered to himself who that devilish pretty girl was who got out of the carriage with Aunt Polly. And Mr. Charles Bowman was not the man to wonder long on such a subject without making an attempt to satisfy his wonder; so, by dint of asking, he soon found out the very pedigree of the young lady—so far away, at least, as to her paternal and maternal grandfathers. When church was over, he, of course, got out as soon as possible, and stationed himself at the door to see the ladies pass out—nearly all young men do that at town as well as at country churches—and when Aunt Polly came along, he, of course, delightedly shook hands with her, and manifested the greatest solicitude about her, and acted in general the part of one who knows he is well known, and who is highly gratified to revive ancient friendship or acquaintance.

"Why, Aunt Polly! I little expected to see your welcome face here to-day. I need not ask you how you do. You look as young as you did when you used to scold me about making your roosters fight!" said he, shaking the old lady heartily by the hand, and giving a sly glance or two at her companion as though to see how she was struck with the appearance of her aunt's young old-friend.

"I don't recollect ever scolding you about that, Charley," said Aunt Polly, "but it's likely I did if you made them fight, and you were a very mischievous boy."

"Ah, I've got over that, years ago, ma'am. The mischiefs I used to delight in no longer please me. Life has become too serious for such things," said the hypocritical Charles.

"I'm glad to hear you say so, Charley, whether it's true or not, and you've been so long a stranger that I don't know about it," said Aunt Polly, who only *doubted* the sudden conversion of her young friend to perfect sincerity. "This is my niece, Alice Charlton. Mr. Bowman, my dear."

"How do you do, Miss Alice?" said Charley, raising his hat and bowing very low. "You hear what your aunt says about me! Why, Aunt Polly, I have hardly been at home for nearly a year. I have been to Alabama, where I am about to settle a new plantation near my father's and brother's places, and from there I went over into Louisiana, where I found a splendid place that just suited me, and on which I intend going into sugar next year. You see I have been very busy, and away from home, and I couldn't call; but I'll make up for it hereafter. Friends are too scarce for me to lose them by neglect."

And the ladies passed on to their carriage, and were seen comfortably seated in it by Mr. Bowman, who then got on his own beautiful mare, a bright sorrel, full of spirit; and as he was a good rider, made her show him and herself off as he galloped alongside of the carriage for about half a mile to the place where he had to turn off to go home.

To save myself the trouble of hereafter selecting for the reader the truth in what Charles Bowman may say, let me here analyze what there was of it in this last address to Aunt Polly.

In the first place, he had been from home exactly six weeks and three days. In the next place, neither he, nor his father, nor brother, had a plantation in Alabama at all. His father had only talked of buying some land there, and he had gone to the State on a frolic, but I doubt if he had been within seventy miles of the land. And, in the last place, the visit to Louisiana, the purchase of the place there, and the scheme for sugar-planting, were entirely imaginary, and invented at the moment.

Let me then warn the reader that he is not to believe anything Charles G. V. Bowman may say. If he hear him say that he loves, or that he hates, that he is sick, or is well, is glad, or is sorry, doubt it; and look for corroborating evidence.

CHAPTER XIII.

TELLS OF MR. BOWMAN'S FIRST VISIT, AND WHAT HE SAID ON THAT OCCASION, AND WHAT SEVERAL PERSONS THOUGHT OF HIM.

THE next day was fair, and Charles Bowman went to Dr. McCleod's. As the weather was warm all the family were seated in the broad passage; the doctor reading, Aunt Polly and Mrs. McCleod busily sewing, and Alice and Flora engaged at a table, intent upon a drawing lesson. After the salutations of the day, Mr. Bowman ensconced himself comfortably in a rocking-chair as near the younger ladies as he could, but not so far from the doctor as to prevent conversation.

"I am told, Charles, that you have been a great traveler of late," said the doctor in his precise and sonorous voice.

"Not very great, doctor," answered Mr. Bowman somewhat embarrassed, for he did not know but that the old gentleman knew the particulars of his movements, and he was, of old, afraid of him. "Not very great, doctor. I made a trip to Alabama."

"Why, I heard that you went to Louisiana too! I have long had a great desire to visit that State. Its population and the general character of its soil and appearance are so different from anything we have, that I hoped you could tell us something about them"

"Well, I did go into Louisiana," said Charles a little

doubtfully, "but I was there only a couple of months, and stayed almost all the while at one place."

"Tell us what you saw, Master Charles," said the doctor. "How did you amuse yourself? Where did you stay?"

"You recollect," said Charles, "Mr. Barrow, who came out here winter before last to purchase negroes, and passed a few days at our house! Well, I went to his house, on the Mississippi River, about a hundred and fifty miles above New Orleans." And then he added, to himself: "How the devil did I get there! Let me see——"

"You must have had some difficulty in getting there," presently said the doctor.

"Oh, not at all," said Charles, by this time ready with his itinerary. "I went down the Alabama River to Mobile, and there I sold my horse——"

"What! Did you go down the river on your horse?" interrupted the doctor, always critical.

"Oh, you understand me, doctor. I went the road on the bank of the river. And when I got to Mobile, a gambler—there are a great many gamblers in that part of the country: this one they called Si Thomas; he took a great fancy to my sorrel nag; you used to know her, doctor; and thought that he could win money on her as she was a thorough-bred, and he offered me eight hundred dollars for her, which I took."

"What! you sold your sorrel mare? Why, I was sure that was she hitched out there at the gate."

"Oh no, doctor! that's her full sister I am riding now," said Charles, quickly.

"Well, may be so. I am not a horse-jockey, and the resemblance is so great that I could very naturally make the mistake," said the doctor: then, after a pause, "Well, what did you do when you had sold your mare?"

"I took a schooner from Mobile to New Orleans, and when I landed in the city I found the steamboat Tamerlane about to leave, and I got on board of her and went up to Mr. Barrow's place," and the young man hurried over this part of his journey, for he had never seen a steamboat, and feared to be called on to describe the Tamerlane. "I arrived there," he continued, "just in the midst of the fishing season."

"The fishing season!" exclaimed the doctor. "I did not know there were fisheries on the Mississippi!"

"Oh yes, doctor. They call it the fishing season, but it is alligators they catch. In August the crop is laid by until October, when sugar-making commences, and as the alligators are then fattest, the whole force of each plantation, and the Creoles, little yellow fellows, along the river, are occupied in catching them for their oil. Why, one good sized alligator will make as much as two barrels of oil, which sells at a very large price. You see, they can't use any other kind of oil for greasing steam machinery, which goes so fast that it sets afire all other sorts. Did you ever see an alligator, Miss Alice?"

"I never did, Mr. Bowman," answered Alice, who, with Flora, had become interested in his adventures, and had altogether withdrawn her attention from her pencil.

"Well, ma'am, it's not a pleasant sight. At first I

was very much afraid of them, but in a day or two got so that I would mind handling one just as little as the negroes and Creoles did. You see, doctor, the river is full of them——"

"Why, Charles," said the doctor, "I thought they generally resorted to the sloughs and bayous away from the river."

"So they do, doctor, in laying time, but after that you will not find a single grown alligator away from the river. The sloughs and bayous are full of young ones, which stay there till they get old enough to come to the river. Well, when the fishing season is about to commence, the planters bait their fishing-grounds near their plantations, and that draws the alligators there in crowds. Of a bright day, if you make a dog howl on the bank, you will see their heads sticking out of the water so thick that you could walk across the river on them. When the first fishing day comes there is a big feast given to the negroes, and about twelve o'clock the hooks are set. They are large hooks attached to a section of chain, and they are thrown into the water out of boats with a bladder tied to each line, and the bladders are all attached to a trot-line, which runs from the bank across the river; and when a bladder bobs down and they find the alligator is hooked, two hands go off in a canoe with a rope which they tie to the line which has the alligator, and then fasten the other end to a windlass on shore, and thus drag the alligator on shore and dispatch him by cutting off his head with an axe."

"I should think that a dangerous business, cutting off an alligator's head with an axe. I have heard that they strike violently with their tails," said the doctor.

"Yes, but you see, as soon as they drag him up on to the bank and get his neck across a log, which is placed there for that purpose, the negroes hamper his tail by ropes and chains they have in readiness; and they are very expert at it. The oil kettles are under a shed near the killing place, and the alligators are tried up as fast as they are caught and killed."

"What do they do with the flesh?" asked the doctor.

"Why, the negroes are very fond of the tails, and they are saved; but I believe they bury the rest of them; for if they were to throw so much flesh into the river the others would not bite at the hooks."

"Humph!" ejaculated the doctor. "It is very likely;" and he turned again to his book, partly to read, and partly to analyze in his own mind, with the assistance of his memory, Mr. Bowman's wonderful story. But Charley, seeing the ladies interested, launched forth on the wings of his imagination into other stories.

"One day," said he, "when we were out deer-driving, and I heard the hounds running, and galloped to head them as they were not coming by the stand where I had been placed, I came to a bayou which did not seem very deep, and made my horse go in. The water was almost swimming; and just as we were in the deepest part a huge alligator rose by the side of my horse with his mouth open. He was just about to seize me by the thigh when I turned the muzzle of my rifle down his throat and fired, and he sank, killed dead, to the bottom. I expect my ball had broken his spine, as he made no struggle. I never was so thankful in all my life as when we got out of that hole. I trembled all over, and I'm sure that I was as pale as death—for I felt so; and I don't mind confessing it to you, Aunt Polly; I got off of my horse, and went down upon my knees, and thanked God with more fervency than I ever did before; and I have had a heap of narrow escapes."

The ladies drew long breaths of astonishment and relief, and looked approvingly upon him for his piety; but the doctor, whose previous ideas had been much discomposed by Master Charles's story, said, "Why, I thought that there were no large alligators to be found away from the river."

"So there are not, doctor, except in laying-time, and that is in October, and had just commenced when we took the drive. It was the last drive of the season, for the alligators are so bad on the dogs that they get so they won't cross the water. There was one of Mr. Barrow's hounds that used to fool the alligators when she wished to cross a bayou, by sitting on the bank and howling. It would draw all the alligators in hearing to the spot; and then she would break and run some distance up or down, and jump in and swim across. Once, an alligator had snapped off her tail just as she got to the farther bank, and always afterwards, whenever her feet struck land, after swimming across, she would jump and howl frantically, as though another 'gator,' as they call them there, had her."

This made open-eyed Flora laugh, and the ladies smile pleased and astonished smiles; seeing which Mr. Bowman entered into other details and anecdotes, no less wonderful, which he had heard or read, and in which he always figured as a spectator or actor, until at last the doctor, who listened closely, though pretending to read, cornered him in a "whopper." It is a difficult matter to corner such a man as Mr. Charles Bowman, whose imagination is as free and subtle as air, and can glide in or out at the least cranny. He was cornered, however, where there was no escape, and he presently acknowledged complacently that *that* story was not true, and he had only told it to entertain Flora; but, he affirmed, everything else he had said was strictly true.

"Humph!" ejaculated the doctor.

But Alice thought it was a mark of great amiability in the young gentleman, who had seen so much of the world, for him to try and please a little girl like Flora, and presently, when the conversation turned to the subject of drawing, she very pleasantly showed her handiwork, and the young gentleman, and she, and Flora, went to the drawing-table, where Flora's progress was exhibited and discussed; and the trio remained together about the drawings, Mr. Bowman amusing, and appreciative, and polite, keeping up a flow of anecdote and pleasant chat until almost dinner-time, when he left, promising to call again very soon.

That afternoon Miss Alice told her aunt that her old friend, Mr. Bowman, was a very pleasant man.

"He always was very pleasant to talk, my dear," answered Aunt Polly; "but it won't do to take all he says for gospel."

And that night as she went to bed Mrs. McCleod was descanting to her husband upon how much Charley Bowman had improved, and upon his ability to support a wife, etc., etc. The doctor, who was grunting as he pulled off his socks, interrupted himself and her by saying, "Well, my dear, are you almost through? When you have finished with him let us converse on some more profitable subject. Charles Bowman is handsome, and is amiable among the women-folk, and his wealth gives him a certain standing among men. But he is accounted what my old father used to call 'a squirt.' You and your cousin may manage as you please, but he should not marry a daughter of mine. I have no ambition to emulate the Evil One, and become a 'father of liars!'"

And after that grim joke, which acted as an extinguisher upon his wife, he put out the candle, and went self-approvingly to bed and to sleep.

CHAPTER XIV.

TELLS WHY MISS SUSAN DID NOT GRADUATE AT THE COLLEGE, AND HOW SHE WENT HOME, AND MR. ECCLES, CALLING TO SEE HER, FINDS ONE OF HIS FRIENDS AND ONE OF HIS ANTIPATHIES ALREADY IN THE WAY.

WHEN the time came for Susan's class to graduate—it was the first graduating class the college had been able to turn out since it had got its charter—she and her mother both revolted at the ordeal. The examinations were well enough, but the standing on a stage, and speaking, and singing, and acting pieces from very mild plays, and the conferring of prizes and receiving diplomas—in short, making a show of herself before a crowd—was not to the taste of Miss Susan; and her mother fully agreed with her. She was not one of those mothers, either, whose taste would have accommodated itself to her daughter's had it been the other way. In that case there certainly would have been a disagreement between them—the first of their lives—and Miss Susan should have had to submit. But the young lady was naturally averse to public display.

Until the college had been founded, and, by means of its occult sciences, had accustomed the people to the reception of new ideas, such a thing as a public "exhibition" (they did not then call it "exhibition," though they now do) of young ladies was unheard of in all our part of the country. But where the "system" goes, in other words, wherever the peculiar civilization of the North is introduced, there is bound to be a shock to retiring female modesty. The Yankee social system is opposed to anything retiring. They live in crowds. Their virtues are dependent upon public opinion for their desirableness, just as are their vices for their heinousness. Drinking and stealing, for instance, are wrong because Public Opinion is opposed to them. The consequence is that they are not so wrong if they can be concealed from the public. Modesty is a stupid virtue, but Learning is superexcellent with Public Opinion, and consequently Modesty must get out of the way for a display of Learning. Modesty! Why, what, after all, is Modesty? Is it to be allowed to stand in the way of Progress, or of the vanity of parents, or of the desire of the neighbors for a little excitement, or admiration, or chance to gossip and criticise? According to their progressive ideas, there is no differences, except physical, between a girl and a boy; and how is it to be known that in the education of the girls the teachers have done their duty if the public shall not be allowed to judge for themselves by a public exhibition of the results of their work? Then, again, how is a system to become known? How is a school to become popular?

But enough of that. Susan could not adopt the new-fangled notion. Words could not convince her of its propriety. She had investigated the grand science of Calisthenics, and feared the other innovations should prove about as showy and empty—about as much of "an advertising dodge;" though that phrase had not then been invented, and she was too refined to have used it if it had been. So she did not get her diploma. When the grand day came, she had quitted the school, and quietly took her place, with her mother, among the audience, where she might hear and see in public what she had seen and heard rehearsed in private, until she knew it all by heart, and was sick of it. And after it was all over, they went to Colonel Christmas's, and the next morning went home to The Barn.

How perfectly splendid the old place had become! The house had received a new coat of the whitest of white, and the shutters had been painted the greenest of green. The trees had grown in all those years since she was a little child until now they were quite forest-like in their numbers and shade; the gullies on the hillside had been filled up; and the whole was like a fairy woodland carpeted with the softest and freshest of grass; and the shrubbery around the house, and the rose-bushes, and flower-plats were in full leaf and blossom, and all was so beautiful and pleasant within and without that it seemed to her that Nature loved her also, and had joined with her mother to do her honor and give her pleasure.

Black Jane, who had been her waiting-maid when both were children, had been carefully educated in all her duties by Mrs. Garthwaite, and was anxiously waiting for Miss Susan to come home, so that she might commence their exercise. Dinah, the cook, had found out some new dishes she wished Miss Susan to try. The dairy-woman had had her dairy newly fixed up, and was proud of it, and wished Miss Susan to see it, and admire her a little for it. Charley, who had succeeded old Tom as coachman, felt it the proudest day of his life when he drove Miss Susan, with "old Mistuss," up to the front door, where Jane, and Dinah, and the dairy-woman, and a whole crowd of other servants, flocked to receive them, and feast their eyes on their young mistress, who, when she alighted, seemed in their eyes a bright and beneficent goddess just arrived on earth.

And when the proper time came, Miss Susan visited the dairy, and tried the dishes, and felt herself petted and admired by her humble friends, and felt all the more gentle towards them for their evident love and admiration.

But there were others to see, and others who would love, and pet, and admire, besides homefolk. The neighbors began to call and pay their visits of welcome, and in a few weeks The Barn was the scene of quiet social gayety for the young lady even more than it had been for the little girl.

Ben went there of course, though too shamefaced to go among the very first. There was quite an assemblage there that day, and the poor fellow, though he had prayed heartily before he went, and had checked his horse and prayed with his hat in his hand two or three times on the road thither, was very much embarrassed. But he went bravely in, and did his devoirs like a polished gentleman, as he was, although he felt that every person present knew the thought and desire of his heart. But after he had spoken to Mrs. Garthwaite, and to Susan, and to some of his other acquaintance, he espied, in a corner, Dr. Sam Stockdale, and unconsciously quoted aloud, but in a low voice, from Job: "And Satan came also among them." Nevertheless, he went up to him and greeted him cordially.

If there was any young man for whom Ben had a fond regard, it was his old friend Sam. He loved him for the noble frankness and loyalty of his character and the gentleness of his disposition, and for the same reasons he feared him above all others as a rival with a girl. It shot a pang into his heart to see him there, and he fairly groaned with it; but though he watched with all the keenness of a jealous lover every word and look and tone, he could remark no sign of love in either the doctor or Susan. They were barely acquainted as yet, and the doctor had come there entirely without design on his part. He had been to Yatton on some business, and was returning with a friend, who was also the friend of Mrs. Garthwaite, and who wished to call as he passed to pay his respects, and, perhaps, to get his dinner—for the two designs are often mingled, and the former is vastly dependent on the latter. He had insisted that the doctor should call with him, and the doctor had done so. Ben's uneasiness was therefore groundless as to the past and present; but, alas! in the future that chance visit was destined to give him an uneasiness to which his present pang was as nothing.

Among the other guests there was one for whom both Ben, and afterwards Doctor Sam, had so hearty a dislike that I must describe her.

She was Miss Maria Jones, a young lady of some twenty-eight summers, of small stature, and prim as starch and stiff silk could make her. Her large round eyes were a pale gray, and her hair of a pale straw-color; her nose was a decided pug, and her lips were thin. She had what I have heard roughly called a "bulging" forehead, over which, as over her nose, the skin seemed to be stretched from some point about the ears so as to be drawn in little folds and wrinkles. It can be readily imagined that she was not prepossessing in her appearance; and her manners were not more captivating.

I always think of her when I see my great-niece—for in some particulars they resembled—but to compare them is "Hyperion to a Satyr." My great-niece is beautiful (and she knows it), and Miss Maria was ugly, though she neither knew nor believed it. But it would be interminable to tell all wherein they differed; the points of resemblance were fewer and more marked. Miss Maria had relatives on and with whom she lived, and who by her petty malice and tyranny were made miserable. So has my great-niece. Miss Maria was as spiteful as a cat—and so is my great-niece; but it is as a princess of a cat. Miss Maria had a little property of her own which gave her self-importance, and of which she took good care that no one else should ever have the slightest benefit—it's just the same with my great-niece, only as her property is rather the larger her selfish ideas are correspondingly larger. Miss Maria always seemed vexed when any little project of happiness for others was going on, and turned up her nose at it, and thwarted it if she could—and that is my great-niece to a dot.

But here was Miss Maria Jones in the parlor monopolizing her dear friend Susan. She and Ben had never belonged to the same mutual admiration society, and when Doctor Sam was introduced to her, she pursed her lips, and bowed her little head so stiffly that he voted her a bitter crab; and after he had talked a little with her, he pronounced her a narrow-minded bore. It was one of those cases of repulsion at first sight, which are always more infallible in their correctness and duration than is sudden love. One can never be attracted to another where their natures are so antagonistic.

"Ah, Susan!" exclaimed Miss Maria, bobbing her little head and winking her round eyes to give them more expressiveness. "You will not be offended at my calling you Susan now that you are a young lady! I always used to call you so when you were a dear little girl. We used to be great friends at the delightful parties given here by your good mother, where we used to dance together; and now that you are at home, and we are such near neighbors, we must be great friends."

"Thank you, Miss Maria," said Susan. "I have no doubt but that we shall be very sociable. You are still living with your aunt, are you not?"

"Oh, yes!" answered Miss Maria. "Dear aunt says she could never get along with those children without me, though I tell her that I am of no use; they don't mind me in the least,—he! he! he!" and she laughed a little laugh which would have made Doctor Sam's flesh creep if he had only known the malice at the bottom of it, and had known that she mentally added that she wished the miserable brats dead. "He! he! he! It is a hard thing, Susan, to take control in the house in which one has recently been a child."

"As for that," answered Susan, pleasantly, "I do not expect that mother will soon give me a chance to try it. She keeps me closely under her thumb, and is a sad tyrant. Do you hear that, mother? Miss Maria says that it is a hard thing to take control in a house in which one has recently been a child."

"I think, my dear," answered Mrs. Garthwaite, "that it would be a hard thing for you to take any more control than you have always had. I am sure that all your life you have controlled this house and all about it."

"Really!" said Miss Maria presently, drawing her full-faced gold watch from her belt, and looking at it (I always did detest the sight of a gold watch in a lady's belt; always felt that it was out of place. What has a pretty woman to do with time? and what difference can it possibly make to one who is ugly?)

"Really, it is near one o'clock, and I expect my poor horses are tired waiting for me. I never like to keep servants or horses exposed to the sun or rain waiting for me." (She ought to have added: "after I am ready to go.") "Good-bye, Susan!" and she gave that young lady a sharp little smouch. "Good-by, dear Mrs. Garthwaite!" and she gave the mother another sharp little smouch: "you must let dear Susan come often to see me, and you must come too, and come soon;" and she bobbed her head, and made a brisk little courtesy to the remainder of the company, and sailed off like a newly-painted, full-rigged toy ship under full sail.

Ben had very little to say to Susan or her mother during this visit. He was uncomfortable, and yet could not complain of his reception from either; it was kind and friendly. He was not Susan's declared lover, and whatever she might suspect of the continuance of his old liking for her, she neither knew what strong love it had been, nor could suspect how very violent it was now. She regarded him as an excellent young man, and one in every respect a gentleman—and that was all. So far, no serious thought of love on either side had crossed her mind. She was therefore self-possessed, and even more than polite, was friendly, and when he got up to leave, both she and her mother expressed their pleasure at having seen him, and said they hoped he would not make himself a stranger at the house. Ah, how cold all this was to the burning fury of his love!

When he came to the office that afternoon he was taciturn, and sat moodily reflecting upon his visit and his love, and often bowed his head upon the table and mentally prayed. After awhile he drew the tobacco out of his pocket (his conscience had been at rest for several days), but when he had pulled off a chew, and went to put it in his mouth, the thought seemed to strike him that perhaps it was wrong after all, and that God would not answer his prayers for Susan's love if he should take the chew of tobacco without being fully persuaded in his own mind. And I left him, when I went home, pondering and mentally praying over that chew of tobacco.

CHAPTER XV.

DESCRIBES HOW MR. ECCLES FELT, AND HOW OTHERS THOUGHT AND FELT, AND HOW HE BEGAN HIS COURTSHIP.

IT was several weeks after his first visit before Ben found himself again at The Barn. The rules by which lovers act vary with their temperaments. Ben was as impulsive and enthusiastic as any man I ever saw, but those feelings were at all times kept in check by his sensitiveness, and were now in a great degree interfered with by the gnawings of his conscience—which is the only expression I can think of to describe his state of mind. The reader will understand its exact value by what I have heretofore said. This morbid state had increased considerably with the increasing perturbation of his mind by love. Frequently upon returning to my office, after an absence of an hour or so, I found the door shut, and upon opening it discovered him confused and suddenly bustling about; and once or twice, either because he was more absorbed or my approach was more noiseless than usual, I found him on his knees praying. Each time that I so discovered him I turned and went out for a few minutes till he could rise and compose himself; for I felt that, earnest as he was, my discovery would annoy him.

The poor fellow had now an additional burden to carry. His belief in an overruling Providence in all the affairs of life was implicit—as it should have been. I found marked in his Bible, and even copied on one of its blank pages, evidently for convenient reference, the texts from Proverbs: "Whoso findeth a wife findeth a good thing, and obtaineth favor of the Lord," and "A prudent wife is from the Lord." He wished to make Susan his wife, and where could a more prudent wife than she be found? But she must come to him from the Lord "who turneth the hearts of the children of men;" and what could he do to make the Lord gracious to him? Could the Lord be gracious to one who sinned so constantly as he did in thought, word, and deed? That if he should marry her it would be to the glory of God was clear enough to him, for it would be, however it should turn out, in the way of carrying out the divine command to increase and multiply; but how could he who was constantly failing in glorifying God in everything else, ask that he should be so blessed as to be enabled to glorify Him in this one thing? Indeed, was not his so insisting upon it a proof that it was not the glory of God but his own gratification he sought? and should not this completely shut his mouth? And he would find himself baffled in an inextricable maze, and would grit his teeth and groan without the power to pray, and with his whole being concentrated upon what he desired more than life, more than his own salvation.

With these feelings, and his natural diffidence keeping him in check, he was very dilatory in making his first visits, and by his actions openly declaring his love for Susan. But at the church door every Sunday he feasted his eyes upon her glorious beauty, as he thought it, and sometimes he mustered the courage to assist her and her mother from the carriage. And whenever the carriage came into town he was sure to know it, and just as sure to find out if Susan were in it, and, if she were, to go, as if by accident, into the store where she was, or to be standing, as though by chance, where she must pass, so as at least to bow and speak to her.

But one day Mrs. Garthwaite coming alone into town he saw her in Mr. Hurlbut's store—poor Marlow had been book-keeper there—and she reproached him for not having come out to see them. Ben felt strangely encouraged by such a reproach. It showed that they valued his acquaintance; and if Mrs. Garthwaite only knew or guessed the feelings of his heart, what more encouraging could he desire than that sweet reproach! Happy fellow that he was! Had God really been gracious to him, and turned the hearts of mother and daughter towards him? But then, how could Mrs. Garthwaite know what he felt? If she did know it, was she not a woman of too much delicacy to make such an open advance? It is said that women have a strange facility of reading the hearts of men in matters of love, and a mother is of all others the most alive to what concerns her daughter, and Susan was an only and a cherished daughter! Yet how could Mrs. Garthwaite know, or even suspect? He had never breathed his feelings except to his God! Had God, to bless him really, almost miraculously, gifted Mrs. Garthwaite with a sympathetic insight to his heart? Hardly, he thought—hardly; the age of miracles was passed. But would this be a miracle?

Here was puzzle upon puzzle, and the poor fellow knew not what to think. Indeed, I doubt if he had not already quit thinking, and abandoned himself to the tumultuous waves and tremulous wavelets of feeling. At any rate, he concluded to commence with his courtship; but not to dash boldly into the waters, to sink or swim. He had not come to that point yet. There were many drawbacks to such precipitation. He would be cautious. He would try the depth of the water, inch by inch. At the worst it was but death. If the stream were likely to prove treacherous, he could draw back in time and die on the hither bank, and if at the supreme moment, when the plunge must be made, he should find it fatal, he could die there. There was no hurry. He could not reasonably expect that a miracle should be performed for him, and he must make use of natural means; and he could glorify God only by using natural means, and using them to the very best advantage.

So he went again to The Barn, in his usual prayerful

mood and with his soul trembling and shrinking within him.

He was met by mother and daughter most pleasantly. They had a high esteem of him, for they could know nothing but good about him. Both knew that his means were greatly increased since he used to come a poor little orphan boy to Susan's parties, and both were glad of it, for he was worthy of all kinds of prosperity. Even had he been as poor as he then was he should have been just as well received, because he was a gentleman, and a good man, whose whole conduct throughout life had been irreproachable; and, after all, that is a far surer passport to the respect of a right-minded woman than any amount of wealth. They knew, too, that he was intellectual, and, for his age and advantages, quite learned. Had he not graduated with high honors from the first college of the South? Had he not been the law-student of their friend Mr. Page, who would never have encouraged him or spoken highly of him in his youth if he had been a dunce or a vicious boy, and who would not now try to advance him if he did not think highly of his capacity! Then, also, he had already made a good appearance at the bar, and many were prognosticating great success for him in his profession; though they said he was rather too serious.

So Susan exerted herself to please him and do him honor, and thought she honored herself by doing so. Young men, against whom nothing can be said, are too rare not to be made much of when they appear; and the women-folk are apt to make much or too little of them; that is to say, the mothers are apt to vaunt them overmuch to their daughters, and the daughters are too apt to have an indifferent sort of confidence in them, as though they were so many old women, and try to please them because they wish to please themselves.

In pleasant chat about old things and new the hours sped on until the sun was going down, and then, when he was about to start, they pressed him to stay to tea; and it was between nine and ten o'clock that night when he came home (he lived with me then), put up his horse, and went to bed, with a glorious future of happiness spread out before him.

It would be a slur upon the reader's capacity if I should attempt to reproduce the conversation at this or at any of Ben's subsequent visits. There can be but two good excuses for detailing a conversation. The first is, that conversation is the necessary form in which certain ideas, comic or serious, must be presented—and in that case the writer has no choice. The other is, that the characters of the parties speaking sometimes can be most strikingly developed by such a form—and in that case the writer has an option. If he be good at narrating sparkling wit and interchange of thought he will adopt the conversational form; and if he be not, he will, if he be a man of sense, content himself with description. I give the reader the credit of having as much sense, knowledge, and imagination as I myself have, and I know that when I am thoroughly acquainted with the characters, dispositions, and present motives of any two persons who are together, I do not need to hear every word they say. If I were writing a novel, and it had to be of just such a bulk, I would fill up with conversations. They make what the printers call "fat" matter, and by their means I should save labor, and both the printers and publishers make money. But I am writing against neither time nor space.

And besides, the commonplace conversations I should have to detail, if I adhered to truth, would hardly be understood by a reader of modern books, who is accustomed to something like this: The lady says:

"Ah, Mr. Fitzgibbons, the periphrastic diction of the patristic writings emulating the νους of the inspired and yet suffering the *non ego* to change positions with the *ego* and become subjective can no longer be regarded as a truly enlightened manner of dealing with Manichæism, or the cosmogony of human aspirations."

To which Mr. Fitzgibbons answers complacently:

"But, my dear young lady, you must ascertain the real definition by employing the τεχνη μαιευτικη and proceed inductively; *prout patet per recordum,* etc."

I acknowledge that even this is but a feeble specimen of modern book-conversations; but it is sufficient to show that in no way should I be justified in detailing the conversations which passed forty years ago between a simply intelligent couple—one violently in love, and the other not yet conscious of his passion.

The sum and substance of the matter is, that if the reader be a person of sense he will know just the style of the talk which passed between Susan Garthwaite and Ben Eccles; and if he be not a man of sufficient sense, or rather imagination, it would make out the couple too unfashionable if their talk were repeated for his sake.

And soon the conversations became frequent. Ben visited The Barn about every ten days, and in a few weeks it got to be that he went every Thursday afternoon. He had, however, made but two or three of his regular visits when his object, before suspected, became perfectly apparent to both mother and daughter, and he began to be looked for when Thursday afternoons came. He generally found other company there; Miss Maria Jones, for instance, who seemed suddenly to realize the need she had long had for young and tender friendship, and had attached herself lovingly to Susan. Of course she saw his motives at once. She had suspected them at his first visit, and Ben was soon conscious that she knew them, and was his enemy.

CHAPTER XVI.

MR. ECCLES, AFTER COURTING AWHILE AGAINST WIND AND TIDE, CONCLUDES TO TAKE A TRIP TO NORTH CAROLINA.

HOW very affectionate Miss Maria would be when Mr. Eccles was present! Her arms were around dear Susan's waist whenever they walked together, and she often whispered to her and giggled, looking meaningly at him, or ignored him altogether, as he walked by them, absorbed by the difficulties of his project, and kicking away clods or pebbles from the path.

In later years I have several times heard Ben allude to those rambles with Miss Maria and Susan, and always with a degree of bitterness which sometimes appeared exaggerated. "That woman"—he always mentioned her in that endearing way—"that woman" appeared to him as having thrown, by some devilish art, her glamour over a lovely virgin, to whom she made herself appear a spotless angel, the embodiment of sincerity and intelligent friendship, while to his unaffected eyes she was a she-dragon, with jutting fangs and hideous mien, which stood between him and his love, gentle and loving to her, threatening and hateful to him. He had read such things in fairy books, and he wondered if they were not founded on fact.

And in the house it was no better. She took it upon herself to usurp the conversation, and argue with him on any trivial or important point she could invent, and to attribute to him ill nature and bigotry when he became excited, stupidity and all sorts of self-contradictions when he remained calm. She seemed to try to make him show himself unamiable when he most wished to appear amiable, and she snubbed him when he seemed at all at ease or hopeful. Often she answered him when Susan was addressed, as though she were her regularly deputed mouth-piece, and as often made nods and winks to Susan not to answer when she intended doing so. In fine, she seemed to take the mind, conscience, and desires, the likes and dislikes of Susan entirely into her charge, and thrust herself forward, and acted and spoke as though she were herself being courted by a lover whom she wished to repel.

All this, apart from its insolence, was vastly embarrassing. It complicated the elements of the problem which Ben had to calculate. It was an interference in what he thought should be the orbit of his planet. It was a serious question how far Susan indorsed her friend. At times, when she was friendly and earnest in her talk, he thought her heart was well inclined towards him, and that perhaps Miss Maria, after all, was not his enemy, or could not affect his Susan; and then, when she seemed to mind the hints and participate in the spirit of Miss Maria, he felt himself almost guilty of treason when the thought intruded itself that perhaps she was more weak-minded and easily influenced than he had believed her to be.

But presently there came another complication which gave him serious pause, and almost determined him to turn back and resign himself to die on the hither bank. One Thursday afternoon he called to see Susan, and she excused herself from seeing him on the plea of headache. Miss Maria was not there, or she would have entertained him in her pleasant way; so he rode back home disconsolate, and suffering heart-pangs at every imagined throb in his sweet Susan's temples. The next afternoon he went again, and found the young lady sitting in the parlor with Miss Maria, as gay as though she had never known what headache was; and, too, when he questioned her sympathizingly about her dear head, she treated it as a mere passing matter of not the slightest moment. But the next Thursday the same excuse was made: Miss Susan had a headache, and begged to be excused. Nor was Miss Maria nor any other company there that afternoon either. It looked suspicious, very suspicious, to the sensitive young fellow. That headache was either very inconvenient, or a mere convenience; and yet she seemed so merry and friendly when he was there the last Friday afternoon that he could hardly believe that she would pretend sickness to avoid seeing him. But how was he to account for the coincidence of the headache with the absence of Miss Maria and all other company?

He concluded that, at any rate, he would not go out to see her until the next regular afternoon, but would contrive to get a bulletin of her health from some other source. Seeing her mother in town the next day he learned in answer to his anxious inquiries that Susan was perfectly well and had gone late the afternoon before to see Miss Maria.

This would have been crushing to an ordinary lover, but it was not so to Ben. To be crushed while there was any avenue of escape never suited his philosophy; and, apart from his abiding confidence that even at the last moment God might intervene to bless him (and in all his agonizing prayers he pleaded God's power and goodness), he had a confused theory about the peculiar nature of woman,—a theory which has led many a poor fellow to act so as that he afterwards should say he had made a fool of himself.

Ben's theory of the peculiarity of woman's character was, in two words, this: that she was inclined to act by contraries; that is, to wish one way and act another. I have now lived my full threescore years and ten, and the result of all my observation is that if there exist any created being which generally acts precisely as it wishes, it is Woman. There are, certainly, exceptions to the general rule. Some women are coy, and most of them are rather catlike when they have the prey safely entrapped; but almost invariably if she won't she won't, and if she will she will, and there is no overcoming or escaping. But that a lover is naturally a fool and not capable of judging he should have no difficulty in knowing exactly whether she will or will not. In all her coyness encouragement slightly preponderates, if she will; and if she will not (mind you, I speak of good, honest women), there is no yielding further than to preserve her own sense of propriety, by being polite, as a lady.

Anyhow, this was Ben's theory, and he made much of it in his reflections. He reduced it as nearly to a science as ever vain theory like it can be reduced, and acted upon it almost to the point that as she was merry his hopes declined, and as she became retiring and silent he became bold and talkative, as though he surely was about to triumph.

Let what I have said suffice for the present about Ben's love, his manner of inspiring it, and his discouragements. A temporary cessation came to the active events of his courtship, and I will therefore occupy myself about other things important in his story. Enough has been said, I hope, to give the reader an exact idea of how he fared in both mind and affections, objectively and subjectively considered—if I may be allowed to adopt that new-fangled mode of speech for which I never before now could find the least use.

One day he came to me to ask my advice about his going to North Carolina, settling up his business there, and removing his negroes and other chattels to our county, where he could have all his interests under his own eye. After his majority, finding his property honestly and well administered, he had allowed the agent in North Carolina to continue his functions and had contented himself with auditing the accounts and receiving his income; but the land in North Carolina was pretty well worn out, to judge by the income, and his negroes would be doubly profitable if placed upon a good place in our county. He said he had learned that young Carraway, who had recently by the death of his father come into possession of a place about three miles southeast of Yatton, near Brown's Creek, and who was a restless sort of body, wished to sell out and move his force to Mississippi, which was then accounted the garden spot of all creation. The place would suit his means and purposes exactly. There was just about enough land for his force, both of the cleared and the uncleared, the place was healthy, and there was a very good dwelling-house upon it. There could be no difficulty in his paying for it; the sale of his North Carolina place would nearly, if not quite do that, as lands were much dearer there than here; and he proposed to acquire and settle it and become a planter as well as pursue his profession, which would not be interfered with by the short distance of the place from town.

I thought the change would be beneficial whether he succeeded or failed in his scheme of marriage, which he at the same time communicated to me as though I, and every other man, woman, and child in town and county, had not long known it. It would be beneficial to his health both of body and mind; for he had not sustained uninjured the terrible strain upon both, or, rather, upon the body through the mind; even if it were not the best thing he could do financially. And then, if he should marry Susan, or any one else, he should have to make the change, perhaps, and so might as well make it now. Taking everything into consideration I advised him to do just what he proposed doing.

And, let me here remark, this is the most prudent advice a man can give another in nine cases out of ten. When he comes to you and says: "My dear friend, it is thus and so; now what course shall I take?—shall I do it? or shall I not?" say to him: My dear fellow, now tell me candidly would you not, taking all things into consideration rather not do it? (or rather do it? as his tone has indicated his desire). And when he answers: Certainly I would! say to him: I thought so, and my advice to you is to do just as you propose doing. Besides that a man generally desires most to do that of two things which is best, this course stops all reproach from him if the affair should turn out badly, and saves a world of trouble.

Ben immediately began preparing for his departure, and in two weeks, as soon as the term (September) of court was over, started on his journey. Of course he went to announce his project and bid farewell to his lady-love; and she neither wept his departure nor bewailed her own fate. She acted and spoke just as a gentle-hearted and sincere woman who has a respect for a man in his position should speak and act in the circumstances. She manifested no surprise beyond asking him if his resolution was not rather sudden; and no interest beyond wishing him a pleasant and profitable journey. Although (and I may as well declare it in so many words) she did not love him, she respected him highly as a man, and felt a kindly feeling towards him for his affection for her—but at the same time felt: oh! how much more she should love him if he would only quit loving her.

The woman is very narrow-minded who does not find cause to be gratified and honored by the pure and ardent love of a good man, however little she may feel inclined to return it, and she must be very narrow-souled if her annoyance at his attentions be not greatly tempered by compassion and respect. She is to him all of earth most desirable; he would live for her a life which should be grand for its labors and unselfishness; or he would die for her, and die willingly, so it were in her behalf and she might bless his memory. How then can she think that love a small matter which so aggrandizes a fellow-mortal as to make him like an archangel, regardless of self? He has created her for himself a Goddess; how can she become so ignoble as to show herself a Fury!

I imagine that Ben started on his journey with a heavy heart.

CHAPTER XVII.

IS DEVOTED TO THE STOCKDALES.

IN the fall, not long after Ben Eccles left for North Carolina, it became absolutely necessary that Dr. Sam should go again to Yatton, on business. I recollect the time when business was just as imperative upon me, and as opportune. Whatever the affair was, it, in his estimation, rendered it perfectly proper in him to excuse himself to those patients who did not need his immediate services, and get other physicians to attend to those who did, and to exercise his boldness and imagination in making excellent excuses to his mother and sisters in order to make the trip. I may be doing the excellent gentleman an injustice, but after he arrived at Yatton I could hear of no business he came for except to go out to The Barn and take tea, and then to go again the next day on a sort of complimentary call, and then again, the second day after, to bid the ladies good-by.

To drop all doubtful modes of speaking, Dr. Sam Stockdale had stood the gradually increasing motive-power of love as long as he could without moving, and he came to Yatton just because he could not help himself. His mind had been fixing itself upon an idea (Susan) with a self-contracting intentness until he felt himself bound to follow his idea, and see whether in all respects she was worth living for, and if she were, whether he could succeed in living for her alone—a man with one fruitful idea.

He was neither so well known to the ladies as was Ben, nor did he have the reputation of being so harmlessly good; his reception, therefore, had a smack of flavor to it of which Ben's was wholly lacking. He had a character of that positive sort which admits of no intrusive idea of gentle, Christian love, when the man who possesses it begins to pay particular attentions to a young lady. It is known and felt at once that he does not come to woo her soul to any other object than himself. There is no sheep's clothing to conceal his wolfish form. He is a wolf (though a sober, respectable wolf) to be run from or submitted to at once, and wholly, when he has made his election of a victim. And it needs no spying and doubtful calculations to tell whether such a character has made that election, or is only inclined to gambol and frisk with the sweet lamb, because he happen to stray into her pasture. These three visits, therefore, told Dr. Sam's intentions more clearly than the first twenty did Ben's, because twenty different reasons might be assigned for the latter's twenty visits, as he was not suspected to be Master Wolf.

I suppose that nothing occurred beyond the usual humdrum of such first reconnoissances; but the doctor went home more full than ever of his idea. The idea had become a fact, a beautiful, living, and loving fact, of which he was determined to possess himself, body and soul, if he could; and he forthwith turned all his thoughts and plans, and even the practice of his profession towards the accomplishment of his object.

The Stockdale family was in some respects peculiar. The old doctor (Dr. Sam's father) had now been dead some six or seven years. He was a fine old gentleman who had his own notions, and everything of his about him partook of his individuality. His great ability in his profession, and the superior quality of his vigorous mind were conceded by all, and a very large practice—more than double that of any other physician in the county—testified to the regard in which he was held. Strangers thought him rough and hard-hearted. Tim O'Flannigan thought so, when the doctor, at his second visit, ordered him to poke out his tongue, and after observing it, bent his shaggy brows, and turned upon him his fierce black eyes, and asked: "Did you take that medicine I left you?"

"No, doctor," said Tim, "I didn't think my stomach could stand it."

"You're a d——d fool, sir! You deserve to die! Shut your mouth! If you were not 'most dead already I'd thrash you, sir!"

But when the doctor sent a man to nurse him, and supplied his cabin with comforts and delicacies he himself could not afford, and told him to go to the devil and quit bothering him when, after he had got well, he asked how much he owed him, Tim O'Flannigan almost worshiped him.

The fact is there are saints for pretty much everything, but I do not know that there is a Gruff Saint in the Calendar; and there certainly should be.

Mrs. Stockdale thought her husband was a saint, of his own peculiar kind, and would at no moment, from the time when she first toyed with his black locks until those locks were as white as snow, have been surprised to see a halo surrounding his head. He must have been a glorious husband; a husband for whom a woman would glorify herself above other women. When I first knew him, though his hair was white, his stalwart form erect and active, his shaggy black brows set over bright black eyes, his sonorous voice, and strong, manly grip of the hand, showed that age had only ripened his strength of body and mind, and mellowed his affections.

But though a glorious husband, he must have been a hard one to get along with; and in truth unless such a man, as he was, is worshiped by his wife, there is no getting along at all in that family; there will be jars and misery in plenty, and finally total separation. For instance:

"See here, Jenny!" he said one day to his wife, looking with a disgusted expression upon a pair of new pants he held before him at arms' length. "I told you to make my breeches with narrow flaps, and you have made a d——d broad concern——"

"Oh, but, doctor," interrupted Mrs. Stockdale, "narrow flaps have gone out of fashion."

D——n the fashion! I beg pardon, my dear. But what in the—ahem! what do I care for fashions? Now see here; if you can't make my clothes to suit me, I'll go off and get a tailor to do it!" and he added, *sotto voce*, looking with increased disgust at the unlucky garment: "It's a d——d shame that I should have to wear such togs as that and not be able to tell whether my breeches are on before or behind, because my wife chooses to follow the fashion instead of obeying my commands!"

Now what mortal woman could stand unmoved such an attack as that except from a man she worshiped? It had in it all the elements of caprice, ingratitude, ill temper, and tyranny; grinding, bowing, crushing tyranny. Here had she done the very best she could to make her husband comfortable, and, more than that, to improve his appearance. Her motives had been pure and disinterested. It was not for the good of his success with the world that he should go so old-fashioned before it, and she had only tried to make him a little, just a little, fashionable, and this was her reward! loud reproaches, sneers, and ill temper! It was enough to make a woman weep—which with the sex stands in place of cursing. She neither could nor would stand such ungrateful oppression if she did not adore the tyrant. Mrs. Stockdale never thought once of rebelling. She knew her tyrant too well even to answer back and excuse or justify herself. "By God! madam," he would have answered, "are they your breeches or mine?"

Almost everybody cursed in those days, so the doctor must not be thought more wicked than he really was. He merely followed an old fashion to which his ardent temper inclined him—just as he refused to follow the fashion in breeches because he had no inclination for innovation.

In the matter of the pants, as in all other matters in which the doctor was concerned (and very few were the household affairs in which he did not at some time, by fits and starts, annoyingly concern himself), Mrs.

Stockdale acted wisely; and she had her reward. She let the matter pass, and after wearing the pants a time or two, he remarked: "Well, my dear, this new fashion is not so bad after all. It is just as convenient and much more decent; though," he added, musingly, looking down at himself, "I should be slightly more like a little boy if the d——d things buttoned to my shirt."

The old gentleman was just the same with his servants and his horses and dogs, and patients, and friends. He knew but one will; and that was his own. The will of everybody and everything else was ignored as though it did not exist, and when a thing was done after any other fashion than his he was astonished and outraged. He was not the only Emperor I have seen in private life, but he was about the best, because he was utterly unconscious of his imperious disposition; and became outraged, not because a thing was not done in *his* style, but because it was not, he thought, done in the right style.

There were two persons, however, who had him in as complete control as he would have had every one else. His two daughters, Sarah and Lily, had him under their thumbs, and he never thought of rebelling from them any more than did his wife dream of shaking off his yoke. But their influence was manifested in different ways. Sarah resembled her mother in person, but had exactly her father's disposition, only it was feminine and refined. Lily, on the contrary, looked like her father—a tall, stately, black-eyed girl she was! but had her mother's gentle and affectionate ways. When Sarah was a little girl she one day seriously informed her father when he had "burst loose" (as Sam called it) about some matter which concerned her dress, that she didn't intend to put up with such language and conduct! The old gentleman was at first amazed, and then gratified at her spirit, and ever after bowed himself to her yoke. Lily, on the contrary, was always her father's darling, and could by her loving ways completely mould him to her will. To one who only knew the old gentleman abroad, it was wonderful to see his gentleness and meekness with his daughters.

With Sam, however, it was different. He had inherited a great deal of his father's strength with a fair share of his mother's softness. It was not long after he was advanced to the dignity of boots that he began to emulate his elder sister's spirit, and to "cut up a little rusty," as our people express it, with his father; and the consequence was that the strong hand came down upon him. The old gentleman had a true respect as well as a tender love for him, and could never act so severely as to cow him, but he was the stronger of the two, and though both made it a sort of stand-off fight, Sam generally had to submit. And, after all, he did not have to submit to much. His father had always made a companion of him, and in ordinary matters had treated him as his equal from his early youth, and let him have his own way, only calling him "an obstinate young rascal" when there was controversy about some minor matter. As an example:

One day when Sam was a little chap, Mrs. Stockdale said to her husband: "Doctor, I got Sam those boots, but he has been fretting about them all the morning, and doesn't wish to wear them."

"Where is he?" asked the doctor; and seeing Sam out on the gallery, sulking, "Come here, sir! What is this row about your boots? Didn't you ask me to get you a pair of those boots at Smith's? Now that you have got them, what's the trouble about, eh?"

"They aren't the kind I wanted, father," said Sam. "They've got blue tops, and I wanted red ones."

"That's a pretty thing to make a fuss about, sir! What difference does it make whether they are blue or red? Tell me, sir!"

"I never did like blue, father. I like red, and I want red; and you know, father, that if you wanted red-topped boots, you wouldn't like to have blue ones," said Sam, sturdily.

"The devil, I wouldn't!" exclaimed the doctor. "You obstinate young rascal, you're as notionate as a girl. Clear out, and change your boots to what color you please. Get sea-green if it please your delicate fancy best. But see here, sir!" as Sam was running off, boots in hand, "if you are so difficult to please, your mother shall put you back into tow shirts again. Look out, sir!"

"Jenny," said the doctor, after Sam was out of hearing, "I don't think it is desirable to thwart a boy's desires more than is absolutely necessary. It's apt to make him rebellious. I have made it a rule to let people, old and young, have their own way."

"How long since you made that rule, my dear?" asked Mrs. Stockdale, innocently.

"Why, all my life, to be sure!" answered her husband. "I always have let you, and the girls, and Sam, and everybody, have your own way. Of course,

I mean under proper restrictions; when your way was the best way; for I should be a fool if I would let any one dependent upon me do wrong if I could help it. But you know now, my dear, that I never do interfere except when I think it is necessary."

"Yes, doctor," answered his wife, "I do know that; but you think it necessary all the time."

"Pshaw!" said the doctor, turning on his heel, and going on out into the yard to regulate matters which were no concern of his, and would, by his "regulation," give his wife all sorts of trouble.

CHAPTER XVIII.

NARRATES HOW THE STOCKDALES GOT ALONG AFTER THE OLD DOCTOR'S DEATH; AND WHAT THEY THOUGHT ABOUT DR. SAM, AND ABOUT HIS LOVE AFFAIR.

THE doctor's house was on the main street of Rosstown, and not far from the court-house. At Yatton there was a large square fenced in around the court-house, and then between that and the rows of houses the streets were a full hundred feet broad, making the town "roomy," as the inhabitants described it. But at Rosstown the same plan was upon a more narrow scale. The court-house square was small, and the streets were narrow between it and the rows of stores. Main street, running east and west, was the principal street for business, and upon it the doctor had, many years before when the population was not half so large, erected his dwelling-house. The tavern was nearly opposite to it, and the principal livery-stable was about seventy-five yards below that. The house was two stories in height, built of red brick, had a narrow little gallery or stoop in front, and very green shutters to the windows. A row of large china-trees made it more quiet, and protected it in a good measure from the glare and dust of the street. As brick houses were then rather more rare than they now are, the doctor's house had a particularly aristocratic and imposing appearance in the eyes of his fellow-citizens; a fact of which the family were not at all disagreeably conscious, although they were as unpretentious as a family of so much character, intelligence, and merit well could be.

Here, after the doctor's death, they still lived. Nothing had been changed, and nothing added to change the appearance of the house, in or out. The same china-trees put forth their lilac blossoms and their leaves together in spring, became gray with dust in the long droughts of summer, shed their leaves in the fall, and kept shedding their berries upon the pavement all the winter, much to the widow's annoyance. Dr. Sam's new gig usurped the place of his father's old sulky in the carriage-house, and a pair of fast-trotting mares and a spirited young riding-horse occupied the stalls of the heavy old carriage horses and the doctor's easy cob. In the parlor and the dining-room the same old-time appearance was observed. Grim profiles, cut in black paper, hung on the parlor walls in little plain gilt frames. There was the doctor's, at full length, with a pair of legs of impossible symmetry; one, with a sharp-pointed boot, standing in advance of the other, upon which the boot was rather more blunt. But the shaggy eyebrows were there, represented by the keenest little cut ever scissors snipped; the bold nose and chin, and the firm mouth were also there. It was, altogether, a very good likeness, and one to make the old gentleman's descendants feel proud of having had such a noble Titan of an ancestor. There was another—of the doctor's mother, a trim old lady, with every frill of her huge cap faithfully reproduced. Mrs. Stockdale was also there, with her features more defined than they were now, that they were somewhat smoothed by age, but not more lovely in expression. Sarah and Lily were also represented with the broadest of pantalets, and the sharpest of little feet showing below their short dresses, and with the longest and most luxuriant of pig-tails falling down their backs. There was a sample or two of the most erudite needle-work, the productions of mother and grandmother, also hanging in frames on the wall. I call it erudite, because such work used to constitute a woman's erudition before the 'onomies, and 'ologies, and Calisthenics came in vogue. In the dining-room the doctor's old gilt-glass decanters, with the accompanying gilt liqueur glasses, stood upon the sideboard, where his favorite coffee-bowl—he would never use a cup—was in the place of honor, and was never touched, except to be dusted and cleaned by loving hands.

But housekeeping now was very different from what it had been in the doctor's lifetime. When his stalwart form was seen, and his stern, sonorous voice was heard about that house, the visitors there were only those who had business, those who were the intimate friends of the family, and those who paid formal visits of ceremony. When those who had business had transacted it, they went away; when intimate friends came, they too knew when to go, and just what liberties to take on the ground of intimate acquaintance; and when formal visitors came, they paid formal visits, and never fished for invitations to take up board or lodging.

But all this was changed. The stern presence which repelled bores was gone, and good Mrs. Stockdale found herself the victim of impositions innumerable. There were country families who came from North, South, East, and West in the county, and some from neighboring counties, and always made it convenient to "happen in" just at dinner-time or at night. They would send their children to town with orders to go to Mrs. Stockdale's for dinner and to feed their horses, or to spend the night with her if they had to remain all night in town; and if they sent a servant in town on business, he had the like orders. There were families in town and in its neighborhood who, while the old carriage-horses lasted, borrowed carriage, and horses, and driver, two, three, or even five times in a week, on the plea that they only wished to use them an hour or two, if the family were not using them. Old Jim, the carriage-driver, used to boast bitterly that he was the only public hack-driver nearer than Augusta. Not only so, it was actually the case that country families having carriages sent their daughters to town with

15

some friendly neighbor going there, and by them sent a request to Mrs. Stockdale to please forward them ten, fifteen, or twenty miles farther up or down the country, as one of their horses was sick, or the crop was in the grass, or the carriage-driver had hurt his hand, or some such excuse. When the new carriage and the fast mares were bought, Dr. Sam took his father's place, and said no! to all such beggars; and once or twice said NO with such a vengeance that they desisted, thinking that he was surely a chip of the old block.

But so long as their mother yielded, neither Sam nor his sisters could stop the other bores without acting more rudely than they thought becoming even towards such conscienceless sponges.

As Mrs. Stockdale kept no cows she had to buy all her butter and milk from the country, and to insure a regular supply she had engaged so much a week from a certain party, a stranger, but who made good butter. One day there had been a failure in the supply, and as she expected some of her country friends, who had called in the morning and had announced that they were coming back to dinner, she was at a great loss what to do. Old Tom Ramsay, the old doctor's faithful dining-room servant, seeing a market-cart up the street, hailed the driver:

"What you got, boy?"

"Butter, sah, an' aigs, an' veg'ables!" answered the simple-looking driver.

"Who do you belong to?" asked Tom.

"Ole Mis' Thompson, sah. I drives her market-kyart to town two times every week."

"You do, eh? Why, I never saw you in town befo'.

What fur you don't come to Mis' Stockdale's sometimes?" said Tom.

"Oh, oh! Ole mis' tole me not to go dar."

"She did, did she? What fur, you 'spect?" said Tom.

"I dunno," answered the driver, "'less'n she don't like her!"

Tom reported this conversation to his mistress when he came home with the butter, and when Mrs. Thompson came that day, with half her family, to dinner (for she and hers were among the most constant and frequent diners and lodgers), Mrs. Stockdale playfully mentioned it to her, thinking it a mistake on the part of the driver, or of Tom.

Mrs. Thompson blushed, and was much confused, but presently answered that she *had* given such an order because she thought that if she sent her marketman there Mrs. Stockdale might think that, as they were intimate friends, she ought to buy from him, and because, also, it might be interfering with ,the person who constantly supplied the family.

Dr. Sam thought that it would have been vastly more becoming if Mrs. Thompson, instead of lying, had told the truth—that as she and hers ate about a fourth of his mother's provisions, she had not the face to sell to her, and did not wish to give to her.

Some of the friends of the family, however, were not so considerate, or, rather, were more considerate for themselves.

Strawberries were at that time not so common a fruit in the country as they now are; and one family near town, reputed well off, used every year to add a nice little sum to their pockets for spending-money by selling them at twelve and a half cents a small plate—about fifty cents a pint. One day Dr. Sam, expecting two or three young lady friends of his sisters' to tea, thought he would play the magnificent, and bought the carrier's whole supply, about eight pints. The boy reported the wholesale transaction when he got home, and the consequence was that four of the members of that family came to Mrs. Stockdale's to tea that evening, so as to get enough strawberries for once, without trenching upon their income.

Now, I am almost ashamed to write these disgusting details as having occurred in the South. We usually give our Northern brethren the credit for all the sharp tricks and meannesses, but human nature is the same here as there, only differently modified as a general thing. But for the sparseness of our population, and the beneficent influence of our system of slavery in preserving the individuality of our people to a greater degree than it can be preserved in a crowded country where universal equality, so called, prevails, I expect that we should present about as great an average, among the masses, of sharp, selfish meannesses as the Yankee can.

However, as I have for some time past in this story cut loose from philosophy of the heavier sort, and as I foresee that a little further along I shall have to return to it again in spite of myself, I will spare the reader any further analysis of this subject, and will return to Dr. Sam and his family.

The doctor—Dr. Sam—was now about twenty-four years old, and had an excellent practice for one who had been only three years at it. Besides the widow's income and that of the children from the estate, which consisted of houses and lands and stocks, and produced a revenue which, though not very great, was large enough for all the comforts and elegancies of the quiet life at that time and place—besides his share in that income, I say, Dr. Sam also received enough from his practice to make it perfectly proper for him to get a wife as soon as he could. Sarah, who was two years the elder, and who had no thought herself of marrying, as she had never yet seen the man who would suit her, and had too little nonsense about her to bother her head and heart about wishing for such a man, used to impress it upon her brother that he ought to marry if he expected to ever be of any account—as if she had really thought she had ever seen a young man of more account than he already was. His mother was used to tell him that she wished to see him married and settled before she died, and she was getting old—though, bless the dear woman, she was but little more than half my present age, and I can't feel old, however I may appear. Lily implored him to marry. She did wish to have another dear sweet sister for a companion although she knew perfectly well, the hypocrite, that Willis Thurston was only waiting for her to name the day when he should carry her away to Yatton and to his sisters as his wife.

Imagine then, if you please, the trembling eagerness of his secret within him to escape when he got back home from his visit to The Barn. It would fly to his lips and make them twitch with suppressed laughter; it would find its way to his eyes and pucker their corners with half concealed mirth; until, after struggling with it a day or two, he could hold no longer, and let it out, to the unfeigned astonishment and joy of the dear ones who heard him.

And yet within two hours from that moment Lily said to her sister: "I told you so!" and Sarah answered that she had done no such thing, but that she herself had first remarked the strange manner of her brother, and had suspected its cause.

"Yes," said Lily, determined not to be put down in that kind of style, "but you know, sister, I was the first to speak of it."

"Well, what of that?" the inflexible Sarah replied, unwilling to share the glory of the discovery. "What of that? I thought it, but did not care to speak where I might be mistaken."

"Never mind, my daughters. I knew it when Sam was so earnest and impressive with his mysterious and contradictory excuses to go to Yatton," said Mrs. Stockdale. And Sarah and Lily yielded the palm to their mother's jealous sharp-sightedness, though each thought that in her way she was entitled to as much credit.

Here now was the first—no, not the first, because Lily's little affair had been discussed and rediscussed before that—but here was the grandest little exciting secret the family had ever had. It was the grandest, because in their, woman's, eyes it was by far a more important matter to the family that brother should marry than that either of them should either marry or die.

It is a curious thing to notice how very important an only son and brother is to a family of women when he is the only male of the family and is at all good and manly. Their devotion to him, and their pride in him are exaggerated to an almost painful degree. Nay, I have seen them go just as far for a no-account, dissipated whelp, whose proper place was breaking rocks at a house of correction. I have known them contribute all their scanty earnings to his vanity in dress, and sit up nearly all night, half starved, to let him in the house when he should come home staggering with drink which he had bought with the wages they had hardly earned by sewing or teaching school, and which he had shared with boon companions. And when such a one has died I have seen them weep themselves almost blind, and always afterwards bewail him as one of the noblest or most gifted of mankind, whose only fault was his generosity and goodness of heart.

And about this matter I must make a remark or two, whether it be in or out of place.

Drunkards are very fond of boasting that it is only the good fellows and the geniuses, or men of great talent who drink to excess; and the women who are so unfortunate as to be allied to them catch the lying cant and comfort themselves with it the best they can. Poor comfort it is, truly! even if it were a physiological fact supported by the best evidence! But there is no truth in it. It is true that great mental ability is usually accompanied by a vigorous vitality and strong appetites, and it is also true that the very amiable are usually also very weak. But that because a man has strong appetites he has a strong mind, or because he is a sot he is therefore amiable, is as false as false can be. I have tested and narrowly observed some of these amiable sots, and can say with perfect truth that they presented the most depraved instances of selfishness it has ever been my lot to encounter among men—the very foundation of whose whole nature is, at best, selfishness. I have repeatedly seen these amiable fellows squander the little money they had made or got hold of in some way, treating themselves and their close acquaintance at bar-rooms and restaurants, when their children at home needed shoes and clothing, and their wives were at home almost frantic to find food for their families. Was that amiability? or was it heartless selfishness? I have heard some of them in a crazed state spouting poetry or quoting Latin and Greek to the admiration and wonder of their companions. Was that genius? or was it the effect of the unnatural excitement of the memory by a poison?

Where one man of really eminent talent has had an appetite stronger than his will, a thousand have had wills stronger than their appetites. In nine hundred and ninety cases out of a thousand it is the will which makes the great man. The intellect is only a tool, and a strong will may make most efficient use of a dull, badly-tempered, or very gapped tool. Where was there ever a great commander, who while he was a great commander was guilty of habitual excess in drink? Alexander? Not a bit of it. He was a remarkably temperate man in all his appetites until just before the miserable close of his career, and I do not know of any other great commander who has even the reputation of having been a drunkard while he was in the really effective service of his life. As for other men of talent or genius the few, comparatively, who have manifested a great weakness for drink, have either overcome it or have had their usefulness crippled and finally totally blasted; while with the mere Good Fellows, if they have kept up their drinking until it has become confirmed, whatever they may have been in public, they were at their homes peevish, and snappish, and unreasonable—the terrors of their wives, children, and servants, horses, and dogs.

But enough of this. The same thing has doubtless been said over and over again before now, and I have repeated it, not as a new thing, but as a fact, which cannot be repeated too often to the rising generation. Fortunately for the Stockdale family their man was worthy of all their devotion. He was a good son, a good brother, a good master, a good physician, and a good citizen, and I take great delight in retracing his career to happiness although I already know it so well.

CHAPTER XIX.

SOMETHING MORE ABOUT MISS ALICE, AND A GREAT DEAL ABOUT THE BOWMANS.

DR. McCLEOD had lived long in the world, and though he had lived very quietly had had his eyes open all the while. He was a connoisseur in motives. To find, analyze, and classify them, had been his labor and his pastime. No bug-hunter ever more persistently and enthusiastically jumped, and stooped, and got upon hands and knees, and peered upon the ground, and slapped the air to secure a new specimen of insect, than did the doctor's imagination jump, and peer, and snap, at some new little motive. The more common he let pass, only classifying them as they flew.

The moment Aunt Polly opened her mouth to speak of Charley Bowman, after she came from church, he knew exactly the idea which was uppermost in her mind, the hidden motive of the impression which the young gentleman had made upon her. And when that night, after the visit, his wife spoke of the improvement of the young man and his ability to support a wife, he knew that she too had the same idea and motive.

It is absolutely impossible for a woman to see a young unmarried couple together without questioning herself about the suitableness of their making a match. Her memory instantly takes a view of all the past of their families, of the present worldly condition of both, of their dispositions, personal appearance, ages, education, social standing, and of all the little stories she has heard about either of them. And if the couple be strangers to her she scrutinizes their personal appearance, manners, dress, complexion, eyes, tones of voice, and sets her imagination to work as to the propriety of their marrying; and if it seem congruous, then as to its probability.

Ask any woman of your acquaintance if this be not the exact truth; and be she high or low, old or young, wise or simple, she will tell you yes, if she tell you the truth—unless she be an exception of a woman, which she very likely, in her heart, may think herself, and may claim to be.

These good, guileless ladies had arranged it all in their own minds. They knew only Charley's good qualities. He was a young man whose family stood well enough in the community; he was very well off, had a fine plantation, with a thriving force upon it; was handsome; sufficiently accomplished for a country gentleman, and was quite amiable. She was a charming girl, pure in heart, refined in her manners, gentle in disposition, and almost a genius; her property was not large, but it was large enough to prevent her feeling that she should go dowerless to her husband, whoever he might be; and then she had black eyes and hair, while his eyes were blue and his hair was sandy.

It was certainly an excellent match; a better for either could hardly be found. And there seemed to be no difficulty in bringing it about. Both the dear ladies knew that propinquity was the surest fuel of love, and opportunity its most certain spark: and here was the propinquity, and opportunities could not be lacking. It was one of those rare conjunctions of fit things, and it seemed "to run on wheels."

Mr. Bowman had promised to call again, and he did call, only two days after. The doctor saw his approach from the front gate, and uttered an ominous humph! but when he came up on the gallery received him politely. There was a little bustle in the passage at the announcement of his arrival, and the hurried tucking away of needle-work, not suitable for strange gentlemen's eyes, and the disappearance of Alice and Flora; but in a minute or two after he was seated, both those young ladies reappeared as fresh and tidy as though they had not before been out of their dressing-room that day. The conversation, at first general, soon became special between the young folk, who had a natural affinity for each other, and the drawings and drawing-table became again the centres of attack and defence, or rather of observation and counter-observation, of feint and counter-feint; for no determined attack had yet been projected, and no defence had been contemplated, or, if contemplated by the young lady, then, almost unconsciously so, only on general principles.

As the experienced and observant reader has been placed in possession of the outlines of the situation, I need not accompany him all the time to mark the consequent movements. His own intimate knowledge shall be a sufficient guide. I wish to say a few words about the Bowmans, as I have about the Stockdales; for it is desirable that everything possible shall be known about Ben's schoolmates.

I cannot say that I ever liked the Bowmans. Although our personal acquaintance was slight, I knew that we were not congenial. Col. Bowman (I never knew how he got his title) always reminded me of Capt. Cartwright, whose daughter my cousin Fitzroy married. He was almost as fat, and quite as pompous, but not half so intelligent. I think he was a native of New York. I'll say he was, at any rate, for as he was not remarkably literary, perhaps Massachusetts might not own him. He came to the South when a very young man, hardly grown, being sent out as a sort of *protêgê* of old Col. Vance, who had for many years done business with his father, who had a shoe factory. Col. Vance was very wealthy; had plantations and plantations; and as the young man was exceedingly respectful to him, and to his sons and daughters, and to his horses, and dogs, and carriages, and carts, and everything that was his, and evidently regarded the whole as sacred, the old gentleman took his worship as an outward sign of inward honesty, and after awhile made him a sort of agent for himself. Mr. Bowman got himself an office on the main street in Rosstown, and the Colonel procured him the agency for several Northern patent machines, and all that sort of thing, with specimens of which he bedecked his office, and obstructed the side-walk in its front. He had samples of the Colonel's tobacco, cotton, and rice, all the finest in the world, spread out on a table in the centre of the office; and upon a railing which he had placed around the Colonel's holy desk, he had a sign in beautiful gilt letters, "COL. CHARLES GIBSON VANCE," in contemplating which he never wearied in the patron's absence, and which he would caressingly decipher when the Colonel was in presence. In the summer he had the Colonel's first blooms of cotton hung at the door, and in the fall his largest ear of corn and largest leaf of tobacco were triumphantly exhibited.

As he was apt at figures, and became a very correct and steady man of business, the Colonel, besides making him a broker for a great deal of his own produce, got for him the patronage of several of his wealthy friends, and also entrusted him with the care of his papers, and finally with the drawing up of his deeds, and the collection of his rents, etc. All this paid handsomely, and Mr. Bowman became Col. Bowman, and also from mixing continually with the very rich, and talking

16

about huge plantations, and huge sums of money, got so lofty he could hardly see common folk and he got him a wife too.

That was one of the crowning triumphs of the fitness of things; which, to tell the truth, is often unlucky rather than triumphant. She was created for him, and he for her. She was the Colonel's cousin, Miss Harmonia Jenkins, poor, except in the awful contemplation of her second cousin's wealth, and proud, with the glory of that relative. She had no pride of her own; she would have thought that sacrilege; any more than she had wealth of her own; which would have been superfluous, and mere dirt beside her cousin's huge edifice.

Now, if there was any one particular thing which Col. Bowman longed for, as the great panacea for all the ills of life, and the great crown of his glory, it was to be in some way connected with Col. Vance's family. He did not care how; he would have married the Colonel's grandmother if the dear old lady had been living and able to consent; or the Colonel's white cook if the Colonel had told him to do so and she had had a drop of the Colonel's blood, or of the blood of any of the Colonel's relatives by blood or marriage. It was the bane of his life that he was not himself of the Colonel's blood, and he almost cursed his ancestors, whoever they might have been (and he knew he had had them, though he did not and could never know their names or whence they came),—he almost cursed his ancestors, I say, because they had been so low in life, or so unfortunate as not to be ancestors of the Colonel also, or had not at least married some relative of some of the Colonel's ancestors. He could never think of marrying either of the Colonel's daughters, though they were fine girls and marriageable, for, besides that the young ladies patronized and detested him, he could not have the presumption to place himself in the direct line of the Colonel's property.

Miss Harmonia was a God-send to Col. Bowman, and also thought Col. Bowman a God-send to her. Her name was itself suggestive of a fortunate marriage; and here was her chance! Who worshiped the Colonel? Col. Bowman! Who was in intimate relations with the Colonel? Col. Bowman! Who was trusted by the Colonel and viewed the Colonel's wealth, and handled the Colonel's wealth, and fully understood and appreciated and bowed down to the Colonel's wealth? Col. Bowman! And so it went on in her head in the catechetical style of "My Mother."

On the other hand, his mind pursued the same exhaustive mode of argument. Who was the only eligible female relative of the great Colonel? Miss Harmonia! Who, because she was the Colonel's relative, was beautiful? Harmonia! Who, for the same reason, was wise and good and in all respects lovely and to be desired? Harmonia! Who kneels with me in worship of the Colonel? Harmonia!

And so they married. The Colonel, and his wife, and daughters, and sons, and many of his servants graced the wedding, and I verily believe that Bowman would have had every overseer the Colonel had, and as many of his negroes as could have been spared from the crop, if he had had his own way, and would have gloried in feasting them all, with their horses and dogs, and thought the money it cost nobly spent.

It was not very long after their marriage that Col. Bowman began to get fat, and then began to yearn for the pleasures of planting life, and the glory of taking his place as a brother with the Colonel and the other agricultural magnates of the land. He had accumulated money, and finding a place (the one he now lived on, near Dr. McCleod's) offered for sale to settle up a succession, he had purchased it, with all its force, just as it stood. The investment had been profitable, and as years rolled on he had purchased other places, two of them for his sons Charles Gibson Vance Bowman and Henry. His wife and he had harmonized perfectly in their desires and schemes. Even her having two sons was, though an accident, in exact harmony with what he wished. He was a lucky man.

But when old Col. Vance died there was a great revulsion in the accordant feelings of the pair. The old gentleman had died intestate, and therefore little Charles was none the better off for his name; and, worse than that, when the estate came to be settled up it was found that the debts were greater than the value of the assets.

Who would have thought it! It was all the fault of those extravagant minxes the Misses Vance, and the reckless expenditures of those dissipated dogs the Masters Vance, and that mean, penny-wise and pound-foolish, hard old woman, Mrs. Vance. They needn't come to Col. Bowman for either sympathy or assistance. Had he not advised them, remonstrated with them, besought them as a loving relative, with tears in his eyes, to refrain from their courses? Had he not warned the Colonel? And the Colonel was a weak old fool for not having taken his warning; for did not he, Col. Bowman, better than any other man, know to a cent and the fraction of a cent just how affairs stood? The old man had despised his warnings, and the young folk and their mother had scouted his advice and remonstrances, and they might suffer the consequences. He was not going to have a set of poor relations whining around *him*.

And when he went to town and met Mr. John Vance he almost shocked himself by saluting him as John, instead of "Mr. Vance;" and William Vance he called Bill, instead of "Master William," and he inquired of them how Louisa, and Jane, and Sally, and the old woman were, instead of respectfully speaking of them as "your respected mother and the young ladies, your sisters;" and he never mentioned his wife's name once to them, whereas always before, and especially if in the presence of others, he had been particular to say: "My wife, your cousin, bade me give her duty to your mother, and remember her with respectful kindness to the young ladies, her cousins, your sisters."

He had grown very fat by the time to which my story has progressed, and was very patronizing, and had a husky and condescendingly gentle voice to almost all who came in contact with him—except when he was tyrannical and rough, and his voice was loud and dictatorial to them. That is a queer freak of man's nature. Such a man as was Dr. Stockdale becomes more kind and sympathetic as he becomes more successful, and a Col. Bowman becomes more harsh and hard and patronizing. But I'll not stop to analyze it here; any thoughtful reader will do so for himself.

There was one man, however, in Rosstown, who put at defiance all the Colonel's coldness and frowns, and whom the Colonel avoided with horror. It was James Ransom; old Jim Ranser, they used to call him. When the Colonel first came to Rosstown he and Mr. Ransom were great cronies. Ransom's father was a very well-to-do planter in my county, but James had taken up the desire to make a merchant of himself, and had been allowed to take a preparatory clerkship in a store in Rosstown, which offered what he thought unusual advantages. Here he was, a young buck of the first year, when Bowman arrived, a stranger; and being of a kind and rather enthusiastic nature in his friendships and enmities, he had taken the new-comer in charge and introduced him to his friends, allowed him to sleep in his room; and, on two or three occasions, had fought his battles for him. But as years passed on and Bowman went up, Ransom went down. His father failed in planting, and was sold out by the sheriff, and the store James was to have consequently vanished. He found himself a confirmed clerk; for he could not understand the energy and perseverance which make a merchant of a clerk. To his comprehension one had to start with a fully-stocked store, or not to start at all. So, as he could never be anything but a clerk, he concluded to be just as jolly a clerk as he could be. The consequence was his losing several clerkships in succession after vain promises of amendment, and he was now "with the dogs," as he himself expressed it; a seedy, talkative, ill-natured or good-natured (according to the state of his nervous system) drunkard.

"I say, Bowman!" he called out to the Colonel one day, when he saw him puffing along the street, "where is it you live?" And as the Colonel made no answer, he continued: "O my Aminadab, you needn't pretend not to hear me. I want to know where you live. I think of taking up my quarters with you next spring when the fishing in the creek is good. I'm sure you'll be glad to see your old friend and roommate. I say, Bo', don't you——"

"Mr. Ransom, I'll thank you to call me by my proper title, sir," the offended and disgusted Colonel replied.

"And what in the hell is your proper title, Bo'? They used to call you Toady, and Lick-spittle, and Sneak, and it wasn't till you took the title of Colonel that anybody ever thought you didn't have your proper title. Now which of your really proper titles must I give you?"

"Mr. Ransom! Mr. Ransom!" spluttered the Colonel; "I'll not submit to such language!"

"You're right, Bo'! You're right, Aminadab! I wouldn't either! I admire your pluck. But now I come to think of it, the boy who used to back you is now before you. So I expect you'll stand it, Bo'; just a little, you know, by way of experiment. I say, my Colonel! what have you been eating lately? You are getting pussy. Been eating whales, eh?"

"Mr. Ransom, I'll thank you to let me pass," said the Colonel, with lofty dignity.

"Pass! Oh, certainly; but it's well the streets are broad, my Colonel. Oh, just to think how spry you used to be about Old Vance's horses when he drove to town!"

By the time the Colonel had borne as much as this (and he had to bear it frequently), he would fairly turn and flee, and if Ransom showed a disposition to follow, would take refuge in some private house, or get in his gig and leave town.

This was Col. Aminadab Bowman, the father of Ben's friend Charles. Ben used to say that he never saw stiffly starched white pants and a broad-brimmed straw hat on a fat man but he thought of him, and felt very small, and yet very contemptuous. I beg pardon for taking up so much room in describing him, but the fact is that there is scarcely a village, town, county, or city in the South but has or has had its Col. Bowman, and sometimes several of them, rivals, at once. And, unfortunately, almost every man in the world has seen a James Ransom.

CHAPTER XX.

WHY MR. CHARLES BOWMAN CONCLUDED TO FALL IN LOVE, AND HOW HE CARRIED ON HIS COURTSHIP.

HE must be a very extraordinary man of whom nothing but good can be said; yet, except that Charles Bowman was reckless of truth, timid of dăn-ger, and an egotist, I have nothing but praises to award him. A more affable and whole-souled young man to those he esteemed his equals or superiors could not be found in all that county. He was gay as a lark;

ready for any kind of amusement that offered itself. He had that common kind of benevolence which always makes a man pleased to see others doing well when it costs him neither thought nor exertion. He could, indeed, at times, when his sympathies were much moved, exert himself to get others interested in a case of charity; but as soon as they became engaged in it he abandoned it to them, taking to himself, and, loud talking fellow that he was, receiving all the credit. As the world goes he was a good-hearted young man, with a proper respect for the feelings and rights of others; but, alas! I fear that in his case, as in so many others, the good-heartedness was merely the effect of a healthy digestion, and the respect for others was the result of fear.

If all this does not appear to the reader to be praise, let him not make his opinion known, or the bulk of the world will call him censorious, and be personally offended.

Alice pleased Mr. Bowman's fancy mightily. He persuaded himself that she was all he could desire in a wife. She was remarkably handsome, had a fine mind, and many elegant accomplishments, and would grace his establishment, as he who aspired to be one of the finest gentlemen of the county should have it graced. Besides that, she was an excellent housekeeper, and would make and keep elegant and comfortable the establishment over which she presided. True, she was not wealthy, and had no near male relative in the world either to add to her wealth or to contribute to the advancement of her husband's influence, but she was of a loving disposition, and her blood was, he admitted, a little better than even that of the Vances, and had a distinctive line a very great deal longer than that of his branch of the Bowmans. Her grandfathers had been men of note in the colony, and their fathers were gentlemen. That much he had learned of them, and when he thought of how utterly unknown his own ancestry must ever be to him, he, like his father before him, was very desirous to ally himself to one whose family was known and respected, whether in the present or for the past.

It was, take it all in all, a very desirable alliance, and he determined to make it, if possible. This determination was not made all at once, like that of one who falls violently in love. It was the result of calculation, and was made after many visits. That want of wealth was a serious drawback; and then, again, her beauty was not of that effulgent character, nor was her mirthfulness of that gay and dashing sort which attract a man to violent transports. The lady was, in fact, in spite of her youth and health, very equable in her feelings, or, rather, very calm in all her manifestations of feeling. She was rather philosophical, as those girls who are grave and take a sober view of life are accused of being, though their dear little noddles may never have been bothered by anything more knotty than the intricacies of a new crotchet stitch or the proper proportions for a pudding. Alice's philosophy was deeper and more learned than that, but she had nothing of the blue-stocking character about her. She had had much sorrow at the death of her mother, and was simply a sincere, affectionate, and domestic woman, whose whole life was ready to devote itself to the good of some other she could love better than herself. She was just one of those rare creatures who are fitted by nature to become either the happiest or most miserable of wives, or the most blessing and blessed of old maids.

She had never before in her life met with a young man so attractive as was Charles Bowman—for he was one of those whose evil qualities can be discovered, unless by chance, only after long acquaintance. He was, too, a neighbor and an old friend of the family, who, indeed, had been partly raised in the family, and his visits were made upon that friendly footing. I suppose the spirit of love came upon her (so far as it did come) by degrees, as it does sometimes upon men—that is to say, when it is produced by propinquity; for all these rules fail when it is of the more sudden and violent sort. At first he was an amusing visitor, then his visits began to be expected, and she was even more particular than usual in her toilet, and then they were wished for; and she imagined to herself what she would say if the conversation should be thus and so, and what she would lead it to in case it should lag, and so forth, and so on; the same old story which has been understood from the beginning until now, and will be always old and always new.

It was with him also the same old story, but not with exactly the same particulars. He went to see her at first because she was pretty, and went again and again because she was interesting, and then he went because he was determined to make her his wife. There were rambles in the garden and in the woods, with Flora always along for company, and there were rides on horseback, and, after awhile, he would come to accompany her and her aunt to church. At home he praised her singing, and never seemed to tire of hearing her sing those ditties which expressed the ardor of love. Upon those he would dwell meaningly, and he would beg her to teach him both tune and words. He grew furiously in love; was never contented away from her. In a thousand ways he showed his passion, and yet when he would sometimes be on the very verge of declaring it in words, his mouth would become dry, and his knees would tremble, and the words would fail.

This was a strange embarrassment for Charles Bowman, and I doubt if he himself quite understood it. For my own part, it is the only evidence I have ever had that he really loved the fair girl. Had he cared nothing for her but to gain her as an elligible wife, he would have been much more composed. He undoubtedly did love her as sincerely as such a man could love; and though he thought she would accept him, he dawdled and delayed with his fate until even Dr. McCleod at last began to weary of his slowness.

As for Alice, she was contented and happy. She discovered new perfections in him every day, and would have loved with all her heart if her natural caution had not intervened. As it was, she thought his loving her, if he really did love her, very pleasant, and that his love, if it were love, was very sunny and genial and pure. She never tired of his presence, and thought often of him in his absence. It did not occur to her that he was delaying his suit too long, for how could she be happier than she already was? And yet she did not abandon herself to the full flood of affection. She loved, and was happy with reserve.

I almost seem ridiculous to myself to be thus, an old man, occupied in describing the progress of a young love. But it is a pleasant subject to me yet, and is environed still by mysteries my philosophy has been unable to solve. Why is it that there is so often such a great inequality in the moral worth of those who love each other? The world does not deceive itself about either, and yet one of the parties is invariably deceived. Every one else who knew Charles Bowman knew his exact worth; some had discovered it, and had communicated their discovery to the others. This is what is called reputation. Alice did not know his reputation with the world, and Mrs. McCleod and Aunt Polly knew it but slightly, for they rarely went from home, and neither at home nor abroad would willingly listen to the discussion of the characters of others. But even if they had known it ever so well, the most patent defects were only such as would be covered, and might be conquered by mighty love. That is, really, the great panacea for all ills, and the curer of all defects, but woman alone pins her faith to it. She follows her own nature in that. She *feels* that "love worketh no ill to his neighbor," and it is all and in all to her.

With what anxious interest Aunt Polly and Mrs. McCleod watched and waited the progress of this love-affair may easily be imagined. Both would often be provoked when visit after visit occurred and they should have to say to each other: "Well, there's nothing settled yet."

"I'll declare," said Mrs. McCleod one day to Aunt

Polly, after the young party had come in from a long walk, and Charles Bowman had left for home without any special manifestations on either part,—"I'll declare I never saw such a man in my life! There can be no doubt in the world but that he's in love, but——"

"Do you really think so?" interrupted Aunt Polly, looking up from her sewing. "I'm sometimes doubtful, myself."

"Certainly I think so, Polly," answered Mrs. McCleod, dogmatically. And then she added, smiling pleasantly: "You are hardly so good a judge, perhaps, as I am. I know that he is; but what makes him delay so is more than I can conjecture. His father and mother can't object. I know that Mrs. Bowman is very anxious to see him married and settled, and only last week she was praising Alice. One thing is certain: if he does not very soon make his declaration the doctor shall call him to account. Neither he nor I, any more than you, Polly, intend to have Alice's affections trifled with."

"Of course not," said Aunt Polly. "But do you think that Alice's affection is really placed on him? I thought I was smart enough to find out all such things, but I'm at a loss this time. She hardly ever talks about him, and yet she seems to like his company very well."

"Think she loves him?" exclaimed Mrs. McCleod. "Why, of course, she does, or will do so if he ask her. Oh, Polly, Polly, you'll never be young again; that's certain!"

"Where do you think they'll live after they are married?" asked Aunt Polly. "I would hate to part with Alice, and yet I would dislike to leave here."

"Leave here!" almost screamed Mrs. McCleod. "Why, Polly, what do you mean? Of course you can't leave here! Plague the man, what did he come here for anyhow! Don't talk that way, Polly, and for goodness sake don't let Flora hear you speak of such a thing! The poor child would cry her eyes out." And the affectionate woman wiped from her own eyes the mist which already dimmed them at the terrible thought of Polly's ever leaving her.

"Yes, but you know, Kitty, that it would never do for Alice to go alone among strangers. She would be so lonesome away from me."

"Why, won't she be with her husband? What are you talking about? She'll be with her husband on his place only two miles off, and you can go over there every day if you choose. The only thing I'm concerned about is what they'll do for a cook. I hardly think his cook is of any account, and it will give Alice a world of trouble to train her. I'll try and get the doctor to let Sally Ann go over for awhile. She can teach the cook, and be of great use to Alice in the preparations for all the company they'll have along at first."

And so the dear ladies went on discussing Alice's affairs and laying plans for her, as all such good women will do on such occasions. Their imaginations, busy with the brilliant future, and their memories with the active past, they soon lose sight of the dull present which plods along bringing with it a future which all their plans and fancies cannot alter.

CHAPTER XXI.

DR. SAM CONCLUDES TO GO A COURTING; AND THE TACTICS HE INTENDS TO EMPLOY.

DR. SAM was no laggard in love, but after his first visit to The Barn, he seemed to think that he must be doubly diligent in his attention to his patients. This is generally the case with energetic men after they have taken a holiday, but he had the additional inducement of love to spur him on to labor. It would be an error to say that he was not an imaginative man—for every man of strong intellect, and especially every doctor capable of eminence in his profession, must have an active and high order of imagination. Our language is deficient in many respects, but in none more than in the words to express the ideas we have of the soul and its attributes. We say soul, spirit, mind, intellect; and we say imagination, fancy; and then we have to explain the idea we attach to each in the particular case. However, he was not imaginative in the sense of being fanciful (I feel that even that qualification needs explanation; but it will have to pass). He took up no "notions," as they are called. His mind was well balanced, and reason held sway over all its faculties. Though he soon loved intensely (and nothing grows in strength so fast as love), he neither saw the face of his loved one on the page he was reading, nor heard the tones of her voice in the music of the winds, the gurgling of the waters, or the singing of the birds. Her radiant form did not appear to bless him when he had done some good deed, nor did a sense of her purity and pleasantness of mind and body render the hovel, or the rags, or the foul diseases of his patients, more loathsome to him than they ever were. He was no laggard, nor had he any nonsense about him, and yet he took his time about going to visit again the lady of his choice.

Why he did so I can only conjecture. Though he resembled his father in the impetuosity of his feelings, I suppose that in such a case as this he felt restrained by delicacy, as well as prudence, from pushing matters too fast. But I imagine that his knowledge of Ben Eccles' love for Miss Susan was one main cause of his hesitation. True, there was no sense in any such reason, and if any one had told him that she was so volatile, or so weak as to be governed by mere attentions and solicitations in such a matter as the bestowal of her heart, he would have been indignant. But a man of honor instinctively avoids interference with his friend in such a matter, and acts as though he really thought he could influence the lady's will.

Now the truth is that so long as he acts fairly there is no interference in the case. The lady may love neither, and reject both; but if she accept either, it is because the other does not suit her so well.

But neither patients, nor friendship, nor prudence could prevent his going again to The Barn before a month was over. Indeed, had he wished to remain away, the advice and urging of his sisters would have sent him there. His love tormented them. If he should be silent, they felt sure he was brooding over his chances. If he were talkative, they were equally certain that Susan was the moving cause; as, indeed, she generally was, for almost all the talk in the little family was about her. Both of the girls knew her quite well; that is to say, had met her several times at Col. Christmas' and elsewhere, in and near Rosstown; and were pleased with her manners, appearance, and conversation, though they had not been so ecstatically affected as they now were.

Lily was especially eloquent in her discussions of the perfections of her sister who-was-to-be. She seemed to think that Susan must necessarily also be in love with her brother, and being in love herself, she had an acute sympathy with her. Did not Susan glorify her brother as she herself glorified Willis Thurston? Did she not invent perfections for him and think him a very wonder of a man? What a precious season they should have singing pæans to their respective Apollos if they could be together! Dr. Sam thought to himself: what a blessing it would be to have Lily with Susan if love be surely budding in Susan's heart! but what a terrible thing if she be entirely indifferent!

Sarah took a more matter-of-fact, but hardly less ridiculous view of the case. Although she had had no experience, she thought her accurate observation qualified her to give good advice in a love affair; and she exhorted and warned accordingly in the most exact and weighty manner. One day, just before Dr. Sam made his second courting visit, Lily was telling him what girls did not like. "A girl," said she, "does not like too much backwardness nor too much boldness."

"Pshaw!" interrupted Sarah, "nor does she like too much candy. I'll tell you, brother, what you must do. It is the great fault of you young men when you wish to please a girl that you treat her like a child or a doll-baby. A sensible woman, like Susan, does not like that. She wishes to be treated like a reasonable being. You must talk sense to her and she will feel complimented by it, and will like you all the more for it."

"How would it do sister," asked Dr. Sam, "if I should get up a discussion with her about pleurisy, or descant upon the exacerbations in typhoid fever?"

"I am not talking nonsense, sir," said Sarah, "and I can tell you that if you go to prescribing calomel for Susan should you find her in low spirits, or in any way give her occasion to think you are making fun of her, you may as well, from that minute, give up your hopes."

"But, Sarah, I really wish to know what I should talk about. The changes of the weather at this season are not sufficiently numerous to afford constant talk, and the crops are soon exhausted. It will not do, I suppose, to talk politics, and you say I must sink the shop; now what shall I talk about? I know nothing of the fashions, and have never been to an opera in my life."

"It makes very little difference what you talk about," replied Sarah, "so you talk sense. I know very well that if a man were to come either talking shop or giggling about me he would disgust me."

"Yes, sister," spoke up Lily, "and I believe that if any man in the world should seem disposed to court you, he would disgust you."

"Good for you, little sister," exclaimed Dr. Sam. "This wise sister of ours wishes to lay down rules for courtship to us, but we know that it has no rules; don't we? You know that the man a woman loves never talks nonsense, and the man she does not love can hardly talk sense if he come as a lover. I'll tell you what it is, Sarah, I am going to court Susan Garthwaite like a sensible man, provided I see I may succeed. If she like me, well; and if she don't like me, well. I haven't the slightest fear of seeming to her to be a fool in either case, for I will always be manly; just as I never can be anything but a gentleman."

And in a day or two afterwards Dr. Sam started off to court Susan in this manly way. His excuses to his patients were made, and were no doubt excellent, but they were too vague for the Rosstownians. They thought they knew the exact business relations of every one of their townsmen—but this urgent affair of Dr. Sam Stockdale's intrigued them prodigiously. Mrs. Fly told Mrs. Thompson—one of the town family of Thompson—that she understood that "old Dr. Stockdale had a large property interest in Yatton, and that the young doctor had to go and see about it;" and Mrs. Thompson, honest woman that she was, replied that she "shouldn't wonder," and assisted in spreading the report as decided truth. Others had it that a medical college was about to be started in Yatton, in opposition to the Rosstown Female College, and the doctor had gone there to examine whether it would pay to accept a professorship. Others, again, said that he had gone to perform a capital surgical operation of a before-unheard-of character. And old Jim Ranser said to a group at a corner discussing the probable causes of the visit: "Dr. Sam has gone to attend to his own business, and you all had better by a d——d sight do the same."

But this time the object of his visit was well known at home, and extraordinarily loving were the words and embraces he received at leaving the loved ones there. Lily was joyous and hopeful, but Sarah and her mother were as grave and impressive as though he were about to start to the gallows.

"God bless you, my son," said Mrs. Stockdale as she kissed him; "you have been a good son, and I know you will be a good husband. I hope your Susan will be kind and loving to you."

"Good-by, brother," said Sarah, kissing him in her turn; "I hope you will succeed; but you mustn't take it to heart if you do not. Girls don't always know what is best for them, but if you manage it right you can't fail if Susan have the sense I think she has."

"Take care of yourself, brother," then said Lily, with her arms around his neck. "I'll be miserable until I know for certain that you are perfectly happy. Can't you write us a note by some one coming from Yatton if you should find Susan too attractive to be left soon!"

Even old Tom Ramsay, who, as servants in such cases always have, had an inkling of his young master's errand, seemed to manifest sympathy with him by an extra pressure of the hand at bidding good-by; and when he remarked: "Mas' Sam, that little gray shows you off mightily," the doctor knew that the old butler was looking forward to having a new young mistress.

Now, they were all very much mistaken in supposing that the doctor's happiness or misery was so near at hand. The rank and file do not always know when a battle is to be fought, and are often deceived by its postponement. It was not the general's intention on this occasion to bring on a decisive action. He was going to view the ground; see where he could post his heavy guns, deploy his infantry, use his cavalry, and find cover for his sharp-shooters.

This use of military phrase reminds me of a letter I once received from a friend, who had served in the army, describing his courtship. I preserved it, and will copy it here:

"You remember my telling you that I was regularly campaigning my courtship. Well, sir, I did conduct the war with consummate skill, quietly and surely making my advances—the little lady herself being the centre of attack, her father the right, and her mother the left wing.

"Monday, Sept. 10th. Every preparation having been made I determined to strike the blow. You may well suppose the time called for all the cool judgment and manhood I could muster for the fray.

"All of my plans having so far carried beautifully, I made a bold and terrific assault upon the city itself, and after about two hours of such fighting as has never been recorded, I drove the besieged back within her strongest works, and captured the key to the whole position, I might hope. Here I massed my artillery, and ceased for the night.

"Sept. 11th. Early this morning I surprised the right wing in his office, and after a tremendous and determined onslaught, which met with a heavier resistance than was anticipated, I finally carried his position in so far as to render him neutral. In like manner I carried the left.

"I now commenced the concentration of my whole force under cover of the works captured the preceding evening. Several batteries of siege guns and mortars were added to those already in position, besides the pieces used in the engagement with the flanks.

"Everything having been most carefully ordered and arranged, the engagement opened about 8 o'clock P.M. with light picket firing, indicating the advance of my skirmishers. Pushing them forward, I found her occupying the inner fort and works protecting the palace, evidently expecting an assault. An hour having been consumed in ascertaining her exact position and ranging for the fray, I ordered a general advance, under cover of the artillery, along the whole line. In an instant after the opening of my guns the grand fort and palace were entirely obscured by a sheet of flame that told the metal of my adversary. My force was equal to the work in hand, and two hours later had captured the fort and all the works, and had demanded the surrender of the palace. She consented, conditionally; that I should give her time to think. I replied, 'Certainly; how long do you desire?' She answered, 'Only six months.' I settled that question mighty quick by throwing a few shells into the palace itself, which brought a final answer, and a royal gun with it."

Now, I call that very clever; and an additional beauty of it is, and therein it differs from the majority of the reports of battles, it was all exactly true as it was meant. And, what is also singular, though he did not marry the young lady shortly afterwards, he was just as happy as happy could be shortly afterwards that he did not do so. *Sic transit!*

CHAPTER XXII.

TELLS HOW DR. SAM WENT A COURTING, AND HOW HE WAS RECEIVED WHEN HE RETURNED HOME.

I NEVER much liked that thirty miles of road between Rosstown and Yatton, though to a stranger to the country it may possess some points of interest. The long lanes of dark-gray worm-fence, without a tree to obstruct the wind or sun, are the coldest of rides in winter and the hottest in summer. In this pleasant autumn weather, however, Dr. Sam had no inconvenience. Even the dust seemed loth to stir in the lazy air as his sturdy gray jogged along at a brisk walk. The sumach bushes with their feathery tufts changed from red to brown, and beginning to incline their points downward, stood upright in the corners of the fences, and the poke-berries hung in clusters on their crimson stalks grown too feeble to hold them upright; and the blackberry briars growing rusty, both leaf and stem, began to look bare as they protruded through the rails, or ambitiously had climbed over their top. When he would emerge from some long lane into a strip of wood, the solemn stillness which seems to accompany the hours when the trees are going into their slumber was broken only by the tapping of the woodpecker, or the melancholy bark of some solitary squirrel in the depth of the forest, and the pattering down of the prematurely yellow and crimson leaves, as they loosed their hold and came fluttering to the earth. Sometimes the road passed through a grove of pines which had sprung up a thicket in some old field, and in a few years had grown to be a forest. The ground was covered with a russet coat of "shatter," as the dead pine leaves are called here, and the air was perfumed with resinous fragrance, but hardly a fly was abroad to give the spot animation. On the doctor trudged, wrapped in pleasant reverie, scarcely interrupted by the grating of his horse's armed hoofs upon the pebbles of the main branch of Big Sandy, near the town, and of the other little creeks which every five or six miles went gurgling merrily over beds of shining sand and pebbles, across the road on their way to the larger creeks. Mechanically he would loose the reins to give liberty to his horse when it would stop and paw the water, and toss its head impatiently to drink. About noon, from the top of a lofty ridge upon which the road meanders for four or five miles, he descried, through the warm, hazy air, the high bluffs which lay like a dark-blue cloud along the farther bank of the river, nine miles (by the road) beyond Yatton, and he knew he was nearing his destination.

Now, I have no means of knowing what were Dr.

Sam's harmonious thoughts, until his near approach to The Barn roused him to sit more upright in his saddle, and check up his horse, to take a look at the distant hills, and remember the exact spot in which he found himself. I suppose that Susan was their subject, and Love the burden of their melody. It is the sweetest of all melodies; that which has been most gladdening since the time the stars sang it together, and shall be the most universal and the most cheering until the trump of the archangel shall announce it perfect, uninterrupted, and eternal. But on earth, alas! the melodious harmony is often interrupted by discords from without and around, which make it sound jangled and out of time.

Dr. Sam, no doubt, was often put out in his harmony by the intrusion of the discordant sounds of the syllables "Ben Eccles." What if Susan loved Ben Eccles! And if she did not love him (the doctor), should he not rather she would love his friend Ben than any other man? No, sir! the doctor must have answered to himself. No, sir! That is superhuman nonsense. If she cannot love me, let her love a stranger; one, of whose qualities I know and care nothing.

This thing of preferring a friend in such a case is all bosh. No man does so. It is humiliating to his self-respect to have one, all of whose weaknesses he knows so well, to be preferred to himself. Either Cæsar or some unknown! is the sentiment of every true lover; to whom friendship in such a case is in the attitude of an alternative, and is an impertinence.

Nor was Ben Eccles the only discord in the sweet strain. Susan might have other beaux; or even if she had not, and did not love Ben, she might feel disinclined to her new lover. Was he her lover, though? Was he not merely going on a tour of observation? And would he not be governed by circumstances in his subsequent proceedings? He thought so, no doubt. I have seen a great many philosophic lovers, but have yet to see one who has successfully practiced his philosophy. To be in love is to persevere in love until a catastrophe takes place; just as with some men to begin to drink is to persevere in drinking until nature can bear the strain no longer. In spite of his manly self-confidence and strong mind, Dr. Sam was just as certain either to be accepted, or by word or conduct positively rejected by Susan Garthwaite, as he was certain to die when his time came. And it would have been just as nonsensical to talk to a man in his condition as to the victim of drink about exerting his will and stopping himself in his career. In both cases it is the will which carries the man on. Change the will of either and he becomes sober.

It was probably the thought of its being near dinner-time which made the doctor check up his horse as he arrived at the front gate of The Barn, and, after a moment's halt, ride on more briskly into town. He did not like to intrude uninvited and unexpected upon the family meal, although he knew he should be kindly welcomed to a bountiful board. Lovers are always more particular than other persons about such small matters. Or, perhaps, he was moved to take the course he did by a judicious care for his toilet, which must have been disarranged by his long ride. That's another point upon which the true and sensible lover is very particular. But whatever the cause, he rode on into town, had his horse put up and fed at the livery stable, took dinner at the tavern, and not until about five o'clock in the afternoon, tidy and spruce, went to make his important visit.

Miss Maria Jones was with her dearest friend in the sitting-room, and her round eyes became a little rounder and more open when Dr. Sam was announced and walked in. He scarcely saw her, and she noticed it. It would be hard to tell what such a woman as she does not notice. She saw him looming large, not as her beau (in that case he would have appeared as perfect and gigantic as an archangel), but as Susan's beau. Beau was the term she always used for lover. A lover was to her the perfection of all things beautiful, and was therefore a beau. She saw, she observed, she solved, and she resolved that Dr. Samuel Stockdale would not suit her, and therefore ought not to suit her dear friend. Such an earnest, single-minded, affectionate, and just man as was the doctor is always tremendous to the Maria Joneses of this world. They are impassable barriers to their plans. A Dr. Sam in the house is, surely, a Miss Maria out of the house, just as when the staunch house-dog takes up his abode in a room, the house-cat takes to the stairs or an open window. Neither Ben Eccles, with his honesty and all-absorbing love, nor Dr. Sam, with his vigorous hatred of humbug and his strong love, was calculated to leave Miss Jones the fond friend and arbitress of her dearest pet; so Miss Jones was determined that neither of them should succeed. The fact is that she was a silly goose not to understand better her own sex, and Susan in particular. She was not the only silly goose I have ever seen who thought her word was law with the king. Theretofore the king had been placable, and she had got to the pitch that she herself must be pleased and must be courted to gain every suit. She had yet to see the king (I mean our dear Susan; it is only a figure of speech),—she had yet, I say, to see Susan implacable; to see her set her head in an opposite course to the one she (Miss Maria) would have her go. Alas, the day when that should be the case!

But at this visit nothing passed remarkable for skill or stupidity. According to the ingenious doctor, he had only come to pay a visit to some friends in the neighborhood, and had thought he would call and see how the ladies were and pay his respects. Pshaw! thought Miss Maria, that man was never cut out for a lawyer. I know very well who the friends are! And when he got to praising his absent friend, Ben Eccles, she thought: Oh, what an artful fellow we have here! He wishes to spy a little; I'll lead him on the wrong track, and she forthwith began Ben's praises in such a way as to make it appear that she feared to embarrass Susan by too much talk on that subject, and presently suggested that Susan had not latterly been in the best spirits, and seemed to be anxious about something.

How low the pulses of Dr. Sam's heart became at this innuendo she seemed instinctively to know, but it was not her cue to give Susan occasion for anger against her on account of open deceit or a false accusation, so she relieved the matter by an "if" and a "but" in talking further about Ben's good qualities thus vindicating her loyalty to Susan, though leaving the doctor in doubt.

Forty years ago, when my memory and feelings were in their vigor, I could have described Miss Maria Jones with every detail of every trait, but now I shall have to leave much of her portrait to the knowledge and imagination of the reader who has seen the world. In spite of her, the visit was pleasant and exceedingly satisfactory to the reconnoitering doctor. Susan was even more beautiful than he had thought her, and her manners were perfection. What a magnificent wife she should make! Beautiful, intelligent, refined, loving, dignified, a good housekeeper, accomplished in every detail of domestic life. "Whew!" Dr. Sam whistled to himself, as he got on his horse to ride away. "Won't I be the most fortunate of men? Ah, I will make my Susan the happiest of wives!"

Mother and daughter were greatly pleased with the visitor. The mother looked forward with no little pleasure to having a doctor in the house. It would certainly be a handy arrangement, even better in some respects than that coveted by a great many excellent ladies of having a preacher in the family. As for Susan, she felt already that Dr. Stockdale was of the material of which heroes are made. She had heard a great deal about him at the Female College, and had often seen and remarked his handsome and commanding presence in church and passing along the street. He was the beau-ideal fondly cherished in the hearts of two or three of her larger companions; and of several (there was no telling how many) of the smaller girls. And now that he had come a courting to her she felt somewhat fluttered, and was disposed to look a little coldly upon her officious friend, Miss Maria.

It was certain that Dr. Sam was very greatly to be preferred to Ben Eccles. In the first place, Mr. Ben Eccles' law, however much he might know of it, was not likely to be of assistance to her mother, and Dr. Sam's medicine was just what the whole family, white and black, were bound to need at some time. In the next place, she liked dark eyes better than gray eyes, and then she liked a sturdy, independent spirit better than one more gentle and sentimental.

I do not affirm that just exactly these thoughts passed through the young lady's mind. The chances are that they never went further than sentiments, as her mind made up the balance of preference for the one man to the other, and did not assume the definite form of thought at all. We all decide in many cases, particularly those of liking and disliking others, upon just such vague reasoning—the reasoning of the heart rather than of the head.

I, myself, like Susan, always preferred Sam Stockdale to Ben Eccles, and yet am even now puzzled to reason out the cause of my preference. Strictly speaking, he was not the handsomer, and if I regard the mere intellect of the two men, Ben had the more. The doctor could be no more loving than Ben, and I doubt very much if he ever could be so devoted to the object of his love. Ben was as highly honorable in all his thoughts and sentiments as was his friend, and they were both just as brave as brave could be.

It is a curious thing that some men bear with them

an aspect or an influence which compels love or fear more promptly, and to a far greater degree, than others who have in a superior degree the qualities which actually give cause for love or fear. I cannot explain it, but I, and all men, can feel it, and all do act according to it. If Dr. Sam and Ben Eccles were now young men they would be in the Confederate army; but although the doctor was just as modest, and no more brave or intelligent than Ben, he would no doubt be a general, and Ben be only a private, or, at most, a captain.

To make a résumé: Susan liked Ben Eccles very much, and so did her mother, but both of them liked the doctor better. Ben was very intelligent, loving, loyal, good, and the doctor was not more so, but the doctor had a spice of the devil, or of an archangel, which we call willfulness, in him, which gave his intelligence, affection, and goodness a twang Ben's did not possess. At any rate, it is convenient to assign this definite cause for the fact. A vine naturally seeks to cling to a high and strong object; though, alas! but a miserable shrub, or a tree already decayed, is often the strongest and loftiest object it can find. So when woman casts around to place her affections, she seeks a strong and noble support, and she never deceives herself, if she can help it. Some men are as strong as others with whom they are compared, but do not look so; some are as good, as honest, and as bright, but do not look so. The woman is apt to choose the one she thinks looks to be the most reliable support, and which will lift her crown highest. Therefore Susan preferred Dr. Sam to Ben, and therefore her mother, in her heart, approved the preference.

(I congratulate myself upon having argued that out completely.)

Susan was not, however, the woman to suddenly make up her mind about anything on which she had the opportunity of reflecting at leisure. She knew the doctor's design, but had by no means already assented to it. There are so many things which make such a hasty conclusion dangerous. It might be that he had some defect of character she had not yet discovered. It might be that he would change his mind, and never go so far as to ask her to be his wife. The prospect of becoming the wife of such a man was not disagreeable, but to conclude that she actually should become so, and upon that to proceed to fall violently or even rationally in love with him, would be imprudent. She would wait, and if it should turn out that he should ask her, and she found that she could love him better than any one else, why then she might say yes, and go on to love him with all her heart.

Miss Susan was a very prudent young lady. To any one, however, who knows the human heart, it is evident that, so far, Dr. Sam's chances with her would be extremely small if some more attractive man should come along. She was just not displeased; and it was the time for the doctor to strike in boldly. After one other visit, made two days afterwards, he determined that he would strike in boldly, and that very soon.

He returned home deeply in love. His mother and sisters met him with sympathetic embraces and a thousand questions. Had he asked her? How had she received him? How often did he see her? Who was Miss Maria Jones? Where did he stay? etc., etc., etc. They were impatient. They were put out when they learned that he had not proposed to Susan; were annoyed when he spoke indifferently of his reception, and hoped he was just dissembling. Altogether, they were not so well satisfied with the campaign of their conquering hero as he himself was, and they laid aside the laurels with which they were secretly prepared to crown him. In fact, Sarah, like a good, patriotic newspaper editor, was disposed to cavil at his generalship, and suggested that he should have done this, and should not have done that, and appeared to consider him a humbug as a lover. She would have acted differently, I promise you. She would have had the young lady at her feet, would have flouted all the Misses Maria Jones in the world, would have *veni*-d, *vidi*-d, *vici*-d with a vengeance!

When she was at the height of her eloquent didactics, Lily said: "Oh, pshaw, sister! Set a woman to court a woman and what a pretty muss she'd make of it! I'm sure brother did the best he could. We are the ones who have gone too fast."

"Speak for yourself, Lily," answered Sarah. "I didn't go too fast; but I'd not have come home without having at least made a bold demonstration and discovered something of how the young lady felt towards me."

"Sister," replied Lily, "if Willis Thurston had proposed to me the fourth time he ever visited the house, would you not have been indignant, and have called him overbold?"

"That's different, Lily," said Sarah. "Brother has known Susan Garthwaite ever since she was a child."

"Yes," answered Lily, "when he was a boy he once went to a party at her mother's. It seems to me that would be a poor ground even to claim acquaintance upon, let alone to presume to claim love."

"Bah! Lily," said Sarah, "you've started on that topic, love, and I give it up. I've had no experience in it."

"That's just what Lily has been trying to convince you of, sister," said Dr. Sam. "When the gentleman comes courting you, if he does not propose at once you will despise him as a fool, and if he do, you will say he is lacking in respect for you, and will grow indignant and wish to knock him down. He will have a sweet time of it."

"Oh, brother, you are so ridiculous!" said Sarah, half impatiently, half pleased, turning away from the conclave. "Manage affairs your own way; but if you don't look sharp some one will cut you out yet, even if Ben Eccles do not succeed."

CHAPTER XXIII.

GIVES AN ACCOUNT OF BEN'S RETURN FROM NORTH CAROLINA, AND DESCRIBES THE GREAT YATTON BARBECUE, AND WHAT HAPPENED THERE.

BEN ECCLES met with a ready sale for his place, which, indeed, had been advertised as for sale several weeks before his arrival in North Carolina. The price was not very large, but it was cash, and was more than enough to enable him to make the two first payments on his new place. He had started with his force, who had their goods and chattels in three covered wagons; one drawn by four mules; one by seven yoke of oxen; and one a two-horse wagon; but, growing impatient, he had left them three or four days' march from Yatton in charge of the overseer, and had hurried on home.

Three days after his arrival they passed through town, a queer procession. Riding in front of all came the overseer, clad in homespun, with a long rifle across his lap and a pair of plethoric saddle-bags under him. His horse was sleek and fat, though a little travel-worn. No one has ever yet seen an overseer whose own horse was poor, unless there were an actual famine in the land. Just behind him, in the middle of the road, and clothed in white homespun, was the head driver, a confidential negro man, who marched firmly along with his old master's (Ben's grandfather's) rifle on his shoulder; and on either side of him, just in the rear, were five or six of the stoutest young men and women, whose eyes rolled and whose heads were turning to see the strange sights in the town. A brindled cur and a long-eared yellow dog, both lank, and with heads down and tails tucked between their legs, kept close to them, and were often trampled on or kicked away. A tussle or two with the vagabond, dissipated town dogs which had rushed at them when they were entering the outskirts of their city, had impressed them with a sense of its being an inhospitable region. Another, a large brindled bitch, preserved her dignity more intact by marching closely by the tar-bucket under the two-horse wagon, which, loaded with the overseer's goods and chattels, and the materials for camping out, followed closely behind the straggling young negroes. The four-mule covered wagon came next. The driver cracked his whip, and cried: "Gee up thar!" with extra fervor. A negro woman nursing her baby sat in the bow looking out, and the heads of four or five negro children could be seen peeping out from behind her and from under the cover at the sides and rear. The feed-trough behind was ornamented with six split-bottomed chairs tangled up with each other. Behind this wagon came the more sturdy and steady of the negro men with axes on their shoulders, and negro women, one or two of them leading children by the hand and placidly smoking their short-stemmed pipes, and a half dozen or so of negro boys and girls, of from eight to fifteen, who were all eyes, and occasionally all mouth, when any unaccustomed sight caused them to exclaim, "Jes look dar!" One negro woman, leading a brood mare, upon which she had mounted her little shirted urchin, followed them, and was followed by the colt, which sometimes walked, sometimes trotted, with head and tail up, in the middle or on either side of the road. The ox wagon brought up the rear. It was loaded and ornamented like the other, except that two or three plain poplar bedstead frames were tied to its sides, and a spinning-wheel accompanied the chairs, tied on behind. Some of the yokes of oxen pulled from each other, and others pressed towards each other, and the leaders rushed to turn every corner instead of decently keeping straight ahead as the driver wished them to do before strangers; and their perverse conduct was the only interruption to the perfect content of every one of the movers. The driver tried to keep his temper and tongue, but the crack of his whip was savage as the near or off leader would find himself impelled by pain to spring forward and thus come straight in the road. A mule or an ox generally tries to do his worst when it has a sensitive driver or rider who wishes it to do its best.

Ben met the procession on the street, and piloted it out to his new place, where he assigned the quarters to each family and single individual. A busy scene of unpacking and arranging then took place, in the midst of which he left his overseer and came into town. He evidently felt unsettled in mind and body. Another man would have busied himself with his new affairs, and never ceased working and directing until he had them all arranged just to suit himself; but Ben was not in a condition to do that. In spite of the healthful distraction and journey he had taken he was very thin and looked badly. He was very nervous, too; could scarcely keep still for a minute, and I noticed his lips often move and his eyes often close as he lifted his hat in silent prayer. He had not yet mustered courage to go to The Barn. Having put it off the first day after his arrival, he seemed to have made up his mind not to go until he had settled his place; and then, lacking strength of will, he appeared to wish to take the occasion of first seeing Susan or her mother when they should chance to come to town; and, finally, he determined to wait to see them at the barbecue.

There had been great talk of the barbecue for three or four weeks before Ben's arrival. It was to be a grand affair; something of a picnic, something of a barbecue, and something of a fishing frolic. It was to be held in a pleasant grove on Brown's Creek, not far from Ben's place, and all the country was invited to attend. The invitation had extended as far as Rosstown and to every other village and neighborhood around; and there was no fear but that there should be a large attendance. The question was not: who would go? but: who could go and who must stay away? And no wonder; for with such managers as the Yatton frolics generally had, and such as it was to have, more particularly, on this occasion, it was counted a calamity not to be able to attend.

There was Col. Carey, and an elegant gentleman he was. Although he was a monstrous long way from being pious, his heart was the teacher of his manners, and his manners were nearly perfect. He was too rich not to be hospitable at his own house, and too hospitable ever to become any richer than he was when he came into his property on becoming of age. He was the chief director and master of ceremonies; and while he directed all, and made each subscriber contribute a fair quota, his own sheepfold, cattle-pen, and fowl-yard were the heaviest sufferers, and his own cellar was the most generous contributor to drinkables.

Then there was Gen. Watkins, the heavy gentleman of the committee, as generous, but not quite so rich as, and much more fussy than Col. Carey. He presided over the cooking, and I would defy a joint to be cooked one instant too long, or to be one moment left unbasted, while he was about. He was despotic over the perspiring cooks, inflexible to the butchers, severe upon the waiters, a very Procrustes to the diggers of the pits, and a Cortez to the fire-makers. When he had the direction of the cooking at a barbecue he always reminded me of the chiefest of the Lords who had the fire made for Shadrach, Meshach, and Abednego, or the head executioner of St. Lawrence.

After these two notables came eight or ten other gentlemen of little less merit, who were to act as ushers, and assistant superintendents. They had charge, under Col. Carey's plan, of the preparation of the ground for the dance, and of the seats and the tables, and collecting the knives and forks, spoons, plates, and cups, and getting up the music, and all the various details of a large public dance and feast.

I really cannot stop now to enter into a history of picnics, which should be honored as a relic of antiquity; a little remnant of the classic ages to which we have clung; although the name we use is by no means classical or euphonious.

Before man had invented the artificialities of evening entertainments, and enervating midnight revelings, in the bright light of the morning of the world, we see shepherds and nymphs mingling in the graceful dance upon the grassy sward, following with measured step the dulcet notes of some Pan-taught swain. The light has never faded from their forms. Fancy repels the thought of their being subjected to the cares and sorrows of everyday life, and clothes them with an immortality of youthfulness and grace.

And the banquets of the Gods! what were they but grand Olympian picnics, in which, far above the clouds, those celestial *gastronomes* were never disturbed by an envious shower, a damper to their enjoyment?

Early in the morning of the great day Ben Eccles rode through the fields over to the ground to see what progress had been made in the preparations. The sun was just rising, a great red globe, through the haze. The tie-vines (*convolvulus*), matted in tangled masses over the dead stalks of corn, displayed here and there among the brown bunches of seed pods their pink, blue, and white flowers, dwarfed by the dryness and lateness of the season; the grass and weeds were for the most part dead and withered, and a general dustiness seemed to be upon everything, even to the unseasonable yellow flowers upon the still green extremities of the pumpkin-vines. Pulling down the bars and entering the wood the dead leaves were crisp beneath his horse's feet, and everything bore the marks of the long, dry, autumnal weather we sometimes have for five or six weeks and call the Indian summer. As he approached the ground his nostrils were saluted by the savory smell of cooking meats, and presently, upon rising a gentle swell, he saw below him a busy scene. The smoke from the long barbecue pits hung in the calm air, and the cooks, in white jackets and aprons, were busy under its canopy basting the whole sheep and hogs and quarters of beef which broiled briskly on their wooden bars over the masses of live coals, spluttering and smoking as the rich juices distilled and fell upon them. Here a party was engaged in fixing forked stakes for the cross-pieces upon which the rough planks were to be laid for the long lines of table; there was another party putting the last pine tops upon the arbor, which was about a hundred feet long; and still another smoothing under it the last loads of sawdust for the dancing floor.

The stand for the musicians had already been constructed in the céntre, so that on either side of them two sets of dancers could be engaged at once, with plenty of room for the full display of their grace or activity.

Gen. Watkins was already upon the ground, busy with the cooks; exhorting, scolding, directing, and fussing about as though he were the only person responsible for the full pleasure of the day. Other gentlemen of the committee were also there, each active in superintending his portion of the work; and Ben soon rode away, feeling that he was an idler upon the scene.

By nine o'clock all was in good order for the reception of the guests, and they began to arrive. At first, boys, dressed in their best, were seen standing about, looking on. No one had seen them arrive. They came upon the scene, as one described it, "promiscuous like," as though they had dropped from the sky, or risen from the ground; or, as old Jim Ranser, who hated boys, said: "like nettle-rash bumps upon a clean skin; you see the blasted things, and they hurt, but you don't know how they came there." Then men began to come singly, and in pairs, and then in squads, upon horses and mules of all sorts of sizes, colors, and values; the older men jogging along deep in grave conversation and turning business-like to find the safest hitching-places for their horses, the younger dashing up more prancingly and talking loudly to each other, some hesitating and some careless where they should leave their steeds. Several smart negroes were on hand, however, in hope to make a dollar or so by relieving all anxiety upon the score of having the horses kept safely; and they showed as keen a knowledge of their customers as ever did the most practiced Jew or Yankee; they knew who would pay best, and they waited on them accordingly.

About ten o'clock the carriages began to arrive, and the ladies on horseback, and the business of the day commenced in earnest. The seats around the sawdust floor of the arbor began to fill with the fair guests, and their attendant cavaliers collected in groups about the arena and the entrances to it, or waited upon them with glasses of cool water, procured with all the speed and bustle such a demand produces on such an occasion.

It would be tedious to describe all the various pranks by which human nature displayed the items of its multifarious compound of good and bad qualities that day: how, before the dancing commenced, some of the girls were continually going from the arbor to the dressing-room, built near it of rough planks and leafy boughs, as though some of their gear needed fixing, but in reality to be admired as they took the short walk which separated them from the crowd; how some of them were too shamefaced even to stand up gracefully until seats could be found for them; how some of the young men were bold and showy, full of vanity and animal spirits, and others were awkward and silly from the same vanity without the animal spirits. I went there early and observed it all, but to recount it here would be but to describe what every one who has ever been in such a scene has observed for himself, and what every one who knows human nature, though he may never have been in the country at all, knows is perfectly natural.

It was an important day to Ben Eccles, and he had come about ten o'clock so as to be there when those should arrive whom he wished to see. He was dressed with great care and with all the skill which the art of tailor and shoemaker at Yatton could accomplish. But he looked rather haggard and preoccupied as he stood one among the crowd of gentlemen at the front entrance to the arbor with his eyes continually wandering towards the road which led to Yatton. Presently a carriage drove up with Charley Bowman's aunt and two cousins, and Charley himself came gallantly along upon his sorrel mare in attendance upon them.

I hardly know whether to fulfill my previous promise to describe these relatives, or to put it off to a future chapter. It will be, perhaps, more artistic to defer it and not interrupt the description of the barbecue, which, it was admitted by all, gave the crowning touch to the glory of Yatton for hospitality.

I cannot say that Ben seemed enthusiastically glad to meet his friend Charley, who, after he had seated his party, went up to him with beaming smile and outstretched hand. But Ben was not in the humor for friendship. No anxious lover can be. Even those dearest friends he may bore with the theme of his love become bores when any other theme is started. Ben had no such friend; unless he had admitted Aunt Polly to his secret and talked it over with her on the two or three short visits to Dr. McCleod's after he had returned from college. I am sure that no one else except myself had been admitted to share it, for the passion seemed to isolate him to itself.

Standing not far from him, and curious to see how he should bear himself through the trial I knew approaching him, I presently noticed him turn a shade paler and close his eyes as though in silent prayer, and I knew that he had seen Mrs. Garthwaite's carriage coming. And, sure enough, it presently drove up with Mrs. Garthwaite, and Susan, and Miss Maria Jones inside; and who, of all men, should presently approach the carriage door to assist them to alight, but Dr. Sam Stockdale, who had accompanied them on horseback. He had come to carry out his well-matured plan of energetic movement.

By a prodigious effort Ben overcame his trepidation and was at the carriage door almost as soon as his friend. Mrs. Garthwaite received him very kindly, and so did her daughter—though a little reserve mingled with her kind politeness. Miss Maria, however, acted as though her feelings were somewhat outraged, and she found herself bound to emphatically decline Mr. Eccles' attentions, and so end the matter at once. The trouble was that she could not consistently with her intentions accept the gallantry of the doctor, and it was a great relief to her when Mr. Bowman came forward and offered her his arm. She had met Mr. Bowman frequently before, and considered him a model young man. Ben offered his arm to Mrs. Garthwaite, and Sam escorted Miss Susan, and they went with them first to the dressing-room, and then found them good seats in the circle around the dancers, who were by that time becoming enlivened with their exercise.

The ice which had kept Ben so long bound was at last broken, but I could not perceive that he made very rapid progress in either thawing himself or in entertaining his companions; and, positively, I feel so acutely his embarrassment that it is embarrassing to me to relate what passed. I had a keen sympathy with the morbidly sensitive and almost hopeless young man, and felt the sinking of heart which oppressed him, when in a few moments and after a few commonplaces had been ventured by him to the ladies, Sam Stockdale came up and led Susan smiling to her place in the new cotillon being formed, and he subsided into her seat beside her mother. I felt the agony and longing with which he watched the graceful form of his love gliding in the dance, and her merry smile bestowed upon her partner and her other acquaintance engaged in the set, or her pleasant greetings to those friends who, passing by, paused to salute her and remark upon her good looks and seeming enjoyment. And above all, I felt the mingled rage and agony with which he saw Charley Bowman reintroduced to Susan by Miss Maria, and, after a few words, lead her again to the dance with apparent alacrity and pleasure.

His effort could go no further. He was completely baffled for the day, and retired from the contest dissatisfied, miserable, and at his wits' end. Thereafter he hardly approached the party, though not one of their movements escaped him. Even at the dinner-table, to which Susan was escorted by Charley Bowman, who had had her hand for the preceding dance and had thus "cut out" Dr. Sam, he kept near to them; but except that he was ready to hand Bowman a glass of the sangaree he was going off to find for Susan, and anticipated him in getting a plate of the breast of turkey, and handing it to him for her, he pretended not to notice her.

The day from which he had anticipated so much was ending in disappointment to him: nor do I think that Dr. Sam found it one of unmixed satisfaction. He had never had any particular respect for his old schoolmate, Charley Bowman, and before the day was over his want of respect had become positive contempt. Whatever fear he might have had of the chances of Ben Eccles was completely allayed, and he felt even more friendly towards him than ever. But Mr. Bowman seemed to place himself in the way, and Miss Susan appeared by no means inclined to thrust him out of the way. She found him agreeable; he was gay and made her laugh; he had no fear of her, and she thought him manly; he had no embarrassment, and danced well, and was handsome, and her sweet friend Maria spoke several times in approbation of him; and, take him all in all, there was no one on the ground in whose company she felt more at her ease and more interested in herself than she did in his.

Of course Dr. Sam had a sovereign contempt for this man, and I fear that once or twice he betrayed it, as though he would wish to inspire Susan's breast with a like feeling—not that he would act ungenerously or disingenuously (I feel sure that he never did a mean thing in his life), but, you know, Susan did not know the man so well as he did, and as he took a great interest in her, it became a sort of duty to let her know that he was not held by every one in the highest esteem. I fear, too, that he even discountenanced the growing acquaintance between Susan and that man's two cousins, who were in public much inclined to manifest and increase it.

Dr. Sam had a contempt for the whole family. They had more bad or indifferent qualities than any other family of the like number he had ever met. He had always thought so, though he had never before admitted it to himself. He did not hate them! far from it. He did not fear them! not he; he feared no one. He had a contempt for them—that was the word. Lovers in their elevation have always a contempt for rivals, or possible rivals, for whom they have no great esteem. So it is with politicians and preachers and fashionable women. They cannot always give the reasons for their contempt; for their rivals may be so far from being contemptible as to be very formidable; but the contempt exists. When it comes to be analyzed it is so nigh akin to hatred that the difference seems to lie only in the distinction.

After the dinner was over (a dinner which I need not say immortalized Gen. Watkins, and by his over-exertions came near making him an angel or saint before his time, if such a fat and jolly gentleman who swore so loudly could ever become an angel or saint except to dinner lovers and a loving family), the dance became fast and furious, and Ben's vexed soul could endure it no longer. It was not his righteousness that was vexed, for though he did not dance himself he did not think dancing a sin; but whose soul would not be vexed if he were condemned to see the girl he loved keeping time to the jumping up and down of others keeping time before her, and smiling upon them, while he is forced by fate or his own awkwardness to stand aloof? When the last grand reel was being formed, and Susan was handing her mother her black silk mittens preparatory to going out into the ring with Charley Bowman, who triumphed to the last, he went hurriedly up to them and bade them good-by; a piece of needless ceremony, which ended, however, in his receiving a pleasant, friendly smile from Susan, which completely effaced all the miseries of the day. She had not been watching him as I had, and had attributed his want of attention to the wrong cause. The kind-hearted girl hoped and believed that he had quit loving her as a lover, and flattered herself that she could now really like and cherish him as a friend. And he, poor fellow, was made happy with a kind of new and blind happiness. It seemed to him that her soul too must be vexed with all the frivolity around her, and that wearied at last she had turned to him with kindly and kindred interest.

We are all liable to mistakes, and I hardly know which made the greater; Ben Eccles when he misinterpreted Susan's smile, or Sam Stockdale when he exclaimed to himself, after seeing the ladies to their carriage to leave for home: "Well, thank the Lord, we're done with that d——d fool at last," meaning, of course, done with Charley Bowman, "and I'll have a chance for a pleasant evening." He and the family, in which Miss Maria was included this evening, as usual, had scarcely seated themselves in the parlor after tea when the gentleman towards whom he had used such a harsh expression knocked at the front door and was admitted, "all smiles and gab," as Miss Maria would have remarked about any one else who had so approached; and was made most welcome.

CHAPTER XXIV.

DESCRIBES SIMON BILLS AND HIS FAMILY, MR. BOWMAN'S RELATIVES; AND TELLS WHAT MRS. GARTHWAITE THOUGHT OF MR. BOWMAN, AND HOW DR. SAM FARED.

IT is no very agreeable task to have to describe Charley Bowman's aunt, Mrs. Bills, her deceased husband, Mr. Simon Bills, and their two daughters, Emily and Louisa Bills. The name is not euphonious, but after their mother's voluntary act in marrying Simon, the poor girls could not help it; though they for several years had been persistently trying to do so. They at least could not be blamed; nor, when the truth was known, was any one inclined to blame the elder lady. The fact is that neither Sophronia Jenkins nor her sister, Harmonia, had had a fair chance. The immense wealth of their second cousin, Col. Vance, not only weakened their own energies, but it dwarfed them in the eyes of the community—just as to be the king's poor cousin is to be confoundedly poor indeed. But the contemplation of their cousin's wealth and their own condition had had different effects upon the two. We have seen that Mrs. Bowman was of the world, worldly; her younger sister was of just the contrary disposition, and was of the church, churchy. And indeed, when Simon Bills, a well-to-do planter of middle age, and respectable standing in the community and in a popular church, took her to himself, years before her sister married Col. Bowman, it seemed to her that she had chosen the better part, and that her reward was beginning.

Mr. Bills was a shouting Christian. I use the word "shouting" rather in a figurative sense, to denote his enthusiastic zeal, than to describe the manner of his devotions. He believed strongly in Faith—which is very different from having a strong faith. Faith was the beginning, middle, and end; and he was so zealous for it that he despised Works, and distrusted them to such a degree that, upon principle, he never performed any more of them than was perfectly convenient, or, rather, than were thrust upon him. Mr. Bills' belief in faith was so strong that he could get drunk conscientiously; and he did get drunk, religiously drunk, every time his faith was aroused more than usual; and the spirits strengthened his furious faith. I would consider myself one of the greatest mnemonists the world has produced if I could transcribe, verbatim, any one of the didactic discourses I have heard him deliver when in that condition. They ran something like this:

"Pedobaptism being a ramification of the great line of argument, which coming from the first, still continues carrying all truth with it, must be considered in a twofold aspect, according as the tenor of the mind which contemplates it, without bias. Hence we see that when John saw the heavens open—no, it wasn't

John, but it's all the same thing, you understand me—when the heavens opened it was Faith which was preached, as it were, that faith which removes mountains, and, therefore, to believe stands in place of to do, for what can man do, the vile worm unregenerate except by Faith? Of course when I argue in this curriculum the grand Arcanum of stated preaching must not be ignored, for what saith the Scriptures? not only seek that ye may find, but likewise how shall they hear without a preacher? Don't you see?"

I am inclined to think that Mrs. Bills never did see that Simon was any the better for his faith, when it had this violent effect upon him; but she bore her burden in a Christian spirit. Mr. Bills was a man who throve in the goods of this world, at least, and, in spite of his occasional excitements, was respected by his brethren, and only laughed about by the ungodly of the community. He was a very wiry and fiery little man, and not over-particular as to when or where or upon whom he should resent an insult or injury. When he was about half drunk, and wholly absorbed in religious argument, it was not safe to show an inclination to jeer him, and the laughers always laughed to themselves.

When Mr. Bills died his widow moved into town, where she purchased a neat cottage residence, and devoted herself to her sorrows and the education of her two daughters. I have no idea that the good woman ever thought for an instant that she had not been the best wife Bills could have had; but it always seemed to me that she rather aggravated his peculiarities of temper and doctrine. He, a man of middle age and thoroughly set in his ways, had taken her, a poor girl of twenty-two, with respectable connections and but slight personal beauty to recommend her. There did not seem to be a show of love on either side; they made a dry business affair of both the courtship and marriage, as though they were acting not from passion but from principle. He appeared to think that he ought to marry for the sake of his comfort, and for increased respectability; and she took him for conscience' sake, as performing the most binding duty of woman, and for her own sake as her first and last and only chance. If she had been of a lively, sunny disposition, I have no doubt but that she would have shed some brightness over his vague and erratic faith.

Such a religion as was his is but theoretical. In its own nature it cannot be practical, for it excludes as sinful everything like action on the part of the believer. It was painful to me to watch the operation of the two opposite errors in which Simon Bills and Ben Eccles found themselves. The one repudiated works altogether, and was miserable in holding that nothing was actually sinful to a man justified by faith; and the other was plunged almost into despair by the impossibility which he found to eke out his faith by his works.

When men set up error as truth they go from error to error in supporting it; and though the first is the more abominable, it would be hard to tell which of these two errors has the more depressing effect upon man's spiritual life. One of the strangest of all mental and moral phenomena is this division of a single truth into two or more gross errors. It is true that we are justified by faith, and it is also true that faith without works is dead, and yet we are not justified by faith in the sense that faith is itself a meritorious work, nor are our works of any merit in themselves, except as they exercise the soul in virtue and are evidences of our faith. We stand justified before God when by faith we appropriate to ourselves the atonement made for us by Christ: it is the atonement made by our surety which justifies us, our faith is merely the hand which appropriates it. On the other hand, it is a self-evident proposition that if our faith do not perform its natural functions, by influencing our conduct, it is but a dead faith, which does not deserve the name of faith at all. The whole may be summed up in this: The atonement of Christ is the grand truth, and by faith we stand, by faith we act.

Now, Mr. Bills believed in faith without works, just as poor Ben Eccles was practically acting on the contrary theory; and Mrs. Bills being but a weak woman, and Methodistically inclined, had the whole matter jumbled up in her head, and at the same time believed both ways and neither way, and did not exactly know what she did believe.

One thing is certain; she never wooed her husband to good works by the pleasantness she might have given their exercise. She was gloomy and sad, and treated this world as a vale of sorrows into which it was a punishment to be placed, and in which the church buildings here and there were the only places of refuge. She was too meek to argue, and too weak not to hang her hands down and snivel when he got drunk, as his increasing confidence in faith allowed him to do more and more frequently. Such a thing as remedying any of the evils of this present life never seemed to occur to her, and Bills, so far from meeting with resistance or guidance from her, found in her nonentity no discouragement of his belief and much aggravation for his conduct. The woman who expects by her tears and other manifestations of weakness to drive her husband from evil courses, does not understand human nature, and if she come about him snivelling, and upbraiding, and irritating him when he is drunk, she is most pitiably and wickedly foolish. It was just this last act which drove Bills from home the day he fell over his mare's head at the pond and broke his neck, and though Mrs. Bills always considered his death as a judgment upon her, and as a lesson and warning sent expressly to her, she never thought that she really was herself the moving cause of his untimely death.

Such had been the uncle by marriage, and such was the aunt of Charles Bowman. As for his two cousins, they were so much like thousands of other insipid young ladies that I do not feel justified in describing them minutely. Emily was a gushing, timid little darling of about twenty-seven, who had large dark eyes and long dark curls, kept an album, and was easily moved to the ecstatics; and Louisa, her younger sister, who had more of her father's spirit, despised nonsense, talked horse and dog, was an authority on the breeds of cattle, and thought herself a Lady Di to ride to hounds. Archie Glenn, who owned Sir Bertram, used to swear she would make a first-rate partner, and had the insolence to try to make her acquaintance and court her, but was ignominiously repulsed, as her tastes were only affected and not real.

Susan had never had any special liking for either of them, but had been too amiable to repel the great admiration they always manifested for her. She was a wise woman so long as she was governed only by her reason; so soon as her heart took the reins she was like any other woman, wise only as it might happen. She never had thought either of them so amiable as she did three or four days after the barbecue, when they came in state, Louisa driving, in the gig to visit her, and after they were gone she expressed her surprise to her mother that they had improved so much.

"I cannot say, my dear," answered her mother, "that I saw any marked improvement. Louisa was boisterous, and Emily talked almost too much about her Cousin Charles."

"Yes, but, mother, you know that she said that her cousin was the only brother she had ever known, and she has good reason for being fond of him; and, besides, she is older than he."

If Mrs. Garthwaite had only pondered the whys and wherefores of that addition: "she is older than he," she might have seen cause to fear that her daughter did not fancy the idea that any love beyond cousinly love should exist between Emily and her cousin. I say "cause to fear," because Charley Bowman was not at all to Mrs. Garthwaite's taste as a son-in-law. Even granting that he was as gay, manly, and generous as he appeared to be, she did not think that he had those other and more solid qualities which make a man contented and secure the content of a wife. The gay in youth, or in public, often become the peevish and ill natured in private, or when they grow older, the manly in speech are often hard and exacting, and dissipation is often the result of careless generosity, just as lavish generosity is frequently the foil of intense selfishness. To sum it all up: Charles Bowman's character appeared to her too light to be solid, and it had the ring of hollowness, and she did not esteem him. She felt that Sam Stockdale was worth thousands of such men, and that Ben Eccles was much to be preferred to him. And besides, she had thoroughly known his mother and father, and had never esteemed them. How could she do so? Their present wealth was no recommendation in her eyes. They had only been lucky and saving. Col. Bowman was to her still Col. Vance's humble servant, and Mrs. Bowman was still Harmonia Jenkins, the poor cousin, and the idea that a son of theirs should come courting her daughter was too shocking to enter her mind without preparation or violence.

What a splendid state of society we should have in the South, and everywhere else, if the good parents were allowed to regulate matters of love and marriage! We have *caste* here, not in its Hindoo sense certainly, but in its English sense, quite as strongly developed as in any monarchical country, though, as we have no titles, it may sometimes be mistaken—never neglected when known. Mrs. Garthwaite knew that Charles Bowman was not her daughter's equal in point of blood, and if she had her way he should never have been admitted to any acquaintance whatever. But Susan did not know it. If she had she would never have given Master Charles any but the most distant bows, and his cousins only stately courtesies. How was she to know that a wealthy and well-educated young man, whose father was called colonel, and was the acquaintance of all the good people she knew, was not on account of the station and peculiarities of his ancestors a fit person for her to marry in case he should love her, and she should return his love? Was he not the schoolmate and the apparent equal of both Ben Eccles and Sam Stockdale, who were the acknowledged equals of any other young gentlemen in any other country?

The fact is that equality is a humbug, and we should have certain titles or marks by which to distinguish who is who. There are certain families of my acquaintance every male in which should be marked by a crop in one ear, and others who should be distinguished by a crop and an underbit; and still others who should have crops and underbits in both ears and slits in their noses, to warn all men who they are. The most preposterous of all foolish ideas is that which makes every one the equal of every one else; and the best proof of its folly is that none but fanatics preach it up and none but idiots act upon it

Mrs. Garthwaite did not ponder the words of her daughter, and did not suspect that Charles Bowman was going to fall in love with and court that young lady. Besides the reasons I have already given for her not doing so, she thought she had heard that the young man was already engaged to some young lady in his own neighborhood. She was not certain who had told her, or who the young lady was, or even that she had, in fact, heard so. It was only a sort of vague impression upon her mind; but sufficient to avert from her any suspicion of his courting Susan.

She did know that Sam Stockdale was in love with her daughter, and, as I have before intimated, she was heartily pleased with the fact. He was in every respect eligible, and she thought her daughter was in a fair way to accept him as the man of her choice. It was very certain that the young lady did not repel him, and had shown no repugnance to his attentions. She even seemed, so far, to prefer his society to that of any other young gentleman who had ever visited the house. She often repeated his dry or comical sayings, and quoted his opinion with respect. Miss Maria Jones, herself, was in alarm about the case, and professed that she could make nothing of dear Susan, but she could not see for the life of her what the sweet girl could find to admire in that great rough doctor, who seemed to care for no one but himself, and lolled back at his ease in the softest rocking-chair, and laughed and chatted as though he thought himself smart; for her own part she was afraid of him, and should not be at all surprised if he would some day snap her head off, or suddenly whip out his lancet and bleed her on the spot; he was a monster whose awful character could not be covered by all the polish of manner he assumed; she knew exactly what all such hard men were; polite enough in society, but perfect brutes to their wives and children; and she'd warrant that if his mother and sisters would tell the truth they were as afraid of him as of death, and would be very glad to get him off their hands and out of their house.

I need not say that Dr. Sam did not deserve this enmity. Although the woman bored him, and annoyed him prodigiously, he tried at all times to be polite to her; and if his politeness was sometimes frigid, or, tc say the worst of it, severely dignified, it was only when she was more impertinent than usual. He did not inconvenience his dignity by trying to conciliate her, neither did he belie his manliness by being rude. But, at the same time, the evident ill will of one who appeared to be Susan's bosom friend gave him some uneasiness; for the most valiant lover who ever lived will weigh the minutest chances, just as the greatest mathematician must take into consideration the smallest fractions; and when, in addition to this, he saw the evident pleasure with which Susan received Charley Bowman the two or three times when he happened on this visit to Yatton to see him come into her presence, he thought he would pause and see how matters were speeding before he pressed his suit to a decision. And so, as his term of absence had expired, he took his leave and went back to Rosstown, leaving Charley Bowman in full possession of the field, except in so far as Ben Eccles might be considered as still keeping it to all comers, though he seemed retired to one corner of the lists.

In about two weeks Mr. Bowman paid a short visit home, as I shall hereafter relate. In the next chapter I will pass over what happened to him at home during the three or four days he was there, to tell what happened upon his return to Yatton—and I hope the misplacement of incidents in point of time shall cause no confusion to the reader.

CHAPTER XXV.

GIVES AN INSTANCE IN WHICH MR. CHARLES BOWMAN ACTS IN CHARACTER; AND THEN SPEAKS VERY PLAINLY UPON A MOST IMPORTANT SUBJECT.

I BELIEVE that I have no arrears to bring up. Dr. Sam is at home puzzled and uneasy about his love affair; Alice Charlton is with her aunt neither puzzled nor uneasy (for a few days—as I will hereafter tell—) about her heart story, for though her lover is absent and engaged in courting another girl, she does not know it, but feels perfectly assured that all is right, and that he will soon return to her. Ben Eccles and his friend Charles can have the full possession of our attention, and we can see how it fares with them without feeling that we are neglecting any one else.

It may readily be supposed that Ben was no match for Bowman in a contest like this; and, indeed, if he were not the person with whom I am naturally most concerned, as I am writing what I know about him, I would before now have taken leave of him in describing this love affair, and would have treated it as a separate story running parallel to his. When I saw how it was going I wished him to quit it, and I know that Susan did so most heartily, but this was his story; it was a warfare from which he would take no discharge, and I must needs follow his fortunes. Nevertheless, I must not be held bound to describe all of his awkwardnesses, and hopes, and fears, his fancied encouragements, and positive or imagined rebuffs; let them be taken for granted. What I was most concerned about was the condition of his mind, which gave me great pain and anxiety, for I always had what I may call a sort of curious interest in him as a study, as well as a friendly interest.

If any one think that he had failed at all in intellect or manliness, let him be undeceived. In ordinary matters his intellect was of the clearest and most vigorous, and of his manliness there could be no question; at any rate, no one about Yatton was hardy enough to question it. Though sufficiently long-suffering, he was not the personification of meekness when it was attempted to impose upon him, or to do an injustice to him or in his presence to another, even though that other were a stranger. He had early imbibed from my father the true doctrine, that whatever Christians should do in heathendom, among Christians they must make themselves respected by a strong arm and a hard fist, cudgel, or bullet, or else have every dog lift his leg upon them, and all their chances of usefulness destroyed. Like my father he fulfilled the command: "Whosoever shall compel thee to go a mile, go with him twain," by going the mile, and then taking his adversary by the ear, and lugging him back to complete the two miles.

Charles Bowman knew his spirit very well, and never dared to ridicule him to his face, or even behind his back if there were any fear that he should hear of it. He knew that at this time, and regarding Susan especially, he might as well rob a bear of her whelps as be guilty of an attack of any sort upon Ben's dignity. And yet he felt that it would be well to place him in an odious or ridiculous light before her; not that he was actually afraid of his rivalry, but it was best, after all, to make assurance doubly sure.

Mrs. Bills, good soul, was a great admirer of Mr. Ben Eccles, and almost imagined she could see the wings budding out on his shoulders. True, he was neither Methodist nor Baptist in his doctrines, but she envied Mr. Snow the possession of such a disciple, just as a continental town envies another the possession of some rarer relic, or an amateur geologist covets a choice ammonite in the collection of another. If he should have taken a fancy to either of her daughters she would have, to use her own words, "jumped at the chance," and a disparity in ages should have been no obstacle. But Ben had never visited them; neither mother nor daughters pleased him. The mother was too good, and he had no place for admiration for the daughters, however admirable the mother thought them.

Not very long, indeed only about three weeks after the barbecue, there was a protracted meeting of the Methodists in Yatton, and a certain preacher, who had a great reputation as a revivalist, and was starring it through the country, happening to be there at the time, attracted large audiences. Emily and Louisa persuaded Susan to go one night to hear him, and as Ben had gone to The Barn to spend the evening, he went along too. After church the girls were vociferous, or rather Louisa was vociferous, and Emily was pertinaciously entreating to Mrs. Garthwaite for Susan to go and spend the night with them, which, her mother consenting, she did, carrying Ben of course in the train to the house. By some extraordinary coincidence, Charley Bowman had happened to arrive that evening, though he did not make his appearance with his cousins until they had got home from church. It may be that he had only been attracted by the fame of the preacher, or had other special business which called him suddenly to town; but Ben always believed that it was a plan between him and his cousins to get Susan to the house while he was there.

However that may be, he came into the parlor soon after they had arrived, and much was the astonishment and joy manifested on the part of his cousins at seeing him, while Ben's soul hardly understood his eyes when they told him they saw a gentle blush mantle his Susan's cheek as she gave the intruder her hand. All was merriment in a few minutes. Master Charles was even unusually gay and witty, and seemed to take a delight in being trotted out and shown off before Susan by his cousins. As it approached the time for retiring for the night, he followed his aunt, who went out of the room for something, and the following conversation ensued:

"Aunt, do you never have family prayers?"

"Certainly I do, Charles, when the girls and I are here by ourselves."

"Well, why don't you have them all the time?"

"The reason is that I do not like to pray aloud before company."

"Well, but, aunt, Ben Eccles is here, and I am sure that he would very cheerfully hold prayers if you would ask him."

"Oh, Charley! how should I ever ask him! It would look so strange, and this his first visit, too, to be asked to pray before those giddy girls!" said Mrs. Bills, her own sense of propriety rebelling against the proposition.

"Pshaw, aunt! I'm astonished at you. You know very little of Ben Eccles, if you do not know that he only lives to do good. Why, nothing could rejoice him more than an opportunity to join his friends in an appeal to the throne of grace. You just ask him, and I'll bet he does it."

"But, Charley, how can I introduce the subject? Nothing would delight me more, I'm sure, than to have Mr. Eccles make one of his beautiful prayers. I know he is gifted that way; and I'm sure it would do us all good. But the request will be so sudden!"

"No, it won't, aunt. You go on about what you are going to do, and come back to the parlor presently; I will lead the conversation, so that your asking him shall be the most natural and graceful thing in the world. After the stirring sermon I heard this evening I feel that a good prayer would be of great service to me, and I'm determined to hear one if possible."

And he returned to the parlor, where presently his aunt followed him, and he led the conversation into a religious channel, and soon got to speaking of domestic piety, and the excellence of spiritual communion among Christians of all denominations and at all times, until at last his aunt found herself almost compelled to ask Ben to lead in family prayer.

The very thought of poor Ben's situation almost makes me gasp, as it did him, and I must pause to fully realize it, and tutor my mind to regard it complacently.

Was ever a poor man placed in such a dilemma! He was one of the most morbidly sensitive of men, and his sense of the ludicrous was exceptionally keen. He was almost dead with love, and at the same time was almost crazed by the religious conflict I have heretofore described. On the one hand was the ludicrous incongruity of the whole affair; that he, a very young man, neither an elder, a deacon, nor a preacher, but a young lawyer, and an ardent lover, should be called upon to perform, in the presence of his lady-love, a gay girl, the functions which were suited to one much older than he, and who had a name and standing in the church! On the other hand was his natural piety, and the dread he now had of doing anything to offend a Deity who was pressing him closely to account for his thoughts, words, and deeds, and was swift to mark his iniquities! All his feelings were in tumult. What should he do? He blushed and stammered, and then turned livid with resolve, and consented, almost cursing his fate in his heart.

It was a hideous struggle, in which the purest and blackest feelings of his heart were mingled in chaos. He read the words of Holy Writ with a secret sneer in his soul; when he raised the hymn he felt like shouting out blasphemy; and though the words of his prayer were smoother than oil, "war was in his heart;" and when he had concluded and said "Amen," he could hardly restrain himself from crying out: "There! and be damned to you, Mrs. Bills! I have settled my fate now!" and the next instant he almost fell fainting with compunction.

When he had gone out of the gate on his way home, he stopped and knelt in a corner of the fence and prayed and groaned over the mutinous and blasphemous feelings of his heart. He felt that God was very angry with him, and that he had perhaps committed the unpardonable sin; and yet the remains of the rebellion were still there, and pray as he might, he could not entirely shake it off. Why should he have been forced to ruin his dearest hopes in this manner! Why had a cup so bitter been given him to drink! God have mercy upon him, and forgive him; he was the most rebellious of men!

And then came a ray of hope across his anguish at the occurrence which made his sense of his sin all the deeper. Might it not be that this very scene which he thought a misfortune should be the means of helping his hopes! Not that he took any merit to himself for what he had done; oh no; for it was his duty, and he had performed it with a wicked heart; but Susan was a sensible woman, and surely she could see the moral courage which had sustained him, and would rather dwell upon that than upon the ridiculousness of the scene!

His mind was chaotic when he rose from his knees and proceeded home. He no longer thought; he felt; and his whole being was pain, dull, heavy pain, with now and then a keen pang which made him groan and sent him to his knees again.

I can no longer persist in describing his condition of mind. It is too painful to me, and must be so to every man who has so felt as to be able to feel with him.

One must himself have felt to be able to sympathize

with others. If I were writing a sensation story with seduction as its theme I should enlist the sympathy of every male who has reached the age of puberty. If I could produce a well-wrought tragedy the whole world would be thrilled, because the whole of mankind are capable of anger, and, consequently, of murder. I am inclined to think that the number of those who can sympathize with Ben Eccles is much larger than most men believe. Of one thing I feel certain : almost every thinking man in Christendom, and every thinking heathen, has had to bear a share, slight or great, short or long, in that same spiritual conflict which now convulsed his mind. It has been a conflict which has divided Christians into many sects, and is the source of all the penances, sacrifices, and other religious rites of heathendom and of Christendom.

The heathen have sought to work their atonement and acceptance with the gods by senseless rites and ceremonies, penances, and sacrifices. Christians have attempted, and attempt to eke out their salvation by the same means, as though any man could merit salvation by works of supererogation. In so far as what they do is a duty, it is but their duty, and they must say, when it is done, that they are, after all, but "unprofitable servants ;" and in so far as it is not their duty, "Who hath required this at your hand ?"

Alas, poor human nature, ignorant of its own freedom, still calls upon itself to worship "in this mountain," or at Jerusalem, to have its devotion accepted ; and, not vain of, but mistaking its own strength, and above all, confounding the infinite justice of God with its own feeble, vacillating decisions, still tries to curry favor with Him, or by hypocritical good works or self-abasement to swerve Him from the right!

The task is vain. God's justice is infinite. Christ's atonement alone is man's justification; for as in Christ God is love, infinite in pardoning mercy to the guilty, and in tender beneficence to the pardoned, so out of Christ "our God is a consuming fire." Ben Eccles was feeling this truth in its agonizing effects as millions felt it before him, and as millions shall feel it yet.

If I were writing a novel or a religious story I would dwell upon this subject and pursue it in all the ramifications which my feeble reason has discovered. An old man, whose life has had its sorrows and whose mind has had its grievous errors to combat, but who has learned with the sorrows and conflicts to love and sympathize with his fellow-man in whom he has always found more sorrow, and trouble, and goodness than rude unkindness, I would gladly relieve, even if it were only one poor fellow-mortal, from the vexations which any error and sorrow must produce. And if I thought that I could do good by changing my story of Ben Eccles into a series of religious disquisitions, I would take him as a text and do my best. But I should bore the reader if he would continue to read, and most likely should deter him from reading at all. Thousands of far more able books than I could write have already been produced upon this particular subject, and first among the thousands is the Bible itself.

If men would only read the Bible itself rather than trust to commentaries and religious books, they should be far wiser. More injury—at least I think so—has been done by taking texts and preaching or writing from them out of the preacher's or writer's own head, with this or that quirk of education, or that or this quiddity of imagination as a guide, than in any other way whatever. Rhetoric is so daring or feeble in its flights; logic is so uncertain in its conclusions from only one premise, and that, perhaps, only a small fraction of a truth; passion is so deceptious in its fury or allurements; pride is so unreasonable in its haughtiness, that the man, however grand in intellect, is apt to be preaching or writing his own crude self rather than the strict truth as it exists. And however careful he may be, and however correct, according to the meaning his words convey to his own mind, he gives most of his hearers but half the truth, and many of them positive errors, as what he says excites predisposed trains of false reasoning or sentiment in their minds.

Understand me. I do not inveigh against preaching. God forbid. So far from it am I that I would that every man were a preacher. The appointed means of spreading the Gospel is by preaching; but it is by preaching the Gospel, and the simple Gospel: Christ, and him crucified. What matters it if by the bias of temperament or education a man also believe in Election, or in Falling from Grace, in Immersion or in Sprinkling, yea, even in the Sacrifice of the Mass, or in Confession, so he believe in Christ's atonement? As I have grown older my charity has been very much enlarged, and I can more fully appreciate the fact that whether in contention about other matters, or in the simplicity of the truth, so Christ is believed, the end is gained. The Atonement of Christ is the one essential, and whoever has that can have or dispense with any other matter of belief. While I bewail the gross errors of almost every association of Christians which usurps to itself the name of THE CHURCH, I believe that where the simple truth, which is the peculiarity of Christianity, is firmly believed, all their errors do not hinder their salvation, any more than their rites and ceremonies, new moons and sabbaths, incense, vain oblations, calling of assemblies, gowns and bands, and other follies, forward or secure it. I thank God that the years of sorrow and conflict which have brought me to old age have also brought me to the quietude which enables me to say: "I know whom I have believed," and to feel assured that the kingdom of Him in whom I believe is broader than the bounds of earthly churches.

But the error of Ben Eccles is the error of every one, church or individual, who preaches or believes that anything in addition to the Atonement of Christ is essential, or is even of the slightest assistance to salvation. The error of Mr. Bills was, not that he placed too much confidence in Christ's Atonement, but that he placed too much confidence in Faith, as though it were itself meritorious—a good work which excluded all other good works. I repeat here what I have before said: without faith, works are dead; certainly; but without works faith is also dead. Whosoever shall have the proper faith will strive to perform its legitimate works—but neither the faith itself, nor the works themselves are of any effect to salvation, but the Atonement of Christ alone is the means and method of justification.

Let us have preaching, then, by all means, and

plenty of it; but let it be the preaching of the good tidings that sinful man can be saved if he will come and appropriate to himself by acceptance the atonement made for him by Christ. We cannot have too much such preaching. It is a gamut which embraces every tone, and from which every grade of music, from that sung together by the morning stars to the mother's simple lullaby, can be formed in endless change of harmony and melody. There is no danger of becoming tired of it, for throughout eternity it shall be the choicest theme of seraphim and saints—the love of God to man in Christ.

In view of that atonement, of the life, sufferings, and death, the burial and resurrection of the Son of God, how mean are all the pompous forms and ceremonies, how paltry all the gaudy paraphernalia which men join to that sacrifice to strive to please God or to cheat him! "Who hath required this at your hand?" Man, and all that he is and has, is God's, who is the Creator, Preserver, and Benefactor; and shall man purchase his Creator's favor, and blind his justice? And, after all, when he brings his empty forms and childish ceremonies, his trivial rites and footy penances, what does he but offer the blind for sacrifice, and the lame and sick! "Offer it now unto thy Governor; will he be pleased with thee and accept thy person? saith the Lord of hosts." Is God a man, that he should feel honored by mass-meetings and laudatory resolutions and speeches? Does he not see into the heart?

"Wherewith shall I come before the Lord, and bow myself before the high God? Shall I come before him with burnt offerings, with calves of a year old? Will the Lord be pleased with thousands of rams, or with ten thousands of rivers of oil? Shall I give my first-born for my transgression, the fruit of my body for the sin of my soul? He hath shewed thee, O man, what is good; and what doth the Lord require of thee but to do justly, and to love mercy, and to walk humbly with thy God?"

Cast down the barriers of the churches, which make a monopoly of religion, disregard the dogmas about non-essentials with which they have environed it, and preach the simple truth of Christianity; and the wisdom of the world shall be set at naught.

It is objected that forms and ceremonies, the shapes and colors of garments, the precise drill for genuflexions, prayer and praise, the size, positions, and decorations of church buildings, inside and out, are necessary to attract the attention and win the hearts of men to the truth as it is in Jesus. Then God himself will do evil that good may come! Avaunt with such blasphemy! Away with such foolish readings of the human heart! Is it true with you, Mr. Objector? No, you say; but it is true with the masses! Are you more human than the masses? have you a tenderer conscience? does sin hang a more heavy load upon you? does punishment seem more dreadful, or salvation appear more desirable to you than to other men? Your objection is unfounded. God is the God of all men, and has put a conscience into all men, and a natural desire for good to themselves, and a natural dread of evil. The earliest church had no such adjuncts as you now find necessary, and yet the gospel spread, and men believed and were saved, thousands in a day! The times have changed, but man has not changed, nor has God changed. His SPIRIT still moves upon the face of the waters, and He can still command: Let there be light! and there shall be light over a whole world, as there is in the hearts of those who now believe. Your adjuncts mislead. They are a snare. They encourage the belief of that very error which now agonized the soul of Ben Eccles. It was in a precisely similar case that Paul wrote to the Galatians:

"Behold, I, Paul, say unto you, that if ye be circumcised, Christ shall profit you nothing. For I testify again to every man that is circumcised, that he is a debtor to do the whole law. Christ is become of no effect unto you, whosoever of you are justified by the law; ye are fallen from grace. For we through the Spirit wait for the hope of righteousness by faith. For in Jesus Christ neither circumcision availeth anything, nor uncircumcision; but faith which worketh by love. Ye did run well; who did hinder you that ye should not obey the truth? This persuasion cometh not of him who calleth you. A little leaven leaveneth the whole lump."

CHAPTER XXVI.

DR. SAM STOCKDALE COMES TO GRIEF.

DR. SAM had very little comfort at home. His love did not fit him quite so easily as it had done, though it was just as warm, and, beside that, his sister Sarah seemed inclined to hustle him with the cold shoulder, and the countenances of Lily and his mother were shrouded with a little cool pity, which was even worse. Sarah's conduct was aggressive, and could be fought and beaten, but that of the others was aggravating, and yet safe from attack; for who can attack contempt?

"Well, Sam," said Sarah, with a fine sneer, "I do think you are a brave wooer!"

"Don't trouble brother, Sarah," said Lily; "the poor fellow has enough to bear!"

"Look ye here, girls!" exclaimed Sam, in brotherly wrath, "you are both too hard upon me; but I can stand your abuse, Sarah, better than I can Lily's compassion. Neither of you knows anything about the case, and I wish to gracious you were in my place for about five minutes. Confound it all! You women who have to be courted think that you could succeed splendidly if you were to court; but I tell you, you would make a botch of it! I know what I'm about, and you don't. I wish neither instruction nor pity!"

And he turned on his heel, had his horse saddled, and went to see a patient.

"You see, sister," said Lily, after he was gone, "he has hope still; and he may succeed after all."

"You are mistaken, Lily," answered Sarah. "He may flatter himself, and try to brave it out with us that he has hope, but he feels that he has no chance, or, if any, but the faintest of the faint. When such a man as brother is, a real man, begins to mope and be uneasy, it is because his affair has gone wrong and can't be remedied. If he could see any remedy, do you think he would dawdle about here and do nothing?"

"But, sister," said Lily, "it is not like brother to mope and pine about what he can't help; and I should think that if he really had no hope he would give the affair up."

"That shows, Lily, that you know nothing of that brother of ours," answered Sarah. "He has some most fantastical ideas in his head about a gentleman's duty. He holds that if a gentleman has paid such marked attentions to a lady as to show her that he wishes to marry her, and she has not been so decided in her rejection of his attentions as to make it insulting for him to still offer them, it is his duty to make a plain declaration to her, and have the affair definitely settled."

"I think he is right in that!" said Lily.

"Perhaps he should be, with regard to some girls," answered Sarah, "for they are very silly, and either do not know their own minds, or are too trivial to manifest them; but I am sure that, with such a girl as

Susan Garthwaite, it is nonsense, or I'm much mistaken. I don't think she's a coquette, and I do think she has already fully made up her mind. I'll tell you what, Lily," she added, "Sam has lost his chance; and that's what vexes me. He will go back to see Susan in a few days, and will return here a rejected man. Mark my words for that! There is no use in talking to him. Let him alone! If he had taken my advice, and had pressed his suit a month ago, he should have been successful; for it only needed a positive declaration on his part to have enlisted all of Susan's thoughts and affections."

I am inclined to think that she was right in that last declaration. Many a matter would not turn out as it does had one of those "if's" been put into execution; but their non-execution was predestined with the event.

A few days after this Dr. Sam came to Yatton sure enough, and came as usual to my house; for, by virtue of my guardianship of Ben, he and I had for years been friends; and, indeed, it was by reason of his visits to me, whenever he came to Yatton, and his friendly unreserve, that I came to know so much as I do about his affairs.

Let it be understood, once for all, that there is very much of the by-play of my story that I do not relate, because it is not necessary, and not sufficiently interesting to be noted as I go along, and because much of it concerns myself. Dr. Sam stayed at my house whenever (except the first afternoon of his first courting visit) he came to Yatton. I was the friend who took him first to The Barn, and about whom I made that cutting remark about calling to get dinner; as I knew that I was innocent of such selfishness upon that occasion, I thought I could safely cut at others through myself. I knew Mr. and Mrs. Bills far better than I have pretended, and knew Charley Bowman well in almost every phase of his life; had lawsuits and settlements in plenty for all of them, for I was their lawyer. I have not thought proper to narrate all these things, trusting that the perception of the reader would be sufficiently acute to discover them, or to suspect them. For the same reason I have not stated in so many words that Ben Eccles was at last settled at his new place, and was keeping bachelor's hall, nor about his visit to Dr. McCleod's after his return from college, nor have I described a thousand other events and persons which had connection with the characters of my story.

But Dr. Sam came to my house as cheerful as ever, although I thought I could perceive in him a sort of mental *subsultus* which boded no good. He had long ago told me of the rise and progress of his love affair, and had often consulted me with regard to it. As I knew my man, and that his asking advice was a mere form of talking about what was nearest his heart, I had always advised him in the manner for which I have heretofore given directions—to act as I saw he was most inclined to act, leaving the decision entirely on his own responsibility. Knowing it to be my doctrine that everything was for the best, he on this occasion propounded to me, with a rather sickly laugh, the question: Whether I thought it would be all for the best whether Susan accepted or rejected him; and I answered him: "Although I admire her very much,

Sam, as you know, I am certain it will be for the best if she reject you. If she accept you, I'll wait and see before I decide about it."

My father gave me just such an answer once, and he was right. I was rejected, and can affirm emphatically that it turned out all for the best.*

Never mind, however, about myself. In the evening the doctor went to The Barn, and as he returned after I had gone to bed I did not know that night what he had done, or with what result. At breakfast the next morning I looked to see upon his countenance traces of joy or sorrow, and only saw the same anxiety he had shown the day before. I left him at my house when I went into town to my office, and when I returned to dinner he had just arrived and was getting off of his horse.

"What cheer, doctor?" I asked when I joined him on the front gallery.

"Nothing cheering at all, Mr. Page," he answered, giving my hand a strong nervous grasp. "Nothing cheering at all. She has refused me; but she is one of the noblest women in the world for all that; God bless her!"

"I'm sorry you did not succeed, Sam," said I, "for she is a sweet girl. But better luck next time. There are plenty of other sweet girls in the world."

---

* This admission makes one believe that Mr. Page in his story of his own life was not particular to tell all of its events, or even all of those which were important. It would have been interesting if the old gentleman had given us a history of his cases of mistaken confidence, as well as of his actual sorrows.—J. C., *Exr.*

"Oh, I know that, Mr. Page," answered Dr. Sam, walking up and down the gallery. "I know that, and I'll get over this after awhile. But I did not know that a woman could refuse a man decidedly and at the same time give him more cause for admiring love than he had before. There never was such an angel; that's my opinion. You must think me very weak and silly, sir," added he, turning off; "but I did love her very much, and, by George!" bringing his fist down upon the banisters, "I love her yet, and it makes me a better and a gentler man to love her. Damn the scoundrel who does marry her! If he treats her badly I'll cut his throat!"

Now this was not very gentle to commence with, and it was a direct threat against his old schoolmate, Charley Bowman; and I knew it, though he had no idea that I did. Why should he have characterized the man she should marry as a scoundrel, and why should he fear her being ill treated if he had not had a sort of conviction that his friend was the lucky man; a man who, he thought, had not the capacity to love her and the magnanimity to treat her as she should be loved and treated?

Of course I never knew the particulars of what passed between Susan and Dr. Sam; but I can well imagine that with her calm good sense and gentle heart, with her high respect for him and her quiet dignity, she appeared to him in refusing him more like an angel of light delivering a painful message and inwardly weeping the while with compassionate woe, than a heartless creature who ruthlessly gave him pain.

After dinner he ordered his horse, and said he was too restless to remain quiet, and, besides that, he was neglecting his business at home. "There's poor Kitty Mason," said he, "who I know will never consent to get well unless I get back and treat her."

"So, sir," said I, "if you had been accepted, poor Kitty Mason would have still had to suffer unheeded by you! Why, no wonder you were rejected! Mrs. Bills would think it was a judgment upon you."

"See here, Mr. Page," said he gravely, "I don't wish you to think me disrespectful; but did you ever see anything in your life you could not find fun in?"

"Certainly I have," answered I, "a great many things; but a young gentleman disappointed in love is not one of them. I told you yesterday that I should consider that disappointment all for the best, and ten years hence you will agree with me. I find nothing in Kitty Mason's case to make fun of, and I can see nothing amusing in the real sorrows in the world; but I do not confound disappointments with sorrows. Man proposes and God disposes, and disposes right. Sin, and physical pain, and death and dishonor are the only real causes we personally have for sorrow."

"I suppose we sin of ourselves; but does not God dispose our physical pains and death and dishonor too?" asked Sam.

"Yes, he does," I answered; "and yet it is right to sorrow on account of them, because they are a part of our burden and it is natural we should sorrow."

"Is not disappointment also part of our burden?" asked he, thinking he had me refuted.

"No, it is the result of our short-sightedness and

folly," I replied; "and our sorrow on account of it is also the result of our folly. Do you suppose that because you have made a miscalculation the world is going in a wrong course? Just wait five or ten years and then tell me what you think of this disappointment—certainly the most grievous that can happen to a man. Let me tell you, Sam, that the worst use to which a man can place his time and feelings is to waste them in grieving over what he can't help. You take my motto: 'It's all for the best,' and I'll warrant that you never in your whole life shall see occasion to regret it. You have failed in getting the girl you love; when you shall marry some other dear, loving woman, years hence, you will be glad that you did fail in getting her."

"Ah, Mr. Page," said Dr. Sam, "Ill never regret having loved Susan!"

"Certainly you never will. To love such a woman as she is equal to a short visit to heaven, and to ever regret it would show that you had been possessed by base and groveling ideas. There is one time, doctor, in which every man, however low, is a gentleman; and that is when he is really in love. His nature is then elevated nigher to divinity; he more resembles the image of God in which man was created than at any other time when actuated by any other sentiments."

No suggestions about its being too late to start upon a ride of thirty miles, about there being no moon, or about the cold wind and threatening clouds, could induce him to remain. He had an excellent horse; he was accustomed to darkness and bad weather; he could stop on the way; in fine he intended to go. So I bade him good-by and he rode away, as gallant a young fellow as ever had bitterness of heart and courage to endure. As I learned afterwards, he did not halt by the way, even in front of The Barn, to apostrophize his cruel fate.

It was a lonesome ride, though black care, the drear companion, was seated behind him. The earliest chilling blasts of December had almost stripped the trees bare; but a few pale yellow leaves lingered upon the extremities of the under branches here and there. Dun fleecy clouds scudded swiftly across the sky from the northeast; such as would betoken snow in a more frigid clime. The golden-rod, with downy seed-spikes, and the dry stalks of other weeds in the bare fields, shivered in the blasts· the sparrows and snow-birds were flitting in the hedges; an occasional flock of rice-birds passed swiftly in undulating flight across the road; a scattered flight of robins, high up in the air, called to each other; or a flock of wild pigeons swooped through the woods, silent and swift, as though they were wandering without object, and could never rest. As the twilight gathered, the robins, jorees, and sparrows chirped, whistled, and fluttered in the briar-patches and cane-brakes in the bottom fields as they selected their roosts, and the husky voices of brown thrushes, scolding at being disturbed by such neighbors, were heard from every clump. When dark night had come down over the scene these voices were hushed, and the chill wind hissed in gusts through the leafless boughs and the dead weeds, or sighed above and around him, burdened only by the dull, distant sound of some idle negro's axe chopping the supply of fire-wood which should have been provided before night. This alone indicated occasionally to his heedless ears that he was passing some habitation on one side or the other of the road. The clouds sped swiftly; the very outlines of the road could hardly be seen; and he rode on steadily, trusting to his horse, and forgetting time and place. The burden of his thoughts was: "My darling Susan! Oh, how can I forget thee! The damned rascal; to think that *he* should be loved by her, the lying scoundrel! Never mind; if he dare to be unkind to her I'll get some excuse and call him out; but he'd never come unless he were shamed into it. I know him of old, damn him! My sweet Susan, you'll never have any one to love you so fervently and purely as I do!" and so on, and so on: of all men a disappointed lover thinks least consecutively and most in a lump.

He arrived at home before his sisters and mother had retired for the night. They heard him call for his hostler, Jim, and knew from the tone of his voice that he was rather surly than gay.

"I told you so!" said Sarah to Lily and her mother; and by that mysterious sympathy which exists between those who live and love together she was perfectly understood; and her mother added, with a sigh:

"Poor boy, how disappointed he must be! See if there is a good fire in his room, Lily; I told Tom Ramsay to have one made, for I felt sure he would be at home to-night. Sarah, tell Tom Ramsay to fix supper for his young master, and to have the coffee strong."

After a little while his firm, quick step was heard in

the hall, and he opened the door of the sitting-room where they had reassembled.

"Hilloa!" he exclaimed, seeing them, "are you good people not in bed yet? Why, mother,"—kissing her,—"what do you mean by keeping such late hours?"

"It is only half-past seven o'clock, my son," she answered.

"Is it possible?" said he. "Why, I thought it was ten or eleven, at least. Well, have you all had supper? I'm hungry? Where is Tom Ramsay? I must have something to eat! Come, girls, bestir yourselves and get your poor disappointed brother something to eat; he needs nourishment."

"Oh, pshaw, brother!" said Sarah, "you are not half so disappointed as you pretend to be. You knew when you left here how it was going to turn out; and I can hardly believe but that you went there, and finding your heart fail, came back contented to abandon the field."

"Indeed, my heart did not fail! I went in like a man and took my punishment as a man should take it from an angel, and here I am safe and sound." Then shaking his finger at them, impressively, "so don't let us refer to the subject again."

They were model sisters, and did not, ever after, first refer to it again; nor did they put on lackadaisical airs of compassion, but let the matter pass as though it had never occurred. They never uttered a word in blame of Susan, except that Lily said to Sarah that she did not admire the young lady's taste if she preferred Ben Eccles or any other man to brother Sam.

Both agreed that it was best as it was, and if she could not love him she was right to tell him so, and not trifle with him or be tempted to marry him because it was advantageous; he would have no difficulty in getting a wife, and there was plenty of time.

It was not until the first soreness was passed that their brother told them one evening that he thought Susan had a special liking for Charley Bowman.

"Oh, what a pity!" exclaimed Lily, mournfully, and wondering; "and he engaged to Alice Charlton, too! Why, brother, how can you say such a thing? She could never show any such preference unless he gave her reason, and how can he do that when he's in love with another girl?"

"In love!" said her brother, with lofty disdain. "You don't know the man, Lily, or you would never use such an expression. *He* love? or *he* stickle at breaking his word? The miserable, lying scamp never told the truth in his life to a man, and how can you expect him to adhere to it with a woman!"

"Pshaw, brother!" said Sarah, almost as wonderstruck as Lily, but vastly more indignant. "You must be mistaken!"

"Mistaken? See here, Sarah, you must think that because I am disappointed I have lost my senses. I tell you that if he were engaged to forty girls he is also courting Susan Garthwaite, and that she will accept him, and they will marry. Confound his picture! if she accept him he *shall* marry her, though the Queen of Sheba should tempt him away. If Alice Charlton had a big brother or her father were alive he would never dream of deserting her; and if he think he can play that game with Susan, I'll show him that though she have no big brother she has me."

"Just let him try it!" he added, talking to himself, and growing very wrathy; "just let him cause her one tear, and I'll break every bone in his rascally carcass!"

And I verily believe that he would have done so. Mr. Charles Bowman, had he had other intentions, was little aware that he was at length engaged in a courtship from which the lady herself could alone release him; nor did Susan know that the strong arm of her rejected lover was a guarantee of the honesty and constancy of her favored suitor which should not fail.

"But, brother," said Lily, "how do you know that she loves Charley Bowman? Did you ask her? or did she tell you of herself?"

"Now Lily, that is too bad!" exclaimed Sam, hurt and vexed. "Sarah talks as though I were crazy, and you talk as though I were a brute! Do you suppose that I asked such a question? Come now; do you really think that I could do such a thing? or do you suppose that she would volunteer such information? Was it not enough for me that she did not love me? and could such a gentle and modest girl as Susan unveil her heart to me, and that, too, for no other purpose than to add to my misery? I'm ashamed of you, Lily. Take her off to bed, Sarah, and make her examine the delicacy of her own heart. Good night, both of you. I must go and see Kitty Mason again. The poor 'creetur' declares she'll get 'on the lift' again unless I see her at least three times a day."

And with that he went out of the room and the

house, leaving with his sisters a topic of thought and conversation which stirred all their womanly sympathies, and caused them to exert all their womanly efforts to search the decrees of Providence for righteous retribution.

CHAPTER XXVII.

TELLS HOW ALICE CHARLTON THOUGHT, FELT, AND ACTED, AND HOW MR. BOWMAN THOUGHT, FELT, AND ACTED; AS NEARLY AS MR. PAGE COULD UNDERSTAND THEM.

ALICE CHARLTON was a woman who had a great deal more vigor of mind and strength of character than she thought she had. The degree of caution infused into some women by the shrinking delicacy of their sense of propriety is absolutely wonderful, and I do not think that it has been sufficiently noted. Such women can never be made the victims of blighted affection unless matters go much farther than they did between Charley Bowman and Alice. That young lady was just one of those women, and that very same delicate sense of propriety gave her also so great a loathing of meanness that even if her whole maidenly love had been engaged it would have changed to contempt upon the discovery of dishonor or baseness in its object. There is no doubt but that she loved Charley Bowman, for I have reason to know that if he had asked her to marry him she would have consented, but her love was not a complete love. It was, as the lawyers say, "laid under a *videlicet* as to time, value, and amount." It was only an inchoate love, though perfect as far as it went.

It would be a little ridiculous to pretend to attribute to a woman a quality which is not natural, though theorists often do worse than that; but if I can understand myself, and make myself thoroughly understood, I think that both I and the reader shall see that what I state is strictly natural and correct. I do not mean that Alice Charlton's love was like a glove, to be put on or off at will, and without effort or pain—that would not be love at all. Nor do I mean that it was a compound, ready to turn to sugar by a proper degree of heat; but that it was that kind of love which can be more accurately described as interest and preference.

She felt a lively interest in Mr. Bowman, and preferred him to any other man she had ever met. A word would have made her feelings love of a more absorbing character, and if she had then married him her love would have become part of her nature, no more capable of being laid aside than would have been her soul while she had life; but the word not being spoken, the interest and preference remained mere interest and preference, subject to be changed by his conduct into contempt. And it is this ability of woman's nature to keep her affections perfectly under control which I find so wonderful. I do not think that a man is capable of such a suspension of affection, for but few, and those the wisest of them, can even suspend an opinion.

I might have expressed all the ideas I have given in

the two foregoing paragraphs with half the number of words, but, bless my soul, if I condense with all my might, my story shall be a short one, and what would become of those readers who wish some one to elaborate thoughts for them as well as amuse them by narrative! My opinion is that most of the reading done in this world is to save the task and annoyance of thinking. I candidly confess that most of my reading has been done for that purpose. Give a man his five (or seven, which is it?) senses and a few fundamental principles, and if he be a thinker, he is instructed, and proceeds to educate himself. But most men are not thinkers; thinking is too slow and painful a process for them. They are assimilators of the thoughts of other men, who say of a proposition that it is true when it accords with their experience and observation (which require only eyes and memory), but could never have collated their experience and observation, and have originated the proposition if left to themselves. It is a positive pleasure to undergo painful thought for such men. It does them so much good to say, why, I knew that before! and it is so flattering to their vanity to be able to believe that they are just as smart as that writing fellow who has set himself up as an author and teacher. It is an author's business to please, and if he set out openly to instruct his good readers he will be sure to bore them. For my own part, in all my disquisitions upon serious matters, I only propose to myself to arouse and combine certain ideas in minds which already know their bases as well as I do myself. I am certain, at any rate, that I am telling them nothing really new.

It is an old, old reflection, as old as thinking itself, that the characters and dispositions as well as the frames and bodily functions of all animated things are perfectly adapted to the conditions in which they shall live, and yet it is very pleasant to discover and watch the instances of this old fact. The characteristic of Alice Charlton, of which I have been speaking, is one of those instances. We speak in condemnation of the coquetry of woman, and yet the vice is even more common with men, and far more hurtful and lasting in its effects. See, then, and admire, the compensation which nature has supplied the woman in that shrinking delicacy which forces her to keep her affections in abeyance.

And, to return to the point of my starting out, Alice Charlton had this compensation in perfection, as all women naturally have it in some degree. When she discovered that Master Charles had proved volatile her love had no blighting process to undergo; it was simply neutralized by the addition of an alkali; and as the alkali was greatly in excess the product became somewhat caustic.

How she discovered his "goings on," as Aunt Polly called them, I do not know exactly. I have been told by some of our young gentlemen who have been at home on furlough from Virginia, that they have often noticed during great battles that any very important event which happens at the extremity of one wing is known to those at the farthest extremity of the other within a very few minutes after; and that though they can account for it through the stragglers and couriers and wounded men, and all that sort of means of communication, it travels with almost inconceivable rapidity, and it is impossible to trace up its course. In the same way, I suppose, the first inkling of this news came to Alice within two or three days after the barbecue, although, as we have seen, nothing decided had been done or said there in the matter. There was no need of supernatural or preternatural manifestations to convey the news. Alice was not a Cæsar, nor was her cause so important to the heavens as that of Rome or Jerusalem. Neighbors brought the gossip, already grown to the full and sharply-defined proportions of accomplished truth, and Aunt Polly and Mrs. McCleod almost believed it at once. Not so with Alice; she had a better opinion of the noblest man she had ever yet seen. It was a slander upon her own acute and accurate perception of character; it was unworthy of him, unworthy of herself, and, besides, she suspected that certain persons were inclined to be meddlesome; at any rate, she knew that the world was given to jump to conclusions and to make the worst of everything. Believe it! Why, it was only four days ago that he parted from her as though he thought the parting were a disaster which could never be remedied. He did not say so in so many words, but what he did say and look amounted to that. He did not go to attend the barbecue; he was not fond, he said, of such promiscuous amusements; he went at great inconvenience to attend to some business for his aunt, a rigid business woman, who was very wealthy, and had (he said, "had very singularly") more confidence in him than in any one else about business matters, and never purchased or sold without his advice. If he went to the barbecue at all, it was to accompany and give confidence to his cousins, who were young and timid girls—particularly Louisa. What folly that her aunt should trouble herself about such a silly report! But never mind; he would himself be at home to go with her on the next Sunday to church; for he had arranged how long he should be gone, and what he would do while he was gone, and when he should return.

But Sunday came and no Master Charles with it. Here was a shade of color to the story; but a thousand things might have occurred to prevent his return; his aunt's business might have been more complicated than he had represented, for he was given to making the easiest of everything; and, besides, she had no right to hold him bound to a day more or less; he was under no obligation to her, and it was really childish in Aunt Polly to harp upon this prolonged absence as though it were a violation of duty.

Monday, Tuesday, Wednesday, the second Sunday, passed away, and still no Charles; and when at last he did come it was on the day after his arrival at home, and was too late for a walk, or for anything more than a mere call, before night, and he talked flippantly, and seemed averse to leaving the general conversation for a more private chat at the drawing-table or near the window, and paid a few compliments that sounded rather far-fetched than sincere, and even referred to her probable marriage some day to some one else; and he left before tea.

Altogether it was a very unsatisfactory visit. He had certainly changed a great deal during his absence. Perhaps he did not feel well, although he was the picture of health; perhaps—well, a hundred things: she would wait for the next visit before she would admit to herself the possibility of the truth of that dreadful story. But at the next visit, nearly a week afterwards, the same scene was re-enacted, though somewhat modified. He was more particular in addressing her and more familiar in what he said, but she felt that he was reserved, and it was evident to her, inexperienced girl that she was, that the silken cord had been broken, or, at least, was unraveling. He even talked gaily about the time when she should be an old married lady and he would come to see her in dread lest his rough country ways should put in confusion her neat household arrangements.

She now fully admitted that the story might be true, and when after the lapse of several days his brother Henry riding by called in to say that Charles had bade him say to the family that important business had called him to Yatton, she knew that the dream—it was nothing but a dream—was over.

When I first heard the particulars of the young man's withdrawal of his attentions from Alice I thought there must be some mistake, for it seemed rather too sudden to be natural, either if what I had previously believed about the sincerity of his affection for her were true, or if it were true that he was determined to have a wife, and was actuated only by policy. It appeared to me that in the latter case he would have been more deliberate in his movements, and would not have been off with the old love until he was certainly on with the new. But I have since been convinced that his whole conduct was perfectly natural—to him. I still believe that he for awhile had what was, for him, sincere affection for Alice—but then, he fell violently in love with Susan; her beauty was the more appetizing to such a youth. I still believe that had he not gone to the barbecue he would have married Alice—but then, he did go, and Susan, to use one of his own phrases, "filled the bill better;" she was just as good a housekeeper, and, moreover, had vastly more to keep house with. I partly believe that he had long had a lurking idea of Susan, and that his conduct was not so sudden and eccentric as it appeared to be. It is rarely the case that the motives for human conduct have not been accumulating long and almost imperceptibly before they attain the strength to make, what we think, a sudden exertion. His going to the barbecue and perceiving the possibility of success only determined his course. Had he stayed away and not seen the chance he would have remained constant to Alice.

Nevertheless, though this previous inclination and this violent love may not have existed to account for his conduct, there are men gifted with such prodigious impudence that no sudden determination for carrying out their own desires need cause surprise. It supplies the place of genius, and they conceive and execute with a rapidity which conquers success. It was certain that, beauty and accomplishments being equal, Susan was a vastly better match than Alice in point of wealth, and a better match also in point of éclat, personal and public. Alice was but a quiet country girl, living in the quietude of a preacher's family away off from town; while Susan was the reigning belle, the toast of town and county—so much for the public éclat. As for the private glory, Alice had no lover, nor was he likely to have any rivalry in his courtship of her, while both of his old schoolmates, Ben and Sam, who had excelled him at school and excelled him after their school-days were over, in point of standing in social life and before the public, here they were both of them dead in love with and avowed suitors of this belle ; and what a triumph if he should cut them out! Sam Stockdale! why, he could out-talk and out-lie him any day, and understood women infinitely better. As for Ben Eccles,—pshaw! he was in nobody's way ; any one could cut out such a timid, half-cracked wooer as he!

I give these as my various readings of the motives and of what passed through the mind of Charles Bowman. The reader can adopt or reject either or all. The facts were as I have narrated them, and I have not sufficient confidence in my own knowledge of human nature to insist upon my reasoning from them. I am rather more certain of what passed with Miss Alice, and, to tell the truth, feel far more complacent when analyzing her excellencies than when trying to trace the devious nature of her false lover.

As I have before said: she had more vigor of mind and strength of character than she thought she possessed. If any one suppose that she fainted or went into hysterics, or that she grew frantic and stamped her little feet with rage, or became maudlin with grief, or misanthropical and sarcastic with grief, rage, and wounded pride, he is much mistaken. She almost made Aunt Polly's head swim by the cool and self-possessed manner with which she ignored that any particular attentions were ever paid her by Mr. Bowman, and all idea that he had ever given cause for any one to believe that he meant to court her.

"But, my dear," said Aunt Polly, looking as though she could not believe her own ears, "you must acknowledge——"

"I acknowledge, aunt, that you are a dear, darling old goosey, who are always casting your eyes up to the clouds as though they were going to rain angels and lovers and other such intangible objects. Wake up, aunty! You've been dreaming, while I've been wide awake all the time. A young man cannot visit here a half dozen times but that you grow delirious, and have visions of wedding-cake and fat turkeys!"

"My sakes!" exclaimed the old lady, alarmed. "I do wonder if the poor child is not daft! Let me see your tongue, my child."

"There, aunty," said Alice, laughing, and then putting out her tongue. "Did you ever see a more marked case of congestion? But let me tell you something, aunty: you will hurt my feelings seriously if you persist in trying to make out that Mr. Bowman made love to me, and engaged my affections and then jilted me. He did nothing of the kind. He came often to see us because we were his near neighbors, and he fancied our company; and as for his having jilted me, it is a shame that you should ever dream of such a thing," said she, her face growing crimson. "He never had the opportunity to do so, and when I grieve for any man, he shall be worthy of it, and I shall have good cause for it."

"But, Alice——" the old lady commenced to reply.

"Don't say 'But, Alice,' aunty. Listen to me. Promise me now that you will never speak of such nonsense again. You don't know how angry I can get sometimes, and I know you would not willingly hurt my feelings. Do you promise, aunty? and will you promise to tell Aunt McCleod that she must never hint at such a frightful thing either?"

"Of course I will, Alice, if you wish it," said good Aunt Polly; "but it's mighty strange! Just to think that I should have been fooling myself all this while! And you didn't care for him, Alice?"

"Not one particle, aunty, do I care for him; I promise you that," said Alice, always truthful, though slightly evasive. "I never did love him, and he can marry just as soon as he chooses, for me. I hope his wife will be happy."

"Well, I'm mighty glad of it, Alice, and that's the truth," replied the old lady, with quick feelings and short memory. "I'm mighty glad to hear you say so, for I always mistrusted him; and I wish Susan Garthwaite joy of him, though she's a monstrous fine girl, from all accounts. I used to know her mother when she was a girl, and she was as well-behaved a girl as I ever saw. Let me see; was she the second? no, she was the—yes, she *was* the second child, I recollect, for the first was a boy, and they named him after his old Uncle Hawkins, and he died when he was a little fellow. You don't remember Hawkins' wife—oh, pshaw! of course you don't; your poor mother was a baby when she died. Bless my soul, what was her maiden name! I'll go and ask Kitty about it."

And the old lady gathered up her sewing, and went

out of the room to find her Cousin Kitty: and so Alice was over the trial, so far as her friends could add to or assuage it. It was but a few days till all the agitation of her feelings was settled, and settled into cool contempt; for Bowman had acted meanly, and even dishonorably. The marble of which she was constructing her idol had crumbled to base lime, and she threw the paltry trash away, and with it dismissed the inspiration which was to give it life and sanctity.

She had not then been indoctrinated into my philosophy, that "it was all for the best," although her healthful nature practically supplied its place very excellently. But I promise you that years afterwards, when she heard that philosophy discussed and applied with certain one or two delightful illustrations, she became a hearty convert to it, or, rather, heartily adopted it; for she was one of those choice beings to whom all things work together for good, and she never could have so opposed the doctrine as to make conversion necessary.

CHAPTER XXVIII.

SHOWS HOW MR. BOWMAN WENT A WOOING, AND WITH WHAT SUCCESS; AND THE EFFECT OF HIS OFFENDING MISS JONES.

MR. BOWMAN went to Yatton, no doubt congratulating himself that he was well out of that scrape. Confound the girl, he thought, I'm not bound to waste my life and my money upon her because she has taken a fancy to me! I'd have a mighty dull existence, with her old aunt always pestering about the house, and old Mac coming over there with his severe manners, and his praying and preaching all the time. Why, it almost makes me feel, when I'm with him and his family, as though I were at a funeral, or at a prayer meeting, and services were just about to commence. What a damned fool I was ever to think of such a match! Why, I'd have been perfectly miserable!

And at the same time Mr. Charles Bowman felt in his heart the uncomfortable consciousness that he had acted the dog; that he was a poor, mean, pusillanimous creature, who had basely deserted a charming and noble woman, whose heart he had won unworthily, or, miserable creature as he was, could have completely won had he not changed his mind; that he was so selfish and so unprincipled in his selfishness that he deserved to be put out of society as no gentleman, and kicked by any one who had sufficient interest in the young lady to kick him. And he shivered when he thought of Dr. McCleod, who, old and preacher as he was, he knew would just as lief kick him as not, if he should happen to be in his presence while in the spirit of it. Might he not meet him while he was in that spirit? That was a serious question. He might avoid it by carefully keeping out of the way; but, taking all things into consideration, might not the doctor seek him? He hardly believed he would; the old fellow was growing old, and was a preacher after all—though, damn him! if he laid his finger upon him (Charles Bowman) he would show him that his preachership shouldn't protect him. But, pshaw! they all had better sense; they would hush up the matter rather than make it public; they had too much pride and reserve to be making a fuss about such a thing. Besides, suppose they did make a fuss, could they point to one single word or action of his which he could not justify as a result of mere brotherly affection! He had been very careful in that matter. He had done nothing and said nothing, in fact, which any sensible girl ought to construe into a serious advance. Oh, damn the luck! let it go; he was well out of it, and shouldn't trouble his head about it. If they chose to do or say anything, let them do so; he didn't care, they couldn't hurt him; he was well enough off to stand their hatred.

Yet he felt that the true reason why he should escape the effects of the doctor's just indignation was that he was a shabby fellow, who, in spite of his wealth, had sunk far beneath the doctor's notice, and that the old gentleman would not notice him even for the sake of his own dignity.

"After awhile," said he to himself, "after a long time has elapsed, or after I shall have married Susan, and shall be able to present myself as it were a new person, with another character, with fresh vouchers, I will see them all; but I'll not visit there till then, for the old fool would most likely shut the door in my face, or order me off the premises."

So Mr. Bowman came to Yatton as he had planned with his cousins, and found Susan at his aunt's, and took occasion to add to his security by inducing his aunt to get Ben to lead in family prayers as I have related. What else he did during the first part of that visit I do not know, except that he was a very constant visitor at The Barn, and always had some walk or ride planned beforehand with Susan, who took great pleasure in the company of the amusing young gentleman. It took but a few days, however, for the bold and dashing wooer to come to the point, and he declared his love to willing ears, and received the plighted word of as sweet a woman as ever lived.

I pass over this love scene very curtly, because, in the first place, I never knew all the particulars, but principally because it did not please me at the time, and pleases me still less now. I hate to record the success of such a scamp in his pursuit of so true a heart. How Susan Garthwaite could have refused the ardent love of so noble a gentleman as Sam Stockdale, to accept the attentions and propositions of so worthless a character as Charles Bowman, passes, I was going to say, my comprehension; and yet I suppose that it can be explained (for such things often happen), and that I should more properly say that it excites my pity. Really, I do not wonder that she should not have returned the love of Ben Eccles, for he was not the man to suit such a girl—not that he was not good enough for her: he was good enough for any woman, so far as moral character, and manliness, and intellectuality, and social position were concerned; but goodness is one thing, and suitableness is another and a very different thing. Susan was a sensible and gentle hearted girl, but she was also a girl of high spirit, and her ambition was of a more worldly character than that of those girls who, like Mrs. Snow, are raised to consider an alliance with the Hierarchy the topmost round in life to which they may attain. She loved a gay, generous, gallant spirit, and thought she was getting one in Charles Bowman, but knew that however charitable and brave Ben was, he certainly was not gay, and that his wife was not likely to lead a very lively and amused life of it. She loved a noble, independent spirit which could and would take its place at the council board and in the fox hunt, at the fray and at the feast, the peer of all other noble, independent spirits—and a precious specimen of the noble, independent spirit she chose, didn't she!

But let the reader work out all that matter of the reasons for her choice for himself—if he will excuse me from doing so. There are some things so plain that it is a bore to relate them. As he, the reader, if I should ever have a reader, has already seen, she was completely deceived. Most women are deceived when they marry, but few are so badly fooled as she was likely to be. Many a woman marries gayety and finds peevishness, marries wealth and finds poverty, marries love and finds only transient appetite, marries generosity and finds stinginess. What Susan should find if she married Charley Bowman my good reader may easily conjecture from what I have already said about him.

Of course Mrs. Garthwaite objected, and was in a peck of trouble. She could not say to her daughter that she should not marry; it never occurred to her that she could say so, though she was greatly opposed to the match. It was the first sorrow her daughter had ever caused her, and yet the dear girl was not to blame; had done nothing wrong; had acted perfectly naturally. What should she do? Where should she turn for relief? Why should Susan have selected this young Bowman, of all other men? There was nothing especial that she could designate against his character, though his disposition and manners did not suit her in general; but he was the son of that mean, odious man and woman who had been the laughing-stock of the country when she was a girl; and how could a gentleman come from such a stock? She would reason with Susan; she would tell her the whole history. But when she began to reason with Susan, she saw that the dear one's heart was too deeply involved, and that it would be only a useless cruelty to tell her the mean things she knew about the lover's parents; that it might, indeed, be the means of putting dissension between her and the dear daughter of her heart.

Miss Maria Jones had now an opportunity to show her usefulness—for the Maria Joneses, much-abused young ladies as they are, have their uses as well as other people, though their usefulness is seldom intentional.

Mr. Charles Bowman in the insolence of his success neglected his friend, Miss Jones; for the sly, the acute schemer had made her his friend from the start. He had flattered her; he had paid her great attention; had treated her as though he knew that all his hopes for success depended upon her; he had recognized the fact that she was arbitress of her sweet Susan's fate; and had so conducted himself as to show her that it was not only to her glory, but also to her advantage, to allow him to conquer; for though he conquered, it should be as her subject, and she should still rule over the conquered province. *Item.*—The Misses Jones are not always so accurate in their calculations of their own strength as such scheming young ladies should be. The idea of a Maria Jones dividing a girl's heart with her husband! Pooh!

However, Miss Jones had given her assent, and, in her way, had given her assistance. She had praised her young protégé in season and out of season; and I must say that Susan was dreadfully in love not to have been disgusted with her. She had done all she could, and he had succeeded; but now where was her glory? Was she not ignominiously thrust aside? Did not her ungrateful subject sometimes make fun of her, almost laugh at her whims, as he disrespectfully called her well-matured ideas, and even hint that she was a sour old maid? Human nature could not endure such base desertion; her complacency became ruffled; her patronage should be changed to enmity!

Susan's fair friend had keen ears, and never forgot what they communicated. She had some time ago heard about Mr. Bowman's courtship of a young lady in his own neighborhood, and though she had then passed it over as a matter to be subsequently investigated, she now determined to get at all the facts. How she manœuvred to get on their track it is useless to inquire, but she did do so, and learned them in all their details, and with a good many details supplied by her own fancy; and she received them, not directly, but indirectly, from Aunt Polly.

It appears that Aunt Polly had an old friend and schoolmate living at Yatton; a good old maid, like herself, though neither so active nor so useful in the world, nor half so amiable. Miss Young, that was her name, Miss Annabella Young had had much more trouble than had fallen to the lot of Aunt Polly. She had trouble about her health, and had had trouble with her youthful affections, and trouble with a wild brother of hers, and trouble with her guardian, and trouble about her property. The troubles with the lover, brother, guardian, and property were over—and a very nice property she had to live on—but she had no cousins whom she would acknowledge, and no dear niece; she took no delight in turkeys and chickens, and despised ducks; she abominated the kitchen, abhorred sewing, and in truth there was very little she did like, and certainly nothing which could assuage the ills of her past life, which still afflicted her, or the present evils of ill health. Yes, there was one thing—and that was, telling the truth. To tell the truth was a mania with her; and the more startling and unpalatable the truth the more she thought it her duty to declare it.

As I have told all I know about Miss Young in another volume,* it will be sufficient to say here that she had kept up a correspondence with Aunt Polly ever since they were separated in their girlhood; for she had an esteem for her old friend which she scarcely bestowed upon any one else; and Aunt Polly esteemed her. At school she had thought her a heroine, a victim of a wicked guardian, and a miracle of suffering fortitude; and had always consulted her in her own joys and troubles, as a congenial spirit—an instance of how persons who have been long separated may mistake each other! Miss Young was in full possession of every phase of Mr. Bowman's courtship of Alice except the last, which Aunt Polly was careful to communicate, with all the apologies she could make for her previous mistake of the matter, but which had not yet come to hand when Miss Maria Jones heard the particulars and read the letters. There it was, all in black and white—the frequent visits, the long walks, the pressures of the hand, the quiet chats—everything but the declaration, and Aunt Polly wrote as though that were a foregone conclusion, or already as good as made—yea, perhaps already made in so many words, only Alice had, may be, too much delicacy to speak of it at once, or, may be, Charles had requested her not to do so just yet as

---

* This shall appear hereafter, if I determine to publish more of Mr. Page's works.—JOHN CAPELSAY, *Exr.*

it would certainly meet with the approbation of all concerned.

Phew! Here were nuts for Miss Jones—nuts which should break Mr. Bowman's teeth! But she was careful not to appear too eager. She knew that she had a difficult game to play; first it would require some skill to get hold of the trumps; for Miss Young had a candidly outspoken hatred of meanness which must be blinded. Thank fortune, she had her blind side—and let the Misses Jones alone for always finding that!

"Oh, my goodness!" exclaimed Miss Maria, with acute horror depicted on every feature, "and just to think that your po-o-r friend and that dea-a-a-r innocent girl should be so deceived by such a monster!"

"I do not understand you, Miss Jones," said Miss Young, bridling up and glancing at her severely over her spectacles. "You will please explain yourself! I am not accustomed to hear my friends called poor, or to have them pitied."

"What!" exclaimed Miss Maria. "Dear Miss Young, have you not heard that this young man—oh, how could I be so deceived! how could I have been so blind! And that dear girl; it will break her fond, confiding heart, when she hears the dreadful news! and her poor mother who only lives in her happiness; her heart will be racked with torment! Oh, that I should live to find such wicked deceit in the world!" and the ingenuous and tender-hearted damsel buried her face in her handkerchief.

"What girl? What are you talking about, Miss Jones?" exclaimed Miss Annabella, leaning back in her rocking-chair. "Alice has no mother alive. What has the young man been doing? Be pleased to be more definite ma'am; you make me nervous!"

"Oh, Miss Young! do you not know what that young man has been doing? and that he is engaged to another? When I first spoke to you about his affair with Miss Alice I thought it was only an amusing jest. Little did I think that he could so deceive me, and that his playful flirtation with a giddy flirt could turn out to be a serious affair with a noble and true woman!"

"I'm getting out of patience, Miss Jones!" exclaimed Miss Young in some wrath. "Explain yourself! Has the young man been courting you? are you engaged to him at your time of life? Speak, ma'am, and tell me the truth!"

Now this was not a very pleasant mode or manner of address to Miss Maria, and at another time she would have resented it even from Miss Young, but now it had only the effect to quiet her agitation—just as a sudden tilt the other way to a bucket of water produces a calm in its waves—so with firm dignity she explained to Miss Young that Charles Bowman was engaged to Susan.

"Ah, Miss Young!" she exclaimed, going off again into sentiment, "I told you that I was the friend he consulted and who knew all his affairs of the heart, and that I took the greatest interest in his success; but I little thought I should hear such a tale as those letters have told!"

"I never would have shown you the letters if I hadn't thought you already knew all about it," said

Miss Young with a little sense of having been taken in; "but I'm glad I did so now. I believe in the cause of truth, ma'am. It must always triumph, however cunningly opposed!" (Some dear good persons *will* flatter their opinions in this way, and in spite of experience will deceive themselves in seven cases out of ten!) "I will go to Mrs. Garthwaite, and expose to her this whole affair; for though it should break her heart she shall never have to say that I voluntarily deceived her even by keeping silence."

"Oh, Miss Young, you are *so* just, and you will do *so* much good! Ah, what a triumph of truth for dear Susan to be thus delivered from the wiles and deceits of that unprincipled young man!" said the gratified Miss Jones.

"I'll go, you may depend upon it!" said Miss Young, rising from her chair with difficulty, and slowly straightening to her full height; "I'll order the gig and go now."

"Oh no, Miss Young, not now. It would be too great an exertion for you after the excitement of the morning, and after your long confinement to the house; and, more than that, do you not think it would be less cruel if I should first prepare their minds for the frightful disclosure?" said Miss Jones, who was anxious on several accounts that the old lady should not precipitate matters. She had to taste the sweets of her revenge in her own way. She must first take a private sip before she allowed Miss Young to come to the feast. And, besides, she had to determine upon her own course, for though she now had the trumps in her hand, she had to play against a wily and unprincipled adversary, who had as his backer one who was solely and wholly devoted to his interests, and she had as an ally only Mrs. Garthwaite, who, even if she won, would sorrow to see her daughter grieve, though for a fancied loss.

The matter required reflection, and Miss Maria was determined to have time for it; so, knowing Miss Young to be as true to time and promise as she was to everything else, she induced her to appoint noon the next day as the hour at which she should call at The Barn with the letters. By that time she said she would have the minds of the dear ones prepared for the damning proofs; and she went out to her carriage and ordered herself driven first through the town to price some goods, and then to The Barn.

Mr. Bowman was in the parlor with Susan and her mother when she arrived. Her manner towards him was frigid, but towards the two ladies tenderly compassionate. Mr. Bowman's attempts to thaw her were treated with a still more frozen disdain, until, at last, apparently worried into saying or doing something with regard to the important matter she was so deeply meditating, she got up to go, and, as she did so, remarked to Susan and Mrs. Garthwaite that she had a most terrible piece of news to communicate to them, and would call again at half-past eleven the next morning. "No," she answered to the entreaties not to keep them in suspense, "I shall be better prepared then to substantiate what I will say, and the matter will keep till then. Good-by, dear Susan! Good-by, Mrs. Garthwaite!" kissing them both with even unaccustomed fervency. "I presume I shall see you again,

Mr. Bowman!" making the gentleman a most stately courtesy, and passing out of the room and house.

Mr. Bowman had not much principle, but he had plenty of timidity, and felt that this treatment and these words boded him no good. Miss Jones was not one of those serpents (he began to picture her as a serpent) which threaten and do not strike. What did she mean? Had she got hold of that damned story about Alice Charlton? Suppose she had; what could she make out of it? Why, nothing at all. Where were her proofs? Alice was too much of a lady to give them; and even if she were not, what good could it do her to thwart him? Pshaw, Miss Jones was ridiculous.

But at the same time he was very uneasy. Nemesis was on his track; a foolish Nemesis, truly, but a very spiteful one; and he need expect no mercy. He must circumvent her if possible; his word was as good as hers. So, by means perfectly at his command, he brought the conversation, which had for awhile languished under the wonder excited by Miss Jones' words and conduct, to his own neighborhood, and to the young ladies and gentlemen there, to Dr. McCleod's family, and to Alice. He spoke of her as a remarkably intelligent young lady, and a great talker and rattle-brain, whose company he liked, because she was so lively: her popularity was very great, and he at one time thought that his brother Henry was much taken with her.

The truthful young man seemed for the moment to conceive the idea that it would perhaps be a capital stroke if he should substitute Henry in his place as the suitor of Alice; but it evidently would not suit; the proof was too easy; so he continued to say that he himself had paid her a great deal of attention in a brotherly way, as she was an orphan and had no brother, but was living there in that hermitage with old Dr. Mac; and he made Susan laugh with his description of old Dr. Mac's sayings and doings.

It was a lame story: the latter part of it did not suit the former; but what did he care? his hearer was not critical, and was easily amused. He had done what he intended; had anticipated the enemy; and if the fight should be upon that ground he had the first occupation, and could choose his positions as circumstances demanded.

Miss Maria's words had partially the effect she intended upon the young man—but their effect upon the ladies was no less discomforting. In spite of her apparent lightness of spirits, Susan had forebodings of unhappiness to come. To say the truth, Miss Jones' manner had been more vehement than she herself intended, and she fully appreciated it when she reflected upon it; but, as she said, "who could endure the cool insolence and hypocrisy of that young man without getting angry?" Susan feared, she did not know what, but was sure it had some reference to her lover. Mrs. Garthwaite also feared, but it was that the terrible news should bring unhappiness to her precious daughter. She wished with all her heart that the young man were away, that the match were broken off by any means; but then the distress and suffering of her daughter—she dreaded that.

Neither of the three reposed untroubled heads upon

their pillows that night (though Mr. Bowman tried a narcotic in the shape of ardent spirits), nor did Miss Jones fare any better. Her indignation, mingled with keen anticipation of pleasurable excitement the next day, kept her long awake. Miss Young, alone, of all the parties to the drama preserved an untroubled breast. Hers was the cause of Truth: and Truth was mighty and should prevail.

CHAPTER XXIX.

SHOWS HOW MR. BOWMAN WAS PUT UPON HIS DEFENCE, AND HOW HE DEFENDED HIMSELF AND WAS DISCOMFITED.

AN ordinary December day in our climate is a poor affair, considered as a winter day. It would do a little better if one could convince himself that it was March or April; but the children and negroes keep one reminded that Christmas is almost here. Generally when it is not raining the sun shines warmly, and even in the shade it is but pleasantly cool to a Southerner; to one just from a northern clime it is like summer. Sometimes we have very cold weather in this month; that is to say, ice forms as much as a half inch in thickness; but this is rarely the case. A few white frosts succeeded by several warm days, then rain, and frosts, and warm, dry weather again, are the common weather of December. This December (I remember it perfectly well) had been very pleasant. During the latter part of the previous month and early in this we had had two or three frosts, and some hard, cold winds from west of north, but then the weather seemed to be settled fair and warm.

It was a cloudless morning when Mr. Bowman rose from his couch, a more miserable man than when he had lain down upon it. The night had not brought refreshment. This may have been partly because he, who never drank to excess, he said, had stopped in town on his way to his aunt's and had taken divers and sundry cocktails and whisky punches, but it was principally owing to facts which he knew, and which he feared others also knew only too well—some of the facts in his history I have narrated. A vague uneasiness tormented his mind even when he first waked up; and when his ideas were a little more clear his impatient exclamation was "Damn the woman!" As he lazily arrayed himself that wish: Damn the woman! passed often through his mind, until when his head felt a little light from the exertion of pulling on his boots he changed it for once to "Damn the liquor!"

He was not in a pleasant humor here by himself. He always needed the charms of company to bring out his amiability, and on this particular occasion needed his breakfast and some strong coffee to establish even his ordinary equilibrium. His aunt and cousins noticed at the table that he seemed crusty and uncommunicative, and they imagined that his love business was not so prosperous as it had been; but they were careful to make no comment, for they knew his humors of old. After breakfast he sauntered out into the sunshine, went to the stable and saw that his horse was well curried, brushed, and fed over again, and that his saddle too, and bridle were thoroughly rubbed; about ten o'clock he sauntered down to the tavern, where he took a hearty drink of Jamaica rum, and came back to his aunt's feeling revived in the inner man and encouraged to look the troubles of the day boldly in the face.

He arrived at The Barn a little after eleven o'clock, and was, as usual, seated in the parlor with Susan when Miss Maria came in state—that is to say, with stately airs as though great affairs depended upon her. A very formal courtesy was vouchsafed to Mr. Bowman and a gentle kiss to Susan, and then she went out to find Mrs. Garthwaite, with whom she was closeted until just before the time for Miss Young's arrival, when both went into the parlor as though they were about to witness and engage in a solemn scene. Mr. Bowman felt that a crisis in his fate was approaching, and tried to despise his adversary; but the effort was vain. She could be despised, but perhaps the facts she brought to bear like so many heavy and light guns might prove irresistible. An ominous silence reigned for two or three minutes, made all the more ominous by the ticking of the great hall clock, the hands of which pointed to seven minutes to noon. Then Miss Maria Jones sent out her skirmishers, and the first dropping shot was heard in the front, followed by others more and more brisk, until the entry of Miss Young was the signal for the opening of the artillery and a general advance of the whole line. It came about something in this way:

"When did you hear from home, Mr. Bowman?" inquired Miss Maria with the greatest politeness.

"I think my aunt received a letter from my mother last week," replied Mr. Bowman.

"Really, you seem to be yourself a poor correspondent," said Miss Maria with a faint hysterical giggle, which was very alarming to her adversary and was altogether unaccountable to Susan.

"I am not so good as I ought to be about it, Miss Maria; and that's the fact," said Charles.

"Why, I should think that one who had so many tender ties to bind him to a neighborhood would like to hear from there more often," said Miss Jones, argumentatively and with gentle interest.

"I don't know that I have any cause to feel uneasiness about them; they are all healthy, and were well when I left home," said Mr. Bowman, evading the point.

"Was Miss Alice also well? though I suppose she was, or you would not have left her! It is curious to me, and to your friends, however, how you can bear to stay away so long from her without writing," said Miss Jones, still politely, but with signs of malice.

"What do you mean, Miss Maria Jones?" said Mr. Bowman, showing a little disposition to bluster.

"Oh, you needn't become alarmed, Mr. Bowman! So far as I know, the young lady is perfectly well. What I mean is that a lover is not usually contented to remain away so long from his lady-love without writing to her, or having her write to him, at least."

Susan had grown very pale, but until now had remained silent, not knowing the specific charge brought against her lover; but now she rose with all the dignity of protecting love, and demanded of Miss Jones to speak more plainly, and say all she had to say. Upon which, Miss Maria, without more ado, then and there, in so many words, announced that Mr. Charles Bowman had long been courting Miss Alice Charlton, and was then engaged to be married to her.

Susan did not faint or fly into a rage any more than did Alice when her trouble came upon her. She was hurt and angry, but was too just a woman to show anger against Miss Maria if she spoke the truth, or against Mr. Bowman, as she might speak falsely. She remained pale and patient, only now and then casting a glance of reproachful interrogation to her lover, who was preparing for an indignant denial and eloquent burst of passion when Miss Annabella Young was shown into the room, much to his temporary relief; for he supposed that the contest would end there for the time, and give him an opportunity to reconnoitre and perhaps parley a little. But much was his dismay when Miss Maria, instead of turning the conversation, saluted Miss Young, almost before she had taken her seat, with:

"I am just telling Mr. Bowman, Miss Young, that I am surprised that he should be contented to remain so long away from Miss Alice Charlton without hearing from her, and telling Miss Susan and her mother that he has long been courting that young lady."

"You told them the truth, Miss Maria," said Miss Young, in her most judicial manner. "I never saw the young man before since he was a child, but I have come, Mrs. Garthwaite, in obedience to the solemn dictates of my conscience, which will neither allow me to deceive nor to suffer another to be deceived when I can prevent it, to lay before you these letters, several of them of very recent date, received by me from my friend Miss Mary Hart, the aunt of Miss Alice Charlton. You will perceive by the post-marks, madam, that they are genuine, and not forgeries," partly holding up her open right hand, "and I am willing myself to take an oath, if you think it necessary, that they are in the handwriting of Miss Hart, who was my schoolmate, and with whom I have kept up a constant correspondence since our girlhood." And she handed the letters over to Mrs. Garthwaite.

"I give the letters to your charge," continued she, "that you may examine them at your leisure. You will find that they narrate the consecutive more striking events of a protracted courtship of Miss Charlton by Mr. Charles Bowman; and the last letters speak of an engagement between them, not declared, but understood, and only not openly spoken of. My friend, Miss Hart, is a woman of singular clearness of mind, and of most perfect sense of propriety, and I hold it to be equally impossible that she should either deceive herself or attempt to deceive me." And the old lady became silent and grim.

Mrs. Garthwaite was, as she appeared to be, in great trouble; her good sense, however, and natural indignation, made her calm and fully equal to the occasion.

"You will perceive, Mr. Bowman," said she, addressing the unfortunate Charles, "that it will be best for you to absent yourself, and to remain absent until we shall have had an opportunity to calmly investigate this most serious charge——"

"But won't you hear me a single word in my defence, ma'am? I deny everything that old Aunt Polly has said," and he cursed her in his heart for a chattering old fool. "She has had the meanest of motives in making this change against me——"

"She has made no charge against you, young man!" spoke up Miss Young. "Those letters were intended only for my eye, and she never dreamed when she wrote them that they should convict you of baseness."

"Mrs. Garthwaite!" exclaimed Mr. Bowman, "she doesn't know Aunt Polly so well as I do. The old woman loves Ben Eccles as if he were her own son, and would do anything to help him. She——"

"Hush, young man!" said Miss Young, "you only stultify yourself. I have heard something of Mr. Eccles' case, and know him to be as highly honorable as is my friend perfectly truthful and sincere. Many of these letters were written before, if I am rightly informed, you ever pretended to cast your eyes in love upon the young lady now present!"

"Mr. Bowman," said Mrs. Garthwaite, "there is no question here of anything but what you have done. You may rest assured that you shall have a fair and patient hearing if necessary, and if you are not guilty——"

"But, Susan!" exclaimed Mr. Bowman, interrupting her. "You don't think I am guilty, do you? You know that I told you all about this myself only yesterday!"

"Yes, mother," said Susan taking his part, "he did so! and I do not believe anything at all against him. I would not believe it if Miss Hart were herself here to declare it!"

"You had better go now, Mr. Bowman," said Mrs. Garthwaite decisively; "we will decide upon this case, and if it be necessary to hear any explanations from you we will call upon you for them. I am not so easily blinded as is my daughter; but you may be assured that you shall have justice!"

"I doubt," said Miss Young, as he was about leaving the room, "if the young man told Susan all that you will find in those letters. However, I have done my duty, and I wash my hands of the consequences. The truth is a precious help in all kinds of trouble, and to have told it is better than to have been crowned with all earthly blessings. I have told it, and am content; but I shall be able hereafter to add one more evidence of its perfection and power to my testimony."

"Yes, you can, Miss Young!" spoke up Miss Maria. "I never saw a more guilty face in my life. He would have stood me down that it was false if you hadn't come with those letters. He couldn't deny them. Ah-h-h! he's a convicted felon!"

"Miss Maria!" exclaimed Susan, indignant. "You shall not speak in that manner about Mr. Bowman in my presence! Please to remember where you are! and before whom you are talking!"

"Why, Susan, my dear," said Miss Jones deprecatingly. "I did not wish to hurt your feelings; but I do not see how you can have any good feeling for a man who has behaved so wickedly as he has."

"You are not the judge in this case, Miss Maria," replied Susan, still angry; "and even if you were you are not the only judge. I will judge for myself if you please, and when I find a difficulty I will refer to my mother for assistance." And the poor girl came near bursting into tears. Her heart was very full of its first woe; a woe which had disgrace attached to it; the disgrace of the man she loved. For she did love him; her heart was singularly captivated by him, and though she had not lost her power of judging, and would no doubt judge in strict accordance with what she saw to be justice and propriety, she was loth to judge; she dreaded to bring her lover to the bar; it was humiliating to do so; and then—it might be dangerous. If he were convicted, what should she do! All was blank to her after that if it should indeed be the result; a dark blank of wretchedness.

It is not my intention to draw a disadvantageous parallel to either of them between Susan and Alice, for I most heartily admired and loved them both; but I may permit myself to say that had their positions been reversed the result to them would have been different. This sounds very much like saying just nothing at all, but what I mean is that if Susan had been in the place of Alice she would have suffered vastly more than Alice did, and that if Alice had been in Susan's place she would have suffered less than did Susan—but that also sounds like a truism—or worse. I must be getting stupid. I wonder if it is not because I am averse to telling the whole truth and saying that my favorite Alice had a more evenly-balanced mind, and though just as strong, more equable affections, than my favorite Susan? I believe that to have been the fact; and yet how very perfect were both women! how lovely, and pure, and great-souled! It seems to me to be almost hypercritical to attempt to find a defect in either of them. I declare that there was no defect in either! They only slightly differed in their excellencies. The two purest gems that ever mortal eyes beheld were not exactly alike, though each were perfect and priceless!

I know a number of gems as perfect as they. Their daughters were almost as perfect, and there is living not very far away one of Alice's granddaughters in whom are combined all the beauties and perfections of both my favorites. Aye, young men, whoever of you may survive this conflict, when you come home you shall have no difficulty in selecting wives and mothers for heroes! The girls who are now at home sewing for you, and going half starved that you may have some food, and poorly clad that you may not go naked, who are praying for you, and glorying in you, are fit mates for you, heroes as ye are. They are not all so beautiful, or so rich, or so elegant in education and manner as were my dear pets, but many, very many of them are just as true and great-souled and lovely.

But, to return to my little Drama; Miss Young soon took her departure, followed by Miss Jones, and mother and daughter were left to themselves. I need not follow Mr. Bowman, whose heat of temper of the morning was but as cream-tarts to his rage of the afternoon—fire mingled with hail; for he shivered for his chances. Let him go, and let us see how the only parties to be pitied passed their time.

By a natural instinct each first sought the solitude of her own chamber, and when there each by a natural instinct as well as an enlightened instruction and a humble heart went upon her knees to implore aid and wisdom from Him who "giveth and upbraideth not." Susan sought aid with tears of deep grief and helplessness; her mother sought wisdom with many a sigh: and when each arose she set with firm determination —Susan, to examine the past and her heart and conduct; her mother, to read the letters and collate the facts stated in them. At last a gentle knock at the door roused Susan from her meditations, and her mother entered with a calm, sad face, and approached and kissed her, saying:

"My poor daughter, I fear it is too true!"

"Do not say that, my darling mother!" exclaimed the poor girl, turning still paler, and throwing her arms about her mother as though for mercy and protection. "Do not say that! There must be some mistake! I'm sure there is!"

"There can be no mistake, my dear," said her mother, handing her one of the letters. "Read that, and then read this, and this," handing her two others.

When Susan had read them, she looked up with woe in her face. There could be no mistake if the letters were true, and it was impossible to doubt their sincerity, at least.

"Now read this last, my daughter," said Mrs. Garthwaite, handing her the letter which spoke of the engagement.

"Oh, mother!" exclaimed Susan, after she had read it, "this does not say that they are engaged! It only supposes that they may be so now, or may be so, or may declare it soon. Indeed, mother, you are too hasty. It may all be explained. Remember what he said about Miss Hart and Mr. Eccles!"

"I do remember it, my dear," answered the mother, "and must acknowledge that it shocked me to hear him unblushingly utter a thing so shamefully false. Most of these letters, indeed all but the very last, are dated before Miss Hart could have possibly heard that Mr. Bowman was paying you any attention; and I regret very much that Mr. Bowman should have attempted to cast such a slur upon either Miss Hart or Mr. Eccles. Even if he were perfectly innocent it was a reckless accusation, but it is to me sure proof that he is not innocent."

"But, mother, may not Miss Hart be mistaken?" asked Susan. "He told me that Miss Alice was very lonely and very amusing, and that he had visited her very often, and may not her aunt have mistaken the object of his visits? Be just, mother, and do not condemn without absolute proof."

"I will not, my dear," answered her mother. "God knows that your happiness is all that I have lived for these many years in which you have been my only happiness; but I do not see how Miss Hart can be mistaken. I do not say that there is sufficient evidence of the engagement, but there certainly is of the courtship; and in his situation, that unexplained, is about as bad as though he were actually engaged. But we will find out all about it now that we are on the track. In the mean time, my dear, I think it best that you should have no communication with Mr. Bowman.

Three or four days will be sufficient to decide the matter, and if he will deceive one he will another in the same way. Admit no interview or communication with him until we shall have heard further. Don't you think this will be the wisest course?"

"Certainly, if you think so, mother; but I am very wretched!" said the poor girl, burying her face in the side of her bed, beside which she was sitting.

"Remember, my child," said the gentle mother, "that you have One to whom you can plead for assistance and comfort, and not plead in vain, although it may be long before the comfort come. You may have a duty to perform, my love, which will require all your fortitude aided by your faith; but recollect that it is your duty because it is for the best."

And with that she went to her own room, where she instantly engaged herself in writing a letter to Aunt Polly, which she then sent by a special messenger, her own carriage driver, Charley, to wit, that same afternoon. Here is the letter; for in my varied relations as friend and lawyer with all the personages of my story, I am not at a loss for the original materials of my narrative:

"MY DEAR MADAM,—You will pardon me for asking answers to a few questions which are of such *great importance* to me that I am not justified in taking another and more roundabout course for discovering the truth. Although it is a *most delicate* matter, I feel well assured that I can trust to *your* prudence and good heart in making a short explanation. Mr. Charles G. V. Bowman has been addressing my daughter, and as a certain rumor has come to our ears it is impossible for her to decide upon the answer she shall give to his suit until she shall learn exactly its truth or falsity. Being put in possession of these facts, dear madam, you will appreciate the propriety of the questions, and the *very great* importance of their being answered *at once.* The questions are these:

"First: Has Mr. Bowman, *at any time,* paid his addresses to your niece, Miss Alice Charlton, *with the ostensible object* of marrying her?

"Second: Has your niece *accepted* him? or, if not, has she *refused* him? or has she a proposition from him *still under consideration?*

"An *early answer* to this will greatly oblige

"Very respectfully,

"Your obedient servant,

"ANNE GARTHWAITE.

"THE BARN, Dec. 16th, 18—."

It will be seen from this letter that though Mrs. Garthwaite had the woman's habit of underscoring her words, she was not one of those who put the object of their letters in a postscript. She had been so long a real business woman that she fully appreciated the importance of clearness and directness; and, besides, it was her natural disposition to go straight to the merits of what she had to communicate or discuss.

And so the momentous day wore through! A great deal of rage, a great deal of anxiety, a good deal of whisky, and a vast deal of conscious meanness on the part of Mr. Bowman; a great deal of wretchedness mingled with a great deal of love, some hope, and a few spasms of natural womanly indignation with Susan; a fair share of sorrow and annoyance, and a mighty deal of cool, calm determination with Mrs. Garthwaite; a strange conglomeration of gratified malice, wounded pride, virtuous indignation, and uneasy cunning on the part of Miss Maria Jones; and, lastly, a calm reliance on the perfection, and almost miraculous ubiquity and interposition of truth on the part of Miss Annabella Young.

Who was in the right?

CHAPTER XXX.

WHAT MR. BOWMAN THOUGHT AND HOW HE CONDUCTED HIMSELF; AND HOW HE AND MR. ECCLES TOOK A SHORT RIDE TOGETHER.

BY the middle of the next day Mr. Bowman found himself sufficiently composed to determine what he should do, and at about three o'clock in the afternoon Susan received a note from him imploring her to see him; only to grant him a few short moments to plead his cause to her, and show how he had been maligned. For he protested upon his sacred word of honor that the whole story was false; that he never in his life had loved any one but her; and that the story of his having loved Alice Charlton, a girl so inferior in every respect, was an absurdity of which no one who knew him could think him capable.

Now I submit it to the reader who understands

human nature, was not that last assertion just fit for a small creature of the Charley Bowman caliber? He could not strive to justify himself without trying to belittle the woman whom it was his greatest honor to have loved—even in his mean way. His attempt at justification was a lie, and he had to tell another to make it symmetrical to himself, who knew all the facts.

Susan, who knew none of the facts, found her heart entirely inclined to believe him; and would have liked nothing better than to hear him plead his cause and assert his perfect love; but she showed the note to her mother, who had, indeed, been expecting such a one all the day. After consultation it was concluded that it was best Mrs. Garthwaite should answer it, and accordingly she soon prepared a reply, and sent it by the messenger, who was waiting for it.

Of course Mr. Bowman was not pleased when he read it, and particularly when he saw by whom it was signed. "Damn her old soul!" was his mental exclamation as he crushed it in his hand after reading it, and turned upon his heel from the messenger. "I might have known she would meddle in the business. She's cool enough, anyhow; and if I have to deal with her in the affair, I'll have made a mess of it, for she don't care a damn for me and doesn't like me. I've known that all the time, damn her!"

The reader must pardon my repetition, here and elsewhere, of Mr. Bowman's language. I have maturely reflected upon the propriety of giving *verbatim* the oaths and other profanities of the characters which a writer has to describe, and have come to the conclusion that where those objectionable expressions are necessary to show the exact character and disposition, they are perfectly allowable; and, in fact, that it is part of his duty to give them. What a mystically over-nice painter he should be who completed a picture of a country cattle-yard swept clean!

Mrs. Garthwaite's reply was as follows:

"SIR,—My daughter has received your note of this date, and has requested me to reply to it. She thinks with me that she must for the present decline your request for an interview. If at any future time she should desire it she will either directly or through me make you aware of the fact. She can, just now, assign no time when it is probable an interview will be productive of any good.

"Respectfully, etc.,

"ANNE GARTHWAITE.

"THE BARN, Dec. 17th, 18—."

Certainly Mr. Bowman could not glean much encouragement from anything in that note. It seemed to cut off all hope; for what could further inquiries produce but perfect conviction? and he know that Mrs. Garthwaite was not a woman who would stop short of the whole truth in her investigation. That infernal Alice Charlton! and that doubly infernal old aunt of hers! how they would gloat over his discomfiture! how they would glory in exaggerating all he had said and done! He admitted that it was perfectly natural they should do so, for he felt that such would be his conduct in similar circumstances. Oh, yes, confound them! if that precious niece could not get him and his acres, fine house, and negroes, no one else should have him and them! He'd ruin her! Yes, by George, he'd ruin her for it! She shouldn't have enough character to get the meanest man for a husband, hang her! (Of course *he* didn't content himself with such words as Confound, Hang, and the rest.) He'd blast her reputation, by George! He'd court her, sure enough, for revenge, and she was what's-its-named fool enough to take the bait. Oh, yes! she'd be mighty glad of the chance; and then he'd leave her—for reasons; and he'd let his reasons be known.

"Oh, pshaw!" he exclaimed to himself in a moment of reflection in his vain rage. "I couldn't do that if I tried, for no one would believe me, and I'd have some damned fool taking up her cause; and besides that, I'm not sure she'd have me; for she's a damned singular girl anyhow, and has plenty of pluck, damn her, to kick me to the devil if she got mad!" Then he lapsed into thought again: "But what a shame it is that I should be euchred in this way, and that too when I held almost a point certain! They can't prove anything, hang them, no matter how hard they try! Am I the first young man who has ever paid particular attentions to a young lady, as a friend? There's the misery of this damned country! you can't go to see a girl twice but that there's talk about it, and if you go three times and don't pop the question, why, damn it, you've got either to explain or to fight, if she's got a brother or a father who is able to fight. It's a wonder to me old Mac hasn't been at me before now. *He'll* come next, for my luck's down on me, and I could be beat if I had four kings and an ace. I know where my mistake was. It was in stirring up that infernal little viper, Jones.

Confound her ugly picture, she had to stick her long nose into it, and she's got as keen a scent as the best hound in the county, hang her! Yes, and when the scent is too cold she'll run by sign. She beats the dogs, by jings!" and he laughed a grim laugh at his conceit; "I wish I had a hound like her, hang her! I'd cut her throat for being too infernally smart. What a confounded fool I was to make the little thing mad! I might have known she would do her best to hurt me. If I had really done anything wrong I shouldn't mind it. If I had really been engaged and broken it off as they say, I shouldn't wonder at their getting their backs up. But I didn't do anything of the sort. Very clear of it. Hang it all! what's the use of my staying here any longer! I'll go off home and let the thing settle itself, as they won't let me settle it. I wonder if the old woman won't go down herself and see Aunt Polly? Phew! what a time they'll have when they get their heads together! and old Mac 'll pray that they may all be delivered from the snares of the Evil One—meaning me, and be blessed to him! And then there's that blasted Ben Eccles! He'll be as pleased as a monkey with the scratches," etc

Such were some of the thoughts which passed through the mind of Mr. Charles Bowman in the solitude of his room after reading Mrs. Garthwaite's note. If any one think that I have exaggerated them, or have made him out a very demon instead of a young man of only ordinary wickedness, he is mistaken. I have neither exaggerated, nor was he, for all that, any worse than tens of thousands of the narrow-souled, selfish, sensual, and lively young men who may be found in all enlightened countries—that is, all countries in which manners and desires do not always agree. They occupy high social positions very frequently; in fact they always do, or aspire to do, so. He is one of a class, and I have tried to paint him faithfully for the benefit and encouragement of his fellows. I have known a good many of them, as clever, social, frank, boisterous, young gentlemen as ever lived; rich too, or at any rate belonging to rich families, or trying to belong to them; but my experience and observation have been that they were as empty of all real good as apples of Sodom.

However, although I have shown a little of the heart of Mr. Bowman, we are now more concerned about his actions and fortunes, and I must confine myself to them. What does the world care for a man's inner life if his outward conduct be correct or amusing! And, fortunately, the world is right—far be it from me to teach otherwise! I should dislike for the world to know all my thoughts, feelings, and imaginations about even the most beautiful, innocent, and perfectly holy of earthly or of heavenly things. I should shrink from its concerning itself about much of my past conduct, though of no importance to it. And yet I am an old man, whose character is irreproachable. I say it boldly and with some pride, that I defy any human being, living or dead, to charge me truthfully with any meanness or dishonorable act, open or secret. When I say "dishonorable act," I mean, of course, dishonorable in a worldly sense; for, alas! I could not make such a boast before my Maker. No, I never in my life have done a mean thing; never oppressed the poor, if I knew it; never defrauded rich, or poor, or the public, of money or duty. Though my grand-niece may hereafter think she can contradict this assertion, I defy her to prove to any sensible person that I was under the slightest natural or legal obligation to leave her my property! She is none of my begetting, thank Heaven! On the contrary, she is my sister's daughter's child, begotten in lawful wedlock and with precious little of my blood in her to judge from her conduct, which is virtuous, and damnable. The virtue of some persons has a sort of hell-fire tinge about it which is to me very uncomfortable; or else it is of the thumb-screw, Procrustean, ice-ribbed sort which——

But never mind that. This is not exactly the time and place to be pleading my private woes; nor, indeed, my outward virtues; except by way of illustration; and having sufficiently done that, let me pass on to my main subject. When I write my own life I will tell all the whys and wherefores about my grand-niece.*

Mr. Bowman, then, was no demon, although his thoughts were mean, and one or two of them were diabolical. I suspect that these last were the effects of excitement, for I have not the least idea that he would have cut his hound's throat any sooner than he would Miss Jones', or that he would have injured Alice as he threatened, even if he had had the opportunity. He could imagine such a thing—was mean enough to imagine such a thing—but, had it come to

---

* Mr. Page's own life has already been published by the publishers of this book.—JOHN CAPELSAY, *Exr.*

the trial, would have had neither the courage nor the abandoned villainy to have put it into execution. A pure and dignified woman has an influence over the Charley Bowmans of the world, which is a powerful shield against their malignant imaginations. And, besides that, it was impossible in the very nature of things that his heart once touched, though ever so slightly, by the celestial fire of love, as I have said that I believed his was by Alice Charlton's noble qualities and beauty, could ever wholly lose its genial glow. It might cool, and become covered with ashes and cold cinders, but a little warmth should still remain; a little tenderness, to change the figure, which could never become callous.

His resolution to leave Yatton and go home turned out, like many other hasty ideas, no resolution at all. In the first place, the solitude of the country would have been utterly distasteful to him, and he was one of those who did not think it gentlemanly to drink by himself. But in the second, and principal place, in the midst of all his misery he had a faint hope that everything should come out right; that is, in his favor. He felt sure that he had had a powerful hold on Susan's affections, or rather, that her affections had taken a powerful hold on him, miserable stick that he was (that is my comment, not his), and that there was a chance that she still clung to him. If so, he had a most to-be-hoped-of ally, and it would not do to be out of the way if anything should turn up.

So at his usual hour for a late afternoon visit he got upon his horse and took the road to The Barn. He had no more intention of actually going to the house than you or I have of sticking our head into the fire; but he thought he could serve two purposes. He might chance to see Susan walking or driving about the neighborhood, and though he would not accost her, what a reminder it should be to her to see him riding about her vicinage disconsolate, as though his body must come and wander with his soul! It would, certainly, be a great satisfaction to him to see her, but it would be a greater help to him that she should see him, and if it should so happen that to speak to her was almost unavoidable, he would speak, and if she were alone he could say more in a few minutes to restore himself to favor than all the mothers and vipers in the world could do in a month to put him out of favor. But, at any rate, if the ride had no such result as this, it would serve, secondly, to blind the public eye as to what was going on; and he would go before it as he usually did—and come home after dark by a back way.

A cunning young gentleman was Master Bowman; and, on this occasion, fate was so propitious as to throw another result in his way, which, though it vexed him greatly at the time, afterwards afforded him much secret satisfaction. He had hardly left the outskirts of the town when he was overtaken by Ben Eccles, also on horseback. Though they had never been cordial friends, there never had been any open enmity between them, and there was, therefore, no reason why they should not salute each other and ride along together as far as their roads should be the same. Neither was in a mood for amusing chat; for Ben's morbid conscience and morbid love were both combating with the demon jealousy. He did not like the frequent visits his friend Charles was making, he heard, to The Barn. He did not think that the young man stood much chance with either Susan or her mother, for he was a notorious liar and braggadocio, if he was rich and gay; and he knew that they preferred truth and courage to wealth and gayety.

He was not certain whether Susan knew the subject so well as he did, and those who lived about Rosstown. She must know it, he thought, and if she did not, was it not his duty to tell her? He was just as far removed from the possibility of doing a mean or officious act as was his friend, Dr. Sam; but it is somewhat singular that both men should have had the same suggestion of duty. Both, however, knew that though it is a capital suggestion, and rarely erroneous when it is about something which concerns only one's self, it may be very suspicious when it relates to some one else, and particularly in such a case as this. The baser temptations of self-interest would more than counterbalance the idea of disinterested probity in the minds both of the lady and of others who heard of it. Might this not be with good reason? At any rate, it was too serious a matter for their own sakes to be undertaken rashly; for while it would have the appearance of raising Mr. Bowman to the importance of a bugaboo to themselves, it might also augment his importance to the lady, and lessen their own chances. All this reasoning did not pass through Ben's head; for when a proposition presented itself he did not always stop to investigate it thoroughly if it looked uninviting; and this looked shabby at the first glance. He would lay it aside to be thought over if there were more occasion than there appeared to him now to be. Mr. Bowman was nothing to him, and could be nothing to her—and yet he did not like his visits; he did not like his becoming acquainted with Susan at the barbecue, and could not imagine what encouragement he could receive that he should go on visiting there—but the impudence of some men was past comprehension!

And so they jogged on, scarcely speaking, each occupied with his own thoughts. We know pretty well what Mr. Bowman's must have been upon the grand subject, and can guess that he was mentally cursing his fate that this dear fool should come poking out there that evening, and planning how he should get out of the scrape gracefully. When they arrived at the lane which turned to the right, about half a mile from The Barn, and led over to Miss Jones' aunt's house, Mr. Bowman checked up and turned his horse's head towards it, saying:

"Well, good-by Ben. I take this road."

"Why, I thought that you were going on to The Barn?"

"No," answered Charles a little crustily; "I am not going there this evening; I have another engagement. Good-by," and he rode off.

Ben felt greatly encouraged. His heart was lightened by the loss of a companion with whom he had so little sympathy, and who gave him so much actual cause for pain. He thought that it was a mistake that Charley's rides in this direction were to The Barn, and reproached himself for his uncharitable idea of exposing the young man's faults to others. It had been a sinful design—for as he had conceived it, was it not a design? And he took off his hat and mentally asked pardon of God for his sin.

Poor fellow! let me not again intrude either upon the patience of the reader, or the more tender feelings of my own heart by describing more than is necessary of his mental malady. Brave, courteous, magnanimous gentleman that he was, it has made my heart ache to have to tell of his unfortunate condition, and show him in positions in which the heartless and ignorant who knew him and the heartless and ignorant who read about him, thought and shall think him ridiculous. Alas, his life had had little sunshine upon it though its way had been generally smooth enough. We speak of physical blessings, kindly associates, and wealth as the most important things for man, and yet a mental cloud or a peculiarity of nervous organization shall make them all worthless, or a burden. Equability of mind is worth them all, and he who has it can bear with resignation, at least, if not with cheerfulness, the absence or loss of wealth, station, friends, or health. From his childhood Ben lacked this placid equability; and when the cloud came the fleeting moments which before were bright became gloomy. A jealous, all-seeing Eye was upon him at all times, and towards it he would often look askance, and with a start drop the pleasure in his grasp; and never was he without the consciousness that every thought, word, and deed was narrowly scanned and necessarily found defective or impure.

But though he was in this wretched state he felt that God was good. He knew He was good; in his pangs of thought he would shout out that He was good; and yet His holiness and justice so overshadowed His goodness that its blessings became painful, and the sources of more and more sin and misery. How could he enjoy the goodness of a holy and just God? Ah, this is a question which has puzzled and tormented many, and wiser men than he!

On the present occasion, after he had penitentially recalled his sinful design, another unreasoning pang of conscience came upon him, and he went like a criminal at large to seek a moment's rest and pleasure, if haply he might find it, and as he neared the house his heart hardened itself as though he would seek it in defiance of the Power which was frowning upon him. The ladies begged to be excused, and he rode back home feeling that it was a providential arrangement to punish him.

It will be perceived that his malady had grown greatly upon him—that he had, in fact, become crazy. True, it was only monomania, but it was a monomania which found excitement on every hand, and would not suffer him to rest. He was as affable as ever, had as much knowledge, and as much keen perception and clear method in business as ever, but at every turn his Enemy met him—an Enemy to be dreaded, and not to be avoided do what he should.

Fortunately—and I hasten to say this for my own relief—there shall be but one or two more occasions to portray his wretchedness, and I feel like hastening on that they may be done with; but I will not anticipate events. Although he is the subject of my writing, there are other persons in whom I take a great interest and whose conduct is so connected with his that it must be portrayed in order that his may be fully understood.

CHAPTER XXXI.

EXPLAINS A POINT NECESSARY TO BE UNDERSTOOD NOW, AND WHICH SHALL HEREAFTER BE MORE NECESSARY.

ALTHOUGH to give the reasons why of something which has gone before is rather an awkward commencement of a chapter—as though that which should before have been last were here placed first—I find it the most convenient place to explain how it came that Ben Eccles and others were ignorant of what had taken place at The Barn; both the engagement and its interruption. It is the most convenient place because that ignorance was the prelude to other events, not yet related, which took place, and were in a great measure dependent upon it, and because I could not tell it before without interrupting my narrative.

I think that I have heretofore remarked that Mrs. Garthwaite was a very prudent woman, and that her daughter much resembled her. They were not only prudent themselves, but, by a natural influence which every one must have observed, all who were accustomed to be about them were more than ordinarily prudent. A gossiping, tattling husband will make a gossiping, tattling wife, children, and servants; and though the same qualities in a wife will not always infect upwards to the husband, if he have the proper spirit he will always by judicious severity be able to repress it and establish prudence in its place. A wife may deprive a husband of his good sense by making him wretched, but not by example. I am not one of those who believe that a bad or foolish wife makes a bad or foolish husband. If the husband be wise and good, the wife shall be the same, or, at least, will keep her wickedness and folly in check.

Example and firmness are great regulators, and Mrs. Garthwaite was a model in respect of prudence; prudence in speech and in behavior. Her servants never tattled to her—as Mrs. Ruggles had taught her servants to do—and had almost lost the faculty of tattling to each other. Hardly one of them had ever been found guilty of confiding to strangers the private and domestic affairs of the family, their intentions and opinions. In every case conviction had been followed by expulsion to the negro quarter and the field, besides other condign punishment. Mrs. Garthwaite had too much just pride to wish her affairs made the subject of general talk, or to desire to hear of the affairs of others; and her servants had become infused with the same pride.

Now Miss Jones, though she would have scorned to think herself the humble companion of Mrs Garthwaite and Susan, and would have been indignant had any one intimated such a thing to her, really had a great many of the traits of an humble companion. In the shade of their authority she was vastly independent towards others, but very dependent towards them—in other words, she was obsequious; towards what pleased them she, knowingly, manifested no displeasure, and what displeased them she never defended. She was, therefore, perforce, prudent in speech and behavior so far as their affairs were concerned; and though, I suspect, she was never formally told of Susan's engagement, but knew it by putting this and that together, as she had a fair talent for doing, she never breathed it until, for a purpose, she told Miss Young.

Miss Young had, so far, had no opportunity of making it widely known, even if, with her love of truth, she had wished to do so. But her love of truth was not characterized by the missionary spirit. It was conservative.

The aunt and cousins said nothing about it because they knew nothing for a certainty, and feared, by talking, to ruin Charley's chances for so splendid a match.

Therefore, as these were all the parties who knew, or were likely to know the facts, the public and Ben Eccles were left to guess—and they had an uncertain subject to guess about, whether they took love or Charley Bowman as the subject. Ben was too much of a without-fear-and-without-reproach gentleman to guess or inquire about the matter, even if he had not had other subjects to occupy his mind; and although he had suspected and regretted the young man's course as a piece of presumption which must lead to mortification, he had not the remotest idea of the real situation of affairs.

And now that I have given the reasons of some things which have gone before, and of some others which are yet to come, I have concluded that it is best to proceed by a new chapter, in which I can really begin at the beginning.

CHAPTER XXXII.

MISS ANNABELLA YOUNG PAYS ANOTHER VISIT TO THE BARN IN THE CAUSE OF TRUTH, AND TRUTH TRIUMPHS AT LAST.

MRS. GARTHWAITE'S messenger got lost. Dark came on when had got about eighteen miles from home, and he turned off at the wrong road. About ten o'clock, after wandering about from plantation to plantation, becoming more and more bewildered, he concluded to stop for the night at a quarter where he was offered hospitality, and found upon inquiry that he was still some twelve miles from his destination. It was between eight and nine o'clock the next morning when he arrived at Dr. McCleod's, and Miss Polly and her niece had left an hour before for Rosstown, upon a shopping expedition.

There was nothing to be done but to wait until their return that evening, for he had been charged to deliver the letter into Miss Polly's own hand and to wait for an answer, with which he was to return with all convenient speed. As Mrs. Garthwaite never manifested over-anxiety, the messenger felt himself at liberty to consult his own convenience, and was therefore well content to remain in such pleasant quarters.

Now, Aunt Polly had gone not only to shop, but also to put in the post-office a letter to her friend, Miss Annabella Young, which she had prepared with much secrecy and pains. It contained a delicate and embarrassing matter—nothing less than the recantation of her foolish mistake about Charley Bowman and her niece; and if any one can find a more embarrassing task than that of acknowledging in a graceful and dignified manner that he or she has heretofore been a fool in a very important and delicate affair, I would like to hear of it. At any rate, it embarrassed dear Aunt Polly; and to such a degree did she feel it that for the first (and last) time she acted secretly, and, as she felt, disingenuously towards her niece. Heretofore she had written and sent her letters boldly, without the slightest thought or fear that their contents should be questioned, and she was much relieved when she had taken a favorable opportunity, while her niece was engaged in the store next to the post-office, to step out of the door, and slyly slip the wretched burden into the post-office box. And it was a still greater relief when, about an hour after, she heard the stage horn and saw the Yatton stage dash gallantly down the street to the post-office door, and bear it away to its destination.

The next morning the important missive was duly delivered to Miss Young, and great was the hubbub it stirred up in the old lady's mind. Indignation was at first the uppermost feeling; and then regret, and a vehement desire to right herself and set the matter right, displaced it. At first her faith in truth was a little staggered; but upon reflection she found the virtue to be positively miraculous in its workings. Why, who would ever have dreamed that here in the very nick of time a letter like this should arrive to remove unmerited blame, and make smooth the course of true love! It was wonderful! The other truth was only a mistake, but here was the genuine article at last; and its triumph should be perfect and lasting!

What a precious set of simpletons we are, to be sure! Miss Annabella was only a type of most of us. We divide truth up into morsels and boast of their magnitude and perfection, and then when other fractions of truth or whole falsehoods are pressed upon us with sincerity, we accept them and suffer our first impressions to fade, or violently rub them out—particularly if they be a little ugly.

There was a bustle in the old lady's household at once. John, the hostler and driver, was sent for, interrogated, and instructed.

"Well, John," said Miss Young, in her slow, precise manner, as the black Phœbus came into the room making more noise with his creaking shoes by trying to step lightly on his toes than he should have done by tramping, "well, John, how are you this morning? and how is Dolly?"

"We's all well, mistuss."

"Have you fed the horse this morning, John?"

"Yes, ma'am; long time ago. I allers feeds him 'fore I eats myself," answered the black rascal, who had that morning bantered a neighbor's hostler for a quarter-race in which he was confident his gig horse should win, and had consequently given the steed an extra allowance with a whole pumpkin thrown in.

"It seems to me that he looks very rough. Are you sure you curry him morning and evening?"

"He been had the lampers, ma'am, but I got ole Joe

to burn 'em out las' week, an' he smoove enough now, ma'am."

"Burn my horse! What do you mean, sir?" exclaimed his mistress, changing her tone to one more energetic. "You get old Joe to burn my horse?"

"Lor', mistuss, you dunno? Why, dey likes it! Dey gums eatches 'em so dat nuffin else can't tetch 'em! I allers has 'em burnt out. Nuffin else won't cure 'em. I done try everything."

"You say that he is well now?"

"Yes, ma'am."

"Have you cleaned my harness well?"

"Yes, um!"

"And brushed out my gig?"

"Yes, um!"

"Are my cushions there?"

"Yes, um!"

"And my whip?"

"Dey all dar, ma'am."

"Well go and get the gig ready, and brush it out again, and dress yourself, and be around at the door as soon as you can."

"Yes, ma'am, I hurry," said the black, going out.

"Do you hear, John? brush my gig out again!"

"*Yes*, ma'am!"

"And turn my cushions over!"

"Yes, ma'am!"

"And dress yourself neatly!"

"Yes, *ma'am.*"

"And"—pausing to reflect—"there's nothing else. You may go."

In due time the gig was around at the front door,

and Miss Young prepared to take her high seat by the side of John, who was dressed in his best.

"Have you examined my springs, John?"

"Yes, ma'am."

"And are they all right? And have you looked at my axle-trees?"

"Yes, ma'am. I seed to it all!"

"When did you grease my gig?"

"Yeste'day, ma'am; an', mistuss, we mus' git some mo' grease. Dubbin's the bes' dey tells me."

"Why, sir, where is all that dubbing you got only last month?"

"Oh, its done used up, ma'am. Dis gig takes a mighty heap o' greasin'!" said the scamp, who had soaked his own shoes and boots and his wife's, and those of some of his chums with the dubbing, which was common property.

"Very well, get some more and take better care of it. Come to me when we return, and get the money. What does it cost?"

"Oh, I reckon a dollar's wuff 'll be enough, ma'am!"

"Very well. Are you ready?"

And after all her interrogations and preparations were concluded, because she could think of no more, she mounted the chair which had been brought out and placed there by her house-woman, and slowly ascended to her place, and was driven off. The house-woman lingered for a few minutes, with her hand on the chair, to chat with a passing neighbor, and then went in and slammed the door, and Miss Young's house was quiet, while her feeble body was being swayed and jolted and her righteous soul was plunged in regret and eager to right herself and the truth. Old Mr. Jackson, who forty-five years before had been one of her admirers, took off his hat to her as she passed him on the street, and remarked to himself that she was showing her age. A little farther down Mr. Jackson's youngest blooming daughter looked from her window and was glad in her heart that she was not such an old fright, and Mrs. Jackson herself, and young Popkins, who were sitting near, echoed the sentiment—that is, if sentiment can echo, which I doubt, though speakers and newspaper men continually repeat the phrase.

It was about noon when the old lady arrived at The Barn. The house was silent, and except for the chickens which were heard from the back yard, seemed deserted. After giving her man particular directions, as that he must keep by the gig, and how he must conduct himself otherwise during her absence—which he took good care to hear and disobey; for she was no sooner fairly in the house than he was back at the kitchen—she went up the steps, knocked at the door with the handle of her large parasol, and was admitted.

There are all sorts of angels, and I suppose that every messenger of good news is an angel for the nonce. Miss Young was certainly an angel to Miss Susan for this day—she ever after respected her as "a well-meaning old woman." It would be entirely out of the question for me to delay to describe the slow and precise manner of the old lady, the very many explanations and comments she gave, and the whole matter and manner of her communication, when the result was so exciting to the principal party concerned. She never paused to remark those things, nor will I. I am getting too old to waste my time in minutiæ when I can avoid them by a few outlines, and I have too many sketches to make. Some writers can fill up two or three volumes with the events of a week in a love affair. It would be too much trouble to go to my library to see how many reigns Tacitus has perfectly described in the same volume of words.

Of course, as the necessary result of this triumph of truth, the poor, forsaken, maligned hero of the hour had to be sent for forthwith. Susan, with love and joy, penitence and righteous indignation in her heart, could not rest until she had expressed it all to him. Even Miss Maria, had she been there, would have participated in the prevailing sentiment, and have wished to hurry up the scene of her own penitence and forgiveness. But she was not there. Her Susan had looked upon her with a cold eye, which sorely grieved her sense of gratitude—if there be such a sense; my observation is that all have it objectively and very few subjectively (another time I can use those wretched words; and I would not swear that I have used them rightly). Mrs. Garthwaite's countenance was not sufficient solace. *That* was only turned towards her justice and intelligence; whereas it was her tenderer feelings which had been moved, and which required recognition. She was therefore not present to have her share in the triumph of truth, which, in truth, proved to be the cause of her final downfall in the affections of her sweet friend, who, though she afterwards looked approvingly upon her act, could never forget the spirit with which it was done.

Good Miss Young was also eager to see the reconciliation, or, rather to right herself and her cause in the eyes of the Victim of Mistake. But Mrs. Garthwaite had no such feeling. She was gratified that her daughter had not been deceived; but was sorry that the match was not broken off. It was a sore disappointment; but she was too wise to show it. There was yet a chance; she did not know what it was, but as they were not yet married there must be several chances. She would bide their time, and if the worst came to the worst—why, she herself had made a mistake, and had been delivered from it.

Do not think it strange that I attribute this last sentiment to so excellent a woman. It was perfectly natural. No just and pure woman can, after time has passed, regard with any degree of regret the early death of a husband whose brutally selfish conduct was a constant reproach and cause of misery. She naturally feels that, as good women are apt to express it, "he has gone from the evil to come," that is, that he was taken away before he reached the lowest depths to which his course would necessarily carry him.

Mrs. Garthwaite did not, therefore, participate in her daughter's joy; but she had lost none of her motherly love and tender sympathy, which would have rejoiced for the joy though the cause of it should break her own heart.

But where was the young man? Who had seen him, or heard from, or of him? He certainly had not left the town? They would dispatch a messenger with a note to him at his aunt's. And it was soon done. Susan wrote the joyous billet, and though she destroyed several sheets of paper before it was to her sense of love and propriety (two mighty difficult senses to reconcile sometimes), it was sent before a half hour had passed from the time Miss Young had arrived.

The messenger did not see Mr. Bowman. He was in his own room, sick, said one of the cousins, but give her the note and she would take it to him. He was sick; not with the pangs of wounded love, but with the disordered head and stomach of a man who had drunk a great deal too much overnight, and although he was by no means a teetotaller, he was not accustomed to such great excesses.

He drank, as did almost every one in the country, more or less, but always some during every day. The fashion of taking a julep before breakfast was then rapidly going out of vogue, but the side-boards were still in first request upon occasions of a visit or a departure, a rain, a drouth, a hunt, a reconciliation, a quarrel, or of anything else which could by any means be made the occasion of a drink. And Mr. Bowman was generally ready to go up to them as frequently as he was invited; but still, he was not a drunkard. I doubt if any one had ever seen him drunk in public, that is, on the streets. He was rather too cautious to get right down drunk: it might place him in a natural position and get him into difficulty.

But the night before he had certainly drunk too much; too much for his health, and almost too much for his prudence, for he had talked in a maudlin way about his being the worst used man in the country, and had hinted to his companions (it was at Barker's room in town, and there were three or four young fellows there besides Barker and Bowman—all wild scatter-brains), he had hinted to them that he could a tale unfold which would make them pity him; he must keep his mouth shut, his honor kept him silent; but never mind, the time *would* come when he should have his revenge. And young Barker swore he would carry his challenge, and Billups and Jimmy Quine said they would stand by him, and Alfred Chives, with a half-drunken sneer, wished to know what redoubtable boy or female his friend Bowman intended fighting, and if he intended eating his enemy if he killed him or her—and other such sneers, all of which Mr. Bowman treated with silent contempt.

Later in the night, after they had drunk still more, there was a quarrel, and Chives had attempted to strike him, and he then made a motion to get at Chives, and there was a great noise and scuffle to keep them apart until the quarrel was settled, and they took a drink together, and Bowman swore that he had none but the kindest feelings towards Mr. Chives, and wouldn't hurt him for the world, and Chives replied that that was lucky, and there came near being another quarrel, which was quieted, and they parted for their homes, Mr. Bowman never missing his way, nor stumbling, but going straight to his room and to bed—to wake up the next morning feeling very badly as I have said.

It was a bad condition in which to receive a note from his lady-love requesting his presence and forgiveness, and all that sort of thing, and he had to get his Cousin Emily to write to Susan that he was very unwell, but thought that he should be able to be at The Barn that evening. Susan received the note, and forthwith pictured to herself that he was an innocent sufferer from her own folly and want of love, and vowed to herself to love him more tenderly than ever, and never to doubt him herself or suffer any one else to doubt him again. And when he did come in the evening, with glassy eyes, and looking rather flushed with the brandy he had taken as "the hair of the dog which had bitten him," as he expressed it, and smelling of cloves, she never once perceived the cause of his ill looks, but attributed them all to herself, and was as miserable and happy as a dear, innocent, tender-hearted girl could be upon such an occasion.

Miss Young had to go home, but Mrs. Garthwaite was there, and made all the requisite explanations, to which he replied somewhat sulkily, as though his honor had been deeply wounded by their distrust. But in the midst of the explanation the answer from Aunt Polly arrived. No secret was made of it, and it was with internal trepidation that Mr. Bowman saw Mrs. Garthwaite open it before him and read it.

The note was not the composition of Aunt Polly herself, although she had written it. When she got home from Rosstown and had read Mrs. Garthwaite's letter she instantly showed it to Alice, and asked her what she must say in her reply. After many pros and cons, suggestions and objections to its exact contents and wording, Alice prevailed upon her aunt to let her compose it, which she did as follows:

"DEAR MADAM,—Your note of yesterday by messenger was received *last evening.* I regret that my absence from home prevented its *earlier* reception by me. I hasten to answer your inquiries in the *same* spirit in which I feel convinced they were *made.* I answer generally that Mr. Bowman's visits *to me and my niece* were always based upon the ostensible object of cultivating our *friendship.* My niece has never either *accepted* or *refused* him, *nor has she any proposition of marriage from him under consideration.*

"I can assure you, madam, that Mr. Bowman is *perfectly free* to act according to his *fancy* so far as *my niece is concerned,* and if it should be that he is about to become connected with your family *she will heartily join me* in wishing contentment and happiness to the lady.

"Very respectfully,

"MARY HART."

This was the note which Mrs. Garthwaite read and then passed to Susan and her lover. The word "fancy" made the gentleman wince a little (and it always seemed to me that Alice intended it as irony, and might have used a more genial word), and the total abnegation and ignoring of all his honeyed phrases, and sweet looks, and assiduous attentions was rather galling to his vanity; but, on the whole, it was vastly better than his guilty conscience feared, and he mentally blessed Aunt Polly, and called her a good, blind old fool. A little reflection, however, convinced him that not Aunt Polly but Alice herself had composed it, and he cursed her for a cold-hearted coquette, who had no more feeling than a statue, and more hypocrisy than the devil himself.

But for the present he was contented, and when Mrs. Garthwaite went out of the room he, as though it was a matter of duty, put his arm around Susan and drew her towards him and she for the first time suffered him to kiss her. Was she not his? Did he not love her, and her alone? Ah, what a happy girl she was! Certainly he might kiss her this once for all the grief she had given him.

But it was a maudlin sort of kiss; not a chaste, loving kiss, but one given by a man half drunk, who thought it was *the* thing and must be done—and who said to himself at the moment, "Oh, how damned badly I do feel! I wish I was back in my room, and had a good hearty drink!"

And he soon excused himself: the excitement of the last three days, he said, had been too much for him, and he really felt very unwell, and must go home. No, he couldn't wait for tea, he felt too badly; but he would come the next day and see his darling, and hoped he should then feel perfectly well.

I am sorry for all this I have been narrating about Bowman and Susan; very sorry. Had I had my own way it should never have happened. She should have married Sam Stockdale, and Bowman should have got a vixen who would have punished him throughout life for his evil qualities. But I did not have the management of the affair; and as it has turned out am glad that I did not. It was eventually all for the best.

CHAPTER XXXIII.

THE AMIABLE CHARACTER OF MR. BOWMAN IS FURTHER ILLUSTRATED, AND MR. ECCLES AFFORDS HIM AMUSEMENT.

A DAY or two after the grand reconciliation Mr. Bowman sauntered into my office where Ben Eccles was busily engaged, and, after some unimportant general talk, asked him when he was going to The Barn again.

"I will go in a day or two," answered Ben, somewhat confused. "But why do you ask?"

"Oh, it's nothing. I only thought that as you are intimate out there I would ask you to present my respects, as I shall have to go home without calling."

"Certainly. I'll do that for you. When do you leave?"

"I thought of starting in the morning. I have been idling too much time about here, and must be at home with my negroes, Christmas. The only reason why I wished you to present my respects is that I know the ladies like you very much, and as I am inclined to think that they do not care much for me, and don't wish them to be any more unfriendly than they are, I thought that if you—if you would undertake to bring me to their remembrance it would be all the better for me."

"You may be sure that I will do so," said Ben with

great gratification, mingled with some pride, and also with much compunction for his previous hard thoughts.

"Please do so, Ben. As I suppose you are to be the lucky fellow I don't know any one to whom I can more heartily wish success. If I had not been such a torn-down scamp I would have put in there myself. But I shouldn't have stood the ghost of a chance. I've found that out."

"Well, never mind about that," said Ben, becoming a little nervous and offended. "I'll be certain to do what you request."

"Ben!" said Bowman, after a short pause and looking thoughtful, "you and I were schoolmates and have been friends for a long time, and I hope you'll not be offended with me if I tell you something which touches your interest!"

"No," answered Ben with a little trepidation, for he could only dread to what such a prelude should lead.

"Well now, I ask you as a friend why you don't act with more energy? I've seen a good deal of the young lady, and you'll wear out your love if you keep putting it off. Why, sir, if I had been in your place, with your advantages, I would have settled my happiness months ago, and should now be married."

"Mr. Bowman," answered the victim coldly, and yet with hope wild in his heart, "I think I know my own business, and have always shown myself able to attend to it without advice unless I asked it!"

"I didn't mean to offend you, Ben. I told you so in the first place. I only——"

"I know. You have not offended me, but at the

same time I would in a friendly spirit ask you to attend to your own business."

"Come; you are angry, and I'll have to leave. But I did not wish you to get mad with me!"

And after Ben, disarmed, had protested that he was not angry, and Bowman had declared over and over again his sincere friendship and interest, the visitor left, and Ben sat alone in deep reflection.

Yes: he had waited just as long as propriety could demand. He had unmistakably manifested his love and intentions long ago; and Susan had had plenty of time to make up her mind. Heaven help him! he could not see much encouragement; and yet a woman's heart and a woman's conduct generally disagreed in such a case. He felt that it had become a solemn and pressing duty to himself and to the lady to make a declaration and conclude the matter. He might succeed! Others thought he should; and if he did, what a blessed man, what an overhappy man he should be! He could not decide upon his chances; they might be very poor, but as woman was so strange, and Susan had not decidedly repulsed him (what could the poor fellow have imagined a decided repulse to be!) he must come to a plain explanation with her. What a miserable, cowardly scoundrel he should be if he *had* gained her affections and would let her timid concealment of the fact deter him from offering himself, and thus render her miserable! It was his duty! and he would do it at once though it should cost him his life. And, ah! it was like walking into the very gates of death to put his fate to the final test. He had rather love on forever in uncertainty than find the certainty of his being unloved; but it was not his choice which should govern; it was Susan's welfare.

And he commenced bracing his mind for the final decision of his dearest hopes. I need not tell the number of times he prayed, nor how he groaned. It would be almost heartless to try to expose all the conflict of his heart and mind which the reader can so well imagine.

The very next day, at about eleven o'clock in the forenoon, he got on his horse and rode out to The Barn. As the visit was at an unusual hour, Susan suspected its object, and gladly descended to the parlor. She was eager for his sake and for her own that he should declare himself, and so end a dream which had from her first knowing of it been a source of disquiet and annoyance to her, as she was sure it had been of anguish to him. She wished to like and to be able to enjoy the company of a man whom she respected so much, and she could never do so as long as he had the idea of courting her. She was glad the idea was likely to be destroyed now. She had given him every rebuff and discouragement that she, as a lady, could give; and in vain. She would now give him every opportunity and every facility to make his proposal; she would even tempt him to make it—so great was her desire to have the matter ended. True, she was engaged to Bowman, but it had been agreed that the engagement should not be made public for a month or two, and in the mean time neither could she endure the persecution, nor ought Mr. Eccles to undergo the disquiet of his suit. Yes, it was best for her own sake as a lady, and as a woman of good feeling, to give Mr.

Eccles his answer, independent of all other considerations, and without reference to a prior engagement—far better than that she should let such a fervent love as his fall to the ground untold, and as though unregretted by her.

It may be thought that Susan had a slight but unacknowledged desire to gratify her vanity by having Mr. Eccles at her feet. But she was above all such pettiness. It was a great grief instead of a triumph to her. She had done all she could to prevent it, and she was now actuated by the desire to spare him continued pain, and the final mortification of seeing another preferred to himself while he was still courting her, and a desire to both get rid of his attentions and conceal her engagement. She had thought, at first, that since he had come and would declare himself, she should, at the first word, tell him that she was already engaged—but had concluded that that would be too shockingly and heartlessly cruel.

She entered the parlor alone and sat there with him alone, talking as he chose to talk. After an hour or two thus spent by her, and spent by him in agonized and vain endeavors to speak the words he had to speak, he proposed that they should walk in the garden. She readily assented, and after a few turns around the walks he managed, with a husky voice, a dry mouth, and trembling limbs to declare his love, and she firmly, but gently, gave him his answer.

The shock, tenderly administered though it was, overcame him. He almost staggered, and then fell upon his knees at her feet, and began praying in a muttering tone, joining her name, and mercy, and God, and love, in a confused manner; and then, while she was in a state of intense alarm, suddenly arose, and looking in a sad and startled manner at her, touched his hat politely and left the garden, got on his horse, rode back to town, and came to my office. I came in soon after he arrived and found him on his knees, praying; he got up upon my entrance and began to laugh, and to talk volubly about what he intended doing with his place the next year, and then about his sins and his love.

In fine, I discovered that his brain was wandering, and immediately persuaded him with authority to go with me to his house in my gig in which I had come to town. Before we started I sent word for Dr. Hutchins, in whom both he and I had great confidence, to come out there immediately. When he arrived, Ben had fallen into a lethargic, almost comatose state, and was at once put to bed, ordered hot foot-baths, etc.

The most skillful treatment and gentle nursing, together with perfect quiet, restored the patient after a few days to his ordinary condition of mind, except that it was more calm and despairing; but a severe attack of bodily illness supervened, attended with much delirium and great nervous excitement.

The natural strength and elasticity of his constitution at last successfully resisted, and he became convalescent. It was the happiest convalescence I ever saw, for with increasing health and strength came increasing peace of mind. The cloud was gone; when it left, or why, or how, I cannot tell—but it was gone. For the first time in years he smiled peacefully, and seemed happy, for his Judge looked with benignant eye upon him. At last, as though he had just awaked from a frightful dream, he saw that his attempt to eke out his salvation by good works was a prolific error, and henceforth he was content. God could be just, and yet by Christ's means could justify sinners. Justice satisfied by Christ was in harmony with love manifested in and by Christ.

A soothing calm came upon his mind; although, as shall be seen, it never lost an impression made constitutional with it by the trouble it had been in so long; and when he got strong enough to relish his tobacco he took a chew between his fingers, and smilingly looking at it he placed it in his mouth, and then shut his eyes and thanked God for all His blessings.

I have said that his long trouble left upon his mind an impression from which it never entirely recovered, and as I shall no more have to depict the trouble, I had perhaps better state the effect, and be done with it. He had got into the habit of praying at all times and places; and it never wore off. The trouble was gone, but the habit remained; in other words, he acted like a crazy man, and was to all seeming intents and purposes a crazy man in that one thing. He would drop upon his knees in the office and pray, and at last would do the same thing in the street or the fields. He appeared to think that no one saw him but a good God, and that if he were seen he was unobserved. It was a curious monomania. In all other respects his mind was clear in all its functions, though by insensible degrees he became more and more mild and gentle in his disposition, until he was almost useless in the rough affairs of life.

We shall see that he yet had hard doubts to overcome, but I have, under the impulse of the moment, anticipated the narration of the effects of the struggle which I have heretofore attempted to describe. I have had a painful task, and feel like indemnifying myself, and the reader who has persevered in reading, by this almost premature avowal that the painful portion of his history is done. Hereafter, though we may pity him for his mania, there will be no painful doubts concerning it. All was calm enough in his mind, and everything was correct in his conduct, if we except the habit in which he became confirmed.

CHAPTER XXXIV.

DESCRIBES THE WEDDING, AND HAS A GOOD DEAL TO SAY ABOUT COGNATE MATTERS.

IT was in early spring that the wedding took place. The wintry winds which whirled about the dead leaves, heaping them here, there leaving bare the ground, had been driven to their northern caves by the fair maid, Spring, who came upon the scene from more southern lands, heralded by warm rains and a more genial glow of the sun; bland zephyrs floating mingled with the sheen; and an emerald carpet spangled with modest star-flowers rose to her tread as she advanced. The gray and russet buds fast swelling big, burdened with joyous load each slender spray, and here and there branches and trees were seen with yellow, silvery green and crimson, dotting the wood. The beeches had begun to wave their banners, the red-buds clothed themselves in rose color, and the dogwood blossoms, growing fast from green to white, gave notice to the rustic fishermen to prepare their tackle. The wild violets, blue and white, covered the mossy banks along the gurgling rills, pendant honey-suckles gemmed with dew fringed the bottoms, yellow jessamines, wild pea, spiderwort, and daisies covered the slopes, and bright verdure and many-colored flowers began to clothe the vales and crown each hill.

And every nook in earth and air was filled with busy life. The hooping cranes circled high in noisy consultation, or, with necks and legs outstretched, took straight their northern flight. In the fields the pitiless ploughshare, upturning the mellow earth, wrenched to the light the nest of the timid field-mouse, and crows and prying blackbirds, heedless of the loud woa! and haw! of the ploughmen, scanned narrowly each furrow to seize the unearthed worm and sluggish snail; and the feathered songsters sent their notes from every hill and brake as they searched about with tender care where each might build its nest. From some lowly bush the gentle thrush poured forth his song of love with bated voice; the gallant partridge strutting on a stump or fence gave out his loudest challenge; in the clumps of hazels and dwarfed oaks the gay redbird flaunted his bright plumage, and the noisy jay delighted his soul with discord; twittering swallows skimmed the verdant meads; noisy martins and trustful wrens peered business-like around the eaves of every house; doves cooed softly, deep in the wood, and from the topmost twig of some bush growing in the hedge the mocking-bird repeated in ecstasy every note he had ever heard or could invent. The white-winged gnats in the sun's first glances weaved their mazy dance in mystic circle. The ants, bound upon industry, commenced to excavate, and bore with unwearied patience their mighty loads of loam and grains of sand; here a scout sped his zigzag course, and there a long dark moving throng took its way in devious line to some new enterprise.

> Here on these weeds with cunning skill, last night
> A spider wove her web, which, misty, bright,
> Like frosted silver, sparkles now with dew.
> These gems will soon exhale and leave to view
> A trembling, frail, attenuated thread,
> To snap by wayward winds or passer's tread.
> So when youth's freshness gems man's hopes they take
> A misty radiance, tremble thus, thus break.

It was in this delightful season, early spring, that the wedding took place—and Susan's heart was in unison with the season. Not a single cloud obscured the brightness of her sky; no obstacle presented itself in her path; all the present was smooth and bright, and all the future a glow of rosy light. She thought that surely there never was before a girl so happy as she; nor was there ever one better fitted for happiness to herself and others.

It was to be a grand affair. Augusta, Charleston, and New York had laid her under contribution for her wedding garments—*trousseau*, I believe they are called by the fashionable—and with air, earth, and sea provided the feast. It was pleasant to see her for days before the time, now in the house with the seamstresses, snipping here, and directing there, and then tripping to the kitchen to consult with Dinah and the assistant cooks. And yet to me, who was there more than once, it was more sad than pleasant. I had been formally told of the approaching marriage, and then informally talked to and consulted about it. To have spoken a word against it could have done no possible good, and must have caused unhappiness, if not ill will; and even if I had been rashly frank, I had nothing tangible to urge why it should not be consummated. If I had said that Bowman was unsuitable, I should have been asked: in what respect? and though I should have mentioned ten good reasons, there was not one of them which could not be palliated or excused. Had I said that he was dissipated, I should have been told that it was only because he had not a wife, and that almost every young man was the same. His lying would have been mere playful exaggeration, the result of an exuberant fancy and a gay disposition; and I could hardly have sustained a specific and marked example of the still more serious defects which I rather suspected and feared than knew to be in his character. But I instinctively felt that they were there, and it was therefore more sad than pleasing to me to see the lovely girl gaily anxious to deck herself for the sacrifice, and to furnish forth a feast for the occasion.

Getting married is a serious affair, though the large majority make a jest of it. It is serious enough for the man who is about assuming great responsibilities; but it is infinitely more so to the woman, whose cares anh responsibilities are much more varied and of infinitely more importance. I, who am a very old man and have experienced and observed almost every phase of human life, may surely be permitted to tell what I know and think about this subject. I well recollect upon my own wedding night wondering to myself at the ignorance of perfect innocence, and at the perfect faith in me my Mary must have to allow me to take her in my arms as my wife. Surely the poor woman who voluntarily subjects herself to a master, to toil for him, suffer for him, and obey him (for all the suffering and obedience, and most of the wearing toil, are her portion), must be looked upon by a gentleman with the greatest admiration and respect! If he knows his own nature he can find nothing in it to call forth such self-abnegation, and nothing which can by any means imitate, much less rival, her act. What is his love compared with hers? what does he sacrifice? what does he subject himself to? Nothing! absolutely nothing! True, it is her nature to do this, but is it any the less admirable for that? I declare that whenever I meet upon the street or elsewhere a woman about to become a mother, I cannot forbear taking off my hat to her and bowing my head in reverential pity.

To gain a juster idea of the case, imagine a pure and sensitive woman, forced by unnatural parents or overwhelming circumstances to marry and submit herself to the embraces and the whims and habits of a man she dislikes. Faugh! what disgust! what unutterable horror must fill her whole being! The violence of ten thousand tragedies cannot equal it; no imaginable situation is so pathetic!

I have actually heard men argue that if the woman

does make a sacrifice for the man it is no more than he does for the woman. Certainly we men must be great brutes when we do not appreciate the delicate sensitiveness and trusting love of the woman. We have no such delicacy, because we are not so innocent. Our love trusts more to a strong arm and a strong will in ourselves, than to any qualities outside of ourselves; whereas the woman is ignorant, loves, and must put her whole trust in us.

Ah, poor women, who have to bear the burden of the race and suffer the pangs of its renewal! we call you fickle and vain, say that you amuse yourselves with trifles, and are incapable of great achievements; as though it were a reproach that she who has so much to suffer should not coyly evade it if she might, she whose lot is so hard should not pride herself upon the charms which serve in many ways to relieve its exactions, and amuse herself with the veriest trifles which can bring diversion and forgetfulness! Kind nature has given these compensations which accord most exactly with her lot in life, and her fickleness, vanity, and triviality render her more attractive and pleasant to man. It is well for her that in addition to her hard lot she has not to find her happiness in grand achievements, in the clash and turmoil of the world. It is her greatest glory that those she bears and those she loves go like men into the strife, and achieve great things!

I fear that the best of men, though they may love intensely, are not sufficiently appreciative and tender to their wives or mothers. I know that Charley Bowman no more appreciated the noble confidence and devoted affection of Susan than would his discordant soul have understood the divinest harmonies sung by a seraph. He gloried in her beauty, her soft, luxuriant hair, her rosy lips, her blooming cheeks, and symmetrical form, and he respected her for her wealth, which was soon to be his own; but as for love, as love should be, pure and sympathetic as well as ardent, he did not know what it was. And she, sweet girl, had crowned him with all the glorious virtues and excellencies man can possess!

It vexes me to think of this marriage, though so many years have passed away since it took place. And yet, of what avail to be vexed or to complain, either at the time or afterwards? In nine cases out of ten such marriages seem as happy as any other. There ensues a little coldness with one party and a little disappointment with the other, and the one contents himself as best he may with the bargain he has made, and the other bows herself to the yoke, and the world wags on, and is peopled, and there is the end of it. Such mismatches are a vexation because the one party requires a more appreciative master, and the other a stern mistress instead of a wife.

But to continue my narrative: grand were the preparations on this occasion, and Miss Maria Jones heard with envious curiosity of all the fine things which had been imported from New York; of the bonnet and veil, of the second-day dress, the morning wrappers and evening dresses, the wreaths, and other tricks and furbelows which are used to set forth a bride and a new wife—but she, with irksome resolve, refrained from going to see them. It cost her many a pang to hear the bridesmaids discuss what they should wear and what they should do, and then to think that had she only made more allowance in her calculations for the variation of polarity she too might have shone in this galaxy. But she was only a looker on; for as there was no social reason for her being omitted she received an invitation. Mrs. Garthwaite was inclined to think that she had made no error, and Susan was not one to bear malice, at any time.

Dr. Sam Stockdale also received an invitation for himself, Sarah, and his mother. I rather think it was sent by Mrs. Garthwaite herself. She always had a singular confidence in the young man. I do not mean that the confidence was undeserved, but that it was singular in that it was so strong and so abiding. He was the man she wished for a son-in-law, and she seemed to feel his disappointment long after its rawness had been covered in him.

"Will you go, brother?" said Sarah to him, when she saw the note inviting them.

"Certainly, I will! Why not?" said Sam, undismayed. "I'm sorry for Susan; but why should I not go to her wedding? To stay away would look churlish, and might afford some pleasure to that dam—I beg pardon, Sarah—to that infernal scoundrel she is going to marry."

"I didn't think you had so much littleness about you, brother, as to hate a man merely because he is successful in what you desired for yourself. You know that the affair with that other young lady was a mistake."

"Neither am I little, Sarah You jump at very

harsh conclusions for a just woman. Even though the affair with Miss Charlton was a mistake, it is not the only reason why I call him a scoundrel; I have known the fellow from his childhood. However, never mind that. I intend to go, and you had better go with me. You can stay with Lily and see how she gets on in her new paradise; and you can see, too, how I behave myself at the wedding. I promise you I will not knock the bridegroom down and take his bride off amid screaming, overturned lights, and confusion—though it would be the most benevolent piece of work I ever did in my life if I should do so. Come, Sarah, get ready!"

And she did get ready; and Lily fairly wept when she saw her, although she had been absent from her only a few weeks, and had already been married more than long enough to have got over the novelty and excitement of bridehood.

"What are you crying about, you silly child?" said Sarah, when Lily's tears had flowed rather longer than the occasion seemed to demand.

"Oh, I'm so happy, sister!" exclaimed the sobbing Lily.

"I should think so," said the unsympathetic Sarah.

And then Lily began to laugh as unreasonably as she had before wept, and Sarah had almost lost her patience before the young wife became calm and sensible as she would have her.

And the young wife, who had also been bidden, and her husband, and brother, and sister, and almost half the county went to the wedding. Ben Eccles was also there. He went as a duty and because he was magnanimous. He had discovered the cruel trick his false friend had played him, and it was with difficulty and after much praying (heartfelt and reasonable prayer it was, unblinded by error) that he had kept himself from taking a summary vengeance. For Susan's sake, at last, rather than from any religious restraint, he had resisted his natural desire. His prayers had been to have wisdom in the emergency so to act as should be best for all parties; for himself, for Bowman, for social order, and, above all, for Susan. For himself, in the abstract, he cared nothing; for the good of social order and for the good of Bowman himself he wished to give the young man a thrashing, which he felt it would be a perfectly proper thing for a Christian to do; but for Susan's sake, to save her the pain of having a meanness exposed in one she loved, and the mortification of having her name brought into a quarrel, and having her beloved insulted or belabored, as he, (Ben) could and would have belabored him, he restrained his just indignation, and upon his invitation went to the wedding as calmly as though it were all according to his wish.

I was there, of course. When I say: "of course," I mean that as I was Mrs. Garthwaite's lawyer as well as her intimate friend from childhood, it was in the social course of affairs that I should be there; and also that if I had not been there I should not be able to describe the affair as I have been doing, and am about to do.

Susan was a charming bride. I do not know a more trying ordeal to which beauty can be exposed than the monotony of color and extreme precision of bridal garments, and I have rarely ever seen a woman who looked so well thus dressed as she did when more negligently and naturally attired. The darlings delight in colors; bright ribbons, cunning knots, and all sorts of pretty little assortments and arrangements to set themselves off with; and they know just which colors and arrangements suit them best. To dress one all in white is therefore unnatural, as I have said, and, to my taste, better suits the bier than the bridal. But Susan was one of those graceful, as well as beautiful, beings to whom every sort of dress is becoming. Let but a dress fit her, and it was at once beautiful, whatever its color or material.

And Mr. Bowman, too, was very handsome. Every one remarked that it was a glorious couple. Even Dr. Sam muttered to himself that if looks were all it was a happy marriage; and when, after the ceremony was over, the bride and bridegroom were separated by the throng around them, and then separated as those should be who desire to be hospitable and not to attract attention to themselves as being weak and love-sick, the doctor watched the gentle bride follow with proud and softened gaze the movements of her husband, he mentally hoped that both might be happy, and mentally registered additional vengeance against the groom if they were not so.

That Mrs. Garthwaite should shed tears during the ceremony seemed to Susan rather weak and ill timed, though she said nothing to her about it. But the poor woman had cause for tears. She knew what her daughter was undertaking so innocently and with such faith, and even if Dr. Sam had been the groom, she would have wept; and the doctor was not the man who had to be trusted—more was the pity.

Mr. Snow performed the ceremony under Mrs. Snow's eye, for she was there looking as much like a fly-away as she had ever looked in her younger days when she had had only four or five babies to take care of.* I believe she was hooked-up all right, for a wonder, but she looked wild and undone about the hair, as though at least two babies had touseled it.

It would never do for me to omit to mention in my description the throng of negroes, principally women, which blocked up windows and doors to gaze upon the marriage of their young mistress. It was a source of the greatest satisfaction to them; not that she was going to be happy, for they took that for granted, or never thought about it; but because her husband had the reputation of being rich. Negroes have even an extra share of human nature in that respect. They have not the slightest respect for poverty in "white folks," no matter how honest and meritorious its possessors may flatter themselves it is. "Poor white trash" they abominate. The rich they sometimes hate, but always respect. For a doctor, or a lawyer, or a preacher to be poor is not at all out of the way in their eyes; they have other claims to respect than mere wealth, and are not included in the term "Poor white trash;" but no one else, who has not plenty of money or property, is excluded.

---

* The reader will find a full description of Mrs. Snow in Mr. Page's life of himself, already published.

JOHN CAPELSAY, *Exr.*

Late in the evening, after the dancing had been going on for some time, and the gallery and hall were full of promenaders, and all the guests had become engaged in amusing themselves as they thought best, I sauntered out into the front yard where, beneath the glorious stars, I could reflect a little upon what had happened, was happening, and should happen. The dew glistened on the leaves of the shrubbery and sparkled in drops on the blades of grass, the katydids and crickets rivaled the music of the fiddles and tamborines I heard behind me, and the hoot of the owls in the distant forest showed that all was undisturbed there. And as I walked, musing, and pleased with the agreeable change, I thought I saw the outlines of a man's form kneeling near a young oak by the garden walk, and as I approached nearer, said: "Well, Ben, so you too seek the delicious calm out of doors," not at all heeding his attitude; for I had learned that he appeared either to be unconscious of the position, or to think that no one could observe it as unnatural. I had to wait a few moments for him to conclude his prayer, and when he had done so he rose from his knees and gave me his hand as frankly as though he had been only standing up engaged in thought, and said: "Excuse me, Mr. Page; I was thinking deeply, and did not hear your remark—though it seemed to me you said something."

"Yes, Ben; I say that you too appear to seek the delicious calm of nature, rather than stay in the house with the young folk."

"Oh, you know that I am very much of an old fogy, Mr. Page. I regret sometimes that I did not learn to dance. I might have been able to add so much more to the pleasure of others; but we are generally wise when it is too late; at least, I am. The bride looked very beautiful to-night, I thought."

"Yes; she is a lovely woman, and I hoped she would have made a different match. I hope that she too may not find that wisdom comes too late sometimes," said I, wishing to draw him out.

"I was thinking of that too, when I made my remark. I do hope and pray that her life may be one of uninterrupted happiness. A woman risks so much when she marries that I wonder more of them do not become old maids. Susan, though, is so prudent and so good that I do not see how any one could ever be unkind to her. You know, sir, that from my childhood I have never admired the person she has married, but it seems to me that her gentle and therefore powerful influence must result in making him kind to her, even if it cannot eradicate his evil habits."

"What are his evil habits, Ben?"

"I do not like to talk about them, sir, for it is possible I may be prejudiced. We all have more or fewer evil habits, and to those who do not like us they generally appear exaggerated."

"I know you too well, Ben, to suppose you would exaggerate, however much you might dislike. For instance, is he not sincere? You can answer me that."

And thereupon, with the confidence he had had in me from his early boyhood, he told me of the manner in which Bowman had urged him to court Susan, and concluded: "I was very angry when I learned the way in which I had been served, and yet I do not know but that I should thank him for having done me a great service. The agitation of the occasion brought on that attack of sickness, which, I can tell *you*, sir, resulted in my gaining a peace of mind to which I had long been a stranger, and for which I had most fervently prayed. What do you think of the efficacy of prayer, Mr. Page?"

"I knew your condition of mind, Ben, but knew that I could do nothing for your relief. I am heartily glad that you have emerged from it; and it should seem that prayer had been very efficacious in your case."

"I do not mean efficacious mentally or spiritually to the person who prays, sir, for no one can help observing and admitting that. I mean, what do you think of its efficacy as regards outward events, matters with which the person's own soul or mind can have no connection—as, for instance, health, or deliverance from danger, or fortune, or the affairs of the outer world?"

As this was not our last conversation upon this subject, and I shall hereafter have a more fitting opportunity to relate my answer and all the points of our discussion, I will not now any longer divert the reader's attention from the wedding, though I have but little more to say about it. I will only remark that I could not get Ben to manifest the least malignancy towards Charley Bowman, although I knew perfectly well that were the occasion to arise he would feel and act almost exactly as Dr. Sam was already vowing in his heart to act. Ben was more gentle and more unsuspicious than was his friend Sam; and that was all.

When we returned to the house supper had been already announced, and Mrs. Garthwaite was looking for me to accompany her at the head of the procession always formed upon such occasions. And after I went to perform my part in that ceremony I had no sight of Ben until, after the supper was over and it was time for the guests to retire, I saw him go manfully up to the bride and take her by the hand, bid her good night, and express the wish that she might have a long and happy life. And I came nearer loving him when I saw his magnanimity, fortitude, and gracefulness on that occasion than I ever came before. Susan, too, seemed struck by it, and I know that she thought of it many a time afterwards when, though her path had diverged so far from that in which her former lover was forced to walk, she had occasion to contrast his former love and sufferings with his subsequent steady friendship and quiet usefulness.

Gradually the candles had burned low in the sconces and candlesticks, the music became more monotonous and languid, the guests began to yawn in the passage and on the gallery, and then there was a search for shawls and bonnets and other coverings, and the rumble of carriages moving was heard without, and the neighing of restless horses, and then The Barn was left to quiet.

CHAPTER XXXV.

TELLS ABOUT SOME OF THE VISITORS THE YOUNG COUPLE HAD WHEN THEY MOVED TO THEIR HOME, AND GIVES MANY WHYS AND WHEREFORES. IT ALSO SPEAKS OF A VISIT MADE BY ALICE CHARLTON TO ROSSTOWN, AND WHAT DID NOT HAPPEN THERE, AND WHOM SHE FOUND WHEN SHE GOT HOME.

MR. BOWMAN had passed gallantly through the courtship and marriage, but there were other ordeals which were to him far more trying, and through which he had reasonable fears that he should not be able to pass unscathed. It was already arranged that the young couple should go at once to housekeeping at his residence near his father's, and it had been repainted, repapered, and refurnished for their reception. The first essay at keeping house alone, and the first introduction into the neighborhood and circle of her husband's parents and friends, with their criticisms, and peculiarities of habit, disposition, and character, were somewhat embarrassing to Susan. But she had no dread, no undercurrent of uneasiness, nor were these matters which seemed to concern her husband at all. In fact he never once thought about either the trouble or the embarrassments of his young wife, any more than he feared he should not have bread and meat, furniture, preserves, and pickles enough, or any other things which might be bought with money. The introdüction of his wife into his neighborhood, where every one knew and distrusted his peculiarities, and, above all, her meeting with Alice, that hoyden, were the matters which gave him an uneasiness he could not shake off.

I am not ascribing to him too much delicacy of feeling when I say this. He had the natural desire that his wife should look upon him as without defect. Her being loved and addressed by other men was too recently possible for him to be able to shake off the fear of being exposed and then brought into comparison with them, and though he should not care how mean he was in the abstract, he must care not to seem mean to one who was not grounded and settled in her affections.

Now you and I know that this was not only nonsense, but a sort of sacrilegious nonsense; a vile miscomprehension of the noble and strong-hearted woman who had married him, and who loved him purely and more than she did her own being; who worshipped him. But what should you have from an animal but an animal instinct?

At any rate, whether sentiment or instinct, whether shame or cowardice, he did dread the time when his wife should become acquainted with Alice. And he wondered to himself how the meeting should take place, for he knew it must occur sooner or later. Would Alice call at his house? At first he was inclined to doubt it, but when he reflected that if she did not his wife would remark it and might be led to suspect the cause, he began to really hope that she would call. "Oh, confound her," he said to himself, "she has spunk enough to call; there's no fear on that score;

but may she not dislike me so that she will not care to come? I do wish to goodness she would come at once and have it over. And I do hope that she will take a fancy to Susan. Not that I care a damn whether she likes her or not, but it will make it just that much easier for me. And I hope that old fool of an aunt will come too. Oh, confound them! let them all come and let's be friends and good neighbors. But what will Susan say when she sees her? and then when she knows her? There's the rub!"

A man must have delicate sensibilities to comprehend a woman's nature. A great brute who must cry out when he is pinched cannot understand the noble hypocrisy—sometimes called fortitude—the peculiar characteristic of woman. Consequently Mr. Bowman had no capacity to comprehend either Alice or Susan. Had he understood Alice he would have known that all her keen senses were alive to extricate herself, even in her own estimation, from the false position in which she felt herself. And had he known his wife he would have known that she was not likely to suspect him, and would hardly comment, unless laughingly, upon the mistaken impression he had given her of Alice; and that even if she did suspect, even if she did know the whole truth, she would treat it as a matter too late to be remedied, and he should never discover the shock to her respect for him the discovery of his deceit (lying) had given her.

It was but a few days after their arrival that Alice and her aunt paid their first visit. In addition to her desire to right herself, Alice had a very natural and lively curiosity to see the young lady who had been so suddenly preferred to herself; and as Susan had just as natural and just as lively a curiosity to see the young lady who had given her so much foolish uneasiness, they were mutually prepared to make themselves most attractive. Both were agreeably disappointed, and, to tell the truth, I think they were the two most glorious women of their generation in our part of the country; and how such a fellow as Bowman should have ever been so placed as to have his choice of them is to me a matter of some surprise and a great deal of mortification. The best gentleman in the world would have thought his happiness and glory of manhood complete with either, and for a Charles Bowman to have had his choice only proves that the most perfect of human beings are subject to errors of judgment, and are never so easily misled as when attracted by the fair seeming of others, and urged by their own affections.

Last night, wearied with writing, I went to bed, and during the night I dreamed a dream which made my soul rejoice. I dreamed that my face was smooth and ruddy, my eyes bright and soft, my hair glossy, and that I had the most beautiful mouth in the world. It was of entrancing beauty, in color, form, and expression, and looking in the mirror I said beau-ti-ful, beau-ti-ful, several times, and admired the movement and the sweet smile which accompanied the pronunciation of the word. Ah, thought I, no wonder that I am beloved and admired by all the young ladies and by the old of both sexes! and as I am so beloved, no wonder that my heart is so filled with love for all.

Alice had once been almost as much charmed with

Bowman as I was in my dream with my own face; but I waked to see a wrinkled, gray-headed, and toothless old man, and she had waked to see Bowman just as unlovely as he really was. And the dear girl, so far from feeling malice towards him, prayed that Susan should never discover his defects and worthlessness, and that the influence of her goodness might lead him to better things.

But all this is not giving a description of the visit, although it was remarkable rather for the feelings of the parties than for anything that occurred. Aunt Polly was perfectly grand in her black silk dress and snowy cap. Her worsted gloves had given place to black silk mittens, and her white apron to one to suit her gown. The ordinary briskness of her movements was changed to a straight and benignant dignity, which she thought vastly becoming the occasion of a visit to a bride who had the reputation of being so fine and yet so sensible. I really cannot tell how Alice was dressed, for, like Susan, whatever she wore became her, and nothing she could choose was ever so extravagant in color or form as to be remarked—though I do not doubt but that either of them could have told to the last detail the color, cut, and material, and even the probable cost, of every portion of the dress and toilette of the other.

Susan, it must be confessed, was a little taken aback when instead of a laughing, boisterous, giddy girl of only ordinary good looks, she met in her visitor a dignified, perfectly well-bred, and almost perfectly beautiful woman—but the disappointment caused no embarrassment. She was as pleasant to her visitors as could well be one in her situation—a new-comer, who wished the hearty suffrages of all, and particularly of her nearest neighbors, and those such estimable persons. Mr. Bowman, himself, who was present, was not so easy when she laughingly referred to him as being here where he was raised, and among his old friends; and was but little relieved when Aunt Polly remarked rather stiffly that she had known Mr. Bowman all his life. It was grazing almost too nearly the subject upon which he was now most sensitive. It was bad enough that Alice's looks and manners gave him the lie; if that other part of his lie came out, what should he do!

To make a long story short, when the visitors had departed, Susan said to her husband: "Oh, what a charming girl! How glad I am that she is such a near neighbor!" and then she archly added, kissing him, "What did you mean by telling me that story about her being boisterous, and only pretty? Why, she's perfectly beautiful! and her manners are most lady-like! You must have been blinded, sir."

All of which was very comforting to Mr. Bowman's consciousness.

But some way or another the fair neighbors, though mutually so pleased, did not at once contract one of those violent friendships which lead to intimacy and constant intercourse. I am inclined to think that Alice, though pleased, did not encourage any such intimacy. She did not directly discourage it, for neither was she one to be impolite, nor was Susan a woman to force herself upon another. The latter would have been perfectly willing for the most fervent friendship, but was rather too absorbed in her new existence to find it unless it were placed so that she could hardly avoid it. Not to encourage was therefore sufficient, and each was contented to think the other worthy of all her esteem and love in case it should occur that the esteem and love should need an object.

This was not, however, the only reason why the friendship did not at once ripen. It will be remembered that it was during the summer before this that Alice had come from Shoccoville to live with her Aunt Polly, and had been first seen at church by Mr. Bowman. For some months, then, taken up with the visits and the dreams, the turmoil and the strife of spirit, she had had no desire to visit and make acquaintance in the county and the immediate neighborhood. The consequence was, that though her fame had spread abroad for beauty, and goodness, and talent, she knew personally but few persons. Except to go a few times with her aunt on shopping expeditions she had hardly left home. Even Sarah Stockdale had never seen her though she went to church every Sunday, and, living on the main street, had an excellent opportunity for seeing all strangers who came to town. She had known Aunt Polly from Sam's childhood, but Aunt Polly's niece was almost a myth.

But the time had come when Alice's retirement was to be disturbed; and as she had neither duties nor solicitude to prevent it she soon had plenty of acquaintances and great popularity—though "popularity" was a word she disliked. One Sunday Dr. McCleod having to preach at Rosstown (as the phrase is, he "filled the pulpit" of the Rev. Mr. Snodgrass, who had to be absent to attend Presbytery), Alice and her aunt went with him. The dear girl was as much the admiration of the Rosstownians as she had been of the Spring Hill congregation; and when the meeting was over Sarah Stockdale, in her own impulsive way, went up to Aunt Polly, saluted her affectionately, was introduced to Alice, and fairly forced the old doctor and his party to go home with her to dinner. And in the same impulsive and powerful way she fairly forced Aunt Polly and the old gentleman to go home without Alice, promising to fetch her herself as soon as she desired to go.

Now the astute reader discovers the whole story at once. Alice sees Dr. Sam and Dr. Sam sees Alice, and both fall vehemently in love and marry at once! That is the plan of the sharp reader, and he is ready to exclaim: "What a splendid match!" But wait a little, my dear sir. You have, perhaps, heretofore found yourself disappointed in your expectations, and you have, at any rate, found that the final arrangement of things is not always in accordance with the apparent fitness of things. You may find it so again. I am writing what I know about Ben Eccles, Aunt Polly's pet; and although in order to tell his whole story I have had to say a great deal about other persons, and to show him sometimes at a very great disadvantage, you must not too hastily conclude that I am going to describe every one else happy and leave him lonely.

The fact is, that even if Alice had met Dr. Sam, neither he nor she was in the mood to fall in love. He was still in the calm which succeeded the violent storm of his love for Susan; and she was tenfold more cautious with her affections than she had ever been before. But she did not see him. There was a great deal of sickness in the country and he was hardly ever at home to a meal; often, except for a few hours at night, not at home at all for three or four days at a time, and his mother and sisters knew of his movements only through the servants, or by sometimes hearing his voice calling for his hostler. It happened that while Alice was there, though he was once or twice at home, he did not know that she was in the house.

When she got home, however, the following Friday, she met Ben Eccles, who had come on a visit to Aunt Polly and the scene of so many years of his boyhood.

CHAPTER XXXVI.

A CHAPTER THE READER CAN SKIP IF HE BE READING ONLY FOR THE STORY.

I DO not know a more appropriate place than this for making a condensed statement of the discussions between Ben and myself about the efficacy of prayer. It would be somewhat unnatural if it did not appear that I did most of the talking; for, apart from personal habit, I was in the place of an instructor, and he in place of one who wished to learn rather than to controvert. It should, doubtless, be to the credit of my modesty if I would substitute another for myself and represent Ben as the instructor, particularly as it may turn out that I was neither a learned nor wise instructor; but I must represent the matter just as it was. The reader can avoid every question, either personal or about the subject-matter, by skipping the chapter; and shall not have to say if he read it that I entrapped him into doing so.

Ben's question was, what I thought of the efficacy, and consequently of the utility of prayer in matters which do not directly concern the mental or spiritual education of the one who prays; for, he said, every one can observe and must admit its personal benefit. I give the idea, not his words.

He had been studying some of the modern philosophers, who, having discovered, as they say, that everything is governed by fixed laws and must happen in accordance with them, conclude that prayer is useless, and therefore foolish. This is, I think, a brief but correct statement of their position, stripped of its verbiage; and it puzzled Ben, as it certainly has puzzled me, and a vast number of men wiser and better than either of us. Every reader will see at once that it was peculiarly of a character to distress one who had gone through such a conflict and had prayed so fervently, and, apparently, so ineffectually as he had; and that it was a difficulty which very naturally and forcibly presented itself to him.

I believe, said I to him, that every modern philosopher worthy of respect admits that there is a God, from whom has emanated what we call nature or the universe, with every substance tangible and intangible, soul as well as body; and there can be no doubt but that what they say is true: that everything is governed by fixed laws. But it seems to me that at the outset there is danger of a misapprehension of terms. The properties of substances are fixed, and must have their effects, and the same effects when the proper conjunctions are made of substance, time, place, temperature, or whatever other incidents may be necessary. An alkali, for instance, will neutralize an acid, and when their relative strength and all other incidents are precisely the same, will neutralize it in the same way and to precisely the same degree. Gravitation is also a phenomenon which has an unchangeable law: that it is inversely as the square of the distance of the bodies that are attracted.

Now, in this sense of law, as applied to the invariable properties of substances, to gravitation, and to every other atom and portion of creation, the philosophers are strictly correct, and no amount of prayer is going to change those laws; nor is there any promise upon which such a prayer can reasonably be founded. The infraction of one of these natural laws will bring its punishment, and there is no escape; and the wisdom, knowledge, and power which have created and placed and continued in operation all of these laws which never change, never conflict, and never, it would seem, can be all discovered, is past the comprehension of finite man.

But when we go higher and attempt to bind the Creator by his own laws, we must make a distinction. God is, indeed, "a law unto himself;" that is to say, He can never do what is contrary to the perfection of His own attributes; He can never be unjust, or unwise, or unholy. But here we must stop. He cannot be included in the "everything" or "all things" of the philosophers; and although He has, according to the counsel of His own will, ordained the laws of nature, there is not one of them which He cannot change, direct, or abrogate, if He, in accordance with His infinite attributes, see fit to do so. That He does not so continually is only a proof of the infinity of His wisdom when he first created and set them in operation, and cannot be used as an argument against His power to change or abrogate. The miracles performed by our Saviour prove His power to do so to those who believe that those miracles were performed; and that He has the power to do so, which must be admitted by every thinker, is a good evidence of the possibility, if not of the probability, of the miracles.

One great difficulty, Ben, in arguing about this and similar matters is, that one does not always know his auditor, and therefore does not know where and how to commence with him. As you believe the Bible, I can use with you what may be called Christian arguments, that is, can take for granted many propositions which it would take volumes to set in order and elucidate to another who does not believe the Bible. Nevertheless, what I have heretofore said is, and what I am going to say shall be, fair argument for all those who believe with the philosophers that there is a God who is the Creator. But there is one point I wish to speak of and lay aside as I proceed.

The philosophers puzzle themselves greatly over "the time when," and say that as God (and consequently all His attributes) has existed from all eternity, it is impossible to imagine a time when creation did not exist; and they talk of the millions and billions of years during which this earth, with its indestructible elements, has been whirling in space in company with other planets and their indestructible elements, until they make one's head ache with trying to imagine "the time when." I will readily grant that no man can imagine a beginning to creation—because it is impossible for any man to imagine *nothing*. Space seems to be an innate idea, if there be no other innate ideas; and space includes within it, bounds. If a man try to imagine Nothing, he imagines Space, as I take it, and that is something, and a thing which includes other things. But because I cannot imagine God without a creation, any more than I can a creation without a God, is no reason why there should not have been a beginning. "In the beginning God created the heavens and the earth," and it is no matter whether our imaginations can or cannot conceive when the beginning was, since we cannot imagine creation without a Creator, or without a beginning.

I will readily grant, then, that no man can imagine a time when only God existed, and there was nothing created—that is to say, will grant that no man can imagine *how it looked or would have been perceived by his bodily senses when that was the case;* when there was neither light, nor darkness, nor atmosphere, nor tangible object. I will, I say, grant this; but at the same time I deny the consequence drawn by the philosophers that therefore God is himself governed by immutable laws of creation. Let me even grant, in order to narrow down the controversy to the point at which I wish to arrive, that God is bound by those immutable laws as to the original frame of the universe and its original elements and laws; yet it is certain that at a recent time the present things and order of things on this earth were created, for the geologists themselves can show irrefutable evidences that that has been the case: the natural increase of the human race proves it. We here, then, have a beginning, which is sufficient for my argument. But recently the creative power has been exerted, and within historical times stars have disappeared which had either existed from the original no-beginning of the philosophers, or had subsequently been created for a certain purpose and then removed. God, the Creator, in this recent exertion of His power, made substances different from those which He had before made, on this earth at least, and, consequently, properties different from those He had before made. I do not say *contrary*, but *different;* for that all, whether the recent, or the previously created, are and were in precise accordance with His wisdom, goodness, justice, and holiness, cannot be doubted.

We see then, Ben, that God, the Creator, has made everything and governs everything by laws, but that He can change or abrogate those laws at His will, when to do so is in accordance with His perfections; and that He has accordingly, at a comparatively recent date, both abrogated and changed, and has also created new and different objects and essences with new and additional, if not different laws. When He created man—whom all allow to be one of the latest of His creations—He gave him a soul and a different body from any previous creation, on this earth at least, and adapted to each other the soul and the body, and the laws which govern them. Remark now, that the farther we remove our inquiries from man the more general and simple are the laws, the effects of which we see, and the nearer we come to him the more numerous and complex they are. So numerous are these laws, and to such complexity does their action upon each other lead, that it can never be hoped that man with his finite mind shall be able even to approximate to any precise generalization of their action. Take, for instance, the health of the human body; an astronomer can tell the exact spot to which any star shall have progressed one hundred and forty-two years and six months hence, but he cannot tell what shall be the state of any one of his own bodily functions in a half hour from that time; and yet his body is the subject of law just as much as is the star. So with regard to all his affairs; his best laid plans miscarry, and often without a definite plan he succeeds. So uncertain, indeed, are all of his own concerns, internal and external, even those over which he seems to have most control, that he has invented the word "Chance," although he knows and sees every moment that no effect whatever can be without a cause, and that every cause acts according to a law.

To admit that God has the power to change, or abrogate, or interfere with any one, or any series of the substances and laws He has established, is sufficient to encourage a man who desires very strongly to hope that He will do so in a given case; but we are not left to hope superstitiously in the matter, nor are we bound to believe that though God has full power over His substances and laws, He ever interferes with them in order to answer prayer. Our hope that our prayers shall be efficacious is based upon the nature of man, and upon the promises of God, as well as upon His nature.

Man has sins which demand contrition, has blessings to give praise for, has dangers to be preserved from, and has benefits to desire, and it is not only his duty to pray, and not only is prayer the becoming act of a creature, but it is also his nature to pray. His Creator has implanted in his heart the necessity of prayer, and all men pray at some times just as naturally as they gasp, or cry out, or are pleased or displeased at other times. Prayer is the instinctive act of an inferior, and we see it manifested in the lower animals towards those stronger than they and towards man. It would be altogether foolish, then, whatever the philosophers may say, to suppose that this instinct, this necessity, is a mere fruitless instinct and necessity implanted in the nature of man only for a moral purpose. Even if we had no revelation we should suppose that there must be efficacy in it, not only morally upon the man himself, but also to procure what he prays for. But we have a revelation which warrants us in praying; for it tells us that our prayers are heard, and promises that they shall be answered if we pray aright and for what is really for our good.

This is an argument, and a sure argument to a Christian, but there are many Christians who need constant reference to it; for their faith in the efficacy of prayer must have some higher authority than their own mistaken ideas and short-sighted observation.

That God can answer prayer, and has promised to answer prayer is a sufficient warrant for a Christian to pray, though he may not understand or even be capable of understanding the whys and wherefores of logic and the subtle reasonings of metaphysics.

It is not necessary to suppose that in order to answer prayer, or to bless or preserve a man, the great Creator, who is infinite in His wisdom and power, and who sees the end from the beginning, has to interfere in the minutest degree with the order He has established. From the beginning He has known every prayer which should be made, and from the beginning He determined, according to the counsel of His own will, which should be and which should not be answered; and from the beginning, without ever the slightest interference, cause may have produced effect, and effect becoming cause produced its effects, and combining those effects with others produced still other effects, so that at the moment the effect should be produced which answers the prayer, or produces the blessing or preservation. If you now say that since it is the case that all things are ordered beforehand there is no need to pray! I answer, in the first place, that you cannot overcome your own nature which impels you to pray; but I also add, that while it is certain that if you do not pray you cannot receive an answer to prayer, it is equally certain that you must and shall pray—the prayer as well as the answer to it has been foreordained.

This may sound to some very dogmatical, and some may even for a moment call it nonsensical: but let me ask such if they think that God has ordained the order of events coupled with "ifs" and "buts," as a chess-player is bound to do? That if the man pray so and so, then such and such a thing shall happen, and if he pray another thing, so and so will happen, and if he do not pray at all, then another and a different thing shall happen? This, if prayer be answered at all, would place the whole destiny of the world, in which effects follow causes in unbroken and certain sequence, at the whim of any one man of the human race. If Hezekiah had not prayed, America might not have been discovered; but as he did pray, the Rothschilds are the great bankers of the nineteenth century.

Man's nature and God's promises lead to rational, faithful prayer, whether God interfere to keep His promises, or have preordained the action of His laws for their fulfillment; and though I think it more probable that the latter is the case, because to the infinitely wise God no interference can be necessary, and because to my finite mind, which is now judging, it appears that the slightest interference might produce uncertainty (so intimate is all the harmonious connection of nature), and uncertainty would have the most disastrous effects upon the character of man, who would not then know what to depend upon—yet, whether the one or the other, whether by preordination or interference, God does answer prayer, and prayer is therefore efficacious.

When we say that God answers prayer, we do not mean that He directly complies with all the prayers made and directions given Him by His creatures. It would be in direct contradiction of His infinite goodness, wisdom, justice, and holiness, if He should do so. But here is what a man can confidently affirm: that "all things work together for good to them that love God;" and that if what they pray for is that which shall be for their good, they shall receive it; and if it would not be for their good, His love will refuse it. This is what the Christian may depend upon. He is not left to any uncertainty about it; and if he have the proper spirit of humble dependence upon the superior knowledge, wisdom, and love of God as to what is best for him, he shall never be disappointed in his prayers; for they will always be coupled with a reference and a deference to that superiority. He never prays for bread and receives a stone, or for meat, and has a serpent given him. Take your own case, Ben. You know it more intimately than any one else can know it. If you have ever been disappointed in receiving what you thought you had a warrant to pray for, has not the disappointment turned out for good to you? Has it not invariably been the means of producing other blessings, and often far greater blessings?

I do not believe that it is always only the prayer of the Christian which brings an answer. The prayer of the creature is often answered by an infinitely loving Creator. The people of Nineveh have not been the only heathen whose repentance and prayers have been accepted and answered.

But I am convinced that there is and has been a great deal of superstition, and a vast amount of arrogance felt about this very matter of prayer. In China when it will not rain, or rains too much, the people upbraid their Gods and beat them ;. and there are, I fear, many otherwise good persons who have the Chinese idea that God owes a duty to them, and who feel reproachful and rebellious towards Him when it is not performed to suit them. This spirit is very different from that humble dependence and confidence a Christian or a creature should feel. God promises and will bestow his blessing temporal and spiritual; but "Thus saith the Lord God; I will yet for this be inquired of by the house of Israel to do it for them; * * * * * * and they shall know that I am the Lord."

CHAPTER XXXVII.

TAKES UP THE STORY AGAIN, AND DISCOURSES LEARNEDLY UPON LOVE.

I REALLY do not know what immediate effect was produced upon Ben Eccles by my attempt to concentrate in one short conversation a subject which has exhausted so many wise and learned brains, and so many large volumes, without being itself exhausted. He was a very respectful young man, and though the conversation (or talk) had appeared tediously long, and my reasoning pitifully meagre, he would not have manifested weariness or contempt. I have always had a fear to enter into an explanation of questions of such great importance, either in conversation or in writing, lest I should hurt the truth by my own ignorance and the weakness of my reasoning powers. But though I cannot expect from the reader the deference paid me by Ben, I feel sure that he will excuse my feebleness on account of my motive, and will grant that though I may have done no good I have certainly done no harm by my effort. I love to try to do good whenever an opportunity offers itself, but at the same time am often glad and frequently doubtful of success when I am through with the effort. I am particularly relieved, however, in the present instance for the remembrance of that talk and the effort I knew I should have to make to reproduce it have been weighing upon my mind almost ever since I commenced to write this history. To give a true knowledge of Ben I had to speak of his doubts, and it is evident that to speak of them, and not to clear them up, or attempt to do so, would be the part neither of a philosophic writer nor of a true friend.

However, I am through with it, and can go on with my story.

Let me see. I left Ben at Dr. McCleod's, where Alice found him upon her return from Rosstown. Well, my dear reader, he did not at once go on his knees to her, nor did she fall violently in love with him. They were a very sober-sided couple. She looked at him, and no doubt said to herself: Well, that's Ben Eccles, is it? Aunt Polly's pet! He's a queer enough looking young gentleman, but I suppose is all that's excellent. I wonder what he's thinking about! And he looked at Alice, and perhaps said to himself: So this is Alice Charlton! Aunt Polly's niece! She's a splendid looking girl, and I'll be bound is a good one! I wonder what she thinks of the efficacy of prayer?

You perceive that every meeting of young folk who are marriageable is not productive of either poetic or any other kind of fire, and you may have seen less hopeful meetings than this produce very joyous results.

Alice had a thousand things to think of with which Ben neither had nor could have the slightest concern, and Ben had abstruse as well as practical sorrows and difficulties which Alice could scarcely have comprehended had she heard them. There was one resemblance between them which, however, served as a cause for no nearer contact of feeling than they at first experienced. Each had had a grievous wound to the affections: with Alice it had left an ugly scar—called contempt; but with Ben, whose wound was a thousand times more profound, the effect had been very different. He had no cause for contempt; no cause for hatred. The object he worshipped was as bright as ever, though less attainable; and though he was no child to cry for moon or sun, he none the less admired it. The fact was, that having loved Susan once he was bound to love her as long as life lasted, and to love her as purely and chivalrously now that she was married as he did when she was a maid. His was no groveling soul to hate the lovely because she could not love him, nor was he so low as to covet the wife or the happiness of another. Far from it, he would—though the thought did not disturb his more unsuspicious fancy—most cheerfully have thrashed his friend Charles had he proved unkind or unfaithful to his wife, or most vigorously have punished any other man who had whispered or looked an insult to her.

But the necessity was upon him to sometimes see his idol. He hardly intended to call at her house, but he loved to be near her, to feel that he breathed the same air, and could render her his protection and assistance if she might possibly need them. It must be remembered that love is a feeling, and not one of the reasoning faculties. His reason could have told him that she felt that she had sufficient protection and aid with her husband near her, and that even if she did not feel so the chances were almost infinite against his having any opportunity to render either, but his love suggested that he might (who knew?) do the loved one some service, and that, at any rate, it was pleasant to be in a place to do so if the chance arose. Love in woman is sometimes a brooding, tremulous, nonsensical, and fantastical sort of quiet hysterics, and in this case Ben much resembled a woman.

As my young readers (always in case I should have any, young or old) may like to hear what an old man thinks of love between the sexes, I will tell them a result or two of my experience and observation. There is a vast deal of humbug in the popular representation of the passion, most notably in the idea that it must be single in its object. That it is most frequently so I grant, but I deny that it is necessarily so. And yet we must distinguish.

To the beautiful we naturally ascribe every good quality. Many a man at sight of a very beautiful woman feels a pang of discontent at the wife who has been good to him and true to him through long years of sorrow, trouble, and, perhaps, of wickedness. I think it is most rarely the case, however, that a further acquaintance with the disposition and mind of the beautiful one does not, if his heart be noble, refreshen the languid love for the faithful wife. Her love for him, a love he can hope for nowhere else, draws him back to her. She may not be so beautiful in face, but her affection haloes her homeliness; her form may not be so symmetrical and graceful, but she is trusting and true. She is his, soul and body; no thought of preference for another, however handsome, ever intrudes into the heart she has consecrated a temple to his worship—unworthy idol! It would be rejected with indignation and a bitter sense of self-insult. He knows it too, and would feel utterly wretched if he did not feel certain of it; and yet his eyes wander away after beauty—and his heart goes with them a little way.

I never saw a woman to be preferred in any way to my Mary. She was to me as beautiful and as holy as the mother of mankind, and the eyes and heart of Adam were not more safe from wandering than were mine. But I know my heart; and if by chance I had seen a more perfect woman, and had found myself in danger of being lured by her charms, even to a sigh of regret, I could have had but one refuge. I could not have gone to principle, or to fear of consequences—for both should have been vain. I should have had to refer myself to Mary's fond affection, to her pride in me, her holiness to me, and her sufferings for me, and to ask myself if I would like this other to take her place; and not till then should my whole nature have risen in horror at the thought.

It is not the man's love nor the wife's beauty which keeps a man faithful; it is the wife's love which binds her husband to her, and, as a corollary, unless she love fondly, yet prudently, there is no trusting his heart at home or away.

Nevertheless, I can conceive a man of such a nature

as that he shall truly love his wife and at the same time have a fond affection for another woman—though it seems to me absolutely impossible that a woman who has a beloved husband living should have such a duality of love. Let us suppose Ben Eccles or Dr. Sam married; should it be thought strange that either should still have a gentle respect and tenderness for Susan, whom he had truly loved? So far from its being strange, I would call it unnatural if he did not feel so. It is not necessary that we should associate crime, or immorality, or even imperfection with this dual love. Neither Ben nor Dr. Sam would wish Susan to be in his own wife's place, nor need he "imagine" Bowman's death and the death of his own wife in order that such a union should take place. He would simply love both women, and love both truly and purely; and if he should have married Susan in the first place, he might have afterwards met a woman, an Alice Charlton or a Kate Bolling, whom he might also not merely esteem and like, but love truly and purely.

This duality of man's love is a subject which in the hands of modern French writers has been made very gross and immoral. But I am convinced that its grossness and immorality are the effect of their own ignoble imaginations; for in the heart of a magnanimous man it may be perfectly delicate and perfectly free from ill-regulated desires.

I have elsewhere written about my love for little Kate Bolling, and it is my love for her which gives me experience in this matter and assists my observation of it in others. If she could see into my heart and discern its gentle and strong affection for her, and should take its tremulous sensitiveness for the love of a lover, she would no doubt be amazed, perhaps somewhat amused, and possibly a little offended that an old man of seventy-six should have such feelings towards her. And yet, although I cannot precise wherein it differs from the love of a lover, I know full well that were I only twenty-six I should love her in the same way, and love my Mary too. I should abide strong in my wife's affection, and yet be jealous of the attentions of others to Kate; I should regard my wife's honor as the most sacred of obligations, and yet be willing to fight and die for Kate's honor; I should go through fire and water for my wife's preservation, and yet would do the same for the safety of Kate.

Of course, I do not mean that I should at once love both equally well. What I started out to illustrate was that love is dual, and that a man may not only at once love two brothers, or two sisters, or two sons, but may also love two women with the same kind of love. I am not comparing the degrees, but the kind of love. If I had had to choose between the two in any given case I would have chosen my wife without hesitation.

This duality of love is certainly true with man, and hence the polygamy we read of in the Bible was natural. But our monogamy is even more natural; for though a man can love two women at once he will always love one much more than the other. We have therefore improved on the ancients in this respect—not that they were wicked, but that we are more prudent than they were. Jacob was a good man (though

I never admired him), but he had a hard time of it with his family; a much harder time than I should think a modern would care to have even if there were no statutes against bigamy. Those statutes would never have been invented but for the greater facilities of travel and the greater prevalence of peace among adjoining nations since Jacob's history has been generally known.

What has led me into this digression about love—a digression which may be foolish in this place, but the substance of which is true for all that—is the fact of Ben Eccles' visit. I imagined to myself what should have been the state of his feelings if while his old love was still strong upon him he had fallen in love with Alice. He did not do so, I know; but suppose that he had! In the first place, was it a possible case? and, if possible, should there have been any conflict of feeling? Hence my attempt to show that it was possible, and could have detracted neither from his manliness nor truth.

Old men are not easily satisfied with problems unless they can work them out in harmonious detail; at least I find that to be the case with myself; and also frequently find, as in this case, that the play has perhaps not been worth the candle.

Aunt Polly made much of her dear boy. She had heard of his sickness and of some of his sorrows, and she sympathized heartily with him, and showed a strong inclination to coddle him up as though he were still a boy, and still only convalescent. Mrs. McCleod and Alice entered into her spirit, and for a day or two they almost worried the sensitive fellow into having his sorrows replaced by vexation—a feeling quite as antagonistic to sorrow as it is to joy; but his cheerfulness and quiet humor soon restored him to a more independent footing, and the visit was prolonged to the satisfaction of all. Ben was now able to join the doctor in the discussion of those high subjects which were nearest the old gentleman's heart and had been his most profound study, and completely charmed him by his acuteness and breadth of intellect, and the great progress in knowledge he had made in the few years since he was a school-boy. Good old gentlemen are apt to be wonder-struck and captivated by pet prodigies; but, indeed, take Ben at this period of his life, when he was nearly freed from his depression of mind, and it would be hard to find a young man more pleasing either to the refined or to coarser natures. Not only was he unselfish, but I never knew any one more fitted to please a selfish companion; for he was unsuspicious of selfishness, and fully entered into the sorrows, joys, and other egotisms which were spread before him, as though they were real and important. And though he had such a keen sense of the ludicrous, and enough gentle, quaint humor in his composition to often put his friends in gleeful spirits, I never knew him to ridicule any one who had confided his feelings to him. This is saying a great deal for his goodness of heart, but no more, I think, than was perfectly warranted.

Fortune seemed to favor him by bringing Susan to pay a morning visit three or four days after his arrival. He was sitting in the passage alone when she came in unannounced, and though he was, for a second, startled, and turned a shade pale, he preserved his composure, and gave her his hand as frankly as though she had never been but his friend, but with a solicitude for her well-being he could only have felt for one who had been more than that. I hardly know how to make my meaning more clear. His frankness was neither bold nor embarrassed, and his solicitude was only shown by his cordiality in asking after her health, and the quiet manner with which he watched her smiles, words, and expression to discover lurking signs of discontent or unhappiness.

He could discover nothing but peace and happiness. No cloud yet seemed to darken over her, no doubts even of her perfect blessedness ever appeared to have crossed her mind. And while he was thankful that it was so, I have no doubt but that his heart would not have been displeased if he could have discovered that there was something lacking in her happiness with which he could at least sympathize, if he could render her, to remedy it, no active assistance. Although he would not have admitted such a charge for an instant, I have no doubt but that he would have felt so —for it is a natural feeling.

Pshaw! Do I not know that when Molly Higgins married, though I was only a school-boy, and at least six years younger than she, I fully expected and desired that she should in a short time come to me and complain of her husband, and admit in her heart, if not in words, that I was the only one who could have conferred perfect and permanent happiness upon her?

Ben was not destined, any more than was I, to see

the immediate unhappiness of the one who thought she could be happy without him. Nor did he, when he went with Alice two or three days later to return the visit, find any cause to think that Susan had either unhappiness or discomfort. Mr. Bowman was present on this occasion—though he had not been with his wife to the doctor's. His friendliness and buoyancy of spirits appeared rather forced when he met the visitors, and so long as they remained there. He had wronged both of them, and felt in his heart that both had a supreme contempt for him. He did not hate either, for the wrong he had done was in neither case of that character which always produces hatred in the wrong-doer. He was only uneasy with them; could look neither straight in the eye; and his wife's evident fondness of him and references to him, and talk about him in the conversation (things which not one good young wife in a hundred thousand can avoid, though she were otherwise a Minerva for wisdom) were rather irritating to him; though her love was in reality his only patent excuse for his former conduct to Alice, and his only refuge from the just wrath of Ben Eccles.

Alice was very much pleased with Ben. She did not have the remotest fear that he should fall in love with her, or that she should grow too fond of him for her own happiness. They walked and rode, and talked and laughed, sketched and read together more like brother and sister than like new acquaintance. Aunt Polly was a tie in which they were quickly united, and in the house, and sometimes in their walks, she made one of as guileless and pleasant a trio as one would wish to find.

The change of scene, and consequent change and excitement of ideas, for a few days prevented any manifestation of his idiopathy; but one day Alice found him upon his knees on the gallery, and her woman's eye soon discovered he was praying, and she slipped noiselessly away. Another time, that same afternoon, she again saw him in that position in the garden. And so it went on, and she began to suspect his monomania, until at last he one day went on his knees and began to pray while they were out walking. There had happened to be a lull in the conversation when he did so, and though she was much alarmed, she neither spoke nor moved until he got up, and continued to converse undisturbed. She had found out that her pleasant companion was crazy—that is the word most commonly used—and though his craziness was of the most harmless and touching character, it was none the less craziness.

Imagine the tender pity which filled her heart at the discovery! She respected him none the less; was none the less pleased with his wit, wisdom, and pleasant fancy and humor, but—but—he was crazy.

Now, it is not easy to prove that men in Ben's condition are really crazy, though all should say they are. In the first place, it will be granted that it is better to pray than to curse; and I will venture to say that four-tenths of the so-called sane persons in the county cursed more than Ben Eccles prayed. So far as the two acts themselves are concerned those who cursed were crazier than he who prayed, and yet no one considered them crazy, though they cursed, as he prayed, almost unconsciously. The reason, then, why he was called crazy, while they passed along as sane, was that he stopped and prayed methodically, and they went along as usual, and cursed "promiscuously and heterogeneously," as poor Ransom used to damn his foes when he got generally angry! The method was the fault; and it does seem hard that a man who is methodical in doing right should be shunned as crazy, while those who are irregularly but frequently violent in doing wrong should be trusted as sane.

If it were not so the fashion to curse, and take up other such habits as senseless and wicked, the number of reputed crazy men in the world would be vastly increased. In fact, it seems that the really crazy are in a majority; and the majority rules. If you should try any man of ordinary wickedness by strictly logical rules, and before a wise and unprejudiced jury, he would be sent to a mad-house—but neither logic nor wisdom rule just now, and very few are not biased by fellow-feeling.

This, after all, though it only shows that others are also crazy who are not called so, is but a reason why slight aberrations, such as Ben's, should be looked upon with great leniency. He was crazy, and a crazy world called him so. But I declare that I would rather be crazy Ben Eccles than have the sanity with which I see thousands of others flatter themselves.

CHAPTER XXXVIII.

CONTAINS AN UNPLEASANT, AND A VERY PLEASANT PORTION OF THE HISTORY, AND PREPARES THE READER FOR ITS END.

I MUST now pass over nearly two years in my history; years filled with events to the personages I have introduced to the reader, but with only such events as occur in the ordinary course of the lives of ordinary persons, such as they were, and as I myself am. Susan was weaning her boy,—a bright, beautiful little fellow, who was just beginning to talk and to walk. They had not been years of uninterrupted happiness to her, though she often, when charmed by the manifold perfections of her son, tried to think they had been. Her husband was neither the patient nor the guileless man she had thought him to be. In truth, she had begun to doubt his word when he spoke, and to suspect his conduct when he acted; and his high, frank spirits in public were a mocking commentary upon his peevish, snappish ways in private. His habits, too, had changed for the worse.

Lying Charley, as he was called far and near, had reached the stage of life and living when men begin to have boon companions (in the ordinary, woman's sense of "boon," which is "carousing"), and often two and three afternoons and evenings in a week witnessed him and them at his own house, or one of theirs, at a dinner party.

A gentlemen's dinner party in those days was a grand and serious affair. Ladies were rarely present, and when they were, the mistress of the house presided at the table, and they all left the gentlemen to their wine as soon as the dessert was ready to be removed. Then the gentlemen drunk long and deep, until the wits of all were unsteady, and many of them staggered in their walk or fell under the table. Mr. Bowman was fond of these parties, but had gone to many of them before he ventured to put his young wife to the vexation and mortification of giving one at his own house. After he had broken the ice, however, and had proved her compliance, he was as hospitable as any of them, and got to think that Susan had no feeling at all in the matter. Because she never reproached him, he would rise in the morning from the bed to which he had barely been able to stagger with her assistance the night before, and begin lying volubly about what was said and done, whom he had helped off to bed, and whom assisted on his horse or to his gig, and how he was complimented on his sobriety; as though she had not seen him, and did not know how very drunk he had been. Or, if he were too sick for much talk, he would complain of his unfortunate idiosyncrasies; that from his earliest childhood he had not been able to eat even two brandy cherries, or a single pickled oyster, without being made violently sick, and all that sort of stuff; when she had had to call his man-servant to pull of his boots, and get him, helpless as a child and comatose with drink, to his bed, where he had lain like a log until nearly daylight, when he had shown symptoms of satiety.

Oh, it makes me angry to write about this, and tell how he progressed; how he made a most particular companion of one of the worst of his acquaintance, a selfish, sensual old bachelor, who lived a few miles off, and about whom some of the most scandalous of stories were told; of how he got to almost living at that friend's house where he was sufficiently well fleeced in private games of poker to make his company acceptable, and where he soon learned and adopted some of the other vices there tolerated. It makes me angry, I say, to write about or even to remember this, when I know the agony such conduct caused poor Susan. The fellow demanded of her the same respect, familiarity, and obedience, as though he were the best of husbands; and she, poor girl, suffered his embraces, and gave him respect and prompt obedience, in hope to wean him from his ways. Wean him from his ways! Alas, he was naturally no gentleman, and did not have the improvable material in him; his nature would have had to be changed to make anything but a gross brute out of him.

As I am so near the end of my story, it will not do for me to attempt to enter here into the details of their domestic life—particularly, as I intend doing so in another place where it is necessary for the completion of my narrative. Indeed, I do so fear to be tedious that the remainder of my story shall be but a sketch, to be filled up by the profound knowledge of human nature, and the perfectly correct taste which I most cheerfully and certainly ascribe to the reader, who has thus far followed me.

Dr. Sam had not been idle during these two years. His practice had increased until it almost rivaled that of his father before him, and he attended to it with an assiduity which made the girls and other women folk say that he was cut out for an old bachelor and was determined not to thwart his nature. There was one young lady, however, who did not join in this talk or opinion. She, about this time, began to be very reserved when Dr. Sam was the subject of conversation, and very grave when she thought of him. Somehow or another she had got the idea that he was more dangerous than he appeared to be, was a sort of snow-covered volcano, was a man who could love with amazing strength, and, moreover, that she was in danger of being loved by him, of being snapped up by him, a gentle lamb by a ravening wolf. Dr. Sam was a wolf still; but he had not in this case, as when he first went to see Susan, put on his wolfish air. Then, he was upon an expedition, a declared and undisguised wolf; now, he was rather playing the part of grandmother. "Oh, grandma, what makes your eyes so big?" "To see the better, my child!" And little Red Riding Hood began to tremble at the answer, she knew not why.

Sarah Stockdale was a loving, impetuous woman, who took upon herself the cares and the welfare of her brother Sam, and could never rest until she had all his cares removed, and his welfare secured, according to her notion. It occasionally seemed to occur to her that her notion might not be his notion; but she would say that she knew what was right, and intended to do it. "Sam may differ with me, but I'll do my best." From the first she appreciated the noble qualities as well as the beauty of Alice, and she never rested until she got her and Dr. Sam acquainted with each other. She was a woman, and therefore was more patient to wait the six or eight months, until the meeting could be naturally brought about, than her father could have been in the like circumstances. He would have lugged them together by the ears, and stormed as though he would box their ears if they had not acted to suit him. She visited Alice, and had Alice visit her several times, until at last, upon one of Alice's visits, Dr. Sam was at home, and the introduction took place. And then Sarah had a fixed point of departure, and felt confident in her navigation. No blind or rash navigator was she, to crowd on sail, and run upon sunken rocks and outlying reefs in trying to make straight to the port. She was wary; oftentimes her course seemed just the opposite to that it should be, and often she seemed to pass the port as though it were not there she wished to go at all; but all the time her eyes were watchful, and she kept the lead going.

"Oh, Dr. Sam, what makes your eyes so soft and bright when you look at me?"

"Loving you, my dear!" was the answer our little Red Riding Hood began to feel in her heart she was to receive. Ah, she knew better than that Dr. Sam was cut out for an old bachelor, or that he intended to become one if he could help himself; and she knew it long before even Sarah had guessed the success of her design; and it made her serious. Here was no lying, volatile youngster to have dreams about! Here was a man! a man who could love and who would love, and who would be loved, and never take "no" for an answer from her. "Grandma, what makes your mouth so big?" "To eat you up!" There was no escaping him; she felt that. The charm was upon her; and though it was by slow degrees, she was yet surely falling to him, and the power of resistance was fast being lost.

There are some joys which fill the heart with laughter, but are too sacred for any outward show of mirth, and I cannot imagine one more holy or of more exquisite delight than that which fills a pure and loving woman's heart when it becomes conscious of the love of a noble man, a great, strong-sensed, imperious master in the world, whose fondest desire is to become a gentle, affectionate, devoted companion to her. Alice became conscious of this love in Dr. Sam's heart by degrees, and without a word of love being spoken by him; gradually the love had filled his being, and gradually it enveloped, and overpowered, and led her captive, and the two were of one accord with no preceding doubt or embarrassment.

I used .to tell Dr. Sam that I understood he had communicated his proposition of marriage to Alice by asking her to engage him as her family physician.

At any rate, they became engaged to be married; and Sarah Stockdale was as important, and in as much of a "feeze," as a young mother over her first baby; far more joyful and agitated than if she herself had been going to marry, and be the sole wife of the king of the fairies. But what gave her joy was woe to the

McCleods, until after more grave consultations, suggestions, objections, entreaties, arguments, and scheming, than were used about the disposal of Napoleon the Great, it was settled that Aunt Polly, until she could reasonably be required to be with Alice, should remain at her old home. Alice did not inquire particularly as to the details of the agreement, nor did Dr. Sam show much curiosity to have the time when, and the causes why, set forth so minutely as a solemn treaty should seem to demand; but that was the agreement, and it is to be supposed that Mrs. McCleod and Mrs. Stockdale, who was consulted, and even Aunt Polly herself, knew what they were talking about.

As this only hitch in the perfect fitness of things was removed, there remained nothing to prevent the speedy marriage of the young couple, and I am greatly tempted to describe at length another wedding; but I spare my dear reader—ah, how I admire his patience, and love his sympathy! Ben Eccles and I were of the few who were invited. To have had a large wedding would not have suited the circumstances of Alice and her aunt, any more than it was desired by them. She should not be a rich bride in her own mother's house, as was Susan, but was an orphan, not dowerless, certainly, but living with the old aunt in the family of relatives. The old doctor, strange to say, wished to have one of the grandest affairs the country had ever seen, and Mrs. McCleod seconded him, and even went beyond him; but Alice had too much delicate sense of propriety for that, and Dr. Sam told them that all he wanted was his wife.

The fact was that Dr. Sam was opposed to a large

wedding-party. As he said, all that he wished was his wife; but, besides that, he thought a large party at a preacher's bound to be a bore. Dancing was out of the question; "Here I sit under the juniper-tree," he said was a confounded sight more immoral than dancing, and "thimble and forfeits" was worse than that; and the conversation of a general assortment, prolonged over four or five hours, was infinitely worse than that, for it would set each at enmity with all the others as insufferable bores, and so destroy the brotherly love which should prevail in every community; and the stuffing and guzzling the guests would have to resort to for amusement and compensation would be a direct effort to create practice for himself, and he would wish to remain quiet at home for a few days; and, take it altogether, he—well, he wished to get his wife, and they might do just as they pleased, but if their consciences were enlightened they would give him his wife and let the party alone.

And so there was but a small company of witnesses invited, among whom were Susan and her husband, who did not come on account of an engagement (dinner party) of Mr. Bowman, which he could not honorably forego—he said. Dr. McCleod performed the ceremony, and Mrs. McCleod and Aunt Polly made a quiet crying match in one corner, and Mrs. Stockdale joined them through sympathy, and Sarah pooh-poohed at her mother, and covertly brushed away a tear or two from her own eyes. Then came the little bustle of embracing, and hand-shaking, and good wishes, and blessings, and after that pleasant chat and a bountiful and delicious supper, and all were just as happy and far more comfortable than a grand wedding could have made them.

And here, with much regret, I take leave of Dr. Sam and Alice. If the reader have for them one tithe of my affection, he will be glad to know that their married life was just as happy as a union based upon virtue and a sincere admiration and respect for each other's virtues possibly could be. If I live to complete the task I have set for myself the reader shall have hereafter to renew their acquaintance and recognize again their excellent qualities. From the time of their removal to Rosstown, except upon the occasions of a rare visit, they passed out of the scenes in which Ben Eccles moved, and I should not be justified in following their fortunes any further.

CHAPTER XXXIX.

MAKES A GREAT SKIP, AND ENDS THE STORY.

RECALL your acquaintance of fifteen or twenty years ago, and trace out the lot of each as nearly as you can. It is likely that the great majority are dead, and of the remainder the larger part have gone elsewhere and passed without your ken; your present acquaintance, if you have remained stationary, are almost altogether new persons, either new to the community or newly grown to notice in it. This was and is now the case about Yatton, and in all of our Southern country of which I have any personal knowledge. Here and there, as I look over the county, I find an old familiar face of fifteen years ago; there are, perhaps, in all the country around a dozen I used to know thirty-five years ago, but not six who were boys with me, or whom I remember even as children when I was first a grown man. Even the names of many of the families which in my youth were numerous and prosperous are now no longer known unless by some registry in the clerk's office of one of the courts. In an old and settled country, like England, this is not so marked, though even there the changes among the people in a few years—changes which, occurring one by one at intervals more or less great, were scarcely observed—are apt to astound when summed up. But here the changes are more frequent and violent. Most are dead or gone; the rich have become poor, the poor have acquired wealth; the known are sunk into obscurity, and the unknown lead the fashion; the handsome have become ugly, and the ugly are now, perhaps, decrepit; thieves have acquired a character as honest men, and honest men are known as thieves; in fine, however still you may think yourself to have stood, there has been little stand-still in others.

A few years have wrought great changes in the lot of those whose history we have followed thus far; and when the curtain rises and we look upon the same scenery we find that there are some new actors, that some of our old friends have changed their rôles, some have been called from the stage forever, and that a new drama is being played. There is The Barn, for instance, the same white, wooden structure we saw before, but within it sits the widow Bowman talking with her mother, who is now quite a gray-headed old lady in snowy cap, but still active, energetic, and as good as ever. And beneath the shade of the large forest trees which embower the house and stretch their huge arms over the whole expanse from the front gate to the gate at the main road, are walking young Tom Bowman, about eighteen years old, and his sister Anne, who is four years younger Their father has been dead nearly twelve years. Tom is at home for the vacation in his college where he has just ended his Junior year. Anne has never been sent off to school, but has received her education from her mother and grandmother, who have both had the ability and inclination to direct her studies—except in music, and a teacher from Yatton comes out three times a week to teach her to bang with more or less precision upon the piano.

I do not intend to describe minutely these young folk (I will do so elsewhere). It is sufficient to say that their mother and grandmother are not only fond of them, but have good reason to be contented. So far Tom has manifested none of his father's bad traits of character, but seems to take, both mentally and in appearance, after his mother. Anne has been so raised that it is impossible she should not be all that is good and truthful.

"I was certain," says Tom, "that I saw Uncle Ben coming over the hill and down the road just now, but he ought to have been to the big gate by this time."

"I expect he stopped when he got to the big oak in the bottom," answers Anne. "He almost always stops there, and generally stops five or six times between town and here if he walks out."

"It seems to me, Anne, that he prays more now than he used to. Isn't it growing on him? You see him all the time and ought to know."

"It depends upon the weather, brother, and the news, and his health, and our health, and a heap of circumstances. When he has much care on his mind he is sometimes three hours coming from town, he stops so often to pray—that is when he is alone."

"Why don't you and mother make him quit it, Anne? I've seen you stop him many a time. Yonder he is now. Hillo, Uncle Ben! Come this way!"

And the person called to, after carefully fastening the gate behind him, goes toward the two, who also advance to meet him. He is decently dressed in black, but his pants are somewhat frayed at the heels and where they rub against the buckskin strings of his brogans, and are rather shiny at the knees, and his dress coat is worn thin at the elbows, and begins to look whitish at the points of the shoulder-blades. His hair is quite gray, and as he strides along towards them, looking to the ground, with his shoulders slightly stooped, and his arms hanging listlessly by his side, one would think him some obedient old dependent who has no will of his own, but moves as he is bid. As he nears them he looks up, and the smile upon his lips and in his eyes is more sad, but just as kindly as when in his younger days he used to love and desire to be loved by all. He has got to be "old Uncle Ben" and "old Mr. Eccles," and yet his real age is not yet fifty. Feeling has made him aged; failures in crops, deaths among his negroes, who were badly managed, purchases of bank and other stocks of '36, not worth the paper on which they were written or printed, consequent law-suits, and the sale of the bulk of his property by the sheriff, have made him poor. For seven or eight years he has been living at The Barn, because he was willing to do so, and because I strongly recommended it to the ladies—for though not their dependent for his support, he was and is wholly dependent upon them for happiness and comfort. He was essential to their security, and is most useful as a faithful friend, and they were and are necessary to him as giving him something to live for and devote himself to. The children have, long ago, got to regard him as their uncle sure enough, and Susan and her mother feel for him the love due to a near relative.

"Is your mother in the house, children?" asks he, when he comes up to them.

"Yes, sir. Did you fetch me what I asked you to get, Uncle Ben?" asks Anne.

"Certainly, my dear; but I wish to see your mother now; I have a letter for her." And with that he passes them and goes on to the house; but Anne runs, and reaches it before him, and has her mother on the front gallery to meet him when he reaches the steps. She is still our dear Susan, though so much older and stouter. The matronly air becomes her; the widow's cap is no deformity. Her hand is still soft and white and dimpled, and her smile is still bright and full of affection. The loss of two of her children in their infancy, and all the troubles of these weary years, of which the death of her husband was the least, have but rendered more gentle and intelligent that spirit which was pure and lovely before: as the blush rose may become a perfect white rose, every tinge of passion has been removed.

"Well, madam, the case of Bowman *vs.* Bowman has been finally decided, and in your favor. I have received a note from the lawyer at Milledgeville, and here is a letter to you from him."

Susan turns a little pale, but receives the letter in silence, and breaks it open.

"Ah, I am so thankful," says she, drawing a deep breath after she has read it. "You always bring good news, Ben; and I am very grateful to you."

"It is I who am grateful to you, madam, for all your goodness," says Ben, with a low bow. "You ought to be glad that justice has been done. Mr. Henry Bowman will have to content himself with what rightfully belongs to him."

Ben's formal method of addressing her mother has long been a source of great annoyance to Anne, who now interrupts him with the inquiry she has made, perhaps, a hundred times before:

"Uncle Ben, what makes you always call ma Mrs. Bowman, and madam? She calls you Ben, and you ought to call her sister, or Susan. You are my uncle, and of course you must be her brother."

"So I am, in feeling, my child; and I hope she knows that. Yes, you ought to rejoice very much, mad——"

"Call me Susan, Ben," says Mrs. Bowman, smiling. "You know I have often asked you to do so."

"Thank you, Su——madam, thank you," says he, bowing and embarrassed; "it isn't natural to me, and I fear you will have to allow me to keep up my old habit. But you are very good."

Presently, Susan goes into the house to communicate the good news to her mother, and Ben, after walking up and down the gallery a time or two, halts at one end of it, and kneels down to pray. Tom, who by this time is seated on the steps, beckons to Anne, and when she has approached, whispers to her:

"Why don't you stop him from that, Anne? You can do so."

"I would, brother, if there were company here, or there were any other good reason, but I haven't the heart to do so all the time; nor would you have if you could only see his face, and knew how happy it makes him to pray. Ma don't like me to keep him from it either, and sometimes has checked me when I was going to do so, or to interrupt him. I often see tears in her eyes when she sees him on his knees, and it always makes her very sad."

I must now dismantle my stage, and pack the scenery away until I shall have to use it again. The play is over. The active part of the lives of some men continues to the end; with others it lasts through one act, and for the remainder of the play they are mere supernumeraries or walking gentlemen. Ben Eccles' part, though essential to the plot, and of the deepest interest in itself, was brief. After Susan's marriage his greatest ambition was to keep away from the footlights.

Had some master-mind understood his story and set out to tell it, the world should have admired its pathos. It was a story worthy of being told; no one knew it but myself, and I have done the best I could. It is, perhaps, the case that I have slighted many parts which should have been more fully developed, and have made too full portions which might, advantageously, have been slighted, or omitted altogether. But different minds are affected by the same object differently; and in what I have slighted, and in what I have dwelt upon, I have followed the bent of my own mind. His history, from the time that I presented him just now to the reader, may be told in few words. In due course of time both Anne and Tom married, and both Susan and her mother died, and then he came to live with me, and lives with me still—an old man before his time, but a harmless, loving old man, gentle towards everything that lives.

There is one point of sympathy between us: We live in the past, before the graves opened to entomb our loved ones; and in the future, when the graves shall give up us and our dead.

www.ingramcontent.com/pod-product-compliance
Lightning Source LLC
LaVergne TN
LVHW020111110826
845151LV00001B/128
* 9 7 8 1 4 2 5 5 4 4 0 4 1 *